GERMANY WAS ONE MAN AWAY FROM DEVASTATION

D-Day was over, and the Allied armies were massing in Normandy for the breakout that would spell certain doom for Nazi Germany.

In Hitler's headquarters in Berchtesgaden, the orders of the Nazi leader grew more and more demented. And throughout the still potent German war machine, discontent grew.

But it was a race against time, and one man alone held the key that could turn imminent ruin into last-minute salvation for the Nazis.

He was Feldmarschall Erwin Rommel, commander of the German army facing the Allies. He had a secret plan—the boldest ever conceived by a fighting general, and one that well might work. But its success depended on his greatest foe: General George S. Patton.

HOUR OF THE FOX

It could have happened . . . it may have happened!

HOUR OF THE FOX

by

Richard Rohmer

A SIGNET BOOK

NEW AMERICAN LIBRARY

PUBLISHER'S NOTE

This book is a work of fiction. Names, characters, places, and incidents either are the product of the author's imagination or are used fictitiously, and any resemblance to actual persons, living or dead, events, or locales is entirely coincidental.

First Signet Printing, August, 1988

1 2 3 4 5 6 7 8 9

To one of the greatest Canadians,
a dazzling legend in his own time,
The Man Called Intrepid,
Sir William Stephenson, CC, MC, DFC, CdeG, D.SC.

Foreword

In 1944, Major-General Richard Rohmer, then a very young Canadian pilot, watched the Battle of Normandy unfold from the ideal spectator's seat: the cockpit of a reconnaissance plane, cruising at low altitude over the battle theater with almost no German air opposition.

In his earlier book, *Patton's Gap*, Rohmer calls the Battle of Normandy "one of History's most important". It reached its climax, near mid-August (D-Day had been on 6 June), when General Patton made his surprise appearance in Normandy in a spectacular, enveloping movement with his Third Army from the western edge of the battle zone, driving swiftly east and north behind the German lines and entrapping the enemy in a pocket with its open neck at Falaise and Argentan—the famous Falaise Gap. Inside the Pocket was the preponderance of German Army of the West, south of the Seine River: the German Seventh Army and, remnanted, the Panzer Army of the West.

All this Rohmer watched from his "box seat" in the air above, as he has told us in *Patton's Gap*. But he was puzzled as he watched, for the Gap, some nineteen kilometers wide, was not quickly closed, and German troops flooded east in a great tide out of the pocket with tanks and guns to live and fight another day, prolonging the war and carnage.

Rohmer has an inquiring mind that must know the reason why, a mind that searches tenaciously for the hard facts and the truth—a first-class lawyer's intellect. He is also a perceptive and analytical thinker who can bridge the gaps in the facts with probabilities. So after the war he undertook intensive research to discover the truth about the events that had puzzled him in Normandy. In the process he found evidence to support the theory that the German Command in the West undertook to arrange in the field an armistice with the western Allies while the fighting in Normandy was in full flood. He has now composed a remarkably vivid and lively account of the events and principal characters involved in this great battle and, theoretically at least, in the attempted armistice.

While the book is appropriately called a novel, the story is set in a solid framework of history, and there are many proven facts to make the theory and invention credible. The German nation was in a desperate state in July and August 1944, with her armies on both fronts, East and West, being pounded mercilessly by superior forces. They were suffering dreadful losses, which the German generals in the field knew could not be long sustained. Hitler had deteriorated to almost total irrationality, indeed madness, after the attempt on his life on 20 July at his eastern headquarters, Rastenburg. Hitler appeared prepared to yield to nothing, time and again ordering his armies to stand and die—senselessly. For the German state there was no hope save through capitulation, but not to Stalin's Kremlin. Hence the attempted armistice in the West—Rohmer's theory.

In these pages Rommel and Patton are brought alive. The highly principled Rommel was, in Rohmer's judgment, ''the most respected German General, not only by the German people, but by the Anglo-Americans as well'', a ''man of integrity and honor''. And Rohmer says that Patton, with all his salty language, was ''by far and away the most able of the American Generals'', the most feared by the Germans. The famed Schwarze Kapelle (The Black Orchestra), formed in 1938 by a group of German officers dedicated to the preservation of the German nation, plays its part in Rohmer's armistice theory, just as it had led the attempt to eliminate Hitler at Rastenburg and so save the nation.

Clearly, at this stage of the war, and before, German apprehensions were focused mainly on the eastern front. Above all, the Germans wished to save their country from being overrun by Stalin's hordes and engulfed in Communism. We in the West, from early in the war, had possessed solid evidence that our Russian ally was not a friendly one. Like the Germans, we began to mistrust and fear the Russians, even as Churchill had from the beginning. By the time the eastern and western fronts met in Germany in 1945, there were many in the West prepared to echo Patton's bitter comment, ''We have been fighting the wrong army.''

The conclusion of Rohmer's story reflects this mood in Germany. His account of the armistice in the West proceeds to the highest level: Churchill and Roosevelt, in accord to stop the slaughter and destruction, are bound to refer to Stalin by reason of the Yalta Pledge of no separate peace.

Major-General Rohmer—the man who caught Rommel—who has had such a distinguished career as an airman, a military person, a public figure, and a lawyer, has become an equally eminent teller of tales, and this is one of his best.

—SIR WILLIAM STEPHENSON
Bermuda

Acknowledgments

THIS BOOK has been in preparation since the summer of 1944 when I took part with all the other combatants in the D-Day operations of 6 June and the ensuing Battle of Normandy, which finished with the closing of the Falaise Gap, 20-21 August 1944.

My appreciation goes to those with and against whom I fought, and to several individuals who assisted in the preparation of this book. Dr. Forrest Pogue, America's preeminent military historian, shared with me, along with other information, his previously unpublished notes of an interview he had in 1947 with Sir Edgar (Bill) Williams concerning Montgomery's order that stopped Patton at Argentan on the evening of 12 August 1944, thus creating the Falaise Gap. Pogue's books, David Irving's classic *The Trail of the Fox*, and Anthony Cave Brown's excellent *Bodyguard of Lies*, along with many other works, were invaluable grist for my fictional mill.

Madaline Webster and her family made their magnificent Bermuda home available to us in the spring of 1983, providing me with a secluded place in which to write portions of the manuscript. Sir William Stephenson, The Man Called Intrepid, whom my wife Mary-O and I had the great good fortune to meet during that Bermuda sojourn, has written this book's Foreword with his usual perceptive precision, but more than that, he has become a close friend whom we much treasure. Dr. Chris Bart of McMaster University undertook significant research to augment bibliographical explorations in the Public Archives in England, where most of the documents that appear in the epilogue were unearthed. And the editing skills of John Pearce, editorial director of Irwin Publishing, and D.G. Bastian were of much value in the ultimate shaping of *Hour of the Fox*.

Special gratitude is owing to Mary-O, whose unfailing support and critic's eye have made all my books possible.

—R.R.

German Military Titles and Terms

Abwehr — German Intelligence Service
Blitzkrieg — lightening war
Feldgrau — troops (field-gray)
Feldmarschall — field marshal
Feldwebel — sergeant
Führer — leader (Hitler's title)
Führerhauptquartier — Führer's headquarters
Führungsblitz — lightning call (telephone)
Generaloberst — senior general
Hauptmann — captain
Leutnant — second lieutenant
Luftwaffe — German air force
Nebelwerfer — mortar rocket
Obergruppenführer — lieutenant-general
Oberst — colonel (*mil.*), group captain (*av.*)
Oberstleutnant — lieutenant-colonel
OKH — Army High Command
OKW — German High Command
Panzertruppe — tank corps
Reichsführer — leader of the SS
Reichskanzlei — Headquarters of the OKW and OKH
Reichsmarschall — leader of Holy Roman Empire; title given to Göring during Third Reich
Reichsminister — federal minister
Schutzstaffel (SS) — National Socialists
Schwarze Kapelle — The Black Orchestra (group of German generals dedicated to overthrow of Hitler)
Stabsfeldwebel — sergeant-major
Unterfeldwebel — sergeant

Unteroffizier — corporal
Wehrmacht — German armed forces
Wolfsschanze — Wolf's Lair (Hitler's retreats)

Prologue

AN ARMISTICE attempt in the Falaise Gap? Never heard of such a thing, you would say, and probably rightly so. That's what I thought until I researched my autobiographical-historical book on the Battle of Normandy, *Patton's Gap*, published in 1981. By the time I was finished I had discovered several pieces of evidence suggesting that there had indeed been a secret armistice attempt.

First let me set the scene. On 15 August 1944, Hitler's Commander-in-Chief West, Feldmarschall Hans von Kluge, failed to turn up at a meeting he had arranged with two of his generals for 10:00 a.m. at the church in the village of Nécy just south of Falaise. Kluge simply vanished until he surfaced at about 10:00 p.m. that night at the headquarters of one of his SS Panzer generals near the Falaise Gap area. It has been said that what happened to Kluge that day would leave history with one of its most fascinating mysteries.

What was Kluge doing that day?

Time magazine reported in its edition of 25 June 1945:

> *The Road to Avranches—One day last August, (Kluge) suddenly left his headquarters on the Western Front . . . With some of his staff, Kluge drove to a spot on a lonely road near Avranches in northwestern France. There he waited, hour after hour, for a party of U.S. Third Army officers with whom he had secretly arranged to discuss surrender. They did not appear. Fearing betrayal, Kluge hurried back to his headquarters.*

The only problem with that *Time* report was that Avranches had been taken by Patton on 31 July; in mid-August there was no way Kluge could have come close to Avranches. A more plausible report would have said Falaise, instead of Avranches. *Time*'s correspondent went on to write:

On the day of the rendezvous, Allied air attacks blocked the Third Army party's route to Avranches. By the time U.S. negotiators arrived, Kluge had gone.

In his book, *Germany's Underground*, published shortly after the war, Allan Dulles, a prominent American lawyer who headed up the American OSS (Office of Strategic Services), the U.S. intelligence agency in Berne, Switzerland, wrote that Kluge made "a futile attempt to surrender to General Patton's army somewhere in the Falaise Gap".

Add to this a sworn statement made by Dr. Udo Esch of the German Army Medical Corps. Esch, who was Kluge's son-in-law, had been director of one of the military hospitals in Paris during the period that Kluge was Commander-in-Chief West as well as Commander of Armee Gruppe B. (Kluge had succeeded Rommel in the latter post after the feldmarschall's injury on 17 July 1944.) Esch was very close to his father-in-law and saw a great deal of him. In his statement made to an Allied special agent shortly after the end of the war, Esch spoke of the events after the assassination attempt on Hitler on 20 July:

> *After this failure, my father-in-law considered surrendering the Western Front to the Allies on his own authority, hoping to overthrow the Nazi regime with their assistance. This plan he only discussed with me, at first, and I doubt that even General Speidel, his Chief-of-Staff, was informed about it.*

As the story unfolds you will find out, as I did, that there was much more to Kluge's disappearance on 15 August than *Time*, Dulles, or Esch might have guessed. But Hitler knew what had happened. That is apparent from the statement he made at a Führer Conference on 31 August 1944, just thirteen days after Kluge committed suicide, having been removed from command and replaced with Feldmarschall Walter Model. Hitler said:

> *Feldmarschall von Kluge planned to lead the whole of the Western Army into* capitulation *and to go over himself to the enemy. It seems that the plan miscarried owing to an enemy fighter-bomber attack. He had sent away his staff officer. British-American patrols advanced, but apparently no contact was made . . . Nev-*

ertheless the British had reported being in contact with a German general.

Hitler's statement was only a hint at what had happened on 15 August. It was the tip of the iceberg.

PART ONE

Rommel's Decision

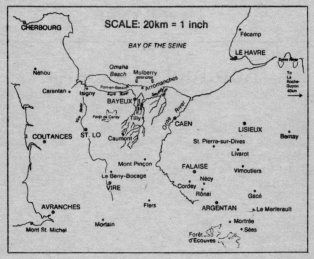

Hausser's Move Toward Arromanches

17 June 1944

THE TENSION in the room was palpable. The atmosphere was to Adolf Hitler's liking. Both Erwin Rommel and Gerd von Rundstedt knew that it was a tactic the Führer often used to keep his generals apprehensive. This meeting was no different. If anything, the cutting edge of Hitler's arrogant haughtiness was made sharper by his obvious unease as he sat on a stool at the end of the long table. Pointedly, he had not invited Rundstedt or Rommel, or for that matter, anyone else in the room, including his own chief-of-operations, Generaloberst Alfred Jodl, to be seated. Except for the two stenographers perched on armless wooden chairs against the wall immediately behind Hitler, it was only he, the Führer, who sat.

He clasped and unclasped his hands, then took off the circular steel-rimmed spectacles through which he had been peering at the large map of France and the English Channel set up on an easel to his left.

"Well, Feldmarschall Rundstedt, you wanted someone from OKW to come to France and see for himself. So here I am, in the flesh." In a short-lived attempt to disguise his foul mood, Hitler smiled at Rundstedt, his left hand automatically coming up to his mouth to cover an array of decayed teeth.

Rundstedt, the Grand Old Man of the German army, the most senior, and with Rommel the most respected, of all German generals, was Commander-in-Chief West and Rommel's immediate superior. He looked down calmly into Hitler's cold eyes showing no sign of nervousness or awe. Nevertheless, he was careful to hide the contempt with which he regarded Hitler.

"Mein Führer," he replied, "at the outset may I welcome you to France, and for Feldmarschall Rommel and myself, I wish to say that you have greatly honored us by coming at great inconvenience to meet with us here."

Hitler's smile was gone as was his patience.

"Yes, yes, Herr Feldmarschall, all that is very nice, but let us get to the point. You wanted me to come here so you could explain to me what is going on. Get on with it. I want to know the current state of affairs and how you plan to throw the British and Americans back into the sea."

"Very well, Sir." Rundstedt was unruffled. "Because Feldmarschall Rommel is in direct command of our forces in Normandy . . ."

". . . and the Fifteenth Army in the Pas-de-Calais area, where Patton's Armee Gruppe is expected to attack," Hitler added to demonstrate his knowledge.

"Of course, mein Führer, of course, Patton's force is very strong but we will be ready for him when he comes."

"And come he will, Herr Feldmarschall. My magnificent flying bombs which are smashing into London at the rate of at least one hundred a day, originate from that area. The fat man with a cigar will be screaming for Patton to do something. I have already heard six flying bombs take off since we've been here. Their engines throb, roar, and pulsate with so much power! But Patton will be too late. With those beautiful machines I will bring England to it knees." The Führer's eyes went blank as he turned that prospect over in his vivid imagination. He blinked slowly like a lizard, then his brain let the eyes come back into focus. "You were saying?"

"I was saying that, as the commander-in-chief of Armee Gruppe B, Rommel should give you his tactical briefing first. Then, if I may add a few words . . ." Rundstedt had been about to make the mistake of inviting Hitler to interrupt at any time to ask questions. He had caught himself in time, knowing that the Führer would be insulted, since he had the power to interrupt in any event—and would do so frequently, if he so chose.

Hitler threw his spectacles on the table and picked up a clutch of colored pencils some staff member had placed there so he could make marks and symbols on the map. These he twisted and rolled unconsciously as he spoke.

"Very well. I will hear you, Rommel. I'm sure you can explain why the Anglo-American forces have not been thrown off the beachhead they landed on ten days ago. No doubt you can tell me what steps you plan to take to drive them back into the sea immediately. Yes, immediately!" His eyes lifted and roamed the ceiling and walls. Rommel knew the Führer well and could tell that his leader was not yet ready to listen—except to himself. Hitler, who wanted to set the stage on his own terms, continued:

"My staff and I have come a long way at great inconvenience to this godforsaken place at your request. Being at Wolfsschanze Two command post for the first time is a painful reminder . . ."

Hitler recalled that the post had been built as a base from which he could direct the invasion and conquest of England, even though he considered it to be much too far back from the coast. He turned to face the map. With his left hand he pointed at the remote command post position at Margival some one hundred kilometers northeast of Paris.

"Here we are over two hundred kilometers from Calais and three hundred from Caen. In reality we are in the middle of nowhere. Mind you the bunkers are large and carefully camouflaged; everything is well furnished; the work rooms are carpeted. Comfortable, yes, very comfortable. Yes, if we can throw the Yankees and British back into the sea, and once the V-1s and the V-2s and the jet aircraft and all the other new weaponry come into operation, the British will be crying for an armistice. It will be an armistice on our terms, and I will direct the occupation, and if need be, the invasion of England, from this place." Index finger of his left hand against the map, he went on: "Except that it's too far from the coast. Jodl, why did we build this place here? Why is it not near Amiens or even Abbeville? Who was the fool who made that decision four years ago?"

Hitler's chief-of-operations, Generaloberst Jodl, was standing to the right, his hands on the back of the second chair in the long row down that side. He shifted uncomfortably. It was not the first time he was required to give a difficult answer with delicacy to a blunt question from the Führer.

Wily and shrewd, Jodl had won his high position mainly because he had an uncanny ability to anticipate Hitler's wishes. He was always thinking one step ahead of him. He had never been known to disagree with the Führer's viewpoint, no matter how irrational or ridiculous, and had great talent for mixing situations, people, and information in a way that enhanced the superiority of Hitler's intellect. As a sycophant, Jodl approached perfection—as did the Führer's chief-of-staff, Feldmarschall Wilhelm Keitel, who was minding headquarters back at Wolfsschanze One at Rastenburg in East Prussia. Jodl would circle this one carefully from a distance before getting to the tender point.

"Mein Führer, while it appears to be remote, Wolfs-schanze Two is well positioned midway between Paris and Brussels, making it close to the seat of government of both countries. Then there are the social and cultural amenities that those two cities can provide."

"You mean bordellos and the like," Hitler snorted.

Jodl chose not to respond but went on: "In normal times there is relatively easy access by air to Reims, only sixty kilometers to the east, which is far better than having to land at Metz, over two hundred kilometers away, as we did yesterday."

"But these are not normal times, Jodl. I was informed that if we flew directly to Reims we might be intercepted by American or British fighters."

'That is true, Sir. They're escorting the medium bombers sent in to attack the V-1 sites in the area and we didn't want to take any chances. Our four Focke-Wulf Condors would make easy targets. However, the air factor was another consideration in locating the headquarters here. As you are well aware, mein Führer, a command post of this dimension and importance could be a choice objective for a hit-and-run paratroop attack, so the farther back from the coast the less attractive that would be for the enemy. Taking all these factors into account, the decision was taken, and I think wisely so, to place your reserve headquarters here."

Hitler tapped the table with his bundle of pencils, his eyes moving away from the map to look at Jodl.

'What you're telling me is that I made the decision myself. It was, as usual, a wise decision. Isn't that right?'' Without waiting for a response, Hitler turned to look past Rundstedt at the stocky, stiff-backed officer behind him.

"Well, Rommel," Hitler barked, "come up here to the map and explain to me why you haven't driven Montgomery and the Americans back into the sea and how and when you will."

From Rommel's left, his chief-of-staff, the ever-prepared General Hans Speidel, handed his chief a long wooden pointer.

Jaw and chest out, Rommel stepped around Rundstedt, stopping two paces back from Hitler and the map. The heels of this highly polished knee-length jackboots came together with a sharp click as he saluted the Führer with a brief bow of his head. Then the pointer was on the map at Caen. Rommel's well-modulated voice, with its distinctive Swabian lisp, held just a tremor of nervousness as he moved the pointer and spoke about the beachhead area from Caen and the Orne River on the east to the Cotentin Peninsula and Cherbourg on the west.

To Rommel, the intent of the enemy was clearly to gain a deep bridgehead as a springboard for a later attack into the interior of France, probably toward Paris. To do this he first had to cut off the Cotentin Peninsula and gain possession of the port of Cherbourg as soon as possible in order to provide himself with a major port with large landing capacity for men and supplies.

"Under cover of his very strong air force, the enemy is visibly reinforcing himself through the port he brought with him at Arromanches. Neither our air force nor our navy is in a position, especially by day, to offer him any hindrance because the enemy has air superiority. Consequently, the forces on the enemy's bridgehead are growing at a considerably faster rate than reserves are flowing to our front."

Without taking his eyes from the map, Hitler broke in: "Normandy's not a bridgehead. It's nothing more than a temporary occupation of our territory."

"Of course, mein Führer," Rommel agreed. "Because of the immense, at times overwhelming, superiority of the enemy air force, I was not able to get the First Panzer Korps, the Seventh Nebelwerfer Brigade, and the antiaircraft corps up fast enough to counterattack the enemy forces after the landing. The enemy has total command of the air over the battle area up to some ten kilometers behind the front. During the day, practically our entire traffic—on roads, tracks, and in open country—is pinned down by fighter-bomber and bomber formations, with the result that the movement of our troops in the battlefield is almost completely paralysed, while the enemy can maneuver freely.

"Every traffic defile in the rear areas is under continual attack, and it is very difficult to get essential supplies of ammunition and petrol up to the troops. Even the movement of minor formations of artillery or tanks on the battlefield is instantly attacked from the air with devastating effect. During the day, fighting troops and headquarters alike are forced to seek cover in wooded areas to ascape the continual bombardment from the air."

Rommel did not look into the Führer's solemn face. He

kept his eyes on the map as he relentlessly painted the black, factual picture not only for Hitler, but also for Jodl and the OKW (German High Command) headquarters staff whom the officers in the field so despised. Those men sat in the remote safety of their massive headquarters near Hitler's at Berchtesgaden, playing with their maps and theories and making the operational decisions that Rommel and his generals had to execute in the field. Rommel, who considered himself handcuffed by the idiocies of Jodl and his staff, saw this briefing as a golden opportunity to get some hard facts through their concrete skulls.

He pressed on: "The enemy has up to six hundred and forty heavy naval guns sitting on battle wagons four to six kilometers offshore, where they are unhampered by any of our U-boats or E-boats. The rapid fire from these guns is so effective that no operation either by infantry or tanks is possible in the area they command. The Americans' equipment, with numerous new weapons and war materiel, is far and away superior to that of our divisions. The enemy armored formations fight their actions at a range of as much as 2,300 meters, using vast quantities of ammunition and with magnificent air support. Parachute and airborne troops are employed in such numbers and with such flexibility that the troops they engage are hard-put to fight them off. Where they drop into territory not held by our troops, they dig in immediately and can no longer be dislodged by infantry attacking without artillery support."

Rommel relentlessly continued his description:

"We must expect more airborne landings, particularly in territory not held by our forces. Our air force has unfortunately not been able to intervene against these formations, as was originally intended. Since the enemy is able, with his air force, to pin down our mobile forces for days at a time, while he himself is carrying on operations with mobile forces and reconnaissance troops, mein Führer, our situation is becoming extremely difficult."

The tip of Rommel's pointer left the map and rested on the carpeted floor between his feet. His litany of bleak information was finished. He waited for the response.

Hitler had listened without interrupting.

"There is one thing you should know, mein Führer," Rommel added, somewhat unnerved by Hitler's silence, "something on the bright side."

"Good," Hitler muttered, "I hoped you'd have something positive to say."

"The troops of all services are fighting with the utmost doggedness and pugnacity, despite the immense materiel expenditure of the enemy. My 17- and 18-year-olds are fighting furiously like mad wolves. But I need reinforcements desperately, mein Führer, desperately."

Hitler looked up into the eyes of his publicly most popular general and said, "I hear you, just as I hear the pleas of my generals in the East facing the Soviets."

Rommel shot back, "But your generals in the East don't have three full-strength Panzer divisions sitting north of the Seine in a special reserve doing nothing when they could be in Normandy fighting!"

Hitler stood up abruptly, stool flying out from under him. His face was contorted with fury as he turned toward the map. He shouted, pounding his fist on the English Channel at Calais, "And my generals in the East don't have an enemy force of over a million men poised to assault us in the Pas-de-Calais area where those three Panzer divisions must go when the attack is made. Remove the Armee Gruppe Patton, and I will let you take the whole of the Fifteenth Army into Normandy. But until then you will fight with what you have! You must fight with what I am able to give you. And you must gain victory by holding fast to every square yard of soil!"

He turned and slumped back on the stool. Jodl had unobtrusively scuttled around to pick it up and replace it. Hitler sighed, briefly winded by the shouting session. His voice now subdued, he said, "I repeat my question: How are you going to drive the Anglo-Americans back into the sea?"

Rommel refused to be intimidated.

"Without reinforcements and without the Luftwaffe, that may not be possible, mein Führer. Whatever I have planned to do has always had to be subject to the approval of Generaloberst Jodl and his staff. Without OKW approval I can do nothing, even as a commander in the field." He turned momentarily to look Jodl squarely in the eye, his bitterness and hatred showing plainly. "What I plan to do is marshal my infantry at Caen, backed up by most of my antitank 88s plus the Luftwaffe's antiaircraft 88s, which regretably are not, but should be, under my command. Then I propose to assemble my Panzer divisions west of Caen but outside the range of the enemy's naval artillery." His pointer was again moving over the map. Hitler watched attentively. 'I will allow the enemy to move southward, but then launch an armored thrust into this flank and fight the battle outside the range of his naval guns.''

''What about the supply port they brought with them at Arromanches, the Mulberry?'' Hitler responded. ''All Montgomery's supplies, troops, tanks have to come in across that port. That's his weak point. If you can capture or destroy it, and the other to the west in the American sector, then you will stop Montgomery and the Americans in their tracks.''

Rommel smiled for the first time.

''Precisely, mein Führer. When I have won the battle here just out of range of the naval guns, I will make an unstoppable armored thrust straight through to Bayeux, straight to Arromanches and the Mulberry. Once I have penetrated the enemy lines with my armored column, there will be such confusion in the enemy camp that they will not be able to call down naval fire for fear of hitting their own troops and equipment.''

Out of the corner of his eye Rommel saw Jodl looking to the staff officer on his right with a smirk of amused derision on his face. Rommel knew the insufferable Jodl would never approve the plan. Bastard! he thought. Perhaps there would be a positive response from the Führer before Jodl intervened. But before Hitler could speak, the screeching of the headquarters air-raid klaxon filled the room, its noise so deafening that no further conversation could take place.

Hitler stood up like an automaton. He turned and walked toward the door, his hands clutched in front of him, the brown trousers of his uniform rumpled, the gray-flecked forelock down over his forehead, the familiar abrupt mustache moving as his tongue sought to remove some food caught between his front teeth. He kept his eyes on the floor except to catch the signal of his aide, who pointed toward the air-raid shelter into which everyone in the conference trooped behind their Führer.

As Rommel entered the brightly lit shelter with its whitewashed walls, scattered armchairs, and sofas, he noticed that the two stenographers were not with the group. If he wanted to say something to Hitler that would not be recorded, now was the time. He moved close to the Führer, who was standing looking at a painting of himself on the wall. When the air-raid siren stopped a moment later, Rommel ventured, "It's probably a raid on one of the V-1 sites, mein Führer. I don't expect we'll be in here very long." Then quickly, "Sir, I've had a long personal association with you . . ."

Hitler turned to face him. "Yes, you have, Rommel. You have served me well from the days when you were in charge of my personal staff and responsible for my safety. You have come a long way since then. Even so, there are people like Rundstedt who think you're not fit for higher command. Are you aware of that?" Hitler could not resist the opportunity to stir up antagonisms between generals. But Rommel was determined to say his piece.

"Mein Führer, I can foresee the collapse of your Wehrmacht on all fronts in the East and certainly here in Normandy. The weight of the enemy force is such that we will not be able to push them back into the sea. It is useless to carry on this way. Surely it is time to consider a political decision."

Hitler pulled himself erect, bristling with indignation.

"Surely you're not suggesting armistice, Rommel, and not to me, of all people! The politics of this war are none of your business. *Your* business is to resist the invasion." Shoving his face close to Rommel's he hissed, "I will hear no more of this, do you understand?"

His putrid midmorning breath made Rommel flinch. He knew he had pushed Hitler to the limit, but still he persisted.

"Yes, mein Führer. As you say. But there is one other suggestion I would like to make."

In exasperation, Hitler rolled his eyes toward the ceiling. "Well, what is it?"

"A visit to the front lines in Normandy. It would be a tremendous morale booster for the troops if they could see you there. Churchill has done this very effectively."

"You don't have to throw that pig Churchill in my face," Hitler snarled through clenched teeth, "and I have more important things to do than go mincing around the front lines whether here or on the eastern front. My place is at Berchtesgaden or Rastenburg!"

And as far away from any risk of being killed or wounded as possible, Rommel thought, realizing, not for the first time, that the man was a coward.

At that moment the building shook and the floor trembled under their feet. Heavy bombs from twenty-four enemy aircraft were exploding on the V-1 launching site one kilometer to the south.

"My God!" gasped Hitler, eyes wide with fear, his hands clutching Rommel's forearm in a vise-like grip. "There's going to be a bomb on top of this shelter!" He looked up at the ceiling. "Surely it wouldn't collapse."

"No, no, mein Führer. There's nothing to worry about. The bombers probably don't even know this command post is here. It's well camouflaged. You're perfectly safe."

Hitler's hands shook as he pulled out a handkerchief to wipe the perspiration from his face.

'I have been through so much, and there is so much to do for the Reich. This is not the time or place for me to die."

Rommel continued to console him.

"You have a long life ahead of you, mein Führer," he said, while thinking, Yes, I am in the presence of a coward. A contemptible man who has sent hundreds of thousands to their deaths but who lives in total fear for his own life.

When Hitler, reassured, turned to look at his portrait again, Rommel had had enough. He nodded curtly toward the self-absorbed leader, and with a barely audible click of his heels, turned and walked toward Speidel at the far end of the room.

For Speidel, the feldmarschall put on a mask of optimism. In a low voice he said, "I just had a chat with the Führer. He thinks my approach is right. He is pleased with the counteroffensive idea and our aggressive planning." Rommel felt no need to tell Speidel what had actually been said in the conversation. It was better to feed him an optimistic line.

Speidel had information of his own. "I understand the Führer will be eating by himself. He'll dine on pills, medicine, and rice. Incredible fare!" Raised eyebrows expressed his disbelief.

"That sounds like something you have to eat by yourself," Rommel observed as the all-clear siren sounded. When its steady whine had ceased, he said to Speidel, "This conference will be finished before noon. Hitler is going to eat by himself, and I can't stomach eating with Jodl and his crowd. After the meeting I will pay my respects to the Führer and we will leave for La Roche-Guyon. Pass the word to Unteroffizier Daniel. We will stop and have lunch at some little village on the way south."

Back in the conference room Rundstedt spoke again, pleading for authority to allow an orderly withdrawal of German forces into the fortress of Cherbourg. Hitler reluctantly agreed but on condition that his force fight for every piece of ground as it moved back. He ordered that the troops holding the fort and harbor were to hold out as long as possible—until mid-July at the very earliest.

As Rommel predicted, the conference concluded at four minutes to 12:00, immediately after the commander of the local V-weapon corps proudly reported that a thousand of the pilotless flying bombs had been launched against London since the night of 12 June. That vastly exaggerated number was designed to bring joy to Hitler's heart, as well as a decoration for the V-weapon commander.

Rommel took his leave of the Führer, explaining that he was urgently required at his headquarters and at the front. Hitler was patently relieved to see him go.

It had been planned that in the afternoon Hitler would tour some of the V-1 sites so that he could be seen gloating over them in the German press. The tour did not happen. Shortly after the Führer had finished his meager lunch, a V-1 launched from a nearby site flew out of control and crashed on a bunker in Wolfsschanze Two, exploding with earthshaking force. Neither Hitler nor anyone in his party was injured, but the Führer was again frightened out of his wits. All plans were cancelled. He departed for Berchtesgaden forthwith, never again to set foot in Wolfsschanze Two at Margival, or anywhere else in France.

The signal reporting the incident awaited Rommel and Speidel when they arrived at La Roche-Guyon shortly after 3:00.

From Rommel there was no reaction. From Speidel, however, there was a curse of regret that the flying bomb had not landed on top of the man whom he was to describe to his colleagues later that day as a crotchety, bent old man, fast reaching the point of raving madness.

18-22 JUNE 1944

LIEUTENANT GENERAL GEORGE SMITH PATTON JR. stood in front of the Michelin touring map of France, scale no. 1:1,000,000, that he himself had stuck on the war room wall at his headquarters at Peover Hall, the remote manor house sixteen kilometers south of Manchester to which he and his Third Army staff had been ordered by Eisenhower. Banished, as Patton saw it.

"Look at that, Codman, look at that." Patton's high, piping voice was incongruous in such a tall, strapping man. His finger pointed at the Caen area where a clerk had traced, using pins and string, that morning's front lines. "Monty's objective was to take Caen on the first day, D-Day, and here it is twelve days later and that son-of-a-bitching little sparrow still hasn't done it. I tell you, Codman, in Sicily I beat him to Messina, and if I'd been leading those troops on D-Day and not Monty, *I'd* have captured Caen on the first day. Remember those goddamned pre-D-Day briefings at his headquarters, St. Paul's School in West Kensington? God, were they ever boring. Monty would always be talking about the need for speed and the need to 'crack about'. And there he is, the little bastard, bogged down right in front of Caen. The Germans have turned that goddamned place into a fortress."

His aide, Captain Charles Codman, knew his general well, and like him, had a sense of humor.

"It seems to me you're both bogged down, Sir."

Patton turned to look through his reading spectacles at his young man.

"You can say that again. I've been in this godforsaken place since the beginning of February—the leader of the fictional First United States Army Group, poised to attack across the Channel with my million-plus men. What a lot of crap. I should have been leading the American forces at the beachhead and not Bradley. And I should be there now, goddamn it, not sitting on my ass in Peover Hall." His eyes looked up at the timbered ceiling in the ancient mansion that had been the seat of several families over hundreds of years. Then back to the map.

"Goddamn it, I'd give my eye teeth to be over there. This war's going to be over before Montgomery or Bradley will let me get into the fight again." For comfort he reached down and patted the white head of his ever-present English bull terrier, Willie. He had found Willie in a kennel on one of his many visits to London, where all the planning was taking place for the invasion of Normandy—Operation Neptune—and the liberation of Europe—Operation Overlord.

As he stood before the map, Patton's mind momentarily went back to Palermo and 22 January 1944. Under attack by the press and in Congress, and in disgrace for his celebrated soldier-slapping incident, he had been removed from command of the American army in Sicily. That day Patton had received his marching orders in the vaguest of terms. The action message read:

> *Orders issued relieving you from assignment this theatre and assigning to duty in U.K. Request you proceed to NATOUSA, Algiers, for orders.*

By now Patton knew not only that his junior in Sicily, General Omar Bradley, was to be the American army commander for Neptune but, as well, that his equal and competitor for glory in Sicily, Montgomery, would command the entire invasion land force. Patton felt crushed. But at the same time he recognized that in the action message the words "assigning to duty in U.K." must have meant what they said. The word "duty" was one of the most significant in George Patton's colorful vocabulary.

When he had arrived in London on 26 January, Patton reported to Eisenhower, who had told him that he would become commander of the Third Army, an army that Patton knew was still in the United States under General Hodges. Eisenhower was vague about instructions. All Patton had felt he was being promised was a minor, de facto military command of an army that would not become operational until some obscure, distant time after D-Day.

In fact for the following months leading up to D-Day, and for some weeks beyond it, Patton's major role had been to play main decoy in a massive scheme of deception—Operation Fortitude—intended to tip the scales toward the success of Neptune. Patton had been chosen as the principal player because he was the only American general the Germans respected. They would be certain that because of his military success in Sicily he would be at the vanguard of any fighting force sent across the Channel for the assault on the French beaches. If the First United States Army Group (FUSAG) was to be credible to the Germans, its commanding general had to be known and respected by them. Ideally he would be the counterpart to Rommel, the German general the Allies most admired.

Patton was therefore the ideal choice to lead FUSAG within Operation Fortitude, whose purpose was to conceal the objectives of Neptune as the main and only point of the invading force. Fortitude South called for the fictional creation of an entire army group comprised of a million men and fifty divisions assembled in the southeast of England near the Channel coast. The idea was to induce the Germans into believing that FUSAG would carry out the main attack in the Pas-de-Calais area, and that the Normandy assault of the two real army groups assembling in southern England, Montgomery's Twenty-first and the American First under Bradley, was merely a diversion.

It was in the Pas-de-Calais that Hitler had lodged his most powerful army in the West, the Fifteenth. The function of Fortitude South was to keep that army in place during Neptune and for as long as possible thereafter, at least until 20 July 1944.

Thus it was that within a few days after reporting to Eisenhower, Patton and his experienced Third Army staff were established at Peover Hall, banished.

By 1 March the organization of his staff was complete, including the acquisition of Willie. The Third Army was in a transitional stage preparing for the move from Fort Sam Houston near San Antonio, Texas, to the gathering ground of England where its new general and his capable staff would whip it into shape along with the other units that would be assigned to it at the appropriate moment. In the war room at Peover Hall, Patton conducted daily conferences with his staff as he enunciated policy and made logistic and administrative decisions.

While unhappy because he had been by-passed at Peover Hall, by the time spring arrived Patton took some satisfaction from knowing that the deception of Fortitude was beginning to have an effect on German intelligence. By March agents reported to their controllers that Patton was in England. FHW (Fremde Heer West), that part of the intelligence evaluation of the German general staff responsible for the western Allies, had stated in a 20 March 1944 bulletin that "General Patton, who was formerly employed in North Africa and is highly regarded for his proficiency, is now in England." Armee Gruppe Patton, the name the Germans gave to his growing fictional force, began to appear regularly in FHW reports.

And by 18 June, as he stood before his map, Patton knew, through Ultra intelligence and other reports, that since Hitler and Rommel fully expected Armee Gruppe Patton to cross the Channel at any time, the German Fifteenth Army was locked securely into the Pas-de-Calais area and out of the Battle of Normandy.

Nevertheless, Patton, at 58 a general "long in the tooth" by Allied standards, was most unhappy "sitting on his ass" in England.

While Patton was looking at his Michelin map that morning, the man he envied most, General Sir Bernard Montgomery, was at his headquarters in Normandy poring over battle maps spread out on the working table in the van he had captured from a German general in North Africa. He had just given the commander of the Anglo-Canadian Second Army, General Sir Miles Dempsey, his orders to mount a further attack against Caen. Dempsey was to capture Caen and provide a strong eastern flank for the army group, continuing the policy of absorbing the enemy reserve divisions in its sector. Montgomery's plan was that he could take Caen in a pincer movement, pushing his forces down on each side of the heavily protected city.

Peering through his spectacles at one of the maps, Montgomery poked his finger at Arromanches and said to his ever-attentive chief-of-staff, Major-General "Freddie" de Guingand, "I'm really worried about these Mulberries. We only have two of them and if we lose them—destroyed by the enemy, by weather, whatever—we'll be helpless. The entire force we have on the beachhead now would have to get out. So we've got to do something, Freddie, we're too vulnerable."

The Mulberries were massive prefabricated portable ports, conceived by Churchill as essential if the invasion was going to be successful. Two had been moved across and put in place shortly after D-Day, one off the American Omaha Beach, the other off the British beach at Arromanches, north of Bayeux. They were made of two hundred floating concrete caissons, the largest of them in the range of six thousand tons, floating bridges, and docks. Each port was protected from incoming heavy seas by some thirty ancient freighters and old warships that had been towed across the Channel and sunk as breakwaters. Even with these Gooseberries, as they were called, Montgomery was concerned about the vulnerability of the invaluable Mulberry ports.

"I'd like you to send Brad an order to clear the Cotentin Peninsula and capture the port of Cherbourg at the earliest possible moment. Tell him my reasoning, that I consider the capture of the port of Cherbourg to be urgent in case we lose a Mulberry. Also tell him that as soon as additional American troops are available, I want him to break away to the south on Granville, Avranches, and Vire. That will take some doing. As I see it, Avranches is the key to the Brest Peninsula."

Montgomery's order was prescient, for on the next day, 19 June, one of the severest storms in decades descended on the Normandy beaches and lasted through to the 22nd. Enormous waves generated by the storm accomplished what Montgomery was worried about: they completely destroyed the American Mulberry. But miraculously, the port at Arromanches was left intact with minor damage. At his morning briefing on the 21st of June, Montgomery heard the bad news from de Guingand.

"So we only have the one left, Freddie," observed Montgomery. "That's our sole life line to bring ashore twelve thousand tons of supplies every day plus troops. God, if the Luftwaffe manages to do it in or if Rommel gets a Panzer spearhead organized . . . That's what I'd do if I was Rommel. I'd collect all my bloody Panzers and make a suicide thrust straight up past Bayeux to Arromanches. So tell Dempsey, and Bradley, too, and also have the air force be on the lookout—for a surprise Panzer attack, a blitzkrieg."

"Let me give you the rest of the bad news about the storm, Sir."

"I'm not sure I'm ready for this, Freddie, dear boy, but if you insist."

Montgomery took off his beret and slumped into his favorite easy chair. The German upholsterers had certainly done a good job for their general.

De Guingand read from a report.

"In addition to the American Mulberry being destroyed, about eight hundred landing craft, tugs, freighters, and other vessels have either been sunk or damaged severely."

"Dear God, that's worse than D-Day! How will that affect our getting supplies across the Channel?"

"The navy says there's no problem, Sir. They've got lots of ships where those came from."

"Good. What's happening in the Cotentin? How is Joe Collins doing? It's absolutely imperative now that he take Cherbourg at the earliest possible moment." Under Bradley, Major General Joe Collins was in command of the American forces in the Cotentin Peninsula. "He simply must crack about and get on with it."

De Guingand's reply was optimistic.

"They're doing much better than they expected, Sir. Evidently there was an infantry division in the peninsula that pulled out just ahead of their arrival."

"Jolly good show. Send word directly to Collins with a copy to Bradley. Tell Collins to crack about, as I say."

"I'm sorry, Sir," his chief-of-staff said, "I'll have to translate 'crack about' for an American. He won't know what the hell you're talking about. I'll tell him to get a 'move on' or, as Gerogie Patton would say, 'Get off your ass.' "

"Poor Georgie," Montgomery mused. "I wonder how he's getting on sitting on his duff at Peover Hall. A pity, Freddie, a real pity. An excellent soldier, a brilliant man, the best fighting general the Americans have, and he's sitting on his duff in England. He'll be beside himself because he's not here . . ."

"Cracking about," de Guingand finished the thought.

20 JUNE 1944

WHENEVER HE returned to the castle at La Roch-Guyon, whether from a trip to inspect the beach defenses, visit the V-1 sites in the Pas-de-Calais area, the Le Havre sector, or the escalating fighting in Normandy, Rommel was always struck by the beauty of the place and was grateful that he had selected it as the headquarters for his Armee Gruppe B. He was particularly pleased with his decision after the trying Führer Conference.

Early in 1944, when he had taken command of Armee Gruppe B, then headquartered at Fontainebleau, he had decided to move the headquarters from the opulence of Paris and into the field closer to the two armies under his command. Rommel believed Paris had a bad effect on his men. They patronized the restaurants, cabarets, brothels, and theaters. And, of course, Paris also offered an extensive black market. For a man like Rommel who did not drink or smoke, did not swear or countenance crude jokes, Paris was not the place to be. Furthermore, Jodl had visited Rundstedt in France early in January that year and had written a devastating inspection report that was widely circulated. Rommel himself was impressed when he read it:

The C.-in-C. West would do well to exchange his Hotel George V for a command post where he could see the blue sky, where the sun shines and which smells fresher. Lower headquarters and officers' accommodations are a danger not only to security but also to inner attitudes and alertness. The bloom of war is completely missing. Deep armchairs and carpets lead to royal household allures. As of March 1, all staffs are to move into their command posts. Unfortunately, these too have largely been built next door to fine chateaux.

Rommel had wanted to use Wolfsschanze Two at Margival for his headquarters. It was remote but sumptuously developed. The place had never been used, but all its facilities, in particular its communications equipment, had been maintained and were in perfect working order. However, as expected, the Führer had turned down his request. As an alternative, Rommel had picked out the castle that had been the ancestral home of the Dukes de la Rochefoucauld in La Roche-Guyon, a picturesque village on the north shore of the Seine some forty kilometers west of the outskirts of Paris.

When he found this idyllic location Rommel was mindful of Jodl's comments about command posts being next door to fine chateaux. The remark did not, however, include command posts inside large chateaux. In any event, while Jodl might inspect the situation in Paris, the chief-of-operations would never lower himself to inspect a mere command post in the field.

So the decision was made. The castle at La Roche-Guyon gave Rommel relatively easy access to all points under his command. He could leave early in the morning in his Horch touring car, go north into the Pas-de-Calais area or west into Normandy, and be back at the chateau, if not for dinner, then well before midnight.

At the centre of the village of La Roche-Guyon was an inn, the Aux Vieux Donjon, with a cluster of houses and shops spreading out from it. At the crossroads was the village war memorial. Moving north from it one entered the Rue d'Audience—a drive lined with sculpted lime trees whose thick branches formed a canopy over the roadway. Tall iron, gold-tipped gates at the end of the drive opened onto the castle's courtyard. Near the gates stood an ancient church, the tolling of whose bell at 6:00 each morning signaled the Angelus as well as the end of the night's curfew.

The castle itself loomed over the village. Behind it rose the towering white face of the cliff that formed the northern edge of La Roche-Guyon. The gray-black slates of the castle's tower roofs peaked almost to the top of the sheer cliff where stood the ruins of the original Donjon tower. From Norman days it had surveyed the winding Seine and its never-ending procession of boats and barges.

In front of the castle lay a long sunken garden and lawn. The stables stood lower and to the left of the main building, while the iron gates of the courtyard entrance were on the right. The entire perimeter of the estate was lined with protective coils of barbed wire. Sentries were posted at key points around the headquarters. The countryside for some distance around bristled with the barrels of 88-millimeter antiaircraft guns in towering clusters like organ pipes.

Rommel had invited the Duke de Rochefoucauld and his family to occupy the upper stories of the castle. They had done so, keeping much to themselves. Nevertheless they enjoyed a friendly relationship with Rommel and those of his senior staff who moved into the remainder of the building. In the cliff behind the castle were deep caves and tunnels from which stone had been quarried for the construction of the castle centuries before. Rommel had these converted into a series of bomb-proof offices, storage rooms, and a communications center.

The main entrance into the castle was through nine-meter-tall French doors, which opened into an oak-paneled corridor lined with paintings of family ancestors. Rommel's office was a spacious, high-ceilinged hall on the main floor. Its double doors opened onto a terrace of rose trees and the courtyard beyond. On the wood-paneled walls hung Gobelin tapestries and oil paintings.

But it was the desk that had intrigued Rommel from the first day he had entered the room. It was a splendid piece of Renaissance furniture, its spindly legs carrying a top of intricately inlaid polished wood. Two hundred and fifty-nine years earlier the Marquis de Louvois, the war minister of Louis XIV, had sat at it to sign the revocation of the Edict of Nantes, which had given members of religious minorities the right to worship and hold political office. The Act of Revocation caused hundreds of thousands of French families to flee to exile in Germany and England.

Rommel sat down at the remarkable desk and ran his hands over its highly polished surface. It was 6:15 in the morning. He and Speidel had just finished breakfast in the ornate dining room, where they had, as usual, discussed matters to be dealt with that day and had made a start on the reports that had come in overnight from the various units in the field. Breakfast over, Speidel had followed Rommel into his office.

When the feldmarschall had settled into his chair, Speidel said, "There's also a signal in from Hausser. His Ninth SS Panzer Division should be in the assembly area by tomorrow morning. They have about another forty-eight kilometers to go.''

Rommel shook his head.

''But they can't travel in daylight that close to the front. The Jabos would have a field day with his tanks and trucks. Just in case he gets foolhardy you'd better send him another order confirming that none of the Ninth's tanks or equipment is to move in daylight. They've come all the way from Poland to be here. It would be disaster if the Jabos destroyed them before they got into action. As soon as the Ninth has regrouped in the assembly-area and Hausser is ready for action, I'll decide where to put them. Probably on Sepp Dietrich's left flank, southwest of Caen.''

''I'll send a signal to Hausser immediately, Sir.'' Speidel was anxious to get to his own office. He had plenty of reading to do from the remaining stack of messages that had arrived overnight. Having culled out the most important, he would come back to Rommel later in the morning to brief him and discuss them.

As Speidel was turning to leave, Rommel's aide, Hauptmann Hellmuth Lang, walked in. He had been with Rommel since March. The feldmarschall had asked for a new aide who was ''a major, a Panzer officer, highly decorated, and a Swabian''. Lang had all those qualifications except that in rank he was only a hauptmann. At his neck was the Knight's Cross, which he had won as a tank commander in Russia.

''Excuse me, Herr Feldmarschall, this message just came in. I thought you should have it right away.''

Rommel took the long typewritten sheet and began to read. Astonished, he looked up at Speidel.

''You won't believe this, Hans. Do you remember the look on Jodl's face when I was talking about moving my troops and armor south out of the range of the naval guns, then attacking the Mulberry at Arromanches with my Panzers? Remember the sneer on Jodl's face? Well, look at this.''

He handed the document across the desk. The tall, owlish Speidel adjusted the circular glasses on his nose and read quickly. A smile spread across his face.

''It's signed by Hitler himself. Obviously he was listening. But the order doesn't give you authority to withdraw south out of the range of the naval guns.'' Speidel reviewed the salient points. ''It says only that you are to assemble a combined Panzer and infantry force in the sector between St. Lô and Caumont. The Panzer divisions will be the Ninth and Tenth SS Divisions of two SS Panzer Korps presently en route. The infantry will be those divisions which in your discretion will form the spearhead of the attack which is to go in as soon as the Panzer divisions are ready. Your objective is to cleave a corridor to Bayeaux and the coast, isolate the British from the Americans and 'Dunkirk' them, and at the same time destroy the port installations at Arromanches.''

Rommel stood up, invigorated. Walking quickly to the French doors, he threw them open to let in the morning air, the fragrance of the roses, and the early rays of the sun.

"I know it doesn't let me withdraw south. But it's enough. It's enough."

Rommel remained in the doorway looking out across the garden, his feet apart, hands clasped behind his back, his black jackboots gleaming in the sun below his gray-green jodhpurs. At the opening of his golden-braided collar hung his Knight's Cross with Oak Leaves and Diamonds—he was proud to be the first German army officer to have received the Diamonds. Below it was the coveted and rarely awarded Pour le Mérite, the highest German award for valor, which he had won in World War I for exceptional bravery and skill in battle. His golden feldmarschall's epaulets glinted on narrow shoulders, and a wide leather belt encircled his field jacket at the waist. He was short and stocky, quite unlike the tall Prussians and aristocrats who populated the upper echelons of the German general staff.

"So, Hans, we must prepare a plan." He spun around, his clear blue eyes flashing. He spoke to Lang. "Find General Hausser. Get him on the telephone. Wherever he is, get him!"

"Yes, Sir!" Lang turned to leave.

"General Speidel and I will want a set of maps for the St. Lô-Caumont area across to Caen and north to the beaches. Tell them to tape them together and put them on the conference table. Then find General Hausser."

"Yes, Sir," Lang said again, striding out the doorway.

Rommel laughed as he moved back toward the sun-filled doorway, drawn there like a wise old dog to a sun patch on a rug. His eyes took in the light morning mist, sun-cut over the yellows and reds of the flowers blooming throughout the courtyard gardens.

He called back over his shoulder, "Well, what do you think, Hans? What happened? That supercilious idiot Jodl obviously thought my plan was a joke. But here we are with the guts of it, signed by Hitler himself."

Speidel didn't move. He crossed his arms in front of him, his brow furrowed.

"It seems to me that you and the Führer were on common ground when it came to destroying the Mulberry port at Arromanches. I think where you lost him was when you spoke of first withdrawing your tanks and infantry out of range of the enemy's guns. That smells like retreat, and the Führer will never give an order to retreat, even to gain a tactical advantage."

Rommel's feet were apart once again, hands tight behind his back.

"You're quite right, Hans. The words retreat or give up ground are simply not in his vocabulary. And the fact that he abhors giving such an order has already cost tens of thousands of German soldiers their lives."

"And will do so in the future."

Rommel's head nodded.

"Exactly." He unclasped his hands. His right hand came around to the front of his collar. Without thinking, he fingered the smooth enamel of his Knight's Cross and touched the sharp points of the Pour le Mérite.

"So, as I see it, Herr Feldmarschall," Speidel continued, "the Führer didn't like the retreat part but decided that your idea of striking the Mulberry was really his idea. I can just imagine the scene yesterday during the Grand Situation Conference when he announced his decision."

In his mind's eye, Rommel conjured up the Grand Situation Conference at Berchtesgaden. It began every day around noon and lasted two to three hours. The only person seated was Hitler. There was one exception. If Reichsmarschall Hermann Göring was in attendance—as he would be today—there was an upholstered stool for him. He was, after all, the number-two man in the Third Reich. There was also his obesity. All the other participants stood around the long red-marble map table, just as they had stood at Margival. Rommel could see them: Goebbels, the little man of propaganda; Himmler, the viper's head of the Gestapo; Hitler's chief-of-staff, Feldmarschall Wilhelm Keitel, tall and broad-shouldered, a monocle clutched in his left eye—totally loyal to Hitler, he was despised by his peers, who called him ''Yes-Keitel'' and ''the Nodding Ass''; Generaloberst Alfred Jodl, Hitler's chief-of-operations, the intermediary between Hitler and his feldmarschalls; and a host of other generals of the OKW staff, all bowing and swaying to the varying moods of the turbulent Führer.

Rommel could see the maps on the long table, illuminated by desk lamps with long swiveling arms. The conference would undoubtedly begin with the northern part of the Russian front and finally move to the secondary situation, the battle in Normandy and the expected attack in the Pas-de-Calais area. The proposal to hit the Mulberry would be glistening in Hitler's memory as the only true jewel to come out of that unhappy discussion at Wolfsschanze Two.

As he conjured up the scene at Berchtesgaden, Rommel mused aloud, ''I can just see it, Hans. There would be no consultation with Jodl. Hitler would simply tell him what he had decided. And now it is up to us to get on with it. Let's go to the war room.''

Followed by his gangling chief-of-staff, Rommel strode down the long paneled hallway into the large chamber he had chosen as his war room. Here he calculated his next moves, plotting the location of his own forces and those of Montgomery and Bradley opposite him. It was here he made his operational decisions and attempted to translate the tactical orders issued by Hitler or by Jodl's OKW staff; these orders usually had no relationship to reality or practicality because they were created by men who had never been on the fighting ground and who did not know the true state of the battle or its terrain. All they had at their distant headquarters were countless maps and charts and the belief that they were superior beings, intellectually and militarily, and that the commanders in the field were lower-level incompetents. Or so it appeared to Rommel.

On the high walls of the war room (once the castle's music room), maps of various scales were hung at levels best suited for the feldmarschall's easy viewing.

The duty officer had prepared the required maps and placed them on the long plotting table in the center of the room. Rommel went directly to them. Speidel stood to his left as the feldmarschall's fingers traced points and areas.

''If we take the road between St. Lô and Caumont as the starting point, it's roughly thirty-five kilometers to Arromanches as the crow flies. Obviously, the spearhead would have to take off northeast and go around Bayeux, probably on the east side of it. It would go cross-country rather than trying to stay on the road system and would probably move out from the Caumont area in order to minimize water crossings. The route to do that would be from Caumont northeast toward Tilly and then straight north.

"That would put the spearhead between the Aure River on the west and on the east the Seulles River, which goes through Tilly. Both of those rivers flow north; therefore, if we could get into the corridor between them, we would have a clean run north past Bayeux on the east side and up to Arromanches."

Speidel nodded.

"The dividing line between the Second British Army and the First U.S. Army runs north and south just to the west of Bayeux. If you want to separate the British and Americans as the order instructs. . ."

Rommel interrupted, "It wouldn't matter if we left a small piece of the British army with their American friends on the west flank. The point is we would have the bulk of the British forces isolated over here to the east between Bayeaux and the Orne."

The sharp sound of the telephone stopped Rommel. The duty officer picked it up, then brought it over to him.

"It's for you, Sir. Obergruppenführer Hausser on the line."

"Good." He was on the best of terms with the much older Paul Hausser. The fact that the Panzer commander was a Nazi and an SS (Schutzstaffel) general did not stand in the way of Rommel's respect for a capable officer. In fact, Hausser and Geyr von Schweppenburg, the Panzer Commander West, had been at La Roche-Guyon two days before for a full briefing session by Rommel on the Normandy front. Hausser, just moving in from the eastern front, particularly needed to know how the command of Armee Gruppe B expected his orders to be carried out. The feldmarschall, who made it a point to know and understand each of the generals serving under him, had been much impressed by Hausser, a tried and true Panzer commander who had seen extensive service against the Soviets.

"Paul, where are you?"

"I've established my headquarters near a small village called Mortrée. It's about thirteen kilometers southeast of Argentan."

"Good. You're well out of range of the naval guns. I hope you have plenty of trees for cover."

"Yes, Herr Feldmarschall. The last thing I want is a flock of Jabos after me. God, they're all over the place. I've never seen anything like it. There weren't any around yesterday; the high winds and rain kept them on the ground. But they're out today. We've already seen several squadrons—Spitfires, Mustangs. I haven't seen any of our fighters yet. What's happened to the Luftwaffe?"

"I'll tell you what's happened to the Luftwaffe. Their fat commander. . ."

"Göring?"

"No, the fat commander in France, Feldmarschall Hugo von Sperrle. He left all his squadrons in the Reich until after the invasion began. He tells me he can now get only three hundred fighters into airfields within range of the front lines, and only about sixty of those are serviceable!"

"Unbelievable!"

"Yes, unbelievable." Rommel was about to add the words, "and the main reason we're going to lose this war". He was intensely bitter about the collapse of the Luftwaffe in the West. But he bit his tongue. It was his duty to keep the morale and spirits of his field commanders up, even if he had to move away from the truth. "Yes, unbelievable, but a fact you have to live with."

Speidel still held the OKW message in his hand. Rommel took it, saying into the telephone, "I have an exciting new order from OKW this morning, Paul. It involves you." He read the order, leaving out nothing. "So your Ninth and Tenth Panzer Divisions are going to be the point of the spearhead. What do you think of that?"

"That's marvelous, Sir, just marvelous. We'll shove those goddamn British bastards right into the goddamn ocean!" He paused. "Sorry about the language, Herr Feldmarschall." In his exuberance, he had forgotten Rommel's distaste for coarse language and was relieved when his commander laughed.

"Good heavens, General, I'm not a priest. If you didn't get excited about leading the force that will defeat the British and destroy their Mulberry, there would be something wrong."

"Well anyway, Sir, the Jabos haven't seen us, and I'm sure they won't. I have all my tanks and vehicles under trees with camouflage netting over them. We even put hay and branches over the track marks in the fields.''

"Excellent. But watch out for the bludhunds. If any of them circle over your position, you're in trouble. There'll only be two of them, perhaps four.''

"What do you mean by 'bludhunds', Sir?''

"Canadian and British Mustangs. They look very much like the ME109. They're reconnaissance aircraft and their pilots are highly trained at spotting. If they find you, they won't attack. What they'll do is call in the rocket Typhoons or Spitfires with their bombs or the American Thunderbolts or whatever they can lay their hands on. Now what about your two divisions?''

There was static on the line momentarily.

"The tanks, trucks, and personnel of the Ninth Division have arrived. Most survived the trip from Poland. However, I lost eight trucks and ten men were killed last evening near L'Aigle about sixty-five kilometers east of here. They had stayed off the road during daylight hours as instructed and spent the day in some woods. But they were so anxious to get here they decided to start off just before dark. That did them in. They were caught by four Spitfires. They went up in flames, every one of them. I think that has taught the whole division a lesson.''

Rommel sighed.

"Unfortunately there will be more lessons to come. When do you think the Ninth will be ready for action?''

"It will probably take four days. It's been a long haul by rail across from Poland. With the last three hundred and twenty kilometers on our own tracks, we'll have a lot of repair work in addition to training. I have to get my people up to battle standards again . . . tactics, radio communications, the firing drills. I would say four days at the outside.

"Then I reckon it's about one hundred and forty kilometers to Caumont by road. And that will have to be done at night. So they'll have seven hours of darkness in which to move 122 tanks, 2,800 motor vehicles of all description, 500 motorcycles, and 16,352 men, the current division strength. It will take me two nights to be in position. So the Ninth should be ready to go, be at the start line by dawn on the 27th, one week from now with the start at last light that evening.''

"And what about your Tenth Division?''

"It's still en route from Poland, Sir. I expect the first

elements to start arriving here tomorrow night. The whole division should be here by the 23rd.''

"That means the Tenth will have only two days to get itself ready," said Rommel. "Training will have to be done around the clock, and repairs, too. Any tanks or vehicles that are not serviceable when you move up to the St. Lô-Caumont area will be left behind. I'll give you instructions as to the exact start line positions and timings later on.''

"What will happen if elements of the Tenth still haven't arrived on the 24th, Sir, when it's time to move out toward the start line?''

There was no hesitation in Rommel's answer. "All the elements of the Tenth that are available on the 24th will move off with the Ninth so they will be in position to start the attack on the 27th. I simply can't commit the Ninth by itself. You will inform me immediately when the first elements of the Tenth Panzer begin to arrive in your headquarters area. One final thing, Paul.'' Rommel looked up at Speidel as he spoke into the telephone. "I will allocate certain infantry, Panzer, and other units to the attacking force. From this point it will be known as the Panzer Gruppe Hausser. What do you say about that, Paul?''

"I'm honored, Sir, highly honored.'' Hausser's voice rang with pleasure. "Panzer Gruppe Hausser will carry out its assignment no matter what the odds. We will bring glory to the Führer, the Third Reich, and especially to you, Herr Feldmarschall. You can count on us!''

"That's what I expect, General Hausser. I want you to give a progress report by telephone to General Speidel every evening around 6:00. This may be our last chance to defeat the enemy and drive him into the sea. So put everything you have into it. Any questions?''

At the other end of the line, General Paul Hausser was in a state of euphoria. He was in his operations tent in the presence of six of his senior officers. Each of them had sat at the conference table listening intently to Hausser's every word, trying to guess what was being said by their commander-in-chief. As the conversation drew to a close, Hausser, the committed Nazi SS officer, jumped up from his chair, elated. "You can count on us, Herr Feldmarschall!'' As he shouted, "Heil Hitler!'' into the phone and lifted his right arm in the Hitler salute, his officers, like robots following their master's command, leaped to their feet. In unison, they returned his salute and roared "Heil Hitler!" in reply.

Hausser put down the telephone. He looked at his veteran Panzer officers, a smile on his face. "Gentlemen, we have been given one of the greatest opportunities ever presented to a Panzer Korps. Let me show you on the map what Feldmarschall Rommel has tasked Panzer Guppe Hausser to do."

Another message was handed to Rommel as he hung up. It was brought by the unobtrusive Luftwaffe staff officer assigned to his headquarters. He was intentionally inconspicuous because of the animosity of the army staff toward the totally ineffective air force he represented. In fact, the man was downright ashamed of its pitiful performance. Nevertheless, because this signal from Luftwaffe headquarters finally contained what he perceived to be good news, he decided he should deliver it himself.

The feldmarschall looked at the man's gray-blue Luftwaffe uniform with thinly veiled contempt. But as he read the message, a smile appeared on his face and his head bobbed with approval.

"Good, very good. A fine piece of work by your reconnaissance people, Oberst."

Rommel knew that huge lump of one-hundred and thirty-five kilograms of massive humanity in Paris with a monocle clamped in its right eye, Feldmarschall Sperrle, would be pleased that the army was finally happy with something the Luftwaffe had done.

He read the message aloud for Speidel and the others in the room to hear.

> *First-light reconnaissance preliminary radio report indicates that portable harbor under construction in American sector of beach near Grand Camp has been destroyed by high waves of storm, 20-21 June. Severe wind and wave conditions still prevailing. Estimate two hundred plus landing and other craft stranded on beach in that area and a hundred plus in British sector to east. Further report will issue when air photographs are interpreted later.*

Rommel was pleased. "This means the enemy now has only one port, the one at Arromanches. He has to put *all* his supplies through it. If we destroy or capture that port, we cut his life line like the oxygen line of a diver. Even if we can't destroy it, the storm will delay the landing of fuel, men, tanks, and everything else. The success of Panzer Gruppe Hausser is absolutely essential now. I'll put the Second Panzer Division, which OKW, in its ultimate wisdom, has finally taken out of reserve for me, under Hausser as well. Speidel,'' Rommel said crisply, ''send orders to the Second Panzer accordingly. They should move up the line east of Caumont opposite the Thirtieth Division of the British and the Fifth Corps of the Americans and await instructions from Hausser.''

He paused, and then asked Speidel, ''What about Cherbourg? That's the enemy's only alternative for a port. The longer we can deny it to them. . .''

''As you know, the Americans thrust right across the Cotentin Peninsula two days ago,'' Speidel replied. ''They're now moving north toward Cherbourg. Fortunately our Seventy-seventh infantry division got out of the peninsula before the Americans cut them off. A most wise move, Herr Feldmarschall.''

''Hitler and OKW don't agree with your judgment. They're throwing a tantrum because whoever gave the order to get the Seventy-seventh out was going directly against a Hitler directive. I wonder who gave that order, Hans?'' He gave Speidel a knowing look. Both of them knew but would never admit that it was Rommel himself who had given the verbal order, of which there was no record.

Speidel continued: ''Our troops are staging a fighting retreat, preparing to fall back into the city of Cherbourg. As you well know, Herr Feldmarschall, they're under direct instructions from the Führer to deny the enemy access as long as possible. The other day he spoke of holding Cherbourg until mid-July.'' Rommel silently shook his head as he thought ''totally unrealistic''. Speidel went on. ''The navy reports there's enough food for eight weeks, but the fortress commandant has only the remnants of three divisions available to him. The last report is of heavy fighting in the approaches to Cherbourg. General Schlieben is under instructions to destroy all of the port facilities and if possible to make the entrances to it from the sea unusable before surrender takes place.''

''So even if Cherbourg was surrendered tomorrow, if the demolition work is done properly,'' Rommel speculated, "it would be several weeks before the enemy could use it as a port. Am I correct?"

"I think so, Sir," Speidel replied. "Perhaps that's a question you should put to Admiral Ruge." The admiral was on Rommel's staff as his naval adviser.

"Yes, I'll get his opinion immediately."

Rommel now directed his attention to the hapless Luftwaffe staff officer. "Well, Herr Oberst, it must be crystal clear in your mind now that the destruction of the port at Arromanches is the key to the defeat of all the Allied forces. What does the Luftwaffe intend to do about it?"

The answer was what Rommel expected. "Sir, on the 18th, the day after the Führer arrived back in Berchtesgaden, Reichsmarschall Göring gave the order to Feldmarschall Sperrle to attack and destroy the port at Arromanches and also the American one under construction." The oberst shifted nervously from one foot to the other. "After my feldmarschall's staff had studied photographs of the ports, they concluded that to attack them with Focke-Wulf 190 fighter-bombers would inflict little damage—well, not enough to make the effort worthwhile. The only way we could be assured of success would be to mass a force of between fifty and one hundred Heinkel and other big bombers. That would be the minimum."

"If you could get them out of Germany and the eastern front," Rommel broke in. "Fat chance."

The oberst was not about to quarrel. "Yes, Sir," he responded and went on. "For accuracy the raid would have to be in daylight. With the thousand-plus Allied fighters now operating from the beachhead and the enemy's heavy antiaircraft strength around the port, the mission would amount to suicide. It could be done at low altitude in bad weather—we'd have to wait for it, for low cloud for escape purposes—even so it would be, as I say, Herr Feldmarschall, a suicide mission."

Rommel interrupted, "But as of this moment you have only one target, the port at Arromanches. Surely your risk is cut in half?"

The staff officer shrugged. "Either way it doesn't matter, Sir. Feldmarschall Sperrle doesn't have the fifty to one hundred bombers available. They're all committed to the eastern front. I'm also informed that even if he had them, he wouldn't be prepared to send them to certain destruction."

That statement astonished Rommel. "Even if it meant the

defeat of the Anglo-American forces? That's an incredible position. A coward's position. My soldiers and tanks are being sacrificed every day! I don't care what your fat master in Paris has decided!'' Rommel's voice was hard with anger. ''I want you to send him a message that the commander-in-chief of Armee Gruppe B demands that the Luftwaffe assemble from the Russian front, or wherever it can find them, a force of bombers sufficient to attack and destroy the enemy port at Arromanches within the week. If Feldmarschall Sperrle fails or refuses to do this, then I will go directly to the Führer. Is that understood?''

''Yes, Sir.'' The oberst did an about-face and almost ran out of the room.

Erwin Rommel was obviously shaken by the statement of Luftwaffe weakness. He leaned forward, hands spread apart, palms down on the map table. His head dropped in a gesture of despair.

''I tell you, Hans, no Luftwaffe support means the enemy is free, absolutely free, with his hundreds of fighters and bombers, to range at will over our approaches to the front lines, destroying and stopping our movements while he can carry on at his pleasure, subject only to the weather and the whims of God.'' He stood, straightened his shoulders, and walked slowly to the courtyard doorway, his back to Speidel.

''There is no possible way I can win the Battle of Normandy. None whatsoever. I have a heavy sense of responsibility. I have my military responsibility. But I also have a responsibility to the people of Germany, just as much as Adolf Hitler has. The German people look to me. I know they do. Above all other generals, they look to me.'' He paused as he thought about the inevitable.

''There must be a political solution, Hans, there must be. We have to have an armistice with the Anglo-Americans. This senseless fighting of this war we cannot win must stop. I know that Churchill and Roosevelt say 'unconditional surrender', but I don't believe them. I'm sure they'd accept an armistice with conditions. We still have the leverage and the strength to force conditions that are acceptable to us. We can negotiate from strength. But if we are totally defeated, we will have no leverage whatsoever; we will have to accept an unconditional surrender.''

Speidel, a sensitive, sympathetic man, was moved by his chief's anguish. He walked toward him, lifting his hand to place on the feldmarschall's shoulder. But he held back, for as close as he felt to Rommel, there was not the intimacy of equals between them.

As he let his hand drop back, Speidel suggested, "Next week, Herr Feldmarschall, next week. Let's wait and see what happens to Panzer Gruppe Hauser. To hell with the Luftwaffe. Hausser will bring it off. The British and the Americans will go skulking back to England, what's left of them, and they'll never come back."

"You're right, Hans." Rommel turned around. Looking Speidel in the eye, he said, "But if the Luftwaffe does nothing and Hausser fails, then I tell you, Hans, I will have no choice. If I don't do it, no one else will. The Schwarze Kapelle armistice plan—I will attempt it with the other generals, whether Hitler approves of an armistice attempt or not. It is my duty to the German people."

24 JUNE 1944

THE ROUGH starting roar of the Horch echoed from the chateau's stables, bouncing off the gray face of the limestone cliff, filling the misty early morning air with a barrage of hostile sound. The noise reached Rommel's ears as he sat at his desk writing the last few lines of a letter to his beloved wife, Lu, alone and lonely at their home in Herrlingen. He usually wrote to her in the evening. It was the best time because it allowed him to clarify his thoughts about the events of the day. But the night before he had been entertaining visitors. And today, as he told Lu in the letter, he would spend most of his time on the road.

He planned to visit the headquarters of the Eighty-fourth Army Korps northeast of St. Lô, talk to the commander and his staff, and get a firsthand look at the battle situation where his forces faced the American Nineteenth and Fifth Corps of the First U.S. Army under Bradley. The St. Lô sector was bocage country, the fields and roads bordered by thick, centuries-old hedges sitting on high mounds of earth. It was almost impossible for tanks, whether German or enemy, to operate in the impeding clutches of the labyrinthine hedgerows. It was infantry country from the St. Lô sector across the base of the Cherbourg Peninsula to its western shore on the Gulf of Saint-Malo. Rommel's troops there were holding the line against the Americans, assisted in no small part by the hedgerows, obstacles not only for American tanks but for enemy foot soldiers attempting to advance.

The drive westerly to St. Lô would be long, uncomfortable, and dangerous. Once he was ferried across the Seine, the distance was two hundred and ninety difficult kilometers.

Rommel could have sat at his sumptuous headquarters at La Roche-Guyon and fought the battle by map and telephone as they did at OKW in Berchtesgaden. But that was not his style. He believed in the principle of visible leadership. He felt he should set an example for his generals and troops by being at the front lines, exposed to danger and unafraid. He therefore drove over the roads of Normandy in broad daylight in his magnificent Horch, its top down, readily visible to his soldiers and French civilians—and to the Jabos, the enemy fighter aircraft with which he constantly played a deadly game of hide-and-seek.

One of Rommel's strengths was his ability to extract high levels of accomplishment from average people. He could be rough on occasion but only with good reason. Never did he bear a grudge, and his anger was rare and short-lived. He had the ability to articulate in a clear and uncomplicated way exactly what was on his mind so that both officers and men understood him. He carried himself with an easy, natural dignity, but also knew when and how to act impressively. His sense of humor was subdued but ever present. All his people, including his field commanders, knew he detested obscenity and crude jokes. A man of indefatigable energy, he was on the move constantly, making frequent visits to the battlefield.

The sound of the Horch starting was the signal that his capable young driver, Unteroffizier Daniel, would have the shiny big touring car in the courtyard in five minutes, the top folded down. With the Jabos roaming the skies over Normandy, ready to pounce instantly on the most delectable of all targets, a staff car, it was mandatory that the canvas top be down to give the spotter, Unterfeldwebel Holke, a clear view in all directions from his place in the back seat. His job was to watch for Jabos in a sky which that day was gray, the high overcast cloud obliterating the sun—conditions that would make it easier for Holke, or for that matter, the feldmarschall himself or his aide, Hauptmann Lang, to spot any lurking enemy fighters silhouetted like soaring hawks against the cloud.

The feldmarschall handed his letter to his aide and went into the bathroom where he relieved himself, then combed back his wispy hair. That morning, the headquarters barber had cut his hair and shaved the sides and back of his head. In the mirror he noted ruefully that his slanted forehead was getting noticeably higher.

Passing through the bedroom, he stopped to pick up his flat uniform cap with its typically German high front and abrupt black peak. He put it on slightly canted to the left and picked up his walking-stick-length, gold-handled feldmarschall's baton, which he always carried in the field. It was his badge of honor and rank. There would be no gloves today. Although the sky was overcast, it was hot even in the early morning. In spite of the heat, Rommel wore his long-sleeved field uniform with its full-length sleeved jacket and high collar with his Knight's Cross and the Pour le Mérite at his throat.

From the look of the clouds, it might rain. He would take his trench coat. Rain or no rain, they would have to travel with the top down in order to maintain the watch for Jabos. It was most uncomfortable to be caught in a storm and have to travel with the rain stinging into one's face like sharp needles and be soaked through the heaviest of clothing. On days when rain was falling or forecast it was Rommel's practice to cancel any planned trip to the Normandy front. Only in the gravest of emergencies would he break that rule. Today, no rain had been forecast, but just in case, he would bring the coat.

Hellmuth Lang was waiting for him in the office, carrying his ever-present briefcase.

"So, the schoolmaster has brought his usual reading lesson for the student," joked Rommel.

"Ah, but I have a very bright student who is always willing to learn."

"Not always, Lang, not always," the feldmarschall retorted as he strode from his office through the open French doors, down the terrace steps to the highly polished Horch, its engine idling smoothly. Unteroffizier Daniel opened the rear door for him and saluted. Rommel returned the salute by touching the gold tip of his baton to the black peak of his cap.

"Good morning, Daniel. No, I will sit in the front seat next to you this morning. My taskmaster, Hauptmann Lang, has brought a briefcase full of papers for me to read. I will sit up front so the wind won't blow everything away. When we get near the battle area and have to take to the back roads to avoid the cursed Jabos, I'll do the map reading."

Daniel moved smartly to open the front door. As Rommel lowered himself into the seat, he added, "We never get lost when I'm map reading, do we, Daniel?" Another joke—on at least three occasions since the start of the battle in Normandy the feldmarschall had misread the map and become lost.

Daniel smiled. "Never, Sir. Never." Obviously the feld-marschall was in a good humor that morning.

Daniel moved on the double around to the driver's side. As he slipped in behind the wheel he turned to the spotter, Feldwebel Holke, sitting in the back next to Hauptmann Lang. "Did you bring the lunch?"

"Yes," Holke replied. "It's in the trunk."

"Good," said the feldmarschall. "If we can manage it, we'll eat on the run. Better give me the maps, Hellmuth. I want to show Daniel the route I want to take. Yes, here we are. When we get across the river, we'll go south to Dreux and then west through L'Aigle and Argentan. I want to drop down there to see General Hausser at Mortrée. Then we'll get on the back roads and make our way northwest toward St. Lô. The headquarters of the Eighty-fourth is just to the northeast of the town. At least that's where it was yesterday. Looks to me about three hundred and twenty kilometers. It should take us about four-and-a-half hours."

"Plus the stop to see General Hausser, Sir," Daniel added as he put the Horch into gear and drove slowly out of the courtyard.

Rommel nodded. "Right. And on the way back we'll stop at Vassy, the headquarters of the Forty-seventh Panzer Korps. A long trip," he said quietly, as he shoved the maps into the door pocket.

"And if the Jabos are out in force, and from the looks of this weather they will be, it'll be even longer, Sir," the young driver added.

Rommel merely nodded. The Jabos would indeed be out in force. Only a fool would be traveling in broad daylight in an open staff car. But he had no choice; as commander-in-chief, he had to do his duty and be seen doing it.

The car passed through the high iron gates of the chateau; past saluting sentries; down the Rue d'Audience under the roof of leaves of the pollarded lime trees; past the Aux Vieux Donjon Inn toward the Seine. A few village men doffed their hats.

The flat-decked, two-car ferry was waiting for them. Its red-faced old captain and his grandson signaled the heavy Horch down the ramp and onto the deck. At the usual spot, amidships, Daniel stopped the car, set the hand brake, and turned off the engine.

Rommel got out and listened to the babble of French orders being given by the captain to his little assistant.

He always enjoyed this half-kilometer voyage across the river. As usual he stood at the bow, feet apart, his hands clasping his feldmarschall's baton behind him. On the high front of his cap, he wore his North Africa glasses, invaluable against the dust on the back roads.

The gray morning light glinted on the ruffled surface of the Seine, accentuating the herringbone-like waves from the bow of a squat, heavily loaded barge. Its deck was just above the waterline as it plowed past them through the murky waters like some ponderous turtle. She was ugly as vessels go, but to Rommel she was a thing of beauty for she was carrying on her decks scores of wooden ammunition crates. They and whatever else was in the vast hold would be offloaded downstream at Vernon. There they would be placed in motor trucks to be carried to the distant Normandy front, where shortages of ammunition were increasing as thousands of shells were expended each day against the ever-stronger enemy.

Near midstream, as the bow of the ferry battered the rolling wake-waves from the receding barge, Rommel turned to look back toward La Roche-Guyon, marveling at the fairy-tale sight of the soaring, slate-topped stone towers at its corners; at its superbly crafted lines sharply edged by the vertical face of the crowding cliff, gray-white in the hampered light of the obliterated sun. At this moment, as often happened when he was working and living inside it, he had a sense of a direct link with the Rochefoucauld who had built the place some four hundred years before, and with his many descendants who had been born, lived, and died within its thick, ever-cool stone walls. How fortunate he was, he thought, a man of humble origins whose father had been a schoolmaster at Heidenheim, to be spending even a small part of his life in a place so opulent and richly overlaid with history.

When they were off the ferry and heading southwest, toward the Dreux, Rommel took the briefcase from Lang, who shouted over the roar of the car's engine and the wind, "The top message is from the Feldmarschall Sperrle about the Luftwaffe attacking the Mulberry port."

"I'll bet I can guess what it says."

He put the briefcase on his lap and took out a thick wad of messages clipped together.

The first one read:

*Have discussed your request for heavy attack against
Arromanches port with Reichsmarschall Göring. In
view of severe shortage of suitable bombers and the
commitment of those we do have to the eastern front,
it is not possible to mount a force large enough to
ensure the destruction of the enemy port. Furthermore, even if a force of sufficient strength could be
gathered, its risk of certain total destruction by over-
whelmingly superior army fighter numbers would make
air attack impossible.*

> Signed
> Hugo von Sperrle
> Feldmarschall.
> 23 June 1944

Rommel shook his head in anger and frustration. That signal was a certificate of doom for the forces under his command. After his bitter experience in North Africa, where he
had no choice but to fight without the Luftwaffe and had
inevitably been defeated, he had sworn he would never engage in another battle without adequate air support. Yet here
he was again, in the same position, if not worse. There was
no hope now of even the slightest tactical air support.
Sperrle's message could not have been more definitive if it
had been done on parchment complete with a fat red wax
seal and ribbons. In Rommel's mind the advice he had given
Hitler a week before was now doubly right. This insane one-
sided battle in Normandy must be stopped. The mindless
bombing of German cities and the killing of thousands of
civilians must be stopped. But Hitler refused even to talk
about the political decision, an armistice.

There was still one opportunity left to throw the enemy
back into the sea. Just one—and it would be a gamble with
almost impossible odds. Everything depended on Paul
Hausser and the armee gruppe that was being formed under
his command. If Hausser could capture or destroy the Mulberry at Arromanches, then with Armee Gruppe Hausser
on the left and the First Panzer Korps under Dietrich on the
right, they would hurl the British into the sea. That done,
the Panzers and infantry would turn west, smash the Americans, and drive them out of France forever.

Yes, there was that one last chance. It must not fail. But
if it did, there had to be an armistice. And apart from Hit-

ler, there was only one other German who could take the initiative with the Anglo-Americans. That man was he, Erwin Rommel, who at that moment considered his duty and responsibility to the German people to be equal to that of the man who had converted the state into his own dictatorship.

As the Horch sped toward Dreux, Rommel scarcely noticed the greening fields of wheat, barley, potato plants, and other crops; the cattle grazing in verdant pastures; the magnificent vistas across the valleys from the hill peaks the Horch was cresting as it thundered across French countryside untouched by war, far from the carnage of Normandy. Finally, with effort, he dismissed thoughts of armistice and Hitler and turned back to read the other messages on the file, including the report from Hausser that the Ninth SS Panzer Division with elements of the Tenth would be ready to move out for the St. Lô-Caumont start line at last light that day, the 24th, and that all forces in Panzer Gruppe Hausser would commence their northward attack at last light on the 27th.

That was good news, indeed. He would go over Hausser's plans for path-finding at night to make certain the Panzer general's tank commanders had a route to follow that would keep them within the five-kilometer-wide corridor laid out from Caumont to Arromanches. Operating one tank at night was difficult enough, let alone operating three hundred as a coordinated battle force. But it had to be done at night; if the armored columns moved in daylight, the Jabos would be all over them like a swarm of mad hornets. Beginning at dawn on the 28th, the Panzers would have to face the Jabos as it was. But by that time the main objective at Arromanches would have been secured; the tanks and vehicles would be able to take cover under the trees in the myriad apple orchards and woods characteristic of the route Hausser's force would follow northward to the sea.

He shuffled through more notes, pausing over a clutch of signals from the commander of the Cherbourg garrison reporting that his troops were fighting bravely but could not prevent further advances of the superior enemy. He also reported that his men had done good work in destroying the harbor's unloading installations, although care was being taken to avoid damaging the shipyards in order that postwar rebuilding could take place. The report stated:

*It does not look good in Cherbourg. But we cannot
expect this type of fortress to hold out for long. The
harbor has been thoroughly wrecked and rendered unusable—it will be interesting to see for how long.*

Again Rommel was pleased. The crippling of Cherbourg
harbor would deny the enemy the use of that port for many
weeks. As he saw it, the whole future of the war and, for
that matter, the destiny of Germany, now hinged on the
Mulberry port at Arromanches.

There was also a report from Rommel's naval adviser,
Admiral Friedrich Ruge, in reply to a question from the
Seventh Army. Could the navy do something about the formations of enemy battleships, cruisers, and destroyers
standing off the mouth of the Orne throwing a never-ending
cascade of heavy shells against the army? Ruge's response
stated that small assault craft—a few motor torpedo boats
and six snorkel U-boats—constituted the entire naval force
in the invasion sector. The snorkel U-boats had at great risk
sunk a few vessels. But the decision had been taken to keep
them in the safety of their pens at Le Havre because to
venture forth now was to invite certain destruction. For these
reasons, Ruge advised, there was nothing the navy could do
about the fleet standing off the mouth of the Orne.

The Horch had just passed through L'Aigle still some
eighty kilometers east of Argentan when Holke spotted the
first clutch of enemy aircraft.

"Four Jabos at 2 o'clock," he shouted. "Range five kilometers. They're at nine hundred meters heading northeast."

Rommel pointed.

"There are some trees about two hundred meters ahead.
Stop under those, Daniel. They'll give us some cover until
we're sure they haven't spotted us."

It was an accepted rule that if you could see a fighter at
up to four to six kilometers, then he could see your big staff
car, truck, or tank. The only thing to do was to take cover
as quickly as possible and stay there until you were satisfied
that the pilot had not seen you, or if he had, that he couldn't
find you. When you were convinced that the Jabo had gone,
you could proceed on your way, but cautiously. Very cautiously—particularly if you were on a dry dirt road. A car
the size of the Horch could put up a rooster-tail plume of
dust that could be seen from the air for kilometers like a
smoke signal. So later on the dirt roads, Rommel and his

party would have to travel at a snail's pace to keep from kicking up telltale dust. The snail's pace was the penalty paid for the good hiding and cover opportunities the back roads provided, as against the open stretches of the main highways, the primary search routes that Jabos patrolled like hungry vultures.

There were two more sightings before they reached Argentan, one by the feldmarschall himself. In both cases they were able to find cover in time. The targets of the enemy's fighters, fighter-bombers, and rocket-carrying aircraft were everywhere. Littered along the highway were scores of burnt-out or still-burning supply vehicles and fuel trucks. There was even the occasional army personnel carrier or tank whose crew thought they had their tracked vehicles well camouflaged or hidden under trees during daylight hours. Some sharp-eyed pilot had seen through their cover or seen tracks the heavy machines left on the field they had crossed to reach the protecting trees, tracks that pointed like a direction arrow to the exact location of the hiding prey.

Halfway between L'Aigle and Argentan, Rommel decided he'd seen enough fresh wrecks to convince him that the Jabos were out in massive force and that he should get off the main highway. At the outskirts of the village of Le Merlerault, his map of the area spread out on his lap, he ordered Daniel, "At the center of town turn left and we'll take the road to the south heading for Sées for about six kilometers. Then we'll turn right on a back road going west. My objective is still Mortrée, General Hausser's headquarters, south of Argentan."

The back road Rommel had chosen was, to his dismay, not hard surfaced, but dirt, which generated great clouds of dust when they turned onto it at speed.

"Slow down, Daniel," Rommel ordered. "Bring it down to fifteen kilometers an hour and see how we do. There's very little wind so any dust we churn up will just sit there."

The speed worked. The amount of dust was minimal.

"Try twenty-five now," Rommel ordered. But at that speed up went the dust again in giveaway clouds.

"I'm afraid that's it, Sir. It looks like fifteen when we're in the open."

"Yes, but there'll be heavy woods ahead where we can speed up and we'll find other back roads on the way that are paved." Discouraged, the feldmarschall shook his head. "There's no doubt it's going to be a long trip. It'll take us another forty minutes to get to General Hausser's headquarters. It's only fifteen kilometers away as the crow flies. And from there up to St. Lô is another 130 kilometers.''

He checked his watch. It was 10:45. They hadn't done too badly so far, but this crawling along was really annoying. If they were at Hausser's headquarters, Mortrée, by 11:45 he would spend perhaps fifteen minutes with his Panzer general then start out again. Meanwhile, he would have Lang work out a back-road route from Mortrée to St. Lô, but using paved roads only—or what he guessed from the map were paved.

The feldmarschall pulled his North Africa goggles down over his eyes as the dust seeped up through the floorboards and billowed around the slow-moving car. In the back seat both Lang and Holke had climbed up on top of the back of the seat, where they sat like heroes in a homecoming parade. From there they could avoid some of the dust and keep a sharp lookout for the Jabos.

The Horch and its occupants were covered with dust when they stopped at the tree-hidden cluster of tanks, trucks, vans and tents that made up Hausser's headquarters. Its location was not in Mortrée but three-and-a-half kilometers to the west off the main highway, in the middle of the Forêt d'Ecouves. The shelter provided by the trees was ideal. They were old, most standing fifteen to eighteen meters high. Thick foliage at their tops formed a sight-impenetrable cover like the vault of a circus tent. What was especially attractive to Hausser about this forest was that the trunks of the trees stood, on average, at least nine meters apart. This provident spacing allowed his bulky Tiger and Panther tanks, personnel carriers, and the motor trucks and trailers that supported them to maneuver with relative ease. It was the perfect safe location for the regrouping of his Panzer divisions.

The staff headquarters officers were lined up in formal order to greet Feldmarschall Rommel. Hausser stood tall and trim in his best uniform and black jackboots. A patch covered the cavity of his right eye, lost in World War I. He raised his right arm to salute his chief—''Heil Hitler''—followed by ''My God, Herr Feldmarschall, you look as though you've come through the North African desert again!''

Rommel lifted the dust-covered goggles from his eyes onto the front of his cap. Daniel stayed behind the wheel after shutting the engine off. It was General Hausser who opened the door for the feldmarschall.

Rommel laughed.

"Yes, but dust is a little different from desert sand, Paul. At least in the desert, the cloud of dust from a moving vehicle is hard to spot from the air and doesn't last long. But here in France's greenest time of the year those cursed Jabo pilots can spot a dust cloud kilometers away."

The feldmarschall stepped out of the car. He took off his cap and banged it against his knee to knock off the dust. Hausser barked at his aide to fetch a clothes brush.

"No, no, Paul," Rommel cut in, "I won't be here longer than fifteen minutes. I'm on my way up to St. Lô, and we'll be on dusty roads again, although I've asked Lang to put us on only paved ones." Rommel smiled as he said, "I'm going to dock him a day's pay for every dirt road he gets us on. Right, Hellmuth?"

The dust-caked Lang grinned as he got out, following Holke, and reached into the Horch's front seat for Rommel's maps. He wanted to look at the maps Hausser's staff had. Maybe *they* would show which roads were paved and which weren't.

"I have coffee for you in my operations tent, Herr Feldmarschall," said Hausser.

"Very good. But first I want to say hello to your staff officers." The feldmarschall put his cap back on and moved to the line of ten officers standing rigidly to attention in their black uniforms with the silver-braided SS patches prominently on their shoulders. Rommel moved down the line stopping to talk briefly to each one, speaking warm words of encouragement. He then followed Hausser into a spacious green bell-shaped tent, where he was presented with a mug of coffee and invited to sit on a hard wooden chair in front of the briefing map.

Rommel took a sip of the hot black coffee.

"Before you begin, Paul, I must tell you that I have a signal from Feldmarschall Sperrle. He says the Luftwaffe can do nothing about an attack on the Mulberry port." Rommel motioned toward the peninsula at the top of the map. "Cherbourg is about to fall, but we have been successful in making the port useless to the enemy. I expect that condition will last until sometime toward the end of August, maybe longer. So the single life line of the enemy is the Mulberry port at Arromanches. If we can destroy that, then the enemy is finished in Normandy.''

Hausser walked to the map.

"We can do it, Sir. I have every confidence in that, with the forces you've placed under my command." He pointed to the Forêt d'Ecouves. "In this forest and in various woods around it I have my entire Ninth SS Panzer Division. My war establishment calls for 126 Tigers and Panthers but the division has only 112. We lost some in Poland and a few on the way here, and there's been no replacement. There are some 2,800 support and supply vehicles, all of course dependent on the provision of gasoline.

"Elements of the Tenth Panzer have just arrived. Almost half strength: 47 heavy tanks, 26 medium, 7 light, and 52 self-propelled assault guns, about 1,000 support vehicles, and roughly 10,000 men. As with the Ninth, Feldmarschall, the Tenth had to get off the trains at Fontainebleau because of air attacks and the sabotage activities of the French Resistance. The long trip across country has been particularly hard on the tracked equipment. As you saw on the roads, we've been hit hard from the air.''

Rommel simply nodded.

Hausser continued, "The Ninth has finished its training and refitting, and I think is in top form. The Tenth is a different matter; about sixteen of its heavy tanks are unserviceable with track problems. We'll just leave them here. As for training," Hausser shrugged, "well, they're just going to have to do the best they can.

"Both the Ninth and Tenth will begin their move northwest this evening at last light. Our objective is to move the whole mass in three separate columns along three sets of roads to the forested area of the Mon Pinçon massif. They will have to get themselves hidden under the trees before dawn. That will be a eighty-kilometer march in seven hours. Advance parties have staked out and marked the receiving areas for each tank commander and each sub-unit. They're all pinpointed on maps that have been distributed. So by dawn tomorrow, the 25th, everything will be in place and hidden, God willing, from the Jabos.''

Hausser approached his next point gingerly. He knew what he was going to say might not please the feldmarschall because it was contrary to Rommel's instruction.

"You had specified, Sir, that the start would be at Caumont-St. Lô, at last light on the 27th, but with your approval, and I hope I may have it, I have decided that the start line should be from the area we reach tonight: the woods around Mont Pinçon and Aunay. And we can launch our attack early—last light tomorrow instead of the 27th.'' He waited for Rommel's reaction. It was immediate.

''I see great advantage to your plan, Paul, because you will have the elements assigned to you from the Second and Twelfth SS Panzer Divisions and the Panzer Lehr. They will be moving west across from the Caen area to rendezvous with you tonight. So the Mont Pinçon–Aunay start line would be good.''

The Panzer general was pleased. ''Exactly, Sir. I propose to pick up from those elements roughly one hundred Tigers and Panthers and twenty self-propelled guns plus sufficient transport to carry fuel, ammunition, and other backup supplies. From the west I'll pick up further infantry and armored personnel carriers and trucks to carry them forward in the attack column. Which brings me to the attack itself.''

Hausser unconsciously adjusted his eye patch. He was getting to the meat of his plan and was apprehensive about Rommel's approval.

''This will be a blitzkrieg attack in the old style. Each of the three columns will be led by Tiger tanks from the Ninth Division and assigned to a separate set of roads in the corridor running northeast from Caumont. We have to stay on the roads at night in order to move as quickly as we can and at the same time be able to see where we're going.

''From Caumont we will run northeast toward Tilly and the enemy front lines. We'll abandon the road to head straight north cross-country using the Aure River as protection on the left flank and the Seulles River on the right. After the tanks will come the self-propelled guns and armored personnel carriers and trucks carrying the infantry. The guns and infantry have been assigned defensive positions along the flanks, on the banks of the two rivers, with orders to keep the corridor open and allow the flow of the supply trucks behind the tanks.

''As you can see, the terrain north from Tilly to Arromanches is flat except for small areas of woods. It's good tank country.''

Rommel broke in. ''You're going to have to move your columns into formation for the start and begin your attack at night. How are you going to cope with the darkness?''

''I made my plan assuming there will be no moon. If we

do have clear sky and some light from the moon, it will be an advantage.''

Rommel nodded. "Exactly. You have to plan for the worst possible situation.''

Hausser continued: "The three columns will proceed on the marked roads, one to the west of Caumont, one in the center, and one just to the east. They'll stay on the roads until they're about five kilometers southwest of Tilly, where the British are located. As the lead tanks approach the front line, the tanks behind will come up to form lines four abreast and about fifty meters apart along a three-kilometer stretch of the east-west road out of Tilly.''

"How are you going to get them formed up in the dark?''

"The leaders will be far enough back from the enemy lines to avoid being seen. Therefore, I've devised a system of green, red, and clear lights, against which each column of tanks will be lined up. In the second line of each column will be Panthers specially equipped with a 20-millimeter antiaircraft gun loaded with tracer shells. These will be fired in the direction given by radio by the column commander. The tanks in the column will follow the line set by the tracers. In addition, there's a red light fitted to the rear of each tank, so each driver can follow the lead of the light ahead.''

"What about parachute flares?'' Rommel's question was a suggestion.

"They will be available at the discretion of the column commander. I have them set up in tanks in the third row of each column. They could be lobbed about two kilometers ahead of the column. When they ignite at about sixty meters and slowly descend, they light up a wide area, but by using them you risk presenting yourself to the enemy as a highly visible target—as you well know, Sir.''

Rommel sipped at his coffee, totally engrossed. "It seems to me that the advantage of letting your column commanders see where they're going and enabling the tanks to keep station means you absolutely must have that light, at least in the opening attack when you're running head on into the enemy's front line.''

"You're right, Sir. I'll make it mandatory to use the parachute flares.''

"And what about backups in case the tanks carrying the tracers or flares are knocked out?''

Hausser pulled out a cigarette and after asking the feld-marschall for permission, lit it.

"I have two backups in each column."

Rommel appeared satisfied. "You have the British Thir-tieth Corps opposite you. What armor have they got in the Tilly sector?"

"The Eighth Armored Brigade along with the Forty-ninth Infantry Division."

"Think you can handle them?"

The Panzer commander nodded. "With the number of tanks, assault guns, and troops you've given me, it would take a lot more than a spread-out British armored brigade to stop us. Add to that the tactical advantage of surprise, and I don't see how anyone can stop us. When we break through at Tilly then we'll have a straight run past Bayeaux to Arromanches."

"Subject to God's will or bad weather," Rommel sug-gested.

"God, the weather, or the men at Berchtesgaden with their heads in the clouds," Hausser responded.

Rommel began to wonder whether Hausser, a senior SS general—whose loyalty to the Führer had been, to that mo-ment, unquestionable—included Hitler in that derogatory remark. If so, there was a flaw in Hausser's personal armor, a flaw that would be of great importance. When Rommel was ready to implement his plans for an armistice attempt, he would have to have the support of all his generals in-cluding SS officers Hausser and Sepp Dietrich. This was the first clue that Hausser was approachable.

The feldmarschall made no comment on what he had heard. Instead he looked at his watch and stood up abruptly. "I must be on my way. You seem to have all the planning in good shape, Paul. Congratulations. Just one thing: get every antiaircraft gun you can lay your hands on into that corridor. As you know, I don't command the Luftwaffe an-tiaircraft units with their beautiful 88s, but Feldmarschall Sperrle does. I suggest you talk directly to him. Tell him I told you to do so. Since he can't give you any air support and refuses to attack the Mulberry port himself, perhaps you can talk him into letting you have forty or fifty 88s from the Caen sector. I tell you, getting to Arromanches and destroying the Mulberry is one thing, but if you do it, the dawn of the 27th will come up like thunder. You'll have every British and American fighter and bomber in the air with only one objective in mind: to destroy your entire force. You'll be concentrated in an easily identifiable corridor. If Panzer Gruppe Hausser can survive that day, it will be able to survive anything. So pray to God for fog, low cloud, and rain.''

"God is on our side.'' Hausser smiled confidently.

"Whether he is or not, Paul, keep in mind that if you drive the British and Americans back into the sea, we'll never see them in Normandy again. Those we don't destroy will become part of the Armee Gruppe Patton, which I expect to come across the Channel in the Pas-de-Calais area at any time. If you destroy the Mulberry port, they might get their troops off the beaches with small craft, but it will be impossible for them to get their tanks and supplies, artillery, and heavy equipment out. It'll be another Dunkirk. Then as soon as that battle is finished I'll move the entire Seventh Army, and the Panzer Army, including your divisions, up into the Pas-de-Calais and close to the beaches there. I refuse to have my Panzer divisions back from the coast by one or two days' march so they can get chewed up by the Jabos before they even get to the battle area. That's where my superiors had them positioned here in Normandy—against my wishes.''

Rommel shook his head. "I tell you, Paul, it's Patton I'm worried about. He sits across the Channel with his million-and-a-half men, waiting to go. All the information indicates that the big assault is going to come somewhere in the Pas-de-Calais.''

"Yes, I understand, Sir,'' Hausser said. "Patton's the reason the Fifteenth Army hasn't been brought down from the Pas-de-Calais—and that's why OKW has brought us in all the way from Poland even though there are four Panzer divisions north of the Seine that still haven't heard a shot fired in anger.''

"There's no choice,'' Rommel admitted. "They must be held in reserve to meet Patton. My quarrel is with Rundstedt and OKW. I want those Panzer divisions close to the beach, not sitting way back.'' Rommel touched Hausser's shoulder with the handle-tip of his baton.

"Never mind Patton. We have our work cut our for us here in Normandy. The fact is, if you pull this off, we may well persuade Roosevelt and Churchill that they should make a conditional armistice instead of sending Patton at us. Then we can concentrate on stopping the Soviets.''

"And if I don't succeed perhaps the time has come to talk about an armistice in Normandy."

Rommel was astonished by Hausser's response. He smiled but said nothing and stood up to leave.

As the two men walked up to the tent entrance, Rommel could sense the urgency outside. Throughout the cavernous woods echoed the clattering and banging of metal on metal, the roar of motors, the sound of generator engines as Hausser's men worked on their majestic tanks and their supply trucks.

"You didn't mention your demolition teams, Paul," Rommel said. "Their explosives have to be planted in the critical places in the Mulberry's structure. And they have to demolish it entirely. I don't want any half-hearted effort. I want the thing destroyed, demolished."

"All organized, Sir. I have twenty squads of ten men each. Each squad is assigned to a special spot on the Mulberry. We have aerial photographs, and our engineers have worked out exactly where the explosives are to go."

"Thank God the Luftwaffe is useful for something."

"We know the weak points and exactly how much high explosive is needed. We will detonate at the extremities of the Mulberry and work in toward the center and across the pontoon bridges to shore. It will be like dominoes. When one piece falls, the next will follow, until the whole thing is down and my men are all safely off it. If anything goes wrong, the men will have to swim for it."

By the time Hausser had finished his explanation the feldmarschall was sitting in the front seat of the Horch, the map spread out on his lap. Lang had marked a "paved" backroads route to St. Lô in a zig-zag of red crayon, a convoluted course into the heart of Normandy.

Feldmarschall Rommel held up his right hand to General Hausser. As it was clasped and shaken briefly, Rommel looked into his one good eye and reminded him, "The future of Germany depends on your success. Whoever is in the lead tank at the spearhead of your columns—he should know that."

Releasing his hand, Hausser smiled and took his chance.

"He already does, Herr Feldmarschall. I will be in that tank myself."

Rommel, who could have refused him permission, smiled.

"If I was in your position, I would do exactly the same thing."

"By being here in the battlefield, spitting in the face of the enemy's Jabos, you are doing just that." Hausser stepped back, left arm clamped to his side. His heels clicked together as he lifted his right arm up, palm down, and shouted "Heil Hitler!"

With that Unteroffizier Daniel began to drive the car forward. The feldmarschall returned the salute in his customary way, touching the tip of his baton handle to his cap. The significance of his refusal to say "Heil Hitler" in response was not lost on Hausser.

As the Horch rolled away from the headquarters of the battle-hungry General Hausser, his counterpart, the commander of the First SS Panzer Korps, Sepp Dietrich, was at his headquarters east of Caen near St. Pierre-sur-Dives writing a signal that would be dispatched to Armee Gruppe B that afternoon. It was a message of desperation. SS Obergruppenführer Sepp Dietrich was a man of tough peasant stock, a loyal supporter of Hitler. He had been with the Führer from the beginning of the leader's rise to power. His Twelfth SS Panzer (Hitler Jugend) and First Panzer Divisions were holding Caen and the line running nineteen kilometers south from it. Together with the Twenty-first Panzer division at Caen and to the east of it, also under Dietrich, they were ranged against the British and Canadians.

Dietrich's three divisions had taken the brunt of the defense of Caen sector from the time of the first engagement there on the 6th of June. His losses in men, tanks, guns, and other equipment had been horrendous as the enemy pitted its massive air, ground, and naval forces against his Panzers in order to break out into the flat country to the east of Caen. There the open terrain, ideal for tanks, would take them to the Seine and Paris.

As his SS chief, Himmler, and the Führer had ordered, Dietrich and his Panzer divisions had held the British and Canadians at bay. But the losses in men, quite apart from tanks and guns, were not being balanced by replacements. And Dietrich, once a Bavarian Cavalry stabsfeldwebel who had become Hitler's chauffeur and one of his personal Nazi executioners, helping the Führer rise to power, could no longer see his losses escalating without bitterly complaining to Rommel's headquarters in the hope that his plight might ultimately affect Jodl at OKW and perhaps Hitler himself.

Dietrich, the pragmatic peasant, was showing signs of

questioning the judgment of the Führer whom he once followed blindly. The tactical errors caused by Hitler's own headquarters combined with the non-appearance of replacements had badly shaken Dietrich's faith. He had talked to Speidel at La Roche-Guyon, pleading for men and tanks, but to no avail. He now had no choice but to put his problems in writing. After all, the military bureaucracy functioned on the written word.

The message that Dietrich was preparing and that Rommel would hear with pain and alarm from Speidel at breakfast the next morning contained figures that shocked even Rommel:

> *Casualties since 6 June 1944: Twenty-first Panzer, 84 officers, 2,513 men; Twelfth SS Panzer, 76 officers, 2,474 men; Panzer Lehr, 78 officers, 2,286 men . . .*

As Dietrich saw it, "The divisions are in desperate need of infantry. The Panzer Lehr has practically burnt itself out."

By midafternoon that day, after several close calls with the prowling Jabos, none of which appeared to spot the great staff car (if failure to attack it were evidence of failure to see it), Rommel and his party reached the command post of the Eighty-fourth Army Korps northeast of St. Lô. Half an hour later, after discussing tactics and the abysmal supply situation with the commander and after several encouraging talks to the headquarters officers and men, Rommel departed. He was dreading the grueling drive back to La Roche-Guyon. A long cross-country trip in a bouncing car over the narrow bocage-lined back roads in the hot blazing sun was bad enough. But, on top of that, the ever-present threat of air attack made the prospect of traveling so unattractive that he actually considered putting it off until dark. However, that would never do. Rommel must never show anyone, let alone his immediate and direct staff, that he was either afraid or tired.

Rommel knew he should not be taking risks. He had lost far too many commanders in Normandy since D-Day. General Erich Marcks, commander of the Eighty-fourth, had been killed in an air attack on his staff car. His wooden leg had prevented him from getting out of the car fast enough to avoid being hit. The entire staff of the commander of Panzer Gruppe West, General Geyr von Schweppenburg, had been wiped out when the headquarters bus in which they were traveling—and from which Rommel himself had alighted only an hour before—was hit from the air. Von Schweppenburg was not on the ill-fated vehicle. General Heinz Hellmich, commander of the 243rd Infantry, had been killed on 17 June in a fighter-bomber attack. On the 18th General Stegmann of the Seventy-seventh Infantry Division had suffered mortal wounds in an air attack.

Again and again on the trip back there were shouts of "Achtung!" from Holke and Lang as they spotted Jabos, and the party quickly took cover and waited. The briefing at the headquarters of the Forty-seventh Panzer Korps at Vassy, some fifty kilometers southeast of St. Lô, gave the feldmarschall the first indication that enemy forces were preparing to mount an attack in the area to the east of Tilly, between it and Caen. Rommel feared that if that attack were to take place, he would be unable to allocate to Panzer Gruppe Hausser the elements of the Second Panzer and Second SS Panzer Divisions and Panzer Lehr. Those elements were scheduled to move to their designated rendezvous point near Caumont that night. Should he let them go, thereby weakening their parent division if the British did attack? The possibility of a British assault was only a guess on the part of the commander of the Forty-seventh Panzer Corps. It was too early to make a decision.

The trip home from Vassy was filled with more of the same devastation that they had seen since midmorning. The carcasses of destroyed trucks and tanks littered the route. And there were approaches, but no attacks, from enemy aircraft.

It was not until twilight, when they reached the outskirts of Dreux, well away from the battle area, that the four men began to feel more relaxed.

The Horch passed through the great iron gates of the courtyard at La Roche-Guyon and came to a stop. A weary feldmarschall, exhausted to the point of numbness of body and mind, walked slowly through the French doors he had passed through fourteen enervating hours before.

At that very moment, the commanders of the Forty-ninth Division and Eighth Armored Brigade of the British Thirtieth Corps and their staffs were busily engaged at their respective headquarters supervising and checking the final pre-attack positioning and disposition of their troops, tanks, self-propelled guns, and armored personnel carriers. Behind them to the north a mass of artillery stood ready to fire.

At H-hour, 4:15 a.m. on the 25th, the darkness and heavy mist covering the Thirtieth Corps front from just west of Tilly, east some eight kilometers to its eastern flank, where it abutted Eighth corps, was lit by the blazing fire of hundreds of heavy guns. The still night air was split by the shrieking whistle of thousands of artillery shells arcing through the darkness and fog toward unseen German targets. British tanks and infantry moved immediately behind that devastating barrage as it began to creep southward farther and farther into the positions held by Second SS Panzer Division on the right or west of the front and by Twelfth SS and the Panzer Lehr on the center and left.

The British plan was to break through the Panzer and 88 antitank defenses and begin an eastward left hook south of Caen to encircle the powerful German Panzer and infantry forces so tenaciously holding that ancient city. Just as General Montgomery had no knowledge of the impending blitzkrieg attack toward Arromanches by Panzer Gruppe Hausser, neither did Feldmarschall Rommel have any knowledge (except for the briefing at the Forty-seventh Panzer Korps headquarters) of the concurrent British plan to attack along a line just east of the intended German thrust. The German attack was now to start northward at last light on the 26th, some forty-two hours after the British start. That forty-two-hour time difference would affect not only the success or failure of Panzer Gruppe Hausser, but also its very existence.

25 JUNE 1944

WHEN HIS alarm sounded at 6:00 in the morning, the feld-marschall found it extremely difficult to get out of bed. His body was still drained by yesterday's trip to the front. He knew he would have been justified in sleeping in until eight or nine. After all, he was getting on. He was 53 and had had a lifetime of ailments, mostly chest problems. But, he told himself sternly, there was no excuse for giving in to the blandishments of his old body. His men were out in the battlefield dying, and here he was in this lush, luxurious castle. It was his duty to get out of bed and to the business of directing the war as quickly as possible. There were reports to be read and decisions to be made. Urgent decisions. If they were delayed, or worse, not made, the cost would be counted in the lives of his men.

His intellect won. Still half asleep, Rommel struggled from his bed, staggered into the bathroom, turned on the bathtub taps. After his bath, he pushed the call button for his orderly, who he knew would be sitting the castle's large kitchen sipping black coffee and smoking, waiting for the buzzer that would send him off on the double to Rommel's suite, carrying the feldmarschall's uniform. The night before, the orderly had taken the uniform and boots out of the bedroom to clean after his master had collapsed into the huge four-poster bed.

By 6:20 Rommel was shaved, hair combed, his uniform on looking neat and crisp, decorations in place, boots gleaming. He thanked his orderly and went into his office. There was a pile of signals on his desk, but he decided to look at them later. Speidel would tell him the important things at breakfast.

In the ornate dining room he found his chief-of-staff already in his usual chair. He had a cup of coffee in front of him and was smoking a cigarette. The lanky Speidel stood up as the feldmarschall entered.

"Sit down, Hans, sit down. Please."

Speidel complied but only when Rommel was in his own chair. The staff waiter appeared and the feldmarschall gave his breakfast order.

Speidel blew his cigarette smoke well away from Rommel, then asked, "Did you sleep well, Sir?"

"Just as if I'd been drugged. I must confess I had a terrible struggle getting up this morning."

"After that ride through hell yesterday, I thought you would have been wise to sleep in for a bit. On the other hand, I knew you wouldn't."

The waiter placed a cup of black coffee in front of Rommel.

"Tell me, Hans, what has come in overnight that I should know about?" This was Rommel's standard breakfast question.

"A message from Dollmann, Sir. He telephoned me at quarter to six."

"Dollmann called you at quarter to six—this morning?" Rommel was astonished.

"Yes, Sir."

"I can scarcely imagine General Dollmann being up at quarter to six, let alone telephoning at that hour from his comfortable chateau at Le Mans. He's a good general, but if he was any farther back from the front line he'd be able to command an army on the eastern front at the same time." Rommel snorted. Dollmann was the commander of the Seventh Army in Normandy. There had been many snide remarks from OKW not only about the distance of Dollmann's headquarters from the fighting but also about its location in an opulent chateau, like some rural bordello. Shades of Jodl's criticism of Rundstedt. "What did he have to say?"

"He wanted to report that the British have opened a major attack on a line east from Tilly for about six kilometers. They started at 4:15 this morning with a creeping artillery barrage. According to Dollmann it's extremely heavy and very effective. Coming in behind the artillery are tanks, which Dollmann estimates to be brigade strength, and of course, infantry. They're coming in between the Twelfth SS Panzer Division, which is holding the west side of our line, and the Panzer Lehr, holding the east side. What's causing Dollmann the greatest concern is that British Jabos are swarming over the area with bombs, rockets, and cannon. The weather is perfect. They go after anything that moves on our side, and of course the Luftwaffe is nowhere to be seen.''

"Have we identified the units opposite Panzer Lehr and the Twelfth SS?''

"It's the British Thirtieth Corps,'' Speidel responded. "Their Eighth Armored Brigade and the Forty-ninth Infantry Division. Probably two hundred tanks, Churchills mostly and some Shermans, and 20,000 men in the infantry division with plenty of armored personnel carriers, antitank guns, and their newest hand-held antitank rocket projectiles—that sort of thing.''

"Does Dollmann think the Panzers can hold? He has 88s to back him up against the tanks and infantry.''

Speidel shrugged.

"I don't know, Sir, and I don't think Dollmann does either at this point.''

"We have to monitor this attack very carefully, Hans. If the British make much headway in the next few hours I might have to change the plans for Hausser's attack.''

"Yes, Sir. The situation should be clear by noon.'' Speidel then gave Rommel the huge casualty figures that Dietrich had sent in the day before. The feldmarschall was shocked.

"I didn't realize Dietrich's losses were that high. If that continues and the Führer doesn't give us any replacements, Dietrich isn't going to be able to hold on much longer. I'll get onto Jodl this morning. The High Command must get us replacements. The problem is they've got their eyes fixed on the East, on the Soviets. They simply don't seem to realize the importance of the battle we're fighting.''

"Keitel and Jodl are just puppets, Herr Feldmarschall. What you're really talking about is Hitler's attitude. Am I correct?''

"Of course that's correct, Hans. You know how I feel about Hitler's leadership. I made that perfectly plain in our conference last week. There was more to that private conversation I had with him than I told you. I explained in no uncertain terms that we were going to lose this battle, and I suggested that it was now time to attempt a political settlement, an armistice, while we still had some leverage.''

"And he refused?''

"Of course he refused. The man thinks only of himself. He is an absolute megalomaniac now. He has no concept of his responsibility to the German people, his responsibility to stop the killing and the bombing on both sides and to keep the Russians out of Germany. By refusing to consider an armistice, he's opening the door for the Russians to walk right in and take over. It will be the end of Germany."

"Unless?"

The feldmarschall took a bite before answering.

"Unless there is an armistice."

Speidel stubbed out his cigarette.

"A lot of people on the general staff think just as you do. They would support an approach to Montgomery." Speidel paused. He had to approach the subject gingerly, not knowing what his chief's reaction would be. "And there are a lot of people who think that the Führer should be done away with."

Rommel stopped eating. His eyebrows shot up.

"You mean assassination?"

Speidel merely nodded.

The knife and fork clattered on the plate.

"Absolutely not. We've been through this before. It would only make the man a martyr. There would be civil war, chaos. No. Arrest him, take him prisoner, have him tried by the People's Court for treason. But assassination? Absolutely not. It would be insane."

The chief-of-staff had his feldmarschall's answer. It was emphatic. But it might change as one disaster piled up on top of another. Speidel would be patient.

"But the matter of an armistice, Sir?"

"That is different," Rommel acknowledged as he picked up his knife and fork and began to eat again.

Speidel remained silent. He poured hot coffee into Rommel's cup and into his own, then lit another cigarette and sat back, blowing the smoke toward the sculptured ceiling six meters above.

Rommel had finished the eggs and sausage. He pushed his plate away and raised his coffee cup.

"I think you know how I feel about an armistice, Hans. As a military man I detest the idea. As a proud German I shrink from the prospect of having to approach Montgomery, cap in hand. But I have to face reality. If Hausser fails to reach Arromanches . . . I am responsible for the military situation in Normandy. Whether it is of my own making or not is beside the point." He drained his coffee cup.

"We both know that it is not of your making," Speidel assured him.

"Yes, and we both know that as the commander of the German forces in Normandy, I must use every means available to me to prevent the enemy from making a break-through.''

''But that may not be possible for long.''

''And that is why I must be prepared to take political action, to negotiate a cessation of hostilities with the enemy.''

''You see no other solution?''

''No, Hans. The only solution is to stop the war while Germany still has some cards in her hand, while we still hold territory. Look at what has happened between the Americans and the Russians, between the capitalists and the Communists. They have taken up a common cause against Hitler. Despite their own tremendous antagonism, their hatred of us has brought them to a marriage of convenience. Once we are defeated there will be nothing to hold them together; there will be an immediate divorce. That will inevitably lead to a war. That war could begin the moment Germany surrenders.

''The only thing that will keep the Russians from sweeping on through Germany and the rest of Europe will be the Americans' overwhelming military strength. Right now, most of the Soviets' armaments are supplied by the Americans, and the Soviets know they, the Americans, cannot move against them. But give the Russians perhaps two or three years and they'll be able to take on the Americans in Europe. They'll have all the aircraft, tanks, guns, and men necessary to bring the whole of western Europe under the heel of Communism and the Soviet dictatorship. After all, Hans, they have their dictatorship and we have ours. Theirs will survive.''

Speidel nodded thoughtfully.

''And under Marxist-Leninist dogma, the Soviets are dedicated to the conquest of the world.''

''Right. And where will that leave Germany? Crushed between the arms of the nutcracker—the Soviets on the east and the Anglo-Americans on the west—that's where. As I see it, Germany must move within the next few days or weeks, while we still have leverage. Germany must convince Anglo-Americans that unless they join Germany in bringing the Soviet war machine to a halt, the whole of Europe will be its target. And we must negotiate with Montgomery before it's too late, before the Russians set foot in Germany, before we have been defeated in Normandy.''

''But not before we know whether Panzer Gruppe Hausser has been successful in its attack against the Mulberry,'' Speidel suggested.

"Yes. If Hausser pulls it off, the Anglo-Americans might even come to us. But if he fails, then somehow we must negotiate."

Speidel called for some more coffee and then went on. "But, Sir, we both know that Hitler has no intention of negotiating. He says he wants to fight to the last house, he wants to fight to the last man, the last bullet. No one is to retreat, and there's no way of coercing him, no way of forcing him to negotiate."

"None whatsoever," Rommel agreed. "Let's see what happens with Hausser. If he's unsuccessful, I'll have no choice but to demand of the Führer that I be given permission to negotiate with Montgomery. As to Montgomery, I'll ask for an armistice and invite the Allies to fight with us against the Russians."

Rommel shoved his chair back. He was about to leave.

"One thing I should tell you about, Sir," Speidel said. "Feldmarschall Sperrle called last night. He wants to come to see you today. I told him I didn't know whether you were going to the front or up to the Fifteenth Army or what your plans were."

"Sperrle? Why would he want to see me?"

"He probably wants to apologize for the collapse of the Luftwaffe."

"He probably wants some of our excellent food and wine, a free lunch. He'll probably clean out the kitchen. I don't think I've ever seen a fatter man."

"How about Göring?"

"No, not even Göring. I was planning to go to the front to see Dietrich, but that long ride yesterday was enough for the moment. Anyway, I'm concerned about the word from Dollmann. If the attack in the Tilly sector is as serious as it sounds, then I should stay here so I can monitor the situation. Tell the Luftwaffe feldmarschall he's welcome to come for lunch. And let me know the minute you hear anything more from Dollmann."

Sharp at 12:00 the gross Feldmarschall Sperrle, all one hundred and thirty-five kilograms of him, moving like a tired rhinoceros, waddled through the towering front doors of the chateau. Rommel escorted him straight into the dining room where the long table was covered with a white tablecloth and the best silver in the house. A large chair for Sperrle had been placed at Rommel's right.

Breathing laboriously, the enormous man lowered his bulk

into the groaning chair and did not arise until it was time to depart. Speidel and Admiral Ruge lunched with the two feldmarschalls. Rommel, who refused to be alone with Sperrle for two hours, had ordered his two senior staff officers to share the burden, which they did reluctantly.

Apart from eating and drinking, Sperrle behaved exactly as Speidel predicted: he apologized for the lack of air support at Cherbourg, which was about to fall at any moment, and for the upcoming assault by Hausser on the Mulberry port. Sperrle's explanation was simple. The ratio of Anglo-American fighter planes to those of the Luftwaffe was more than thirteen to one—4,000 to 300. There was nothing he could do about it. All the decisions were in the hands of Göring and the Führer, who had eyes only for the eastern front. If fighter planes were to be diverted to Normandy, Hitler himself would have to make the decision. Perhaps Feldmarschall Rommel, one of the Führer's favorite generals, might be able to persuade Hitler. If the Führer would give Sperrle, say, a thousand machines, which he knew Hitler had because Göring had told him so, then the Luftwaffe could give Rommel the support he needed. Sperrle could destroy the tactical fighter airfields and aircraft that the invading forces had set up on the beachhead.

So that's what the fat man wanted: to ask Rommel to get something from Hitler that Sperrle himself could not get. Then, of course, there was the magnificent lunch. He had wanted that, too. Just before the meal was finished, one of Rommel's obersts entered the dining room, taking great care to make as little noise as possible so as not to distract Feldmarschall Sperrle, who was in full flight with a story about Göring. Rommel followed the oberst with his eyes. Sperrle, his monocle clamped firmly in his right eye, jowls shaking, belly heaving as he talked, his wine glass going to his mouth every few seconds, paid no attention as the officer leaned over to whisper in Speidel's ear. Speidel listened expressionlessly and then asked to be excused. Rommel nodded his assent as did Sperrle.

Speidel hurried out of the room, leaving Rommel to fret over why he had been called away. While Sperrle droned on, Rommel's mind was elsewhere. He was thinking about General Schlieben, the commandant in Cherbourg, who that morning had received Rommel's order to fight to the last man. Schlieben's reply that morning had appealed for Luftwaffe support, but Rommel had decided against it. Whatever was done at this stage would be far too late. Cherbourg was written off. If any Luftwaffe sorties were flown, they would be more effective in support of Hausser and the heavy fighting around Caen.

Rommel also thought about Hausser, who would be getting ready to begin his attack the following evening. The SS Panzer general had reported that morning that the planned move to the starting area had been completed before dawn on the 25th. So far there was no indication that the enemy had detected their presence. All Rommel could do now was hope that someone in Hausser's force didn't become careless and leave a tank or vehicle exposed that would give away the whole show.

Then there was the troublesome call from Dollmann about the British attack at Tilly. Speidel had been trying to get further word out of Dollmann but with no success. Perhaps that was what had taken Speidel out of the room.

Finally the meal was over. Rommel escorted Sperrle through the front door and down to his awaiting Mercedes. Then he was gone. Not a moment too soon. Rommel hurried back up the steps. As he made his way to the war room, his jackboots banged on the polished hardwood floor of the long corridor, the sharp noise ricocheting off the walls like gunshot.

"What's going on?" he demanded of Speidel.

His unflappable chief-of-staff was standing at the far end of the room by a map of the Caen sector. As Rommel approached, he replied, "It was a call from General Dollmann, Sir. The enemy attack from Tilly is along a seven-kilometer-wide sector and with what he claims to be an overwhelming armored superiority. He says that the enemy has cut an approximately five-kilometer-wide and two-kilometer-deep breach between the Twelfth SS Panzer Division and the Panzer Lehr Division here." Speidel pointed to the small map. "I've also had a report from General Dietrich. . ."

"They're his divisions," Rommel broke in. "He'll know the situation far better than Dollmann."

"Yes, Sir. Dietrich reports that he cannot counterattack, and he can't regain the previous position with the forces available to him."

"If Dietrich says he can't, then there's no question about it. Where are the elements of the Second SS, Twelfth SS, and Panzer Lehr I assigned to Hausser? Have they moved yet?"

"They went to their assigned area at Caumont last night. They're in place there now."

"Damn!" Rommel muttered. It was the only time Speidel had ever heard him use the word. "If Montgomery had called me and personally asked me to weaken my defenses by moving seventy tanks off to the side so he could break through, my timing couldn't have been any better."

"They're only thirteen kilometers to the west of the Tilly sector. You can order them back, Sir. They'd be in place in an hour, two hours at the outside."

Rommel pointed to the French doors and the bright sunlight that streamed through them.

"In broad daylight?" There was a hint of sarcasm in his voice. "The whole lot would be destroyed before they moved one kilometer. Look at this weather, Hans. There isn't a cloud in the sky, every Jabo the enemy has would be in the air attacking."

Speidel immediately covered his tracks.

"I didn't mean move them in daylight, Sir. I meant tonight."

Rommel's mind was working furiously.

"No, it's too early to make that decision. We'll have to size up the situation at last light. Then I'll decide what to do. The problem is, the damage has already been done. If Dietrich can still hold the enemy, then I'll have to continue my gamble with Hausser. Remember the attack on Arromanches is a Führer Order."

"But you're the commander in the field. You've ignored Führer Orders in the past."

"Only when it's been expedient, Hans, only when it has been expedient. And here in this place it is I who decides what is expedient, not the Führer. As of this moment, the objective of Panzer Gruppe Hausser has priority. I will keep it that way until the situation in the battlefield compels me to change my mind." He turned away from the map and walked to the doorway. There he stood, looking out, feet spread, shoulders back, his hands together behind him. To Speidel and other members of the feldmarschall's staff, this was a familiar pose. It was as if Rommel found strength and inspiration in the sunlight. Without turning around he ordered, "Hans, contact Hausser. Ask him if he can move up his attack time by twenty-four hours to last light this evening."

"I've already done that, Sir," Speidel responded.

"Good. And the answer?"

"The answer is no, Sir. He's still waiting for the infantry and paratroops, elements out of Eighty-fourth Korps and Second Paratroop Korps. They've had trouble getting organized and have a long way to go. He must have them in place before launching. Some of their trucks have been caught by the American Jabos. They've had many casualties. He expects their move to be completed tonight. He has his own organizational problems with the night signals. He needs the additional twenty-four hours to cure those and brief the Eighty-fourth and Second commanders on their part in the attack."

Rommel was silent as he considered his alternatives. Then he turned around to face Speidel.

"Give Hausser a warning message. Tell him I may order him to attack tonight with or without the infantry."

"But, Sir," Speidel protested, "without the infantry, we'd never be able to hold that corridor open. The enemy would be able to cut off the armored spearhead from behind. You might lose the whole force!"

"I know that, my dear Hans. So will Hausser when he gets the message. In exchange for the destruction of the Mulberry port, I might have to sacrifice the entire Panzer Gruppe Hausser. It is not a decision that I have taken, it is a decision that I might have to take."

"Would it be wise, Sir," the cautious Speidel asked, "to request the approval of OKW?"

"To ask permission of those dunderheads to send Panzer Gruppe Hausser in without infantry?"

"Yes, Sir. It might be prudent."

Rommel snorted with derision.

"Those inexperienced jackasses wouldn't know what I was talking about. Furthermore, I've been instructed by God to carry out the Mulberry operation."

"By God?" Speidel was bewildered.

"Of course," The feldmarschall smiled. "I have the personal order of the Führer himself to slice through to the coast and take the Mulberry port."

At 6:00 p.m. on 25 June, Rommel made his decision. Even though they were withdrawing gradually in the face of the intense enemy attack, Dietrich's Twelfth SS Panzer Division and the Panzer Lehr—now split by the British forces—were nevertheless holding a tight cap on the southern end of the enemy penetration southeast of Tilly. In Rommel's judgment, there would be no breakout by the British, notwithstanding the depth of their initial thrust and his expectation that the attack would continue in strength the next day.

The order went out to Hausser:

Maintain original schedule, last light, 26 June for attack start.

When Rommel dictated the order to the war room clerk, Speidel asked, "What about the Twelfth SS and Panzer Lehr elements that have been given to Hausser? Should they go back to Dietrich? God knows he needs them."

Rommel shook his head. "No. They will stay put. Dietrich has held on without them. They will remain as part of the Panzer Gruppe Hausser."

"But Feldmarschall, Dietrich is pleading for reinforcements!"

Rommel was beginning to lose his patience.

"For heaven's sake, General, I know he is. But I can't give him any. Isn't that clear? I have to destroy that port, and Hausser can't do it unless he has the maximum strength in tanks and men."

Speidel persisted.

"But what if. . ."

The feldmarschall had been pushed too far. He hit the table with the palm of his right hand.

"I have made my decision. I know you're a great philosopher, Dr. Speidel, but I'm simply not going to stand here and argue theoretical 'what-ifs'. These are difficult decisions. You may disagree with them, but I am the commander. I have made my decision. I want it carried out immediately."

His chief-of-staff was recognized as one of the cleverest German staff generals. Certainly he was one of the most highly educated. He was also a pragmatist who recognized that he had pushed his chief to the edge.

"Yes, Sir," was his reply.

The feldmarschall's anger subsided immediately. The incident was forgotten.

"Good. Now what I must do is monitor the situation very carefully. I have a suspicion that Montgomery still hasn't shown his entire hand. The Tilly attack may just be an opener."

26 June 1944

THE EVENTS of the next day were to prove Rommel correct. The British attack the day before had indeed been just the opener.

At 6:30 on the morning of the 26th, his breakfast with Speidel and Ruge over, Rommel went with his chief-of-staff to the war room to look at the latest messages from the field and higher headquarters. At that very moment, the enemy launched another major assault. The British Eighth Corps, holding a five-kilometer line immediately to the east of the Thirtieth Corps, began an intense southward attack behind heavy artillery fire and air support hampered by a lowering sky. Taking the brunt of this strong tank-led thrust was Sepp Dietrich's First SS Panzer Korps.

The first reports of this new initiative were in Rommel's hands shortly after 7:00. It was now clear to him that Montgomery's plan was to break southward through Dietrich's defenses to the west of Caen, then swing east well south of the city. He would then do a hook to the north on the east side of Caen to encircle and entrap Rommel's forces tenaciously holding the city and the sector to the north of it.

Rommel had no choice: he ordered the Seventh Army and the First Panzer Korps to throw everything they had against the tip of the southward thrust of the British. The breakthrough had to be prevented at all costs. He knew that the heavy rain that had started to fall during the morning would create a severe tactical disadvantage for the enemy's tanks as they maneuvered for firing position and attempted to advance through the once-dry fields of Normandy, now turned into a sea of treacherous mud that would catch and hold them like flies on flypaper. And with luck that same rain and cloud would impede, if not totally prevent, the enemy from using his deadly fighter-bombers and rocket-carrying Typhoons.

The feldmarschall's mood was somber and subdued as he

checked the reports from Dollmann and Dietrich on the battle maps in the war room.

To make matters worse, the news from Cherbourg was bad. With heavy support from artillery and naval gunfire and their unchallenged air force, the Americans had broken into the city the day before, capturing two of the main forts and securing the area around the arsenal. Just before lunch, a quiet affair during which the feldmarschall had very little to say to anyone, word came that the inevitable had happened. The commander, Schlieben, had surrendered after the dominating fortification, St. Sauveur, had been secured by the enemy. Even so, the fighting was not finished. Isolated groups of soldiers had taken seriously Rommel's order to fight to the last bullet and were still offering strong resistance.

During the afternoon Rommel talked to Dollmann and Dietrich and to Jodl who informed the feldmarschall that the Führer was getting concerned about the British attack.

Rommel tried to sound optimistic as he said to Jodl, "Please tell the Führer that I'm confident the line will be held. He should know that his young men in Twelfth SS Panzer Division, the Hitler Jugend, have turned the area in their front into one big death-trap for the enemy. They are fighting like tigers everywhere."

"I will tell him that. He will be pleased to have that encouraging news, particularly about the Hitler Jugend. Now what about Hausser?"

"What do you mean?" Rommel replied. Jodl had the annoying habit of asking incomplete questions.

"The Führer wants to know if the attack of Panzer Gruppe Hausser will be launched on schedule at last light this evening."

"As of this moment, 21:10 hours, I have not altered Hausser's instructions."

"Does that mean that you might change your instructions, that you're thinking about it?"

There was an edge of sarcasm in Rommel's voice.

"My dear Jodl, it may be difficult for a general who is not a field commander to understand this, but it is fundamental that a field commander must be prepared to change his orders to his fighting troops at any time. He must be able to respond instantaneously to the actions of the enemy in any fluid battle situation. I have to assess what Montgomery is doing minute by minute, and if I have to issue new orders to Hausser or Dietrich or Dollmann, I will do it. But as of this moment, I have not changed Hausser's instructions. And as of this moment I do not intend to do so, but I may receive information in the next five minutes or the next hour that will compel me to change those instructions. Do you understand what I'm saying?''

Jodl did not like being lectured by lesser beings, even feldmarschalls. It was on the tip of his tongue to say so, but he thought better of it when the insistent call buzzer on Hitler's line sounded. ''I must go, Feldmarschall. The Führer is calling me.'' With that he hung up, leaving Rommel to get on with the business of running his war.

At 8:47 that evening a telephone call came that Feldmarschall Rommel knew had been inevitable. His appraisal of the tremendous battering the Panzer units were taking from the massive assaults of Montgomery's armor, vastly superior in numbers as they were, made him realize how desperate Dietrich's position had become. Rommel was in his office, sitting at the desk, scratching out a letter to his wife when the telephone rang. Told that the call was from Dietrich, he feared the worst.

The blunt Panzer commander got right to the point. ''I've kept you informed, so you have some idea of the hammering we're taking. The fact is I can't take any more without reinforcements. I've lost close to fifty tanks today.''

''Yes, but you've destroyed more than sixty of Montgomery's.''

''There's a difference, Herr Feldmarschall. He can afford them. He has sixty replacements in the field right now. And he has hundreds more where those came from. And I've lost more than five hundred men today. These are highly trained men. Men who know how to operate tanks, know how to maintain them. I don't have any replacements for them. Look, the 18-year-olds in the Hitler Jugend are fighting like madmen. Everybody—my tanks crews, the kids manning the 88s and the other antitank guns, Dollmann's infantry—every one of them is fighting like a madman.

''And we're holding them, Herr Feldmarschall, we're holding them right across the goddamn board. They've pushed us back anywhere from three to six kilometers, but they haven't broken through. They will though, Herr Feldmarschall, they will break through unless you give me some reinforcements as quickly as possible. What I need, Sir, is Hausser. You've got him sitting over there south of Caumont with more than two hundred tanks ready to start on some wild-goose chase the Führer dreamt up. You and I, Herr Feldmarschall, know he'll never make it. This rain will turn the whole of his attack area, from Caumont right up to the beach at Arromanches, into a goddamn quagmire. For a blitzkrieg he has to have dry, solid terrain. His attack cannot succeed. Why not send him and his tanks here to help me stop these bastards in their tracks? If you don't, those goddamn Englishmen will be by me, through me, and out into the flats east of the Orne. And if they do that, they'll be *behind* my tanks, *behind* my entire force north of Caen. And that will be it! That will be it!''

Rommel leaned back in his chair, face toward the ceiling, eyes shut as he listened to Dietrich's hard words pounding into his brain. The lead tanks of the three columns of Panzer Gruppe Hausser would be moving out at last light—in only an hour's time. There was no putting it off. The decision had to be made then and there.

Rommel stood up. The words he spoke into the telephone were slow, measured, and clear. When he was finished, he asked, ''Is all that perfectly clear, Sepp?''

At the other end, Sepp Dietrich was delighted. ''Thank you, Herr Feldmarschall!'' he shouted. ''Thank God we've got somebody with brains, somebody with guts enough to make a decision without having to go cap in hands to OKW. But I don't think the Führer will be too happy when he finds out you've abandoned his pet project.''

''I'll tell him in due course, Sepp, when I'm ready. Perhaps sometime tomorrow.''

''After you've done it. Aren't you afraid the Führer might fire you?''

''He already has good grounds for doing that, but he hasn't done it yet. I'll talk to Hausser now. He has been warned to stand by. Sepp, I want you and your staff to know that I'm doing my utmost to get reinforcements for you. I have your signal showing your casualties. I've already talked to OKW about it. I've been screaming at them for tanks just the way you're screaming at me.''

''I know you're doing your best for us, Herr Feldmarschall. If you can't get those reinforcements, nobody can.''

The conversation was finished. Still standing, Rommel signaled the headquarters switchboard operator, directing him to call General Hausser. Evidently Hausser was standing by, as instructed, for within two minutes he was on the line.

Rommel shouted over the static, "How are things going, Paul? Are you set to begin?"

"Yes Sir, everything's set. All the briefings are finished. My only concern is the rain. It's been pouring down all day. It and the mud might slow us down a little bit, but I'm confident we'll be all right."

The feldmarschall chose his words carefully.

"I'm afraid you won't have to test your confidence, Paul. The Mulberry will not be destroyed by you. I need you to help Dietrich hold the line against the British. If I don't get you over there, the possibility of a breakthrough is very high. On top of that, Dietrich and I are of the opinion that the mud would stop you in your tracks. So Panzer Gruppe Hausser is kaput, finished. And so is the last chance to throw the enemy back into the sea. It is gone forever, Paul."

Hausser's disappointment was extreme.

But he admitted, "I must say I have been really worried about the rain. Dietrich knows this territory like the back of his hand. I don't. If he thinks I would get bogged down in the mud, then I would have to accept his opinion."

"Either way, Paul, the Mulberry operation is off. Now these are your instructions on the disposition of your force." He told Hausser to return all borrowed elements to their original divisions and to move his Korps, the Ninth Panzer Division and elements of the Tenth, east into the path of the oncoming British Eighth Corps, between Panzer Lehr, which would shift to the right, and the Hitler Jugend, which would shift to the west.

"These orders will be followed, Sir, but it will take time to prepare a new plan and issue orders to my unit commanders."

"No question. You have to plan properly and carefully for this move. It is imperative that you move tonight if you can possibly do so. But I don't want you to think about traveling cross-country in broad daylight even if it is raining and there's low cloud. If the Jabos catch you in the open, they'll come after you even if the ceiling's only thirty meters. The only thing that will protect you is a good, solid fog. The longest I can give you is twenty-four hours. You must be on the move at last light tomorrow at the very latest. You don't have far to go, only about twenty-five kilometers, and you can go straight up the main highway through Villers-Bocage that runs into Caen. Subject to the weather, Montgomery, the whims of the Führer, and acts of God, your divisions should be in the line and fighting tomorrow morning or at the outside on the 28th.''

''I can see no problem in meeting that schedule, Herr Feldmarschall. My men are keen and fresh. But they're going to be bitterly disappointed by the cancellation of the Mulberry operation. In fact, those with me here look devastated by what they've heard. I can tell you I've got a bunch of long-faced people here.''

Rommel could visualize the scene. He also knew what Hausser said next was intended to boost the morale of the men listening to him. ''But do not worry, Herr Feldmarschall, we are the Schutzstaffel, the SS. We are the elite Panzer troops, the very best of all the Panzer units in the armed forces of the Third Reich. We will carry out our orders . . .''

''Whether you agree with them or not, eh Paul?''

''Exactly, Sir. For the Führer and the Reich. Heil Hitler!''

28-29 June 1944

JUST AFTER 1:00 on the morning of 28 June, Hausser reported that all his available units were in the line and in action.

"Bloody hell," Montgomery spat out as he heard the news in his van. "Where have they come from? The Ninth SS Panzer Division and reconnaissance elements of the Tenth, you say?"

"Yes, Sir. They've come in from Poland," replied Brigadier Bill Williams, Montgomery's intelligence officer. "Just arrived. They're fresh and they've had lots of battle experience."

"No wonder we've been stopped again. Rommel's got eight Panzer divisions against me in the twenty miles between Caumont and Caen. Why can't the damned RAF or the Canadians knock them for six with their bloody rocket Typhoons?"

"You have to see them to hit them, Sir. The entire battle area's heavily treed, and Jerry gets his tanks hidden with no problem at all. He won't move in daylight unless he's forced to."

"I know that, Bill," the general said peevishly. "God, it's frustrating. And look at what's happening. They're counterattacking from the southwest and starting to take back the ground we've just won. Won't the bloody press have a field day again? They'll be after me like a pack of yapping jackals. I can see the headlines now: 'Monty Bogs Down Again.'"

The brigadier, an erudite Oxford don, knew his little general well. When Montgomery was in one of his self-pitying tirades, it was best to keep quiet until spoken to.

"What they can't understand is that I'm trying to attract the bulk of the German armor to the Caen sector, the pivot sector, so Bradley can break out more easily when the time

74

arrives. I'm succeeding with too great a measure, I'm afraid.''

Neither Montgomery nor the press knew at the time the true measure of that success, the breakup of Panzer Gruppe Hausser and with it the removal of the threat to the Arromanches Mulberry.

''Tell Freddie to come to my van immediately.''

Williams picked up the field telephone and cranked its bell box vigorously.

Major-General Freddie de Guingand was in the van three minutes later. His chief briefed him on the situation and then instructed, ''Send word to Dempsey to cease the attack. He is to concentrate for the time being on holding the ground he's won, beating off those bloody counterattacks. I want him to regroup and have the infantry hold the line so he can withdraw his armor into reserve, so they can get ready for renewed thrusts. Tell him to pass the word to all units—well done.''

Monty shook his beretted head, looking crestfallen. ''All right. The operation is terminated.'' His Eighth Corps would stop and lick its deep wounds sustained from the mauling by Dietrich's Tigers and Panthers and by the brutal 88s.

Early on the morning of the 29th, Dietrich's headquarters and then Hausser's reported the sudden lessening of the enemy's attack and his apparent return to a defensive holding posture.

The reports to Armee Gruppe B were made by the two SS Panzer Korps commanders rather than General Dollmann, the commander of the Seventh Army. At 3:00 that morning, at his command post in Le Mans, Dollmann had committed suicide by swallowing poison. His chief-of-staff, General Max Pemsel, reported the death as heart failure. The cause of Dollmann's suicide was the premature fall of Cherbourg. Hitler had ordered the Cherbourg commander, General Schlieben, to carry out the battle for the crucial port to the last man giving no quarter. Schlieben had followed his Führer's instructions, but Hitler had discovered that someone higher in authority than Schlieben had secretly ordered the strong Seventy-seventh Infantry Division out of the Cotentin Peninsula before the Americans cut them off. Obeying orders, the Seventy-seventh had escaped just in time, and so was not in the Cotentin to keep Cherbourg from falling into the hands of the Americans, who were in desperate need of the facility.

Hitler was beside himself. Whoever gave the order did so against his explicit instructions. Despite pressing inquiries from OKW, none of the headquarters staff would admit to giving such an order. In frustration, the OKW had appointed a fact-finding committee of a general and the chief judge of Western Command. They were ordered to investigate the fall of Cherbourg and allocate blame for the secret order.

On the evening of 28 June, the findings of the committee were in Hitler's hands. The accused general was Dollmann. Hitler had immediately accepted the report. After receiving word from Berchtesgaden that Hitler blamed him for Cherbourg, Dollmann had sent a telegram to his Führer denying that he had given the order and citing the involvement of others in his command decisions. That done, Dollmann had taken the standard course for German generals who had fallen into dishonor.

Rommel was not at La Roche-Guyon when the report of General Dollmann's death arrived shortly after 6:00 a.m., and when the reports came in from Hausser and Dietrich advising that they had stopped the enemy. Rommel had left La Roche-Guyon late morning the previous day. Word had arrived from the headquarters in Paris of the Commander-in-Chief West, Feldmarschall Gerd von Rundstedt, that he and Rommel had been ordered to report at Berchtesgaden at noon the next day, the 29th, for a conference with the Führer.

Later in the day Rundstedt's chief-of-staff, General Blumentritt, had spoken to Rommel.

First they discussed Dollmann's death. Rommel made no admission, but his conscience was deeply troubled. It had been he, not Dollmann, who had given the secret order for the Seventy-seventh to leave the Cotentin.

Then Blumentritt told him about the Führer Conference. Rommel was curious.

"Who else will be there? Any idea?"

"It looks as though a copy of the order also went to Feldmarschall Sperrle."

"That means that the commander of Navy Group West, Admiral Krancke, will probably be there, too. My guess is that Hitler's bringing in all his senior commanders in the

West to tell us that we're not running the war properly and how we should be doing it."

"I don't know, Sir," Blumentritt admitted. "I do know that Feldmarschall Rundstedt has asked the Führer for directives for future fighting. With Armee Gruppe Patton expected to attack across the Channel at any time, it would help if we all knew what the Führer has on his mind."

"Well, I'm sure we'll know after the conference. Whether it will make any military sense is another question."

That criticism worried Blumentritt.

"I must remind you, Herr Feldmarschall, of something you know very well. The telephone calls of senior officers have a tendency to be monitored."

"I know that, Blumentritt, but for the sake of Germany and the German people, I think that those of us in high command in the battlefield have to speak up. We have to give the Führer military opinions in no uncertain terms."

"Regardless of the consequences?"

"Regardless of the consequences. Now, when is your feldmarschall leaving? It's a long drive to Berchtesgaden, probably eighteen hours."

"He's not looking forward to it. I've booked accommodation for him in Frankfurt. He'll spend the night there, then go on first thing in the morning."

"I'm going to drive to Ulm. My home is near there at Herrlingen."

"I'm sure your dear wife will be happy to see you. What about your son?"

"I will arrange to have Manfred released from his anti-aircraft battery for the night, so I'll see him, too. When is your chief leaving?"

"He's going to leave at noon."

"Noon. It is of the utmost importance that I have ten or fifteen minutes with him before we get to Berchtesgaden. There may be no opportunity to talk once we get there. Can we set up a rendezvous point on his route east, which I assume will put him on the main highway D33 to Metz?"

After the rendezvous point was agreed on, Rommel quickly ended the conversation with Blumentritt. He still had to pack, and a good hour's head start was needed in order to make his way through Paris to reach the meeting point east of the city.

This trip was not to be taken in the stiff-springed, windy Horch but in the big, smooth-riding, hard-topped Mercedes.

After a last-minute discussion between Rommel and Speidel, the Mercedes swung through the iron gates of La Roche-Guyon, the feldmarschall's pennant fluttering prominently at the front, Daniel behind the wheel, the feldmarschall seated comfortably behind him, and his staff officer, Major Eberhard Wolfram, on his right.

Two hours and fifteen minutes later, at the first crossroads beyond Montmirail, about one hundred kilometers east of the heart of Paris on the main highway to Metz, Daniel reported, "There he is, Sir, about a kilometer ahead."

Rommel had been reading. His eyes quickly focused ahead. "Yes, that is he. Just pull in behind."

Rundstedt's car, also a Mercedes, was pulled off to the side at the precise point Rommel and Blumentritt had agreed on. Before Rommel's car came to a stop behind the other vehicle, Rundstedt got out of his car and walked back to greet the much younger feldmarschall. They stood on the edge of the pavement as they talked, unconcerned about traffic, for there was very little of it—only a few German military vehicles, whose drivers slowed down at the sight of such important cars.

Cordial greetings out of the way, Rommel went immediately to the point. "As I have told you, Sir, I believe this war must be brought to an end immediately while we still have some leverage. I think you are of the same opinion. I propose to tell Hitler exactly that in no uncertain terms. And if you agree with me, I'd like to have your support."

The old feldmarschall, his large watery eyes looking down at the younger man, was almost fatherly.

"Yes, I will support you. There is no doubt in my mind. We don't have the men or weapons to cope with the overwhelming force that the Anglo-Americans have already put on their beachhead, let alone what is sitting in England waiting to be brought across. But that so-called armee gruppe of Patton's that our intelligence people are always telling us about—I have a suspicion that it's a lot of hogwash. . . . "

"Abwehr reported only two days ago that there are still sixty-seven divisions in Britain of which at least fifty-seven are allocated to Patton's force," Rommel countered.

Rundstedt shook his head.

"When I see Patton on the beaches somewhere between Calais and Le Havre, then I'll believe it. But that's not really the point. The point is that even without that force attacking us, Montgomery is going to defeat us in Normandy. In any event, Erwin, I will support you. But a word of caution. You must remember that I am an old man. I am 70 going on 90. I am the most senior officer in all the German armed forces. If I stand with you on this, there will be consequences for both of us. The Little Corporal will not want to hear what we have to say. He will not accept our opinions. On top of that, he will regard them as treasonous since they are opposite his.''

Rundstedt paused as if taking Rommel's measure. ''I simply want you to understand that if you are as tough and direct with him as you were at the conference at Wolfsschanze Two you may find yourself dismissed. And even though I have been critical of your ability to handle high command—and you know that I have, I've never made any bones about it—I think that at this stage in the war you are the best person to direct the battle and, at the right time, handle the armistice proceedings.

''You may have to try for the armistice whether the Little Corporal agrees with it or not. Look, I may be the most senior of German generals, but you are by far the most respected, not only by the German people, but by the Anglo-Americans as well. As I see it, they would detest dealing with Hitler—it would be like trying to handle a berserk, poisonous snake—but with you they would know they were dealing with a man of integrity and honor.''

Rundstedt placed his hand momentarily on Rommel's shoulder.

''So, Erwin, I know you no longer have much respect for Hitler. God knows, I lost mine a long time ago. And I know you're going to be blunt with him. But remember, the people of Germany need you. Don't let them lose you because you can't win a shouting match with a man who has all the power, and who is paranoid, mad, and jealous of your accomplishments.''

That caught Rommel off guard.

''Jealous? Hitler jealous of me? I can't believe that.''

''You should, Herr Feldmarschall. Hitler is very much aware of your enormous popularity among the German people. He is jealous of your accomplishments as a fighter and a leader. He knows full well that if there is any attempt at a coup against him in which the military has a part, it is you who will emerge as the leader. Think about it, Erwin.''

Feldmarschall Rundstedt had said more than he had intended. Before Rommel could reply, he said briskly, "We must move on, Erwin. It's a long way to Frankfurt and a long way to Ulm and Herrlingen. Please give my best wishes to Lucie and tell her that I was asking about her."

"Thank you, Sir, I will. And thank you for your advice. It is most valuable. But whether I can follow it remains to be seen. We Swabians are pretty pig-headed, you know." He smiled.

Rundstedt returned the smile, saying, "And sometimes you look like it, too."

Rommel was not quite sure how to take that remark.

"I'll see you at Berchtesgaden, Sir, at noon tomorrow." With that he transferred his feldmarschall's baton to his left hand, took a step back smartly, and raised his right hand to his cap in a crisp, military salute, a token of respect the much younger feldmarschall felt at that moment for General Feldmarschall Gerd von Rundstedt.

Back in his Mercedes, Rommel said nothing for the next half-hour as the car moved steadily eastward, positioned on Rommel's instructions about a kilometer behind Rundstedt's vehicle. No sense giving the Maquisard two feldmarschalls for the price of one. He sat silent, ruminating on Rundstedt's advice. Major Wolfram wisely did not press his chief with attempts at conversation but sat looking out the window to his right as the lush French countryside and ancient villages swept by.

Rommel dropped Wolfram off just before midnight at the Deutscherhof Hotel in Ulm, where the major's wife was waiting for him. Then he and Daniel drove on the short distance to Herrlingen, where the feldmarschall was joyfully greeted by Lucie and Manfred. There was not much time left in the night for talk, but the three were happy to be together for however brief a period.

Rommel had always been honest with his family about what he was doing and what the future looked like. He felt they had a right to know, and furthermore he often received intuitive guidance from the way they reacted when he talked about the problems he was having with this person or that— or, in this instance, how he was going to approach the Führer. He had, of course, shared with them the depth of his disillusionment with Hitler and his belief that the man had totally abandoned any interest in the German people.

Now he told them of his intention to speak frankly to Hitler at the Führer Conference. The young Manfred listened carefully to his father, as he always did, but did not offer any opinion. He knew, though, that his father might not survive a confrontation with Hitler.

There was no reticence, however, on Lucie's part. She also knew the consequences of crossing swords with Hitler. When she and her husband were finally in bed together in the early hours, he asked her, his voice almost a whisper, "Should I do it, Lucie? Should I forfeit our future because I think someone has to stand up to this madman and tell him that, for the sake of Germany, the war must stop? If the man turns on me he can destroy us. I could be court-martialed. I could be tried for treason, demoted, perhaps even executed."

She stroked his face gently with her fingertips, feeling the long day's growth of stubble. A white stubble, she had noticed as they talked downstairs.

"What you must do, my darling, is follow the dictates of your own conscience. If you must stand up to Hitler for the people of Germany, then you must do so. It's a silly thing to say, because I know you'll do it anyway, but don't worry about Manfred and me. We love you and we're proud of you. Whatever you do and whatever sacrifice you have to make, we will share that sacrifice with you gladly. We believe in you. We're your family. Do you understand?"

She moved her hand again up the side of his face. Startled, she stopped her hand. She felt moisture. The moisture of silent tears. But Erwin Rommel was never moved to tears. Nor would she ever remind him that he had once cried in the dark before the dawn of the day he last set eyes on the man who was both his leader and his enemy, Adolf Hitler.

Their sleep together that night lasted little more than three hours. The alarm rang at 5:00. By 5:30, the feldmarschall, Lucie, and Manfred were in the big Mercedes. Unteroffizier Daniel, bleary-eyed but alert, was once again behind the wheel. At the Deutscherhof, Rommel tenderly said goodbye to his family—a kiss for Lucie and a manly hug for the tall, lanky Manfred.

"I may never see you again," he whispered as he held his son momentarily.

Wolfram had said his goodbye to his wife and turned to enter the car after his chief. Lucie briefly held Wolfram's arm, asking him to do something she knew he had not the power to do.

—"Take care of my husband, Major. Don't let anything happen to him."

Whenever he drove through the tall fir forest that enclosed the winding mountain road approaching the town of Berchtesgaden and Hitler's home, the Berghof, perched on the mountainside above it, Rommel never failed to be impressed, if not awed.

The Berghof loomed out of the side of the Bavarian mountain like one of the ancient fortresses standing everlasting watch over the Rhine, except that Hitler's aerie was not made of stone and slate but of modern concrete and steel shaped in soaring lines and angles by Albert Speer, Hitler's architect. Speer had become Hitler's trusted confidant, and in later days, his armaments minister, the only civilian functioning in the OKW as part of the Führer's otherwise totally military entourage. As Rommel's eye took in the still-distant Berghof in the gray, overcast morning of 29 June, its distinctive shape had been almost obliterated by the camouflage nets that had been draped over it and its adjacent buildings in an attempt to blend its mass into the side of the mountain. Even so, the place evoked a sense of majesty and power, just as Hitler had intended. But for Rommel that morning, the power that the Berghof now symbolized was an evil one, and he approached it with ominous foreboding.

Some five kilometers beyond Berchtesgaden stood another structure, a fortress in its own right, placed there to allow its ruling members easy access to the Berghof. The Reichskanzlei—the headquarters of the German High Command, the OKW, and the Army High Command, the OKH—was the primary base of operations of Hitler's military chief-of-staff, General Feldmarschall Keitel, chief of High Command of all German armed forces, and of the insufferable Generaloberst Alfred Jodl, the chief-of-operations. Rommel was always amused when he heard Rundstedt contemptuously refer to Keitel as "Hitler's head clerk", or claim that it would be impossible to find a more obsequious ass than Jodl, who was a laughing stock among the generals in the field. In his determination to acquiesce to Hitler's every wish, Jodl had ordered that there be no criticism of any of Hitler's schemes in the presence of the Führer even if Hitler had specifically asked for expert opinion. "Jawohl, mein Führer" and "Certainly, Sir" were the phrases used most frequently by Jodl in Hitler's presence, words that the arch-sycophant insisted all others use as well.

Also in that sprawling structure was the headquarters of the army chief-of-staff, General Kurt Zeitzler, another man who had many qualities the feldmarschall disdained, particularly his insensitive, coarse manner. Undoubtedly, Keitel, Jodl, and Zeitzler would be at today's Führer Conference, all standing like fawning peacocks around their black-mustached mannequin of power.

Daniel slowed the Mercedes down to a crawl as they approached the heavily armed SS sentries at the Berghof's entrance gate in the valley floor. All the troops assigned to guard the complex were of the elite SS Adolf Hitler unit. With the insignia embroidered on the left shoulder of their jackets, they stood guard at all doors, operated the telephone system, monitored all calls, and had complete responsibility for fending off any attempt against the person of the Führer. They patrolled the barbed-wire barricades and manned the smoke generators that could quickly blanket the entire area with a fog-like cover as a defense against air raids. In their black uniforms and black steel helmets, the proud SS Adolf Hitler men, armed to the teeth, were everywhere, or so it seemed to Rommel.

After producing special passes at the gate—even Rommel would not be allowed in without one—Daniel drove the Mercedes slowly up the steeply winding road through the dense forest of fir trees, stopping under the *porte cochère* at the front entrance to Hitler's fortress home.

Returning the smart salute of the SS guards, Rommel walked quickly up the long marble steps. Major Wolfram accompanied him on his right, but one deferential step behind, carrying the feldmarschall's briefcase.

It was five minutes before noon, the hour at which the Führer Conference was supposed to start. But instead of taking them to the main conference room, the officer who greeted them at the door led the feldmarschall and Wolfram to the spacious, comfortably furnished waiting room. There Rommel found Rundstedt, Sperrle, and Krancke. Even the old soldier Rundstedt showed signs of nervous apprehension at the prospect of another meeting with the Little Corporal. He expected it to be like the last one, filled with tension and animosity and made unpredictable by Hitler's increasing tendency to rant and rave, his temper flaring and subsiding like a fountain.

The assigned hour came and went. Then 1:00. At 2:00, stewards brought in coffee and sandwiches.

Shortly after 3:00, Goebbels, Hitler's henchman and master propagandist, emerged from the conference room. He chatted briefly with Rundstedt and the naval and air officers, then took Rommel aside. The feldmarschall was a favorite of his and the object of one of his most successful publicity campaigns. It was Goebbels who had staged the mass reception in Berlin that immediately followed the ceremony at which Hitler had presented Rommel with his feldmarschall's baton. It was the diminutive Goebbels who had walked at Rommel's left in the small, proud company of a dozen Nazi feldmarschalls and generals who had escorted the new feldmarschall into the packed hall where some five thousand people stood and cheered as their hero was escorted to the podium to receive their tumultuous accolades. Through Goebbels' efforts, Feldmarschall Rommel had accumulated much more than military rank and authority. He had acquired such prestige, honor, and glory in the minds of the German people that he had become a person capable of great political power, the power to influence and lead public opinion, power sufficient to propel him into the position of leadership of the nation should Hitler fail or falter or by some disastrous event disappear from the scene.

Knowing this, Goebbels was much more solicitous of Rommel than the other senior officers, leading Rommel to believe that he was talking to a friend, a friend who could influence Hitler. Rommel therefore told Goebbels what he intended to say to the Führer and why. The wily Goebbels nodded as he listened, inducing Rommel to think that he was hinting approval. Rommel was convinced that he had won an ally who would stand with him in the Führer Conference.

On the question of how long it would be until Hitler would summon them, Goebbels was, as usual, noncommittal, saying only that there was an emergency on the eastern front and that Hitler was engaged with Keitel, Jodl, and others, including Himmler, many of whose SS Panzer divisions were involved. With that, the slight little man, his white brass-buttoned uniform jacket hanging loosely about him like a shirt on a scarecrow, his gaunt, narrow gray face grimly set, took his leave of Rommel and scuttled back into the conference room.

About an hour later, the SS Reichsführer, Himmler, appeared. The pattern was much the same, Himmler eventually taking Rommel aside to ask about the performance of his two generals, Dietrich and Hausser, and their divisions. Once again Rommel used the opportunity to explain his intentions and ask for support. Once again the reaction was noncommittal. The bald, flat-faced Himmler peered through his round, steel-rimmed spectacles at Rommel and at the end of his proposal was evasive. After all, Rommel's proposed statements would undoubtedly border on the mutinous in Hitler's mind. On the other hand, if it appeared that the Führer was showing signs of accepting Rommel's position—a miracle that Himmler could not bring himself to think would happen, but then Hitler *was* thinking so erratically these days—it might be good to get on the bandwagon early.

When Himmler returned to the conference, Rommel was standing in the doorway to the waiting room. He could hear a snatch of Hitler's voice, high-pitched, screaming with fury as the door opened for Himmler, then quickly shut behind him. The feldmarschall shook his head as he thought, with some despair, By the time we get in there he'll be in such an emotional state, it will be impossible to reason with him—not that I ever could.

It was not until 6:00 that the summons finally came. Hitler had kept his four senior officers in the West cooling their heels for six hours. Their staff officers were left behind to wait even longer as Rundstedt strode into Hitler's presence followed by Rommel, Sperrle, and Krancke.

For most people, the conference room was like a torture chamber. It was much larger than most of the conference rooms at the Berghof and so had come to be called the Great Hall. On its paneled walls, tapestries were hung to absorb sound. Officers in the room not directly engaged with what the Führer was doing or saying were therefore able to stand in little clumps and carry on their own conversation without disturbing Hitler. If their conversation got too loud, however, the Führer would lift his head and look in the direction of the offenders, whereupon all would be silent momentarily.

In the center of the Great Hall and down its length ran the long map table of reddish marble. There was only one chair in the room, and that was Hitler's. Everyone else was obliged to stand, just as at Wolfsschanze Two. There was, however, the stool available for the ponderous Reichsmarschall Göring. As Sperrle lumbered into the conference room behind him, Rommel wondered whether the gross Luftwaffe feldmarschall would be able to last for the however many hours the conference would take.

The large picture window that opened on a superb vista across the valley was, as usual, closed, and all light shut out. There was a slight smell of gasoline fumes that had seeped up from the garage under that part of the Berghof. The ventilation system, which could have removed the smell and the stale air that hung in the room, was not in operation. Hitler claimed the ventilated air gave him headaches and weak spells.

Rommel had walked stiffly through the open double doors of the Great Hall a step behind Rundstedt, who now moved to the right side of the map-covered marble table. There at the far end of it sat Hitler, glowering at the four men entering his sanctum. Once more Rommel was startled by how much he had aged: the black, white-flecked hair and closely trimmed mustache, the slightly trembling hands, the ashen, waxy face, and the tic in one eye. He was leaning forward on the table. The light gray, double-breasted, beltless jacket was rumpled as if he had slept in it. His tie was slightly loose at the collar, and his hair hung down over his forehead like a curved spring. Behind him in a corner by the window sprawled his Alsatian dog, Blondi, a vegetarian like her master.

In the corner behind Hitler and to his right stood Göring's upholstered stool. It was not in use today. Ranged down the far side of the table, looking confident in their usual places of protocol at the pinnacle of German power, were Hitler's senior advisers. Yet there was a certain look of unease about them as they eyed the people responsible for carrying out Hitler's, the OKW's, and the OKH's orders in the field. They shifted their weight constantly like a bunch of toy soldiers, for they had been standing in Hitler's presence for at least six hours with no respite except for an occasional furtive dart in the adjoining toilet. In the line of protocol stood Himmler next to Hitler, then Goebbels, Keitel, Grand Admiral Dönitz, Jodl, and Zeitzler.

Standing against the wall some three meters behind their masters, like a school of variously hued fish, were their respective staff officers, mostly obersts whom Rommel did not recognize.

There was one civilian present in addition to Reichsminister Goebbels: Martin Bormann, the powerful secretary of the Nazi Party, who would disturb Rommel's concentration with his constant note taking.

Both Rundstedt and Rommel were intrigued by the unexpected presence of Feldmarschall Hans von Kluge, who stood not at the marble table but unobtrusively next to Göring's stool. Kluge, who had suffered injuries in an automobile accident on the eastern front and had been invalided home for some months, was a favorite of Hitler's. He did not come forward to greet them when they entered the room. He merely nodded to them, a sign they both returned. The reason for his presence was to be disclosed three days later.

Hitler, looking solemn, did not stand to greet his field generals, nor did he offer Rundstedt, the most senior soldier in the German armed forces, any explanation or apology for the six-hour wait.

The day had not gone well for Hitler. He was in a foul mood and almost at the point of exhaustion after the tirades and furies of the long afternoon. But since it was he who had summoned his western commanders to the Berghof, he now had to turn his mind away from the disasters festering on the eastern front to that bothersome new battle area the British and Americans had created at his rear.

He was now doing what he had vowed he would never do: fighting on two separate fronts. Before he discarded his non-agression treaty with the Soviet Union, he had made sure his western front had disappeared with the ignominious casting of the British into the sea at Dunkirk. That had freed all his forces to be thrown against the inept—as he saw them then—Russians. The British were back again, like fleas returned to a dog, and they had brought with them their egotistical American allies, Roosevelt's army of amateurs. If he had been able to concentrate solely on Normandy, he would have had Montgomery and Bradley and all their sniveling troops packing back to England within a week. Instead his mind was filled with the problems of the eastern front, and he had had to leave the battle in Normandy to the bothersome incompetents standing in front of him.

"Well, Feldmarschall," he snarled at Rundstedt, "when we met only twelve days ago, I gave you instructions on how to conduct the battle. And here you are back again, in less than two weeks, looking for instructions on how to fight your battles. In the meantime, the Anglo-Americans are pouring men and equipment into Normandy. Division after division, thousands of tanks and guns, aircraft by the hundreds. And what have you done? You've fallen back, given ground, retreated.''

His eyes shifted to Rommel. ''And you, Rommel. I gave you the simple task of driving a wedge of armor up to the beachhead and destroying that infernal Mulberry port. You yourself suggested that it be done, and contrary to the advice of Jodl, I ordered you to do it.'' He waved his hand wildly. ''And what did you do? You put Panzer Gruppe Hausser together. You put them at the starting point. Then what did you do? Contrary to my explicit orders, you canceled the operation and instructed Hausser to move over to Caen to help Dietrich, when Dietrich could have held the line against the British attack by himself.''

''But, mein Führer . . .'' Rommel started to protest. Hitler would have none of it.

''Please be so good as not to interrupt me!'' he shouted, his face red with anger. ''Then there's Cherbourg. I instructed you to fight to the last man in Cherbourg. I told you to hold the line, to fight for every piece of ground so that the Americans would be denied the port they so urgently need. And what did you do? You let Dollmann order the Seventy-seventh Infantry Division, one of the most powerful in the whole German army, you let Dollmann order them out, and they left the peninsula. The task force blamed Dollmann, who fortunately died of a heart attack—or so they say. But Dollmann was under your command, Herr Feldmarschall. As soon as you knew the Seventy-seventh was moving, you should have stopped them. And then when I ordered you to counterattack against the Americans in the Cotentin Peninsula, you did nothing. If you had counterattacked as I ordered, you would have trapped the American general, Collins, and all his troops. You would have cut them off from the rest of the American forces to the east and from their supply line.''

Hitler shook his head and looked morosely at his hands spread out on the smooth, cold surface of the red marble. ''It was extremely hard for me to be forced to give up that attack on the Americans. All we can do now is counterattack at Caen against the British and eat our losses. The only piece of good news I've had today is that among them Reichsführer Himmler and Hausser and Dietrich have stopped the British in their tracks and forced them to retreat. That's the SS for you. Sepp Dietrich. Now there's a man.

Did you know that he was once my chauffeur and assisted me by purging some people who were intent on removing me from the leadership? Yes, that's what happens to people who plot against me. They are purged, Feldmarschall, just the way you purge cockroaches from a kitchen." He giggled for a moment and nodded his head. "Yes, and the ones you kill are replaced by new ones. I know. I know.

"And what can we conclude from this, Herr Feldmarschall? I'm saying that everything would be all right if you would only fight better." With that stinging insult on the table, and giving no opportunity to the angry Rommel to respond, Hitler turned his attention to Rundstedt.

"So you want directives for future fighting? I'll give them to you and they do not involve retreating and they do not involve surrender. The first essential is to bring the enemy attack to a halt as a precondition for cleaning up the bridgehead. Dietrich and Hausser have at least done that. By the way, I've appointed Hausser commander of the Seventh Army in place of Dollmann. I'm sure both of you would approve. Reichsführer Himmler will appoint a new commander for the Second SS Panzer Korps shortly."

Himmler nodded, eyes blinking. Hitler took his steel-rimmed spectacles out of his jacket pocket and fidgeted with them as he continued.

"The next thing is that the Luftwaffe—that's you, Sperrle—must create a constant state of unrest over the enemy bridgehead using the latest types of aircraft, my new jets and rocket bombers, which are to engage and destroy enemy aircraft. I've already communicated this directive to Reichsmarschall Göring. He is also to continue sea-mining in order to hit at the enemy's supplies and render their warships' stay in coastal waters as uncomfortable as possible. This is also a job for the Luftwaffe, because you have no ships or submarines to do the job, Admiral Krancke." He did not want or expect an answer from the admiral.

"The destruction of the enemy's battleships is absolutely essential. The fire from their big guns has been creating havoc starting from D-day. There will be special bombs employed for the engagement and destruction of those battleships by the Luftwaffe.

"Then there will be the creation of antiaircraft nests on supply roads in order to make road strafing impossible for the enemy Jabos. To this end, old aircraft cannon and other antiaircraft weapons will be installed in well-hidden nests along the supply roads between Paris and the battle zone. This is the kind of idea that you people should come up with, Feldmarschall Rundstedt, you or your staff. It shouldn't have to come from me. Why do I have to do all the thinking?''

There was an uneasy shifting in the room as the Führer stopped, walked over to Blondi to pat her head, then returned to the table.

''The next matter is also for the Luftwaffe. There will be provision of one thousand fighters from new production in order to achieve their superiority over the beachhead area for at least a few days a week. By my calculations, with the fighters then available, if they could fly three sorties a day, a total of up to fifteen hundred sorties a day could be flown.'' He was twisting the spectacles furiously as the words flowed.

Hitler next looked down the table to his right at his naval chief, Grand Admiral Dönitz. ''Employment of all available naval units, including torpedo, E-boats, and U-boats as well as midget submarines. What about it, Admiral? What do you have available?''

All eyes turned to Dönitz, who had so much gold braid on his arms it was almost obscene, Rommel thought. The graying admiral, wan and exhausted from the interminable standing and the Führer's never-ending monologues, was startled when he realized he was expected to reply. However, he had little trouble in answering.

''The number of craft I have available, mein Führer, is extremely small. Admiral Krancke''—he nodded toward his junior across the table—''informed me yesterday that he has only one torpedo boat in Le Havre. In addition there are twelve E-boats there and only six U-boats with snorkels.'' The snorkel was an air-breathing apparatus that allowed the submarine to stay submerged for long periods. U-boats without snorkels were much more vulnerable because they had to surface often in order to charge their propulsion batteries.

''Pathetic, Grand Admiral. Pathetic.'' The Führer shook his head.

''I know it's pathetic, Sir. But the allied Jabos have literally blasted my channel force out of the water. The feldmarschalls aren't the only ones who have problems with the Jabos.''

Hitler's piercing gimlet blue eyes now shifted to Rommel.

"Well, Feldmarschall, you were anxious to interrupt me when I was speaking. Now you may have your say. I assume you have cleared with your superior here whatever it is that you want to propose."

"He has, Sir," Rundstedt said.

"All right, but don't waste my time trying to give me reasons or excuses for Cherbourg or the Mulberry operation."

By this time Rommel had overcome his anger at the crude criticism leveled at him. He would not give excuses or reasons. Besides, what he wanted to say was of overriding importance. He had prepared himself for this moment for days. Rommel squared his shoulders, stuck out his jaw, and began.

"Mein Führer, I speak not only as a commander but on behalf of the German people—to whom, like you, I am accountable. It is our political situation that concerns me."

The Führer pounded on the table, screaming, "Feldmarschall, you will not speak of the political situation!"

Rommel would not back off. "Mein Führer, my duty to my country dictates no other choice."

"Did you not hear me?" Hitler screamed again.

After the second admonition, Rommel complied and spent the next ten minutes explaining the tactical situation from his perspective, using the Normandy maps on the table for reference.

When he had finished, but before Hitler could speak again, Rommel went back at his primary objective. "Mein Führer, I repeat, I am obliged to talk about the political situation. Clearly we are being overpowered by the Anglo-Americans. Clearly we cannot win. Now is the time to seek a political solution with the Anglo-Americans while we still have some bargaining power. With the situation as it is here in the West and as it is on the eastern front, how can you imagine, mein Führer, that the war could still be won? In the interest of the German people . . ."

Hitler's head was bowed. His anger erupted like a volcano as he stood up slowly, eyes and mouth bulging with fury. His body shook as he attempted to control himself. Finally he shrieked, "Get out, Rommel! Get out!"

Rommel instinctively took a step back. He turned to look at Himmler and Goebbels across the table. If they were ever going to speak to support him, this was the moment. Instead, both averted their eyes. The silence in the Great Hall was total except for the snoring of the oblivious Blondi.

Rommel had no choice. He drew himself up, clicked his heels and gave the prescribed Hitler salute with his right arm. "Heil Hitler!"

The Führer said nothing. He stood, knuckles on the table surface, staring madly into Rommel's eyes. The feldmarschall did a smart about-face and marched quickly down the long Great Hall and out the double doors without looking back.

It was the last time that Erwin Rommel was to lay eyes on Adolf Hitler.

2 July 1944

IT WAS a quiet, pleasant Sunday morning in the Paris suburb of St. Germain-en-Laye. General Feldmarschall Gerd von Rundstedt had just come back to the house, known as the Pavillon of Henri IV, after a delightful walk in the adjoining park. The manicured green grounds dropped sharply away to provide a panoramic view of Paris, hundreds of meters below, as it spread out to the east, to the Seine and its bridges, and to that symbol of the City of Light, the Eiffel Tower.

As he walked back toward the house, enjoying the morning sun, he stopped outside the Pavillon to absorb its beauty. It was a compact, cream-colored stone building, its windows green-shuttered, its roof of shining slate reached by masses of ivy that climbed its walls. Over the front entrance stood a glass canopy. On the end wall was a black and gold plaque depicting a baby's cot with the words in French, ''Here was born Louis XIV.''

Rundstedt knew his days here were numbered. Hitler would soon remove him as Commander-in-Chief West, and he would have to leave his historic headquarters.

His conviction stemmed from the tumultuous conference at Berchtesgaden three days before, from the fact that he had acknowledged to Hitler his support of Rommel's position before the little feldmarschall spoke in the terms that Hitler had immediately described as defeatest, bordering on treasonable. In fact, it was justification for Hitler to dismiss both of them. When the two discussed the situation before they left Berchtesgaden at dusk that evening, they had agreed that Hitler would undoubtedly do exactly that.

To make matters worser, Keitel had telephoned him yesterday, anxious to talk about the continuing bad news from the West, the fall of Cherbourg and new attacks by the British. He wound up asking Rundstedt plaintively, ''What shall we do? What shall we do?'' Rundstedt had sharply and

recklessly replied, "Make peace, you fools. Make peace!"
As he put the telephone receiver back in its cradle, Rundstedt knew that he had just taken the cap off the bottle. In his mind's eye, he could see the sniveling Keitel rushing to the Little Corporal with the news of what he had just heard. Hitler would then pronounce that that was the last straw, that the old man had to be removed and replaced with some man more bent to his will than the crusty, 70-year-old Rundstedt. Furthermore, Rundstedt now knew exactly who his replacement would be.

The old soldier stopped a moment longer to relish the sight of the Pavillon. He had had enough of the idiocies of Hitler and the men of his OKW. He yearned for the peace of retirement when he could return to his home in Germany and tend his rose garden. He looked with pleasure at the display of ruby red roses on the bushes that he had trimmed only yesterday. Then he walked under the glass canopy to the front door, which was opened by the usual sentry. He stopped by a long mirror in the hallway. Facing it he adjusted his Knight's Cross at his throat, ran his fingers across his mustache, and pulled down on the bottom of the jacket of his beribboned uniform.

As he did so, he heard a door open down the hall near his own office, then footsteps. He turned to face his young aide who stopped in front of him and came smartly to attention, heels clicking together, eyes wide as if he had been startled or shocked.

"Herr Feldmarschall, one of the Führer's adjutants, Oberstleutnant Borgmann, is here. He has a message for you from the Führer himself."

Rundstedt nodded. So the time had come.

He entered the huge, gilt-covered chamber he used as an office, strode across the room past Borgmann, whose Hitler salute he ignored, and went to sit at the ornate table that served as his desk. When he was comfortable, he looked up at the young officer standing rigidly at attention. "Well, Borgmann, you have a message for me from the Führer?"

"Yes, Herr Feldmarschall, but first I have been instructed by the Führer to present this on his behalf."

From the leather letter case he had been holding under his left arm, he extracted a flat, purple-velvet-covered box. Rundstedt recognized it immediately. It was the standard container of military decorations presented by the Führer himself.

"The Oak Leaves to your Knight's Cross, Herr Feldmarschall. The Führer regrets that he cannot be here in person to present them to you in recognition of the great and faithful service you have performed for the Führer and the Third Reich."

Rundstedt took the box and opened it. The small golden oak leaves joined at the stem glinted against the purple velvet. He would be pleased to wear them above the Knight's Cross, even if they did come from the Little Corporal.

The old feldmarschall shut the case and put it on the table. "Please tell the Führer that although I am unworthy of such a high honor, I am grateful that he has seen fit to present it to me."

"Yes, Herr Feldmarschall, I will give him those words exactly."

"Now is there anything else?" Rundstedt knew there was.

"Yes, Herr Feldmarschall," Borgmann replied as he extracted an envelope, which he handed across the desk. "It's from the Führer himself, Sir."

Rundstedt took the pince-nez glasses from his inside jacket pocket and perched them on his nose. Holding up the letter-opener to slice the top of the envelope, he wondered what words the Little Corporal had used in order to justify the deed.

The letter was written on one page in Hitler's own hand. It was short and to the point. Hitler recognized Rundstedt's advancing years and failing health and so had no choice but to relieve him of his command so that he might enjoy the fruits of a well-earned retirement. The man chosen to replace him was, according to Hitler's letter, a loyal, highly experienced, and capable officer.

It was, as Rundstedt expected, Hans Günther von Kluge. Given Kluge's lurking presence at the Führer Conference, Hitler had obviously made his decision to move Kluge in after the first confrontation at Wolfsschanze Two on 17 June. Yes, Clever Hans, as people called Kluge. In Rundstedt's opinion he was a pliable character who never stood up to Hitler and was no competition for him, which was undoubtedly why he was one of his favorites. Kluge was getting on. He was 61. He had been the commander-in-chief of the Fourth Army in the Polish invasion and had been in France. In July 1940, Hitler had promoted him to feldmarschall and sent him to the eastern front, where his Fourth Army at Rostov suffered the first real defeat of a German formation in the war. As the eastern battle went from disaster to disaster, Hitler made Kluge commander-in-chief of Armee Gruppe Center.

As everyone knew, on Kluge's 60th birthday, 30 October 1942, Hitler had written a personal letter of congratulations and sent him a large amount of money to enable him to improve his estate. It was also intended to buy his soul. In the fall of 1943, Kluge had been seriously injured in an automobile accident on the eastern front and incapacitated for several months. Now here he was, a confirmed Hitler sycophant who had abnormal difficulty getting along with his peers—here he was, taking over from Germany's most senior field officer.

The fact that Kluge was difficult to get along with was well known. His most famous demonstration of this had occurred when General Heinz Guderian, the renowned tank expert, returned to the eastern front as Inspector-General of Armored Forces. Kluge had had a shouting match with him, then challenged him to a duel with pistols and invited Hitler to serve as his second. Hitler to serve as his second? How ridiculous! That kind of infantile judgment called for sacking, not seconding, but the Führer had merely ordered Kluge and Guderian to resolve their differences in some other way.

So, Rundstedt thought, here was the pompous, aristocratic Kluge, coming from the eastern front where he believed the *real* war was being fought, to France, where he believed commanders had been sitting for years in their plush, comfortable chateaux, living a life of opulence and luxury, out of the danger of battle. And now Kluge was to be the superior of Rommel, who was not of the aristocracy or the upper-class but was instead simply a lower-class Swabian. Rundstedt could not help but pity Rommel. Except that after that scene last Thursday, surely Hitler was dismissing him, too?

"What about Feldmarschall Rommel?"

Borgmann was perplexed. "I don't know what you mean, Sir."

"You know perfectly well what I mean. Is someone delivering a letter to Feldmarschall Rommel today telling him that he's dismissed?"

"I have no idea, Sir," was Borgmann's honest reply.

"The reason I'm asking is that I am expecting Feldmarschall Rommel at any moment. At 11:00 we're going to the funeral of another general the Führer has dismissed, General Dollmann. If you had a letter for the feldmarschall you could have given it to him here and saved yourself a lot of time.''

But there was no letter. After Rommel's insubordinate display at the Berghof, Hitler had wanted desperately to dismiss him. At his Grand Situation Conference the next day, at which Keitel, Jodl, and their usual staff were present, Hitler had ranted and raved about him, threatening all manner of dire consequences, including dismissing him and turning him over to the People's Court for trial on charges of high treason.

But as the Führer came to the close of his twenty-minute rambling monologue on the subject of the ungrateful Rommel for whom he had done so much, his cunning mind began to look at the other side of the coin. How would the German people take it if Rommel was sacked? Hitler couldn't pawn him off on the basis of his age or health. Nor could he dismiss him for incompetence, for Goebbels' propaganda machine had made Rommel the most popular of all German generals. Certainly there were his failures at Cherbourg and with the Mulberry operation. But would they stand up at a court-martial? Because that's what he would have to order if he dismissed Rommel for incompetence.

And who would replace Rommel as commander of Armee Gruppe B at this critical moment? Who would he put in his place to face Montgomery? How would it look to the enemy, to that evil, corrupt pair, Churchill and Roosevelt, and to the decadent Eisenhower; how would it look to them if he sacked both Rundstedt and Rommel in the midst of the battle? Surely the enemy would sense that they had Hitler's organization and the German general staff in total disarray and take it as a sure sign that Hitler believed he was losing the battle. That would never do.

Thus, much to Rommel's own surprise and that of Rundstedt, the popular feldmarschall was not sacked. Rundstedt had no knowledge of these events or of Hitler's rationale. He had long since given up trying to analyze the decisions of the Little Corporal. But he knew that Rommel was still a marked man.

''Please communicate to the Führer, Herr Oberstleutnant, how grateful I am for the honor of the Oak Leaves. I will wear them with pride—if ever I wear my uniform again.'' He stood up. ''One final word.''

''Yes, Herr Feldmarschall.''

''While I go now to my home to tend my roses—and indeed I look forward to doing that—the Führer should know that I stand ready to serve Germany again whenever he needs me. And mark my word, that time may not be long in coming.''

3 July 1944

THE WORD from General Blumentritt, now Feldmarschall Kluge's chief-of-staff, was terse. The feldmarschall would pay his first visit to the headquarters of Armee Gruppe B that afternoon at 2:00. No, he would not come for lunch. He would confer with Feldmarschall Rommel and his senior staff—senior staff only. The Commander-in-Chief West required a thorough briefing on the fighting.

At 1:55, Rommel, accompanied by Speidel, went down the long corridor to the entrance to await their new Commander-in-Chief. Rommel did not carry his feldmarschall's baton. After all, this was to be a working meeting with their new chief, a get-together, so to speak. As they waited in the sunlight, Speidel asked, "You've met him. What do you think he's really like?"

"Well, Hans, he has the same first name as you do, so that's a good start." They laughed. "First of all, he's Prussian and of the old school, and you know what that means. He'll be opinionated and uncompromising. Some people who knew him in the East said that he was pliable, easily influenced. Others said he was hard as rock. Some say he's wise, some say he's dumb."

"But what do you think?"

"I think he is clever. Clever Hans, they call him. I think he is tough; I think he is highly opinionated. The worst thing is that he is extremely difficult to get along with. You've heard about the Guderian affair, haven't you?"

Speidel laughed. "Indeed I have."

"Well, add to that the fact that he's coming from the eastern front with years of experience in battle. Like all the generals who have served there, he will think we've been wallowing in the lap of luxury and know nothing about battle. And he'll think he can clean the situation up in Normandy in no time. Just watch."

"And what does he think about you?" Speidel ventured.

Rommel clasped his hands behind his back, threw his chest out and chin up. "I really don't know what he thinks of me or for that matter what he knows about me. But if I was clever Hans von Kluge standing in the corner of the Great Hall last Thursday and watching the way I handled the Führer under those dramatic and theatrical circumstances, then I wouldn't have a very favorable impression. I would say that the Rommel fellow is bullheaded, independent, defeatist, and worst of all, disobedient. I'm sure that Hitler, Jodl, and Keitel had already told him that, and my performance would only have confirmed it for him."

The sound of outrider motorcycles and the roar of the Mercedes command car they were escorting could be heard in the distance.

"So you see, Hans, I expect our relationship with Feldmarschall Kluge to be extremely difficult. He's nine years older than I. He is senior in rank. And he's an aristocrat. I'm only one step up from being a peasant. We shall see, Hans, we shall see."

Two helmeted outrider motorcycle drivers guided their machines into the courtyard, engines and exhausts making a raucous, screaming roar. The black, squat Mercedes, feldmarschall's pennant flying, followed immediately, swinging around the courtyard in a horseshoe pattern to stop precisely in front of the main entrance.

Speidel stepped forward to open the rear door, coming smartly to attention as he held it.

The new Commander-in-Chief West, crouching down to get through the car doorway, stepped out. When his feet hit the ground he straightened his ramrod body to its full six-foot-two height. Up went his right arm as he barked, "Heil Hitler!"

Rommel was startled by the full formal regalia that Kluge had put on for this occasion—gleaming boots, medal ribbons, neck decoration, and towering hat, of course with his feldmarschall's baton in hand—instead of the working dress that Rommel wore and had expected of his chief. Startled also by the unexpected Hitler salute, Rommel did something Speidel had not seen him do before. It must have been an involuntary reaction. His feldmarschall lifted his arm and gave the HItler salute in response.

Kluge then removed his cap to reveal brushed back, steel-gray hair. Beads of perspiration dotted his high, rounded forehead. His large, slightly bulging eyes looked down at the diminutive Rommel, then swept around the courtyard and up and along the breathtaking towers and curves of the magnificent old castle.

In his deep, perfectly accented Prussian voice, Kluge's first words were not a gentlemanly greeting. "I must say, Rommel, that for a working-class Swabian, you certainly have excellent taste in castles."

Rommel's welcoming smile disappeared. He glowered as he replied, "I did not have the accidental good fortune to be born to the aristocracy as you did, Herr Feldmarschall, but I can assure you that lack of good luck has not affected my good taste. May I show you inside, Sir?" he offered.

The "sir" was expected by Kluge and gratified him. Under no circumstances would Kluge invite this lesser-in-all-respects feldmarschall to call him by his first name.

"Thank you, Rommel." Kluge tucked his cap under his left arm and took his baton in his right hand as he walked up the two steps to the huge doorway, his long legs taking giant steps while Rommel walked quickly beside him, trying to keep up.

They strode down the corridor, heels clacking on the hardwood floor. Kluge, his head swiveling to take in the paintings of the Rochefoucauld family members looking imperiously down on them, said, "Take me to your office first. I wish to have some words with you. Then you may take me for a tour of this fascinating place."

Rommel ushered his visitor into the splendid hall he used as an office. The two were followed by Speidel and Oberstleutnant Hans-Georg von Tempelhoff, Rommel's 36-year-old, blond-haired operations officer. Rommel had earlier asked the younger officer to accompany him when he was showing the feldmarschall about. Since Tempelhoff was of the aristocracy and a veteran of the Russian front to boot, Kluge might feel more comfortable with him along.

Inside his office, Rommel was about to introduce Speidel and Tempelhoff when Kluge ordered, "Shut the door." Tempelhoff promptly did so, giving a slight shrug of apology to the group of other staff members, including Kluge's, left standing in the corridor.

Kluge threw his hat and baton on the desk, then walked behind it to sit in Rommel's chair. There was no invitation for Rommel and his men to sit. Kluge had spent a week in the heady atmosphere of the Führer's Berghof and had attended every Grand Situation Conference. If the Führer used the technique of not letting people sit, then he, Kluge, would do the same. It was very effective, he thought, in making absolutely clear who was boss. To make certain Rommel learned the lesson, Kluge intended to break a paramount military rule: that a senior officer must never criticize an officer under him in the presence of that officer's juniors.

Settled in the chair, he looked squarely at Feldmarschall Rommel. "I have the personal mandate of my friend, the Führer, to clean up this mess in the West and throw the Anglo-Americans out of France." Teeth clenched, voice hard, Kluge then spoke words that appalled Rommel and shook his loyal staff officers. It was as if Kluge were speaking to a wayward young lieutenant rather than a brave feld-marschall. "You will have to get used to taking orders and obeying them for a change. That's item one."

Rommel bristled. "You can't speak to me that way."

"I am speaking to you that way, Herr Feldmarschall. And the second thing is you will never, I repeat never, go around me directly to the Führer. Do you understand?"

This was too much for Rommel to take, especially in front of Speidel and Tempelhoff. Rommel turned around, his back to Kluge, saying, "Please be so kind as to leave, gentlemen. And I don't want what you've heard repeated. Understand?"

"Yes, Herr Feldmarschall," they said in unison.

As Oberstleutnant Tempelhoff put his hand on the door to open it, Kluge shouted, "You do not have permission to leave. I am the superior here, and when I am here, I will give the orders!"

Rommel whirled about to shout his violent objection just as Kluge added, "Now get out, both of you."

When the door was shut, Rommel leaned across the desk, his face red with anger. "Listen, Herr Feldmarschall, you may be the Commander-in-Chief West, you may be my su-perior officer as of today, but you are in my headquarters and I am the feldmarschall. When I'm in my headquarters, I give the orders to my staff, not you. The fact that you're a Prussian, born with an aristocratic silver spoon in your mouth doesn't mean that you can come into my establish-ment and criticize me in the presence of my staff. That's unforgivable. It doesn't give you license to behave like an uncivilized boor. It's no wonder that everywhere you've gone your staff has hated you, your colleagues have detested you.

It's too bad that Guderian didn't have the duel with you and win it. It would have been good riddance.''

That did it. Rommel's thrust struck deep into Kluge's ego. He hauled himself out of the chair, his face, filled with venom and hatred, as red as the roses in Rommel's garden. Wagging his finger at Rommel, he snarled, ''You insufferable little Swabian asshole. How dare you speak to me like that! You're probably the most inexperienced feldmarschall in the whole German army.''

''And you don't know what you're talking about. The British are the toughest enemy in the world.''

''The British! You don't know anything about fighting until you've met the Russians. I'll have the British and the Americans back in the sea in a week. You have the men, the equipment, the tanks, everything, and you haven't been able to do it. I'll show you how to do it, and you will carry out my orders.'' He hit the desk with the palm of his hand. ''And you will not go around me and go directly to Hitler. If you do, I'll have you court-martialed!''

Rommel smiled with disdain and turned on his heel to walk to the doorway. ''Really, my dear Feldmarschall? I wonder what the Führer would have to say, if I went around you to him. I wonder.''

Kluge was calming down. He knew he now had the whip hand. He laid it on Rommel cruelly, who again had his back to him, and was standing by the doorway, feet apart, hands behind his back, heels lifting together in a short rhythm.

The heel-lifting stopped abruptly when the Commander-in-Chief West retorted, ''I already have the authority from the Führer to take whatever disciplinary action I deem appropriate against you for whatever cause, and that includes a court-martial, Herr Feldmarschall.'' He sat down on the chair again.

''Now that we've had our slanging match, Rommel, and we understand each other a little better, I suggest that we get on with the business of running this damned war and defeating the enemy instead of ourselves. I'm aware that you think you should have replaced Rundstedt and not I. But that's Hitler's decision, and he's made it. So let's get on with it.''

Rommel turned to face his loathsome new military master, his eyes narrow with hatred, his body taut from the tension.

''Now take me to your war room.'' Kluge's voice was

almost conciliatory. "I expect a full and comprehensive briefing from your staff."

"Very well, Herr Feldmarschall. Who knows, I might even participate myself."

"I expect you will. I must have all the information you can give me. Tomorrow I will start a tour of the front to see for myself. It may take me a day or two to assess the situation, but when I'm ready, you will come to my headquarters. I'll be ready to give you what Feldmarschall Rundstedt wanted from the Führer: directives for the future fighting. And when I say directives, I mean exactly that. You've had your own way for far too long and you've botched it badly. The Führer has personally instructed me to do what you have failed to do: hold fast at any price and destroy the enemy."

As Kluge stood and picked up his cap and baton, Rommel was on the verge of a response, a defense of his conduct of the Battle of Normandy. But his judgment told him it was futile to argue with this Prussian megalomaniac who clearly intended to destroy him. This pompous, prancing peacock had his mind made up and there was nothing he could do—at the moment—to change it. The only thing that might change his thinking would be a tour of the front. There he would come to grips with reality: casualties of more than one hundred thousand men since D-day and virtually no replacements; hundreds of tanks lost and no replacements; and the Jabos, hundreds of them, and no Luftwaffe. The man would have to see for himself. The best thing Rommel could do was to button his own lip, finish the briefing as quickly as possible, and get the Prussian strutter on his way back to his own headquarters. And may God have mercy on poor Blumentritt and his staff at St. Germain-en-Laye.

Two hours and fourteen minutes later, after curt formal farewells and an exchange of Hitler salutes, Kluge's command car, its motorcycle outriders leading the way, drove out of the castle courtyard, leaving Rommel and Speidel standing at the entrance. Seething, Rommel turned to walk back into the castle.

"Come, Hans, we have work to do. I must construct my defenses against that Prussian swine and his patrons at OKW. Find the adjutant, Hauptmann Kaboth. I will prepare a memorandum on what has happened since D-day. I want to pin the blame exactly where it belongs: on the OKW, OKH, the Luftwaffe, the supply system, everybody. If Kluge is laying the ground to attack me with a court-martial . . . Hauptmann Kaboth's shorthand is very good. I'll dictate a first draft and then you can give me your comments.''

"Certainly, Sir." Speidel looked compassionately at his beleaguered chief.

The feldmarschall looked up and down the hall to make sure no one was within earshot. Then he spoke in a low voice. "And the time has come to make plans for an approach to Montgomery. We must lay out plans for how it's to be done, and the form of it, the proposal. Are you with me on this, Hans?"

Speidel's response was firm and immediate. "Absolutely, Herr Feldmarschall. To go on like this is sheer madness. I'll go find Kaboth."

Rommel entered his office, leaving the door ajar for the adjutant. He went directly to his desk, sat down, found paper and pencil, and began scribbling notes on the points he wanted to cover. At first it was difficult for him to concentrate, an unusual problem for him, but he had listed ten items by the time the adjutant arrived. Rommel looked up, motioned him to the spindly chair across the desk, and went on with the making of his notes. When he had written down the fourteenth point he sat back and looked at the list. It seemed to cover everything.

"So, Herr Hauptmann, are you ready to begin?"

"Yes, Sir."

"Good. This will be a memorandum. I don't want it addressed to anyone. It's just a memorandum, with a preamble as follows: 'The reasons why it has been impossible to maintain a lasting hold on the Normandy coast, the Cherbourg peninsula, and the fortress of Cherbourg, are set out below.' ''

It took the feldmarschall more than an hour to dictate the first draft as he thought out each point and made corrections, all the while pacing around the room like a tiger in a cage, pausing occasionally to look out over the garden. Finally it was done. His litany of complaints was exhaustive.

But it was not until 5 July that Rommel was fully satisfied with the document, afer he and Speidel had spent hours discussing the points and editing.

He dispatched two copies of the memorandum. The first went to Kluge with a covering letter:

To C.-in-C. West,
Herr Generalfeldmarschall von Kluge,

> *I send you enclosed my comments on military events in Normandy to date. The rebuke which you leveled at me at the beginning of your visit in the presence of my Chief-of-Staff and Ia, to the effect that I, too, "will now have to get accustomed to carrying out orders", has deeply wounded me. I request you to notify me what grounds you have for making such an accusation.*

> 　　　　　　　　　　*Signed,*

> 　　　　　　　　　　*Rommel,*
> 　　　　　　　　　　*Generalfeldmarschall.*

Despite Kluge's injunction against going around him and communicating directly with Hitler, the man known as the Fox of the Desert nevertheless made sure that the Führer had a copy of the memorandum. He did so by sending it to his friend and Hitler's adjutant, Rudolf Schmundt, whom Rommel called "John the Apostle". He knew that Schmundt would place his memorandum before Hitler. And so Schmundt did.

6-7 July 1944: Patton

GENERAL PATTON shouted at the loading crew running his jeep up the ramp into the fuselage of the C47 transport, "Don't bend my goddamn jeep! I'll sic Willie on you if you do!"

It was a mock threat because obviously the general was happy as hell. He was chatting animatedly with Captain Codman and Sergeant Meeks, his personal orderly who had been with him since 1942.

Patton looked at his watch. It was five after 10:00. He lifted his head to look at the clear blue sky. The weather had been rotten—rain and low cloud—for the past three days, but now there wasn't a cloud. "Beautiful morning. Generals' flying weather, Codman."

"Yes, Sir. Perfect all the way to France. Can you actually believe that you're going, Sir?"

"It's about time, goddamn it. Bradley needs me over there. He sure does. I know that area like the back of my hand. All he has to do is put my Third Army in the field, and I'll show him how to break out of that goddamned beachhead."

As Codman well knew—he'd heard the story many times—Patton and his wife, exactly thirty-two years before, had made an extensive tour of Normandy while on their way home from the Olympic Games at Stockholm where the general had competed in a military contest called Modern Pentathlon winding up fifth in the field of thirty-two contestants. With his prodigious memory, Patton had retained complete recall of the Normandy terrain he had covered. He was sure he could put his special experience, which none of the other generals had, to good use if they would only let him get over there. He had been totally frustrated by being held in England as the head of the fictitious decoy, the First United States Army Group (FUSAG). But he knew Fortitude was working, that the Germans believed he was going to lead the Army Group Patton across the Channel at any time now and so were still holding their Fifteenth Army in northern France, out of the battle in Normandy.

Patton's Third Army was coming together rapidly. His divisions were assembling near Southampton ready to follow him across to Normandy. He had spent a great deal of time visiting his units, inspecting them, and making colorful speeches.

At his final inspection the day before, Codman had listened to his general give one of his blood-and-guts speeches to the troops. "I'm not supposed to be commanding this army; I'm not even supposed to be in England. Let the first bastards to find out be the goddamned Germans. Some day I want them to raise on their hind legs and howl: 'Jesus Christ, it's that goddamned Third Army and that son-of-a-bitch, Patton . . . ' "

But the name of the game was the Germans should not find out that he was in France. That would let Hitler know there really wasn't an Army Group Patton.

The young captain of the aircraft—he looked like a schoolboy to Patton—came down the steps of the C47, walked over to the general, and gave him a smart salute, "Sir, the aircraft is ready to go. Everything's tied down, including your jeep. So if you'd like to get on board, Sir."

"Thank you, son. Come on, Willie," he said, picking up his dog. "You and I are going to France."

At 10:25 the C47 was airborne. It was almost a year to the minute from the time Patton had left Algiers for the Sicily that he and his then equal, Montgomery, would conquer. Escorted by a clutch of fighters, the C47 made an uneventful trip across the Channel to a narrow airstrip behind Omaha Beach.

As soon as the aircraft was on the ground and shut down, Old Blood and Guts stepped out of the aircraft, followed by Codman and Meeks, to be greeted by several hundred American soldiers who had just been flown in. Naturally he would seize the opportunity to speak to these young boys, pump them up. When his jeep was out of the aircraft, he mounted it and began, his shrill, high-pitched voice reaching out across the crowd of khaki. Jokingly he told his audience that he was the Allies' secret weapon. In a serious vein, he cautioned them that his presence there was indeed secret and they could not tell anyone they had seen him in France. He left his audience fired up when he finished by saying, "I'm proud to be here to fight beside you. Now let's cut the guts out of those Krauts and get the hell on to Berlin. And when we get to Berlin, I'm going to personally shoot that paper-hanging goddamned son-of-a-bitch, just like I would a snake." There was no mistaking that he meant Adolf Hitler.

He then sped off in his jeep down the road with his driver, Sergeant Mimms, at the wheel and Codman, Meeks, and Willie in the back. They were heading for Bradley's headquarters a few kilometers away in a field south of Isigny.

His old friend, Omar Bradley, welcomed him warmly, as did Bradley's deputy, General Courtney Hodges, and General Joe Collins, the Seventh Corps commander. Collins had come to Bradley's headquarters to discuss problems with the southward attack, which had been launched on 3–4 July toward St. Lô. Progress had been especially difficult because of the numerous water obstacles and bocage. By 5 July the southern edge of the flooded area had been breached by the Americans, who were only to be met by the enemy counterattacking in strength.

It was a particularly difficult time for Patton as he listened to Bradley and his generals and watched them move their fingers around the maps, difficult because he could not put in his five cents' worth and wasn't invited to.

He and Bradley had dinner alone that evening in the latter's tent. As they sat down to eat, Bradley joked, "Sorry I don't have your favorite wine for dinner, Georgie."

"Next time, Brad, next time. When you come to my headquarters—wherever the hell that is—I'll make sure we have a nice white wine for you. After all I haven't anything else to do but go look for wine and food until you make the Third Army operational, bring my divisions across from England, and give me my Eighth Corps back. And listen, thank you for bringing me over."

Bradley nodded and said, "As I told you, I want you here as a backstop in case something happens to one of my generals. And I'd like to have you available for advice—when I need it. Anyway, Eighth Corps is doing a hell of a job on my right flank. As you saw this afternoon, I've given them the objective of La Haye-du-Puits. But they're having a rough time, Georgie. Casualties are very high and the Krauts are really tough. On top of that, Rommel has decided his western flank needs some reinforcement: I've just had word that Second Panzer Division has been identified against Seventh Corps Eighty-third Division and is heading for St. Lô. Rommel has moved the Panzers from the British sector around Odon, so things are hotting up.''

"What about Monty? He was supposed to take Caen on D-Day, and here it is a month later.''

Bradley was reluctant to be critical. "He's having a tough time. No question about it. He has at least four Panzer divisions between him and Caen and 88s by the carload. He's got a big operation scheduled to start tomorrow evening. He's going to call in the big bombers to hit Caen. Then he's going to send in Dempsey's armor after that. He just has to get moving. You've seen what the newspapers are saying.''

Patton nodded, "I sure have. The U.K. press is really on his back because he's not making any progress. He's not moving, but you are.''

"Well, that criticism isn't fair, Georgie, because it's Monty's plan to attract as much German armor as he can on his front at Caen so the Germans will put as few tanks as possible against us and make it easier for us to break out. As he puts it, he will continue to pivot on Caen. And he's certainly attracting Rommel's attention there.''

"And you've got a new SS Panzer division that Rommel has just moved over here.''

"True. But Monty's got another problem.''

"What's that?'' Patton was all ears.

"Ike was just over here.'' General Dwight D. Eisenhower, the genial U.S. general, was the Supreme Commander of the Allied Expeditionary Force and thus was Montgomery's superior. "He's very unhappy with Montgomery's performance, and the amazing thing is that so are Ike's top staff people, and they're all British: Tedder, Coningham, and Morgan. In fact—and Georgie, this is just between us—those three are pressuring Ike to take over as Land Commander and get Monty the hell out of there.''

"Fire Monty?'' Patton was astonished. "Jesus Christ, Brad, that would be like removing God. The uproar that would cause in England would be incredible. We'd have Monty's troops shooting at us instead of the Germans.'' He shook his head in disbelief. "Listen, Monty won't win any popularity contests, he moves with the speed of a South Carolina crab, and he likes to fight by a set plan. God, don't I know that. But, Brad, he's a first-rate professional soldier. Goddamn it, he proved that in North Africa against Rommel. I tell you, if Ike tries to fire him—and you know what the press will say, that Ike hasn't got a battle record and here he is trying to fire the greatest British battle hero to come down the pike since Nelson—I tell you there'll be all hell to pay. Sure it's easy to sit on your ass in England and look at the maps and decide that if you were running the battle instead of that little son-of-a-bitch of a cocky rooster, Monty, you'd do it differently. Christ, I've been doing that since June 6th—it's easy to do that.''

''I couldn't agree more,'' Bradley responded, ''but the fact is that Ike is listening to Tedder and those people, and he's reading the British press.''

''Son-of-a-bitch. Look, I'm going to go over and see Monty tomorrow morning. Pay my respects. After all, he is the Land Commander, and I want to thank him for bringing me over here.''

''I don't think you have to thank *him* for that.''

Patton laughed. ''Sorry, Brad, you did it and not Monty, and I've already thanked you. But as a matter of protocol I should see him, and if I can help his ego by thanking him—what the hell.''

''Fine, but just a word of caution, Georgie . . .''

''Which is?''

''Monty's not a flashy dresser. In fact you might find him in a sweater and trousers, no rank badges, nothing.''

''But that goddamn ever-present two-badge beret . . .''

''Why not? It's his trademark. But the point is, don't go dressed up like a damned Christmas tree!''

First thing in the morning, Patton bumped off in his jeep eastward to pay his respects to Montgomery. He had paid attention to Bradley. Instead of his shiny steel helmet he wore his wedge cap. In place of his jodhpurs he had on plain trousers, and the cuffs weren't even tucked in his combat boots. However, the ivory-handled revolvers were there, one on each hip. A fellow couldn't go too goddamned far.

General Montgomery's headquarters were still at the Chateau de Creullet at the village of Creully, thirteen kilometers east of Bayeux, but he did not reside in the chateau. His personal van was isolated, well away from the remainder of the vans that comprised his command post. Even that of his chief-of-staff, Freddie de Guingand, stood at a respectful distance.

On arriving at Creully, Patton found that Montgomery was not there. In fact he had gone to visit Bradley to discuss the First U.S. Army's mounting problems. So Patton followed him back. He found Montgomery getting ready to depart with de Guingand and Brigadier Bill Williams, Monty's intelligence chief whom Patton had met during the briefings in England.

Montgomery was clearly in a hurry to get back to his own headquarters. "It's wonderful to see you, Georgie, and I wish I had more time, but I've got this bloody great attack on Caen scheduled for tonight, and this is the first time I've called on the RAF heavy bombers to give me a hand. So there are still a lot of details to look after, you understand, old chap."

"Don't worry about it, Monty," Patton smiled. "At least I've had a chance to see you and pay my respects to my boss." Then he put the big question, the one he hadn't raised with Bradley the night before—but now he had both of them. "Tell me, Monty, when is the Third Army going to be operational? When are you and Brad going to let me at those German sons-of-bitches?"

Montgomery shifted uneasily, looking at Bradley. "Well, that question's a little difficult to answer, old boy. As I understand it, Ike's looking at the 1st of August, and the plan as it now stands is that on that date your Third Army will take the field with the First Army. Brad will become the commander of the Twelfth U.S. Army Group, putting him on an equal status with me, and I will relinquish the land command to the Supreme Commander, who will move his headquarters over here. Now the timing on that may change because Ike has a very large staff, a very large staff indeed"—his lips curled with a hint of contempt—"so there may be an accommodation problem. We had hoped at the beginning that we would take Caen relatively intact and they could have moved in there, but of course that's gone down the tube. So my guess is you've got at least a three-week wait, Georgie. But remember," Monty cautioned, "your being here is a secret. I can't stress that too strongly, old chap. Absolutely essential, you know. Got to keep Hitler thinking you're going to come charging across the Channel to Calais."

No sense sulking, Patton thought. At least I'm here. "Don't worry, Sir." With his ingrained professionalism, Patton had no problem using the word "Sir" to his superior, Montgomery, or for that matter, his recent junior, Bradley. "Lots of luck on your attack tonight. I hope you take Caen and roll that son-of-a-bitch Rommel right back to Berlin.''

From that meeting Patton went directly to his secret Third Army headquarters in a picturesque apple orchard in Néhou near the Douve River in the Cotentin Peninsula. Néhou had been taken from the Germans on 16 June by men of his own non-operational Third Army attached to Collins' Seventh Corps. Collins had captured the critically important port of Cherbourg on 26 June.

The need to keep Patton's presence in France secret weighed heavily on the minds of Bradley's senior staff. Bradley's intelligence officer, Colonel Monk Dickson, acting on the instructions of his general, called a press conference of the war correspondents, American and British, attached to the First Army's headquarters. These were men who understood the need for security. When the correspondents had assembled in the intelligence tent, prepared for what they hoped was a big story to rush back to their offices, they were somewhat taken aback by Dickson's brief statement. ''Gentlemen, I don't know whether any of you have seen what you took to be General Patton around here with his dog. You were mistaken. Good morning, gentlemen.''

The hint was understood and accepted. There was to be no mention of Patton's presence in France until more than a month later, 15 August, when simultaneously with the announcement that General Patton was commanding an army in France, the Senate Military Affairs Committee in Washington finally confirmed the acting lieutenant general's permanent promotion to the rank of major general. Coincidentally, 15 August was to be the most significant, the most dangerous, and almost the most rewarding day of General Patton's battlefield career.

6 July 1944: Rommel

AT THE same time that General George Patton was delivering his fiery speech to the surprised American troops at the airstrip at Omaha Beach, Feldmarschall Erwin Rommel was only sixty-five kilometers to the east visiting Sepp Dietrich at St. Pierre-sur-Dives.

The previous day Rommel had traveled in the Horch from La Roche-Guyon to visit the new commander of Panzer Gruppe West, General Hans Eberbach, a pleasant, resilient man, an old friend, and like Rommel, a Swabian. On 1 July the Führer had dismissed Eberbach's predecessor, Leo Baron Geyr von Schweppenburg, because of his attempt to withdraw his Panzer forces and evacuate northern Caen.

Rommel had broken his own rule against traveling in the rain in order to go to the Panzer Gruppe West headquarters in the Forêt d'Ecouves. There had been gusting rain squalls and low scudding clouds all across Normandy, reaching as far east as la Roche-Guyon itself. Armee Gruppe B staff had telephone several headquarters in the battlefront area and confirmed that there was virtually no Jabo activity due to the weather.

Rommel had made the decision shortly after 8:00 in the morning. They would keep the Horch's canvas top up most of the way, at least until they were about forty kilometers east of Eberbach's headquarters. From that point on, since there might be a stray Jabo despite the weather, they would put the top down but leave the side windows rolled up. That would give a bit of protection to Lang and Holke. Rommel and Daniel in the front would be protected by the windshield.

The four of them had set out wearing heavy plastic rain cloaks, expecting that it would be wet and uncomfortable when the top was put down. And it had been. The rain had fallen in gusting thick sheets on the brown and green French countryside and stung the faces of the two soldiers in the back seat as their slitted eyes constantly swept the sky for the appearance of any Jabos foolish enough to be flying in the thirty to sixty meters between the low cloud and the undulating land.

Once at Eberbach's headquarters, Rommel had reviewed the entire battlefield situation with the new Panzer commander, encouraging him to hold fast the strong bridgehead west of the Orne River at Caen and reminding him of Hitler's instructions that there should be no retreat.

The foul weather continued on the 6th, though the meteorologists had predicted a change. Once again Rommel broke his rule in order to be seen at the front. He particularly wanted to meet the rugged and reliable Sepp Dietrich and review Dietrich's defensive tactics and the disposition of his tanks. Equally important, Rommel wanted to get a reading of Dietrich's attitude. Did he feel there was any chance of success, of holding the Anglo-Americans, or was it time to think about the German people and the possibility of attempting an armistice? The approach to Dietrich would have to be cautious indeed. After all, the Panzer general was an SS man and one of Hitler's close supporters. A wrong word to him at the wrong time would find its way immediately to Hitler. The inevitable result would be instant dismissal and disgrace.

Rommel had had no qualms about raising the matter of an armistice with Eberbach. After all, the man was a confidant of his, a practical and realistic Swabian, an officer who trusted his feldmarschall completely. Eberbach had reluctantly agreed that some drastic action had to be taken soon, even an armistice, if that's what Rommel felt was necessary.

But what would Dietrich say, and was it safe to open the matter with him?

By the time Rommel's Horch was halfway to Dietrich's headquarters, it became apparent that the meterologists were right. The clouds began to lift, even though the sky remained completely overcast. There were now perhaps three hundred to four hundred and fifty meters between the ground and the cloud base, more than enough room for the Jabos to begin operating. The Horch's canvas top came down at Bernay with the improvement of the weather and the increased danger that accompanied it. When they reached the village of Livarot, some fifteen kilometers to the east of Dietrich's headquarters, the rain stopped completely, and blue patches were seen between the breaking clouds. Between Livarot and St. Pierre there were four far-off sightings of Spitfires, which moved like clusters of distant ducks sharply silhouetted against the gray sky.

Although the people of St. Pierre-sur-Dives had become accustomed to seeing the famous feldmarschall's car driving through the village, the men still doffed their caps as it passed. That morning the feldmarschall acknowledged the gestures with smiles and by touching the peak of his cap with his baton. In his heart Rommel knew that the French detested their German conquerors, but perhaps these signs of respect were an indication that the people liked him as an individual.

At Dietrich's headquarters—some twenty camouflaged tents under trees in an orchard on the outskirts of the village—the Panzer general greeted his commander in his own gruff, yet pleasant, way and escorted Rommel into the large operations tent, complaining about the heat that was beginning to return after the rain.

"The rain gives three kinds of relief, eh, Herr Feldmarschall? First from those goddamn Jabos, second from the heat, and the third from the dust. Right, Herr Feldmarschall?"

Rommel laughed, taking off his cap and noticing the perspiration that covered the leather headband inside it. "Yes, Sepp, the dust that can betray your life, the heat that can make you perspire and stink, and the countless Jabos like swarms of angry bees."

"Exactly, Sir, exactly," Dietrich nodded, and turned to the map on the table to brief Rommel. His stumpy index finger jabbed at the city of Caen north of the bend in the Orne River. "The important thing is that I'm holding the bastards out of Caen and west of the Orne. And what's more, I'm going to hold them there. They landed one month ago today. They've been pouring men and equipment out of the beachhead. I don't know how many men they've got there now . . ."

"Intelligence estimates say about three-quarters of a million, plus hundreds of tanks and airplanes."

Dietrich snorted. "It shouldn't matter a damn, Herr Feldmarschall, since my new Panther and Tiger tanks are much better than their American Shermans and the English Centurions. That 88-millimeter gun in my tanks is the deadliest and most accurate weapon in this war. Its range and accuracy are just fantastic. My Panzers can pick off Montgomery's tanks long before they can move into shooting range with their little pop guns.''

Rommel nodded. ''The way you have your antitank 88s in defensive lines on the high ground outside Caen to the west and north—well, it doesn't matter how many tanks they send in, they'll never get through your screens.''

''Don't be too sure, Sir. My problem is numbers. Numbers of tanks. Numbers of men. Hell, I'm getting no replacements at all. I gave you the figures. My attrition rate is appalling. My 88s and tanks are superior, but it's Montgomery who's got the real numbers. I can pick off his tanks, but he just sends in more. And those goddamn Jabos with their rockets. I don't know how long I can hold those lines, Herr Feldmarschall.''

Rommel nodded. ''I understand perfectly. My problem is really the same as yours: nothing coming in for replacements—not only for you, Sepp, here against the British . . .''

''And the Canadians. Don't forget them. They're tough bastards, let me tell you!''

''Yes, the Canadians. And the same over to the west against the Americans. No replacements for my tanks, my troops anywhere.''

''Well, I don't know much about what's going on over there against the Americans. That's your job, Herr Feldmarschall, and Eberbach's and Hausser's, now that he's succeeded Dollmann. Poor old Dollmann. Do you really think he had a heart attack?''

Rommel was cautious. He knew that to Dietrich the death of others meant little—he had personally murdered many fellow Germans for the benefit of the Führer. ''Right now, all the evidence is that it was a heart attack. But if it was suicide, he had good reason. If he'd gone back to Germany, the Führer probably would have had him tried by the People's Court for treason. So maybe Dollmann did take the cyanide pill. I don't know.''

''What would you do, Herr Feldmarschall, if the Führer relieved you of command and summoned you home for some act you had done, some disobedience or some failure, real or imagined? I suppose these days it wouldn't matter if it was imagined, because it's quite clear that the Führer is more and more out of touch with reality.''

Rommel was startled to hear Dietrich criticize Hitler.

Here was the first clue that the SS obergruppenführer was disillusioned and that he might get Dietrich on his side. He continued to listen intently.

"Yes, all the Führer's decisions these days are made on the advice of those idiots, Keitel and Jodl, who have never even been to the battlefront. Yet there they are, making decisions and giving advice, poring over their stupid maps and paying no attention whatsoever to what we tell them, sending us no reinforcements." Dietrich stopped for a second. "Sorry, Sir. But when I think of those pompous, idiot assholes at Berchtesgaden . . ."

Rommel lifted his head to look at Dietrich. "Are you including the Führer in that description?"

Like a boxer, Dietrich looked him square in the eye. "I am first among the Führer's henchmen that are left, and as such I have earned the right to judge his actions, Herr Feldmarschall. And yes, at this moment as I stand here in this field, in this tent in Normandy fighting an enemy who is destroying my tanks and killing my men, I know the only likely result is defeat. It has to be unless I get replacements, and I know he won't give them to me. So yes, Herr Feldmarschall, I include the Führer among the inept assholes of Berchtesgaden." His face was hard-set, his eyes steely. "And I am quite sure, Herr Feldmarschall, that the opinions I have expressed are strictly between us."

Rommel returned his gaze. "Of course, Sepp, of course. You have my word on it."

Dietrich averted his eyes as he pulled out a package of cigarettes from his tunic pocket. "What I was attempting to ask you, Sir, was simply what you, as a man of honor, would do if Hitler dismissed you? Would you go back and face the music or would you do what scores of other generals have done in this war: take the pill?"

There was no hesitation. "I would never take that route. It is the path of weakness, the easy way out. If I had done something for which I should be tried and punished, then I would accept my punishment. And it may well be that one day I will have to face the music, as you put it. You see, Sepp, I have a plan. Yes, you can call it that, a plan, or perhaps a better word would be proposal, a proposal that I intend to put before you and my other generals some time in the near future, the very near future. The risks involved in what I have in mind are very high. If something goes wrong, the Führer's wrath would strike me down like a bolt of lightning. But I would be ready for that, Sepp, because the action I propose to take is for the sake of the German people, and I have a high responsibility to the German people.''

''And to Hitler?''

''And to Hitler, because I have sworn an oath of allegiance to him. But my first allegiance and responsibility is to the German people.''

Dietrich shrugged as he puffed on the cigarette and turned back to the map. He did not ask what the proposal was. If Rommel wanted him to know he would tell him. ''So what about the overall situation, Sir? For the thousandth time, I need replacement tanks and I need replacement men. Without them . . .'' He shrugged.

Rommel drew his hand across the map from the Cherbourg peninsula to Caen. ''The overall situation is very simple. In a word, it's a disaster. Since the 6th of June, I have lost 100,089 officers and men, and I have received 8,395 replacements. I have lost 215 tanks . . .''

''And more than half of those losses were mine, and all I got was 17 replacements.''

Rommel went on: ''I have been talking to Jodl every day, shouting at him for replacements, and I can tell you I'm getting nowhere. The Russian front has priority and that's that. As for our supply system, the people who are running it are a bunch of incompetent fools. I need gasoline and ammunition at the front, and the new Quartermaster West, Oberst Finckh, is just sitting around with his finger up his nose. The problem is the idiot isn't under my command. You want my overall assessment? It's disaster.''

Rommel took up his characteristic pose, shoulders back, feet apart, his baton clasped in both hands behind his rump. He knew what he was about to say would sound ludicrous.

''Yesterday I told Eberbach to be prepared to switch two of his Panzer divisions to the north into the Pas-de-Calais area if there's a new invasion by the Armee Gruppe-Patton—or to the Seventh Army if there is a big breakthrough by the Americans in the St. Lô area.''

Dietrich was appalled. ''But if he has to do that, there is no possibility I will be able to hold Caen.''

''I know that. What you would have to do is fall back across the Orne and, using your 88s, your remaining Panzer division, and your infantry, concentrate on preventing the enemy from crossing it.''

"But you don't really think there will be a second invasion, do you? My guess is that the Anglo-Americans have committed their full forces here in Normandy."

Rommel had been getting his intelligence information about Armee Gruppe Patton from Speidel, who in turn was being fed intelligence by Oberst Alexis von Roenne, the High Command's top expert in foreign armies West. On 6 June—D-Day evening—Roenne had issued a secret summary of the situation: "Of approximately sixty major formations in southern England, at most only ten or twelve divisions, including airborne troops, are so far involved in this operation." On 16 June, German radar operators in the Pas-de-Calais area had reported the same kind of deceptive radar signals and electronic jammings they had found just before the invasion of Normandy. According to Speidel's information, there were still fifty-six divisions waiting in England under Patton. And then there was the Cramer story.

General Hans Cramer, who had followed Rommel in Africa, had been the last commander of the Afrika Korps. He had been captured in May 1943. From Africa he had been taken to England, where his health began to deteriorate. The British had decided to allow him to be repatriated through the Swedish Red Cross. In May 1944 he had been taken from his South Wales prison camp to the Combined Services Detailed Interrogation Center in London's Kensington Palace Gardens.

According to Cramer, his route had taken him through southeast England, the area lying directly opposite the Pas-de-Calais sector. There he had seen enormous build-ups of aircraft, armor, guns, and shipping. Furthermore, he had been received by Patton himself in his capacity as commander-in-chief of the First United States Army Group, FUSAG. During a long luncheon he had overhead conversations between Patton and his staff about the upcoming assault by the FUSAG force against the Calais area. The American general and his staff did not realize that Cramer could understand and speak English and so were apparently unguarded in their conversation.

Rommel replied, "Of course I think there'll be a second invasion. Between the Cramer report and what I'm getting from OKW, there is no doubt in my mind that we can expect an assault from Patton at any moment. That's why the Fifteenth Army must be at full readiness and kept in the Pas-de-Calais, complete with supporting Panzer divisions, and why the additional reserve Panzer divisions are north of the Seine instead of committed here.

"It's very simple, Sepp. If it wasn't for the Armee Gruppe Patton ready to strike with a million men and massive weaponry, you could have all the replacements you need. You and I would be able to drive the Anglo-Americans back overnight. But Patton hangs over our heads. He is by far the most able of all the American generals. I have no choice but to be ready for him."

To return to La Roche-Guyon, Rommel instructed Daniel to go east to Livarot, then on through Broglie, Conches, and Evreux. This had become Rommel's favorite route back from his frequent visits to Dietrich. In the opinion of his senior staff, using the same route was a dangerous practice. The car was becoming well known to the citizens of the towns and villages through which it passed. At any moment the feldmarschall could be a target for the Maquisard. But he had ignored the solicitous advice. When he left the front he wanted to take the shortest, most comfortable route home.

Furthermore, he could not bring himself to believe that he presented to the people of France, or to the Maquisard, an enemy image worthy of hatred. He had committed no act of murder, torture, or cruelty against French citizens. On the contrary, he had conducted himself with the utmost respect for the rights of the French people, allowing for the circumstances of the war and the fact that they were indeed a conquered people.

He could understand why the Maquisard might attempt to assassinate an SS general or a Gestapo agent. But he and his fellow generals were not Nazis, nor were they politicians. They simply served the duly authorized government of Germany. True, Adolf Hitler had swept away all vestiges of the democratic process and had become the dictator as well as the Supreme Commander of the German armed forces. But it was wartime, and Hitler and his Nazi colleagues held total political power. Therefore, the German General Staff, including Feldmarschall Rommel, took orders from the Führer, even though they themselves were not members of the National Socialist Party. Erwin Rommel had no problem with that line of reasoning. So the possibility of an attempt on his life did not enter his mind as his Horch roared through the familiar villages.

6-7 July 1944

AT ABOUT 8:30 on the evening of that clear, sunny day, there was an ominous lessening of artillery fire into the German positions in the northern reaches of Caen and immediately west of it on the Orne, the sector that Rommel and his generals knew Montgomery so desperately coveted. After all, it was D-Day plus thirty-one, and Montgomery's prize objective that he had hoped to take on invasion day, Caen, still had not been seized. As the enemy fire slackened, then ceased, the troops of the Hitler Jugend, the infantry divisions, and the Panzer units in Caen braced themselves for the attack to come. They had full confidence that they could withstand any tank or infantry assault that Monty could launch against them. As Rommel had put it, they were fighting like tigers. And they were holding.

It was later recalled by the few survivors that at about 9:30 the quiet that came with the foreboding lull in the firing allowed them to pick up a distant rumbling coming from the north, like the thunder of a faraway storm and far more ominous than the silence. Weak at first, it began slowly to rise in volume, a deep, constant, roaring sound, filled with undulating nuances that gave it a certain symmetry to a listener trying to judge its source.

Then suddenly it all came together. At low level and independently, six—or was it eight?—of the dreaded enemy Mosquito Pathfinder bombers appeared as if out of nowhere against the golden colors of the evening sky, rocketing in from the direction of the beaches to drop their red and green marker flares with precision. The aircraft were instantly met by a cascade of tracer shells from the carpet of light anti-aircraft guns and by the black bursts of 88-millimeter shells all hurtling skyward in an envelope of deafening sound. The troops on the ground beneath and between the marker flares dropped by the Pathfinders now knew what the distant roaring noise was. It was the sound of high-flying, heavy bombers approaching en masse.

Furthermore, the instant those brilliant flares appeared in the sky above them, every man beneath knew that he was looking death in the face, knew that he was in the target area on which the oncoming bombers—how many, a hundred, two hundred, a thousand?—would shower their massive, lethal bombs. But there was no escape. None whatsoever. The German infantry, tanks, and guns were immobilized in the wreckage of the houses and buildings in Caen, the ancient city they were dedicated to defend against the equally dedicated Canadians.

The marker flares on which the bomb aimers in the advancing flood of British and Canadian aircraft would set their sights made a rectangle over the northern part of the city. It was approximately three kilometers east and west and more than one kilometer deep and included the city core and the major concentration of Dietrich's Panzer forces, the antitank 88s, and the Luftwaffe's antiaircraft 88s. This was the center of Rommel's main force defending Caen. To attack them head-on on the ground was tantamount to suicide. There had to be some other way, and Montgomery had found it: British and Canadian bombers, Lancasters and Halifaxes, attacking by the hundreds on a pinpoint target, for the first time in daylight.

And now the rubble of the city the German forces had turned into an impenetrable fortress became an impassable trap. With the brilliant flares hanging in the evening air like the myriad eyes of a malevolent argus about to strike at them with every device of death and destruction, screams of warning echoed through the gutted buildings of the target area. "Head for the cellars! The bombers are coming!" German soldiers and the few remaining French civilians rushed down stairways into any cellar, tunnel, or protected area they could find. There they crouched in the darkness, waiting.

Above, the men in the tanks, the powerful Tigers and Panthers, had no choice. They were sealed in their metal behemoths like sausages in cans. The troops manning the antiaircraft guns could not run either. Their targets were moving inexorably into range, a long line of aircraft, stretching north as far as the eye could see. It would be like shooting ducks in a gallery. Their altitude was in the range of 1,500 meters. They were not in any kind of formation but rather a long stream, each at a different height, spaced carefully so that the bombs released from one would not fall on another aircraft below. The men in the Luftwaffe anti-aircraft batteries had never seen such massive numbers. Such beautiful targets. They would fire their 40- and 88-milli-meter guns at them until they ran out of ammunition or were killed.

A moment before 9:50 p.m., the first bombs from the British and Canadian armada were dropped; the last fell slightly more than forty minutes later. Between those times some 2,560 tons of explosives thundered into the target area. The ground shook incessantly as if in an endless earthquake. Fountains of earth, rock, brick, wood, men, guns, tanks, and vehicles shot high into the air. The screams of the injured and dying cut through the dense mixture of dust and smoke that enveloped Caen like a thick fog. Every building and standing structure in the target area was leveled. All communications terminated. The shock effect on the troops that had not made it to shelter and even among many of those who had was overpowering. Many were driven mad by the concussion and appalling noise and rushed frantically around in the dust and smoke-filled open areas until they were smashed by a bomb or cut down by shrapnel.

Several hundred antiaircraft 88s outside the target sector kept up an incessant barrage against the slow-moving enemy bombers, which had no choice but to fly straight and level on their bombing runs. Each of them provided a superb target for the maliciously accurate 88 shells. Scores of the Lancasters and the Halifaxes were hit, some of them bursting into exploding balls of flame and debris that fluttered lazily down to the earth. Others lost wings or other sections and cartwheeled across the sky in a downward curving arc like great geese shot dead on the wing.

Circling high above the stream of bombers were some fifteen squadrons of British and Canadian Spitfires ready to pounce on any gaggle of Focke-Wulf or ME109s that might be scrambled from bases near Paris. The eyes of thousands of German troops around Caen searched the sky for the Luftwaffe fighter aircraft they were certain would appear. But they looked in vain. With their virtually complete air superiority, the enemy had pinned Sperrle's fighters in their lairs by launching attacks against their airfields by British-based fighter-bomber squadrons just as the lead aircraft of the horde of slower bombers crossed the English coastline heading for Normandy.

The evening sky, now reddening as the sun dipped below the horizon, was a kaleidoscope of thundering bombers: the smoke of thousands of exploding 88 shells appeared magically out of nowhere like balls of black wool; countless bright burning tracer shells carved their upward paths toward the never-ending line of bombers; and mortally injured aircraft made their final sickening descent, many of them disappearing into the maw of the very inferno they had created. And in the center of this holocaust the white canopies of scores of parachutes burst open, silhouetted against the black matte of the bursting 88 shells. Dangling from the parachutes were terrified men, some injured, floating helplessly down through the raging wall of flak being thrown up by the deadly Luftwaffe antiaircraft batteries. The last aircraft dropped its bombs in the gathering darkness shortly after 10:30. Like the others that had survived the gauntlet of withering antiaircraft fire, it kept heading south beyond the concentration of flak, then wheeled slowly eastward, then north, back to its base in Britain.

Its departure brought curses from the hundreds of surviving Luftwaffe men manning their literally red-hot 88 guns, because they had failed to shoot down the last enemy swine. As the guns went silent, the sounds of the marauding bombers could be heard receding into the now-dark sky. So could the screams from the wounded and those trapped in the debris of the devastated buildings.

In the ruins were the survivors of the Twelfth SS Panzer Division, a unit led by an aggressive young colonel, Kurt Meyer. His troops were youths, an average age of only 18-and-a-half years. With the light of their torches barely piercing the thick pall of smoke and dust, Meyer's SS began to salvage what Panzer and Tiger tanks they could and the 88s and other guns that had been thrown around like toys during the incredible onslaught.

While they worked frantically to find useable equipment, other troops and medical orderlies came in from outside the target range and joined the search in the rubble for survivors. For those who had remained alive, the respite from the deafening noise, concussion, and firing of the guns brought the euphoric relief that they had indeed lived through it, that the worst was over, and that they could now regroup.

But what came next was as lethal and destructive as the bomber attack. It was an artillery assault from the guns of the battleships standing off the Normandy coast and the many divisions of heavy field artillery to the north of the city. Their fire, however, was not concentrated in the target area but was directed against gun emplacements and fortifications to the west, north, and northeast of the city.

The bombardment began shortly after the bomber attack ended and shattered the gun-quiet that lay over Caen. Accompanied by the distant roar of the big guns that fired them, hundreds of lethal shells whispered toward their targets through the darkness filled with concentrated cargoes of high explosives. They struck in flaming mushrooms, blasting destruction everywhere. For the Germans it was as if the world had turned into one massive, unceasing roll of concussions and explosions, fire, and unbearable noise.

With this new onslaught, the Luftwaffe gunners opted for survival deep in their dugouts, as did all the other German troops in the area. They knew that the air attack and the artillery assault had to be the precursors of a major offensive by the Canadian and British forces, though they also knew it would not begin until the northern edge of the barrage started to move south toward Caen. When that line started to creep forward, the enemy infantry and tanks would be just behind it.

The relentless barrage continued through the night. It was not until the first of the sun's rays appeared that the barrage line began its move south. The ground attack had begun. As the line moved southward past them, the surviving German troops began to emerge cautiously from their dugouts and trenches. Their uniforms were caked with the dust and dirt, their faces grime-smeared, their senses battered by the mind-stunning artillery barrage that had just passed them by. Now as they poked their heads out into the cordite-filled air and early morning, dust-laden mist, the message was passed by word of mouth and radio: "Retreat into the city, maintaining a rear-guard action."

Authority for that order had been given by Speidel to Hausser, now in command of the Seventh Army, and to Eberbach. Both field generals had frantically telephoned the headquarters of Armee Gruppe B several times after the artillery barrage had begun but before Rommel, who had left the Caen front shortly after 8:00, returned to La Roche-Guyon, totally exhausted, close to midnight. They wanted permission to retreat and regroup regardless of any Hitler order forbidding such action.

To Speidel the situation was perfectly clear. There was no choice but to salvage the outlying forces beyond Caen by bringing them back into the city, devastated though it was, and then to make an orderly withdrawal to the southern part of the city across the Orne. That would still leave a bridgehead to the west of the Orne southwest of Caen.

When Rommel walked into his office at the castle, Speidel was there to tell him of the horrendous attack that had started at Caen just after he had left and about the decision he had made authorizing the withdrawal.

Rommel was tired and reacted with unaccustomed testiness. The Caen attack he would have to deal with. But first there was Speidel's action.

"You have no authority to give such an order, General! A withdrawal or retreat is expressly forbidden by the Führer himself!"

"But, Herr Feldmarschall . . ."

"There is no sense arguing about it. Your decision may be the right one . . ."

Speidel stood his ground. "I think it *is*, Sir. My God, our people are being torn to shreds!"

"I know, and, yes, your decision was the right one from a tactical point of view. But you and I both know that you can't make that kind of a decision without the approval of OKW. Now get onto Jodl right away. Tell him that you made the decision in my absence, that I agree with it but that I will only approve of it if the Führer agrees."

"But Sir, with all the discussions we've had about armistice with Montgomery, I don't understand your concern about getting Hitler's approval."

The feldmarschall was exasperated. "Look, Hans, this is not the time for me to be fired by Hitler. I must stay here and stay in command. If I do something like this without Hitler's approval, I'll be yanked out of here just the way Rundstedt was. You understand?"

Speidel saw the point immediately. "Yes, Sir. Of course. I'll get onto General Jodl immediately." Speidel shook his head. "He won't like being wakened in the middle of the night."

Rommel had no sympathy for Jodl. "I've told him before, and I'll tell him again if necessary: there's a real war going on. Anyway, if he and Keitel would let us make our own decisions in the battlefield, then he wouldn't have to be wakened in the middle of the night.'' He started toward the door. "I'm going to the war room. That Caen attack sounds bad.''

Speidel reached Jodl on a "lightning call" at 12:35 in the morning. To his astonishment Jodl, even though he had been wakened from a deep sleep, did not appear to be upset. He sounded a little groggy but seemed to understand everything Speidel was saying. He listened to the Caen status report without interruption. Encouraged, Speidel explained that in Rommel's absence he had given authority to withdraw from the city across the Orne. He added that he had waited until the feldmarschall's return and his concurrence with his action before requesting approval from Generaloberst Jodl.

"From what you have told me, Speidel, there was no alternative. As I see it, either Hausser's and Eberbach's forces are going to be totally overrun there, or we give them the chance to get out. Let them get across the Orne. Put up as strong a rear-guard action as possible. Get as many tanks and guns back over those bridges as you possibly can, then make absolutely certain those bridges are blown. Is that clear?''

"Perfectly clear, Herr Generaloberst.'' Speidel could hear the tone of relief in his own voice.

"One more thing, Speidel. The next time you want to give an order of retreat or withdrawal when your feldmarschall is not there at your sumptuous headquarters, remember that it is only myself or the Führer who can give such an order.'' Jodl's voice was hard.

"Yes, Herr General.''

"So you will not give that order until, and not until, you have my approval. There will not be a second chance. I will let this incident go by simply because there appears to be no alternative to the withdrawal. But just don't try it again.''

8 July 1944

THE ORDER for Operation Lüttich was given by Hitler himself on the afternoon of 8 July.

Rommel arrived back at the chateau late that night totally exhausted after a frantic day at the Caen front working with Eberbach and his other generals in the repositioning of their guns and tanks. The begrimed, weary feldmarschall could see that Speidel, his usually phlegmatic chief-of-staff, was agitated as he stood, boot heels together, hands by his side, right hand clutching a sheaf of papers. Rommel could tell Speidel was excited by the flushed face, and the rapid opening and shutting of the eyelids behind those thick glasses. He wondered what had stimulated this highly intelligent man, an intellectual whose mind worked on a different plane from his. Rommel admired Speidel's intellect and begrudged his education. In fact, in his own way he stood in awe of his chief-of-staff and knew that in some ways—though never with any overt disrespect—Speidel took advantage of it.

"How was the day, Herr Feldmarschall?" Speidel asked.

"I spent most of it at the Panzer Gruppe headquarters, working out the regrouping of the 88s, setting up new antitank lines on the high ground. The situation there is very bad, Hans. Montgomery threatens to cross the Orne, and our defenses are so thin." Rommel shook his head in despair as he laid his cap and baton on the desk and started to unhook his flat collar. "And no reinforcements. Nothing. The situation is impossible."

His eyes went to the papers Speidel was clutching. "What's that you have? Some brilliant new battle plan by OKW guaranteed to throw Montgomery back into the sea?"

Speidel hesitated for a moment, caught off guard by Rommel's perceptive remark.

"As a matter of fact, that's exactly what it is, Sir. It's an order from the Führer himself."

He moved toward Rommel holding out the papers but the feldmarschall waved him off. He walked around the chair behind his desk, slipping off the Pour le Mérite and his Knight's Cross. He opened his jacket at the front showing the edges of the braces that held up his jodhpurs. Slumping into the chair, eyes and cheeks drooping with fatigue, he protested, "I can't read that stuff, Hans. I'm too tired. I'll read it in the morning. Just tell me what's in it."

"It's obviously something that madman at Berchtesgaden has thought up himself," Speidel said derisively.

"Just tell me what it says, Hans." Rommel sighed. "What are the orders?"

"What he's done, dreamt up with all his funny maps and the misinformation his stooges feed him—he's given order for Operation Lüttich. It is supposed to be a surprise attack in massive strength—a night attack. It calls for four SS and three army Panzer divisions against the British at Caen. He's talking about a hundred thousand men and five hundred tanks. And in order to make the surprise complete, the plan calls for no artillery support!"

Rommel was bolt upright, all signs of fatigue gone. "My God, he must be out of his mind. Where am I going to get seven Panzer divisions? The ones I have are barely holding the line at Caen, and they're being chewed up like grist in a mill. And infantry? I've got the Seventh Army strung out like an elastic band."

Speidel held up the papers. "The order says that you can have the Fifteenth Army's reserves of one Panzer division and six infantry divisions. That's all of the Fifteenth's reserves."

"That in itself is madness, sheer bloody madness. There is Patton with his armee gruppe ready to strike against the Fifteenth Army, and the Führer is ready to take away their reserves, all the reserves."

Speidel nodded. "Patton has more than sixty divisions in his force. When he strikes, you'll need everything you can lay your hands on, Herr Feldmarschall. Those reserves should be left where they are."

Rommel stood up, leaning forward, the palms of his hands resting on the smooth desk top. "I have no choice, Hans. This is a Führer Order. I have no choice. I must obey."

"But, Sir, quite apart from the numbers and where they would come from, there's the matter of surprise. How could you launch an attack like that and have any chance of success without artillery support?''

Rommel snorted as he straightened up and fell back into his chair. ''Easy, my dear Hans. You just shut your eyes and go. The problem is you can only go at night. Otherwise the Jabos will kill you as soon as you start to move. It's the same problem we had with the Panzer Gruppe Hausser. Without the Luftwaffe we have no alternative but to launch at night.''

''Ah, but the order says that the Luftwaffe will supply air support on the biggest possible scale including the new secret weapon, the ME 262 jet fighter. It says that the first of these will be ready by the time you're ready to strike.''

''What kind of time has the Führer given me?''

''Ten days.''

Rommel put his hands over his face as if trying to shut out the world. ''Ten days. Ten whole long days. God only knows what the enemy can do in that time.'' He dropped his hands to the arms of the chair. ''This Operation Lüttich is sheer madness, absolute and utter insanity. This whole war is insane. Something must be done to stop it now, Hans, now!''

Speidel rolled up the order in both hands. The opening was there. ''The members of the Schwarze Kapelle believe as you do, Sir. They believe the time has come. General Stülpnagel decided today . . .''

''So that's where you were today. With Stülpnagel.''

''Yes, Sir, I was.''

Speidel had spent the day in Paris and had only just returned to the chateau after a lavish dinner with General Karl-Heinrich von Stülpnagel, the military governor of France and one of the leaders of a clandestine group of German generals operating under the name of the Schwarze Kapelle, the Black Orchestra. They were dedicated to the removal of Hitler in order to save the German nation from complete destruction.

Rommel was no stranger to the Schwarze Kapelle movement. Speidel, soon after joining Rommel as his chief-of-staff and after listening to his feldmarschall talk in despairing terms about the political and military policies of Hitler and the Nazi regime, had told Rommel about the existence of the organization and had invited him to meet its leading members.

On 15 May 1944, the feldmarschall had attended a meeting of senior western generals at a lodge in the Forêt de Marly, a favorite hunting spot of Louis XIV. It was ostensibly called for a discussion of the defense measures to be taken on the Channel coast; but in fact it was a Schwarze Kapelle conference.

Rommel had been impressed with the rank and power of the men he met around the table that day; also by the fact that they were dedicated, as he was, to the preservation of the German nation, and to that end, to the overthrow of Hitler and his national socialists. The movement had begun in 1938 and was now moving inexorably from discussion toward action. Around the conference table with Rommel and Speidel had sat Stülpnagel; General Heinrich Baron von Lüttwitz, the Second Panzer Division commander; the military governor of Belgium, General Alexander Baron von Falkenhausen; and the commander of the 116th Panzer Division, General Gerhardt Count von Schwerin. Lüttwitz and Schwerin commanded the two most powerfully equipped and best trained Panzer divisions in the West.

The conspirators' seriousness of purpose had been increased by the news that the Gustav Line in Italy had just been pierced by the Allies and that the prospect of the German Tenth Army's being annihilated there was great. Furthermore, in the East the Soviets were not being held by the crumbling German forces.

On that day at Marly they had focused on several matters: what had to be done to work out an armistice with the Allies; a plan for arresting Hitler and for his trial by civilian courts; when German forces would evacuate all conquered territory in the West; and the need for a revolution against the Nazi government, ideally before the Allied invasion.

Rommel had not rejected the concept that he would be the leader of the rebellion because, as they had urged upon him, of all the German generals he was the one who had the highest esteem among the public and the army. But there had been one point at which he had balked. He did not believe that Hitler should be assassinated. He would have no part in such an act, for he believed that would only make the man a martyr and that his death would bring civil war. His opinion appeared to be accepted, and no further discussion of an assassination took place—at least in his presence.

But today, the 8th of July, Stülpnagel, Speidel, and others had decided that there was no choice; they had to make a last-ditch effort to persuade Rommel to support the assassination attempt, which was in its final planning stages. For even if the attempt was successful, unless Rommel agreed to lead the rebellion and the armistice attempt, civil war and the complete collapse of the German nation could result. Rommel was the key. He had to be brought on side.

As Speidel saw it, the insane order from Hitler and OKW that he now brandished just might convince Rommel that Hitler was mad and that the only way to stop him from causing the death of countless more German civilians and soldiers was to kill him.

But it was not Speidel who would speak to Rommel of these matters. No, Stülpnagel and Speidel had decided that someone else should make the final approach. That was why Speidel now continued by saying to Rommel, "The plans that we agreed on at Marly are progressing well. General Stülpnagel wants you to be fully informed about the proposal for an approach to Montgomery, so on behalf of the general, I'm asking that you receive his emissary tomorrow. We need your involvement and advice in the last stage of the planning."

He did not add that what they really wanted to know was where Rommel stood. If he was still against the assassination, what would his position be if they did indeed kill Hitler? The assassin had been selected, Oberst Klaus von Stauffenberg, a long-time member of the Schwarze Kapelle and of the German General Staff, an officer who was a walking wreck. With the Tenth Panzer Division in Tunisia, he had been strafed in the open by a pair of American Thunderbolt fighters. His left eye had been destroyed and his right one badly damaged; the trunk of his body and one of his knees had been skewered by shell fragments. His right arm was lost, as were the third and fourth fingers of his left hand. Even so, he carried on with his duties, and with full dedication to the Schwarze Kapelle.

"Who is this emissary you want me to see? Why can't you brief me yourself?"

Speidel shifted uneasily. Rommel knew the answer would be direct yet evasive.

"It's because I am not at the center of things. Furthermore I'm not a leader of the Schwarze Kapelle, merely a supporter."

"Also you would be more comfortable if someone else

talked to me about this, wouldn't you?'' Rommel gave him an opening.

''Exactly right, Sir.''

''So who is it you want me to see?''

''General Stülpnagel's adjutant, Oberstleutnant Caesar von Hofacker. He's Luftwaffe, Sir.''

The feldmarschall raised his eyebrows, ''Only an oberstleutnant and Luftwaffe at that. And you really want me to see him?'' There was a hint of incredulity in his voice.

''I know you think it should be someone of seniority, like General Stülpnagel himself, but Hofacker knows everything that's going on in Berlin and Paris and has the full confidence of all the leaders, including Stauffenberg.''

Rommel nodded. ''Ah, yes, Stauffenberg, I've heard of him. Badly mangled in Tunisia. So he's in on this too, is he?''

''Very much so, Sir. In fact he's been given the responsibility for Hitler's arrest when the signal for Operation Valkyrie is given.''

''Valkyrie?''

''Yes, Case Valkyrie is the code name for the plan to seize political and military power in all major German centers once Hitler has been taken.'' Speidel had no intention of telling Rommel that the true plan was that Hitler would be assassinated. ''It's far less noticeable to have a young oberstleutnant visiting you on apparent staff matters than to have General Stülpnagel or any one of the other leaders come here.''

''You say his name is Hofacker? I know a General Eberhardt von Hofacker. He commands a Württemberg infantry division.''

''Yes, Sir, Feldmarschall, that's his father.''

''Good. When you're dealing with an officer of such a low rank, it makes it easier when you know the quality of the man.''

''So you will see him, Sir?''

''Knowing you, you've already selected the time for Hofacker.''

Speidel smiled. ''Yes, of course, Sir. Ten o'clock tomorrow morning.''

Rommel nodded. He knew that Speidel had set him up. Not that it mattered.

9 July 1944

AFTER A hasty breakfast and a briefing on the reports from the Normandy battle area, Rommel returned to his study where he carefully read through the Führer Order, which set out in elaborate detail Hitler's rationale for the execution of Operation Lüttich. As he read, his disbelief and chagrin grew. The force that the Führer now ordered to be put together to face the mightily entrenched enemy was the force that ought to have faced Montgomery and the Americans within forty-eight hours after they set foot on shore on 6 June. Now the objective was totally impossible. It had no relationship with reality.

Nevertheless, Rommel had no choice. He would ask OKW that morning for two Panzer divisions from the Fifteenth Army rather than the one, and eight infantry divisions rather than six.

On the other hand, there was no need to rush. Hitler had given him ten days to put together the Operation Lüttich force and mount an attack at Caen. Furthermore, an infantry or Panzer division would need several days to get itself together and en route.

Rommel's most difficult problem was this: if he was to put together a force of a hundred thousand men and five hundred tanks, how would he be able to hide them from the eyes of the ever-searching Jabos, especially the highly trained fighter reconaissance pilots, the bludhunds? The hawk-like vision of those men had been honed by more than a month of battle. They had the uncanny ability to track down and find guns, tanks, vehicles, and tents hidden under trees despite the most elaborate camouflage the feldgrau could put together.

There were only two areas where an assembly would be even remotely possible. The first was in the large forest area some twenty kilometers to the east of Caen, astride the main highway to Lisieux. The second was the Forêt de Cinglais, lying on each side of the highway leading south toward Thury-Harcourt, about fifteen kilometers from the front.

If he could assemble his men and tanks and guns and equipment in those two forest areas without being discovered, he could then, under cover of night, move those forces up the highways, spreading his strength evenly to the east and west of Caen, provided that he had crossing points over the Orne River. It was imperative, therefore, that the bridgehead and crossing points be maintained on the west bank of the Orne. As of that morning, 9 July, his Panzer Army and the Seventh Army were still in place to the west of the Orne facing the Second Canadian Corps and the British Twelfth and Thirtieth Corps. To the northeast of Caen they still held ground to the west of the Orne opposite the Second Canadian Corps and the British First Corps as far north as Colombelles.

But at the center of Caen there was no hope. The Canadians were forcing their way to the river. It was now a question of preventing them from crossing it, at all costs.

Rommel initialed the Führer Order and walked down the corridor to the war room, where he remained monitoring reports and giving orders, his mind totally engrossed in the crisis of the battle as he worked with his commanders in the field, as closely as telephone lines and the secret code machine would permit.

In the midst of this tense situation Count Caesar von Hofacker arrived at La Roche-Guyon. It was with considerable reluctance that Rommel tore himself away from the war room to receive in the privacy of his study the handsome lawyer in Luftwaffe uniform.

"You have something to say to me?" Rommel asked curtly.

"Sir, I'm here as the emissary of General Beck and Oberst von Stauffenberg and also General Stülpnagel. They have instructed me to tell you that the plan for Operation Valkyrie will be carried out six days from now, in accordance with the principles agreed on at Marly in May. They ask that you confirm that you stand ready to participate as you agreed at that time. A memorandum has been prepared." He undid the front of his jacket deftly and took out an envelope. "This sets out your part in Operation Valkyrie, particularly the need for orders requiring the evacuation of all territory in the West, but only, of course, after suitable armistice arrangements have been made with the Allies. The

116th Panzer Division under General Schwerin—which is still under your command in the Pas-de-Calais area—will be available to you to contain any resistance by the SS Panzer divisions at the Normandy front.''

Hofacker laid the envelope on the desk. Rommel eyed it. "Who prepared this memorandum?"

"Walter Bargatsky. He is a lawyer on General Stülpnagel's staff. He is responsible for the legal planning for the execution of Operation Valkyrie, the assumption of power, the promulgation of a temporary government . . .''

"Which would be led by General Beck, I assume?"

Hofacker nodded. "That is correct, Sir. Oberst Stauffenberg will be responsible for the arrest of the Führer and Goebbels, Himmler, and Göring.'' He was under explicit instructions to tell Rommel only that Hitler was to be arrested, not that he was to be killed. Stülpnagel had wanted Hofacker to tell the feldmarschall that the plan was to assassinate the Führer, but this morning, on the last-minute urging of Speidel, he had backed off for fear that Rommel was not ready, that he would refuse to participate at all. Rommel's prestige and presence would be essential in dealing with the Allies and in keeping order after the revolution. It was better to lie to him now and have him enmeshed to such an extent that he would not be able to back out once the operation was set in motion, whether Hitler was assassinated or not.

"The most urgent thing, Herr Feldmarschall, is the matter of the plan for the approach to Montgomery. The plan must be prepared immediately.''

"Obviously, Hofacker, obviously. If Valkyrie is going to take place in a week, there will have to be two parts to the plan. The first has to do with the mechanics of getting notice of an armistice offer to Montgomery, then getting negotiating teams from both sides together. The second has to do with my generals, including my SS generals, Dietrich and Hausser. I'll have to try to convince them to support me.''

Thinking about his generals reminded him of the battle situation. He wanted desperately to get back to the war room.

He pressed on: "Dealing with the generals—I can do that myself. My relationships with Hausser and Dietrich are excellent, and they above all men know how badly we in the West have been treated by Hitler. Where I need help, Hofacker, is on the legal side of things, on the wording of the armistice offer. There should be no problem in getting a letter across the lines to Montgomery; we can organize a truce under some pretext. We've already had one—a week ago in General Lüttwitz's sector the Americans gave us back some prisoners they had captured at Cherbourg. They broke in on the radio circuit of a section of Panzer Grenadiers speaking German and talked to the commander. They wanted to give back to us a number of women, mostly nurses, whom they had captured at Cherbourg. General Speidel authorized a local truce, which began at 3:00 in the afternoon. The women were exchanged at 3:10, and the guns were silent in that sector for a full four hours. Four hours, Hofacker. If we were prepared, we could negotiate the armistice in that period of time. We could rig a truce through a cooperative division commander like Lüttwitz and in the process get a letter across to Montgomery—or by radio contact well in advance we might even arrange a meeting."

"Why not a letter to Eisenhower, Sir?" Hofacker asked. "He's the Supreme Commander."

"Eisenhower? No, no, he's not the man. He's not the battlefield commander. We've got to go to the man who's in command of all the land forces, American, British, Canadian, everything—the man I would have defeated in the desert if the Führer had given me replacement tanks and if I'd had Luftwaffe support. The exact same situation that I'm faced with today. If I can make an armistice deal it has to be with Montgomery."

Rommel picked up the envelope and took out the two-page, typewritten memorandum. He read it slowly and carefully, grunting from time to time when he came to points of special significance. When he was finished he put it back in the envelope and returned it to Hofacker.

"You keep it. I know what it says. This lawyer Bargatsky, he writes very well, and he obviously knows the legal points. Would he be able to prepare a draft—mind you, it would be draft only—for me to send to Montgomery? I'm not saying that I will use it, but it would certainly be helpful. He could set out the terms and conditions we agreed on at Marly, such as the withdrawal of all our forces to Germany in consideration of the recognition by the Allied governments of the new Beck government. There would not be the laying down of arms in the usual way but rather a truce and withdrawal. Our forces would retain their equipment so that we could immediately commit them to the fight against the Russians and keep those swine out of Germany.''

Rommel paused and looked directly into Hofacker's eyes.

''He should also cover the details of the armistice: when it is to go into effect, all that sort of thing. We would offer a complete evacuation of all the territories we hold in the West. The army would withdraw to the old Siegfried Line. The Anglo-Americans would immediately stop the bombing of Germany—the quid pro quo for that would be the shutting down of the V-weapon bombardment of London. The armistice would not require the unconditional surrender that Churchill and Roosevelt had fixed in their minds. Instead it would be an armistice with peace negotiations to follow.

''I know Montgomery: just as sure as I'm sitting here, he'd be prepared to accept those terms and a separate peace apart from the Russians. He's no fool; he knows that the Russians want to subjugate the rest of the world to Communism and that they'd take on the Anglo-Americans at the drop of a hat. So what about it? Can you have your friend Bargatsky draft such a letter?''

''It will be delivered to General Speidel sometime tomorrow afternoon, Sir,'' Hofacker replied, smiling. ''Tomorrow afternoon at the latest.''

Rommel stood up, signaling the end of the meeting. Hofacker saluted simply by clicking his heels and giving a slight aristocratic bow of his head.

''A question, Sir,'' he said. ''How long do you think you can hold out against the Americans in Normandy?''

''At the most two to three weeks,'' Rommel replied without hesitation, ''then the breakthrough may be expected. We have nothing more to throw in. Now if you will excuse me, Oberstleutnant Hofacker, I must get back to the war.''

12 July 1944

THE FOLLOWING days merely confirmed the bleak report Rommel and Speidel were preparing for Hitler on the situation in the West. There was no staunching the daily loss of men and materiel. As the Anglo-Americans increased in numbers and resolve, Hitler and OKW seemingly decreased in any desire they might have to counter with fresh troops and equipment.

At his morning breakfast with Speidel, Rommel was unusually quiet and reflective. The two men ate without talking. As they were finishing their coffee, a feldwebel appeared with a message.

"Yes, what is it?"

"A message from the Commander-in-Chief West, Sir."

Rommel took the message and began to read it as the feldwebel clicked his heels.

"Bad news, Sir?" Speidel asked tentatively.

"I really don't know. Feldmarschall Kluge wants to see me this afternoon. He has asked if it is convenient for me to see him. The wording doesn't sound like him at all. Strange." He instructed Speidel to relay to Kluge's chief-of-staff that he would be pleased to meet General Feldmarschall Kluge. "Suggest 17:30 hours. Also suggest he have supper with me."

As the afternoon wore on Rommel was preoccupied with thoughts about Kluge. He had never met such a rude, arrogant swine. But Kluge was his commander, and like it or not, Kluge's orders had to be obeyed. A dreadful man. Why did Kluge want to see him? Was it to give him another insulting dressing-down? This time he would not take it. He would simply walk out. Or did Kluge want to give him a set of battle orders the instant expert had conceived to defeat Montgomery's forces in a single stroke? Probably a combination of both, he thought.

Kluge was scheduled to arrive at 5:30. Rommel would

change into his full dress regalia, complete with medal ribbons, in order to match the strutting feldmarschall. In fact, he would outdo him, because it was he, Rommel, who wore the Pour le Mérite at his throat, not Kluge.

At 5:27, Rommel stood at the entrance to the castle. He had instructed Speidel that he wanted to greet the Commander-in-Chief alone and that the two of them would have dinner unaccompanied. Rommel did not want a repeat performance of the shouting match in the presence of his staff. If they were going to have at each other again, they would do so in the privacy of his office or in Rommel's room where the dinner would be served.

Feldmarschall Rommel was satisfied with his appearance. His high-faced flat hat sat squarely on his head. The gray-green fabric of his freshly-sponged dress uniform was carefully pressed. The knee-high jackboots below his jodhpurs shone as they never had before. On his left breast were two multi-hued rows of medal ribbons.

In his usual stance, feet wide apart, hands behind his back clutching his baton, he began to feel the steamy humidity, but ignored the discomfort. He was concentrating on how he would handle Kluge this time. Whether Kluge had him court-martialed for it or not, he decided he would stand his ground. His emotions were firmly under control. It was a cool, determined Erwin Rommel who waited in the summer's heat to meet his commander and foe.

He knew the punctilious Kluge would be sitting in his black Mercedes, perhaps one kilometer to the east of La Roche-Guyon. Its engine and that of the two motorcycle outriders would be idling as they sat under the shading leaves of some huge tree. Promptly at 5:28, Kluge would give his driver the order to proceed. In turn the driver would shout the order to the outriders. In precise formation, like a pair of small black ponies pulling a hearse, they would move off at a moderate speed designed to put them into the castle's courtyard at exactly 5:30.

Rommel checked his watch when he heard the first distant staccato sounds of the motorcycles. He did not have to check his watch one minute and ten seconds later when the three vehicles swept loudly into the courtyard. It was 5:30 exactly.

Rommel came smartly to attention as the feldmarschall's car stopped broadside one meter away from him. Rommel made no move to open the door. For any other feldmarschall, he would have done so without hesitation, as a matter of courtesy. But not for Kluge.

The point was not lost on the Commander-in-Chief West. Sitting in the dark reaches of the long vehicle, he waited for his driver to get out, walk smartly around the back of the vehicle, and then open the rear door.

Kluge stepped out, straightened up to his full height, and gave a perfunctory Hitler salute. Rommel, somewhat surprised, returned it with the crispness and energy he had expected from Kluge.

That exchange over, Rommel was again surprised when his visitor smiled at him, stepping forward and offering his right hand in apparent friendship. Caught unawares, the stocky feldmarschall seized the huge hand. It was at that moment that he noticed that Kluge had on his work tunic instead of his formal uniform with its medal ribbons. When the Prussian feldmarschall spoke, it was clear to Rommel that he was a different man from the one who had confronted him just three days before.

"It is very good of you to receive me on such short notice, Feldmarschall Rommel." The smile was still there, though now a shade grimmer. "My tour of the battle area has taught me a great deal, and I have come to tell you . . ." He looked around and saw that no other person was present except for his own driver. "I have come to tell you that I was very badly misled by Keitel and Jodl and . . ." It was apparent to Rommel that he was about to add "the Führer", but thought better of it.

"They misled me very badly. Yes, very badly. Not only about the conditions of our troops, but about the tremendous losses in tanks and guns, and about the replacements. Yes, the lack of replacements. They gave me quite a false picture. Not only about the battlefront but about you, Erwin." There was no expression on Rommel's face as he looked up at Kluge. His use of the name Erwin was an obvious attempt to bring himself down to his junior's level, but at the same time it was a clear signal of his sincerity. The junior feldmarschall would now wait for the invitation to call his superior by his first name. Would it come?

"They told me you were arrogant, incompetent, and that you repeatedly disobeyed instructions from OKW and from the Führer himself. They said that more often than not you gave them the wrong information about the state of the battle in order to further your own interests and justify your demands for more men and equipment.'' He squared his shoulders and came to the last difficult part. "So when I came here three days ago, I had completely inaccurate information, and that is why I acted as I did. I have visited all the field headquarters, I have talked to all your generals. I have seen with my own eyes. I now know that the information I was given at OKW was completely wrong, about the battle situation and about you, Herr Feldmarschall. So I have come to offer the hand of friendship, to tell you that I will not interfere with your battles and your decisions in the field and to tell you, man to man, that I apologize.''

Feldmarschall Rommel hid his astonishment as he accepted the apology and agreed to let bygones be bygones. At the dinner the two of them shared privately, the commander of Armee Gruppe B spoke quite openly with his commander. They exchanged information, opinions, and confidences. The past was behind them.

But the invitation from Clever Hans to call him by his first name did not come that evening. Indeed it would never come.

15 July 1944

"I SIGNED it this morning, Paul, just before I left," Rommel told Paul Hausser, who had replaced General Dollmann as commander of the Seventh Army. The tall, graying SS general, his peaked forage cap square on his head, black patch over his right eye, stood with Rommel in a grain field next to the orchard where he had relocated his Seventh Army headquarters. He had abandoned Dollmann's chateau near Le Mans for a location much closer to the battle area.

Rommel had come to regard Hausser as the most stable and reliable of his commanders. He had an air of calmness and determination about him, an SS man from the beginning who had always shown himself loyal to the Führer and to Himmler, the architect and head of the SS.

"I should have brought a copy for you but there just wasn't time."

Hausser chuckled. "It's all right, Herr Feldmarschall. Even if you'd brought it, I would have had difficulty reading it with this one eye of mine. But tell me about it. I'm interested in anything that you say to the Führer about the mess we're in."

Rommel turned to ensure that none of Hausser's staff were within earshot. Three or four stood nearby talking. Best to move away a few paces.

"Come, Paul, let's walk along the edge of the field so we can have a little privacy."

As they walked, a light wind made waves in the golden grain that rose to the tops of their jackboots. Above them, the intense July sun was partially obscured by lumpy white clouds that covered more than three-quarters of the sky.

"Our new Commander-in-Chief paid me a second visit three days ago," Rommel said.

The amiable Hausser snorted. "I hope it was more pleasant than the first one. When he came here to visit me I can tell you, Sir, he got an earful. I gave it to him full blast.

Shortages of ammunition, shortages of fuel, shortages of food, dreadful casualties. I'm sure Dietrich and the others did the same. He went away from here stunned. Perhaps I should say, more stunned.''

"Oh, well that explains it," said Rommel, as they walked side by side. "When he came to see me on the 12th he was a changed person. He really had his tail between his legs. Not at all the peacock who had come from two heady weeks with the Führer at the Berghof."

Hausser shook his head. "What a place, the Berghof and that loony bin, the OKW. It must be like a three-ring circus there, all of them dancing and prancing in front of the Führer, trying to curry his favor, whipping up crazy battle plans for us poor bastards in the field. The problem is, Herr Feldmarschall, that the Führer has become as mad as the rest of them. Just as mad as the rest of them," he repeated, talking more to himself than to Rommel, who carefully noted the remark.

"Well, at least Feldmarschall Kluge and I have reached— how shall I put it?—a reconciliation. He now understands what I've been trying to say to OKW. Indeed, his attitude is so different now that I feel I could raise the question of approaching Montgomery for an armistice before it's too late."

Hausser stopped in his tracks. He turned and looked down at Rommel with his one good eye. Instead of the anger Rommel had expect, Hausser's response was curiosity.

"An armistice? What do you think his reaction would be? Positive, I hope."

"Yes, I *think* it would be positive. But they tell me with Feldmarschall Kluge you never really know what he's going to do. They say it depends on whom he was talking to last."

"And is that what you want to talk to me about, Herr Feldmarschall—an armistice with Montgomery?"

Rommel stared up into Hausser's one light-blue eye. "Yes, Paul, that's exactly what I want to talk to you about. But let us deal with that question after I tell you what I've said to the Führer."

They resumed their slow walk.

"Our much-changed Commander-in-Chief West *politely* asked me to prepare a written report on our battle prospects. With Speidel's help that's what I have done. Only instead of addressing it to Feldmarschall Kluge, I addressed it to the Führer. I signed it this morning and sent it off to

Kluge. In three or four days, I'll prod him to make his comments and pass it on. In the message, first I described in detail the calamitous situation we have in Normandy. Then I told him that his proposed Operation Lüttich was impossible.''

Rommel changed course and headed for an apple tree at the orchard's edge to escape from the hot burst of sun that had just hit them.

Standing in the cool shade he continued: ''When the report was in its final form, I added a concluding paragraph. When Speidel read it he almost had a stroke. I intended it to be an ultimatum to the Führer and that's exactly what it is. 'Everywhere our troops are fighting heroically,' I said, 'but the unequal struggle with the enemy is drawing to its close. In my view the political consequences of this have just got to be drawn.' ''

Hausser's response was similar to Speidel's. ''My God, Herr Feldmarschall, 'political consequences' means you're telling Hitler that he should seek an armistice. That's the same thing as putting a gun to your head or a cyanide pill in your mouth. He'll go berserk!''

''I know that, Paul, I know that. Speidel drove the same point home with a sledge-hammer. So I agreed to take out the word 'political'. But still I've given the Führer an ultimatum that says, If you don't seek an armistice, I will, whether you agree to it or not. What do you think of that, Herr General?''

Hausser did not hesitate. ''There's no choice. There has to be a political solution and an armistice here in the West.''

Hausser did not add the words Rommel was looking for and had to hear.

''Whether the Führer agrees or not?''

''Absolutely. Whether the Führer agrees or not. What's more, you are the only man who can bring it off.''

''So you will support me if that's what I have to do?''

SS General Paul Hausser drew his lean body up to its full height. ''Yes, Herr Feldmarschall. I will not only support you, I will follow you, and so will all my troops.''

During their walk and then as they were standing beneath the apple tree, Rommel's highly experienced ears and eyes had been monitoring the sky for the sounds or sight of enemy fighter aircraft. The only ones he had heard or seen were in the distance, well away from the hundreds of Luftwaffe flak guns that covered the whole area around Caen like ants on a plate of sugar. The Jabos were far enough away that they would not be able to see any part of Hausser's well-camouflaged headquarters or the Horch, which Daniel had parked under one of the countless apple trees.

Suddenly, just as they were halfway back to the staff car where Hauptmann Lang was waiting, talking to a small group of Hausser's officers, alarm signals rang in the feldmarschall's brain as he heard from perhaps three kilometers to the southwest the staccato fire of 20- and 40-millimeter aircraft guns.

He stopped talking in mid-sentence and grabbed Hausser's forearm. Both men turned to face the sound of the flak. Strange, Rommel thought, unable to see any tracers from the flak guns nor what they were firing at. Not really strange, he quickly realized. It meant the aircraft they were shooting at were down low, undoubtedly as close to the ground as they could fly at high speed.

Then the first snatches of the undulating thunderous noise of fighter aircraft engines reached their ears. Almost immediately the undulating ceased as the sound grew stronger. Still the enemy aircraft, whatever they were, could not be seen, hidden as they were behind a far copse.

The noise increased, and the tracking flak came into sight. The trajectory of the tracer shells was almost horizontal to the ground as the gunners trained their sights well ahead of the Jabos. Even though they knew exactly where they were coming from, neither Rommel nor Hausser could see the planes, nor could they guess how many of them there were.

Then the Jabos were on top of them. Two of them—as if out of nowhere, their propellors and wings almost touching the tops of the tall trees. Their shining nose spinners and the 20-millimeter cannon mounted in each wing were pointing straight at Rommel and Hausser. In a split second Rommel remembered the shallow ditch that he and Hausser had crossed when they left the grain field to go into the orchard.

Shouting "Into the ditch!" Rommel took two running steps and flung himself flat into the air, arms outstretched like a diver doing a belly flop. The stagnant green water at the bottom of the ditch flew up like a fountain as he and Hausser hit its surface.

As he dove in Rommel could hear the staccato thumping of the two 20-millimeter cannons of both Spitfires as they spewed a torrent of lethal shells at the unexpected targets of tents, men, trucks, track vehicles, and guns that suddenly appeared before them. At the speed they were traveling, probably four hundred kilometers an hour, they were able to get in only a two-second burst. Nevertheless, the damage they wrought was devastating.

A gusher of earth erupted from the side of the ditch one meter from Rommel's head as a cannon shell plowed into the moist ground. Glancing up, Rommel glimpsed the camouflaged belly of one of the Spitfires with the distinctive Allied white and black recognition stripes at its wing roots.

As soon as the aircraft were gone, the feldmarschall struggled cautiously to his knees. He was soaked from head to foot. He looked around, wondering if the planes were being followed by others or if the attackers were wheeling to come in for another strafing run. Because of the intensity of the defending flak, he doubted they would return, if indeed they had survived their low-level run. There were no aircraft in sight or sound. Quickly his eyes turned to the headquarters area.

A huge billowing cloud of dust lacerated by streams of black smoke, shafts of flame, and upward rolling fireballs blanketed the entire area. The blasts of exploding fuel tanks mingled with the screams of injured and dying men and the crackling sound of flames devouring tents, vehicles, camouflage netting, and the trees that had earlier protected them so effectively from the searching eyes of enemy pilots.

Rommel was momentarily transfixed by the scene even though he had seen it all many times before. He was startled by Hausser's voice behind him saying, "It looks to be clear, Sir. There were just the two of them."

"Right," the hatless feldmarschall agreed as he struggled, dripping, to his feet, his baton still clenched in his right hand. He looked around for his cap and found it on the dry ground at the lip of the ditch. Before he put it on, he used both hands to sweep off mud and water from the front of his jacket and whipcord jodhpurs. Now he had to get to his men. He picked up his cap and baton and, without a glance back at Hausser, walked quickly toward the growing holocaust.

Inside the envelope of smoke, dust, and flame he saw burning vehicles and tents, and men milling about. Everywhere was total chaos. Without a by-your-leave to Hausser, Rommel took charge, galvanizing every able-bodied man, including Hausser, within earshot.

"Get all the tents down that are near the fire. You men

there, move quickly. The damaged vehicles and personnel carriers, anything that can move—move them out. Don't just stand there. Where are the fire extinguishers? Get them out of your vehicles and start using them. You men, get buckets from the kitchen. Make a chain, use the water from the ditch. You, get the medical people on the double, stretchers, ambulances.''

In half an hour's time the spread of the flames had been controlled. Any fires, mostly in armored vehicles, that could not be extinguished were allowed to burn themselves out. The injured were on their way to field hospitals. The situation was under control.

Miraculously, Admiral Ruge, Kramer—the replacement spotter for Holke, who was ill with the flu—and Unteroffizier Daniel had survived unscathed. The only injury in the feldmarschall's party was to the Horch. Its right front wheel had taken a direct hit from one of the 20-millimeter shells that by some fluke had failed to explode. If it had, the entire car would have been written off. As it was, the wheel was shattered and the tire shredded, but the joint to the axle untouched. Daniel, who had changed more flat tires on the Horch than he could remember, replaced the shattered wheel and tire with the spare from the right front fender. In no more than five minutes, the car was ready to go—and so was the feldmarschall.

In an unusual gesture for him, he offered his hand to general Hausser. ''I apologize for taking charge at your own headquarters, Paul, but as you know, it's a failing of mine.''

''If it's a failing, Herr Feldmarschall, you can fail here anytime,'' Hausser smiled.

Rommel shook his head as he waved his baton toward the devastation. ''If this is what two Jabos can do in two seconds, can you imagine what a few squadrons of them could do if they caught us assembling five hundred tanks and a hundred thousand men for Operation Lüttich?''

Hausser frowned. ''Or what they would have done to my Panzer Gruppe Hausser if they'd caught us before we launched?''

''The attack that never was, you mean. I still think you could have done it, Paul. You could have gone all the way to the beach and destroyed the Mulberry.''

''Who knows, Herr Feldmarschall? There's no use looking back. We have to look ahead. It's up to you now. As you say, the important thing is for the Anglo-Americans to get to Berlin before the Russians do. So don't bother going cap in hand to Hitler to ask for approval, just do it!''

''It will be done within the week.''

The only other SS general Rommel would have to talk to was Dietrich. He planned to do that on the 17th. He had had absolutely no trouble convincing his own army generals, whether infantry or Panzer. He had visited them all during the past three days. But the SS generals were another matter, although Hausser had not been a problem.

Rommel and Admiral Ruge next visited the survivors of the Sixteenth Luftwaffe Field Division who were still in the front line against the Canadians at Caen. All their 88-millimeter antitank guns had been destroyed in the savage RAF and RCAF bombing attack, but they were still ready to do battle using Panzerfaust bazookas.

Enemy shells whistled down in a never-ending stream. The crash and thundering of weapons and shells shook the ground and filled the air with the pungent smell of cordite mixed with the stink of death and dust, always dust. Here, in the face of death, Rommel walked fearlessly among his men, lifting their spirits.

Then it was on to see General Edgar Feuchtinger, commander of the Twenty-first Panzer Division, at his headquarters in an orchard just southeast of Caen, so close to the city that Rommel had little to fear from the enemy Jabos; the intense concentration of 88-millimeter antiaircraft guns and hundreds of lighter antiaircraft weapons ensured that the Jabos avoided that sector like the plague. But once his staff car was anywhere to the east, south, or west of Caen, the Jabos would be roaming, usually unimpeded, looking for trucks, gun emplacements, anything German that could be destroyed. The most succulent of all targets was a staff car.

Feuchtinger had committed himself to Rommel's cause during the feldmarschall's last visit. Now Rommel simply wanted to give the beleaguered general some encouragement and tell him that he was pressing for Tigers and Panthers to replace the tanks that were being chewed up by the enemy, and for tank crews and supporting infantry to replace the hundreds of men destroyed in the massive attack on Caen.

There was something else Rommel needed to say. ''Intelligence tells us that the enemy is going to try a major operation across the Orne and to the southeast—right across your line, Edgar—for the 17th of July. Another massive assault, probably with bomber support. So get your people dug in well and set up as many defensive lines as you can, so that if they break through one line they're immediately met with another. You've got to do that in depth because if they break through here with their armor then they've got nothing but the wide open plains ahead of them straight to the Seine and Paris.''

Feuchtinger nodded. ''Yes, Herr Feldmarschall. I've already had that information and my orders from General Eberbach. We're doing exactly as you say.''

''Very good. You know, Edgar, this attack—if it comes in on the 17th—will be designed to force us to draw all our strength, particularly our Panzer strength, into the Caen sector. It leaves me weak in the Western sector against the Americans, but I can rely on the bocage country, the hedges, to help Hausser's infantry forces and what tanks we can spare to keep the enemy pinned down there. What troubles me most is that the new attack date—it's only two days from now—coincides with the most favorable date for the assault of Armee Gruppe Patton. I think the two events are locked together. If they both happen at the same time, it will be a disaster. On the other hand, there's one thing we can all look forward to: the arrival of General Schwerin's 116th Panzer Division. Feldmarschall Kluge has finally ordered it to the Normandy front from the Pas-de-Calais area. It should be in place in full strength before the big attack on the 17th. Then we'll have nine Panzer divisions, or what's left of them, in the Caen sector to hold the British and Canadians.''

''Do you think that will be enough, Herr Feldmarschall?''

Rommel shrugged and looked at his watch. ''It's late. It's time to start back.'' Rommel walked toward his Horch just a few meters away. Ruge was already in the back seat waiting. Unteroffizier Daniel had started the engine and was holding the left rear door open for his feldmarschall to get in.

As he settled into the rear seat, Rommel turned to Feuchtinger, standing stiffly beside the car, waiting to give the Hitler salute as his commander departed.

''You know the answer to your question as well as I do, Edgar. And so do Kluge, Jodl, and the Führer.'' With that, he tapped Daniel on the right shoulder with the baton, the signal to get going.

They traveled east through St. Pierre-sur-Dives where Sepp Dietrich's headquarters was located, but did not stop there. It was Rommel's practice to visit a headquarters only when warning had been given of his arrival. Then on to Livarot, then Conches to the Seine, and the ferry across to La Roche-Guyon.

As they drove they passed the charred skeletons of scores of trucks, tanks, personnel carriers, horse-drawn carts, and other vehicles that had been destroyed by the Jabos and shoved off to the sides of the roads. They also passed hundreds of trucks laden with munitions and supplies hidden under trees and woods, waiting for nightfall to continue toward the front lines.

About eighty kilometers away from the front lines, Feldwebel Kramer, sitting in the front seat next to Daniel, spotted several enemy aircraft. One passed at low level almost overhead, but the pilot evidently did not see them.

In the company of his trusted friend, Ruge, Rommel often was philosophical. During the long drive back that evening, the top of the Horch down and the roar of the engine and wind muffling their conversation, Rommel talked to Ruge about how life would be changed by a sudden peace or armistice and about the absurdity of continuing an aimless war. As with Hausser, Rommel mentioned his ultimatum to Hitler. "I've told him we're going to be defeated and he should look at the political situation."

"And if he ignores you?"

"Then I'll have no choice. I'll collapse the western front—and quickly because we're running out of time. The Soviets are at the threshold of Germany, and I tell you, Friedrich, we must do everything in our power to make sure that the Anglo-Americans take Berlin and not the Russians."

Ruge, as usual, was cautious. "But if you take that course of action, you'll be starting a revolution."

"Exactly, my dear Ruge, exactly!" Rommel exclaimed. "And I have the best authority in the world for that proposition. In *Mein Kampf* Hitler himself says: 'When the Government of a nation is leading it to its doom, rebellion is not only the right but the duty of every man. Human laws supersede the laws of the State.'"

Rommel suddenly noticed that Admiral Ruge appeared to

be most uncomfortable. He was restless, almost squirming, and kept peering ahead and to both sides. The Horch was hurtling down the D140 Highway from Bernay toward Conches, traveling at close to one hundred and ten kilometers an hour.

"For heaven's sake, Friedrich, what's the matter? You look as though you're sitting on a hot poker."

"I am sitting on a hot poker, damn it. We're in the heart of Maquisard country. They've made several attacks in this area in the last couple of weeks."

Rommel laughed. "So that's it. You're afraid the Resistance fighters are going to attack us. Come, come Friedrich. They wouldn't dare attack a feldmarschall's car, let alone mine."

Ruge shook his head. "That may be your opinion, but it's not mine. Look, you use this route regularly. Everybody in these villages knows that. This morning as we barreled through Conches, people were waving at you and lifting their hats. There wasn't a soul who didn't know that the great Feldmarschall Rommel in his big car had passed through town. And they know that, because you're a creature of habit, you're going to come back the same way. So if the Resistance wants to get you, we're sitting ducks in this fat, open car with the top down and an engine that's so loud they can hear it for kilometers."

All the while he was talking, the admiral continued to search ahead with is eyes.

Suddenly he shouted, "Did you see that! A glint of metal in the bushes up there about one kilometer ahead on the right. Did you see it, Kramer?" He punched the shoulder of the lookout in the front seat.

"Yes, Sir, I saw it!" Feldwebel Kramer shouted. "It might be a gun!"

Ruge, his face white with fear, turned to Rommel. "For God's sake, let's not take any unnecessary chances. Let's turnoff at the road up here. There's one coming up about a hundred meters ahead!"

Rommel could not bear to see the admiral so panic-stricken. His judgment told him he should just drive straight on, but for Ruge's sake he shouted to Daniel, "Turn right at this road!"

Daniel had to slam on the brakes to make the turn. The tires screeched and the rear of the huge Horch fish-tailed.

Just as the car began its turn to the right, Ruge saw a

slight puff of smoke from the place in the bushes where he had seen the flash.

In a split second a clean round hole magically appeared in the Horch's windshield immediately in front of Kramer's head. No sound was heard above the noise of the wind, the engine, and the screaming tires.

As the car finished rounding the corner, Kramer slumped over against Daniel, pulled there by the force of the sharp, fast turn. When his head hit Daniel's shoulder, the two men in the back seat could see blood beginning to gush out of the hole in the back of Kramer's skull. The Maquisard bullet had passed through cleanly. It must have missed Ruge's head by a fraction.

Not realizing what had happened, Daniel struggled to control the big car. Kramer's body was still being pressed against him. The transition from pavement to dirt caused the vehicle to skid almost sideways down the road with the front wheels jammed hard left to counter the slide. Finally the rear wheels held and Daniel straightened the car out. When he put his foot on the brake, Rommel screamed, ''For God's sake, don't stop. Kramer's been shot! Get moving as fast as you can!''

Then the next bullet came. This time they heard it. With a sharp popping noise it entered the left side window about a foot in front of the feldmarschall's face and went out through the window of the right front door.

''Move, Daniel, move!'' Rommel shouted at the top of his lungs. ''Get down as far as you can!''

Unteroffizier Daniel dropped his body below the level of the protective metal of the door, keeping his head up only enough to see where he was driving.

In the rear seat, Rommel and Ruge hunched forward, their heads between their knees. Both knew that the thin steel body of the Horch was no real protection against the sniper's high-powered bullets, but both instinctively felt safe by ducking.

As Daniel pressed his foot hard on the accelerator, the powerful motor roared and the rear wheels spun, throwing up great clouds of billowing dust. The distance from the sniper increased, but Rommel wondered if they were really out of his range. Rommel, a highly competent marksman himself, had already concluded that there was only one person shooting at them, someone with great skill and accuracy, probably using a telescopic sight. They would never have survived a group of snipers. Perhaps, however, the single marksman was with a gang armed with lesser weapons. If so they would have produced a lethal fusillade if the car had driven into their trap. Thanks to Ruge, he would never know.

Rommel's question about range was answered when he heard a sharp crack somewhere in the front end of the Horch—the familiar sound of a high-powered rifle bullet meeting impenetrable metal. They were still accelerating, probably just hitting eighty kilometers an hour. Would there be another shot?

Faster and faster, still accelerating. No bullets. Still no bullets.

Daniel now had the speed up to one hundred and thirty down the narrow dirt road. They had to be out of range.

Rommel sat up, his hat still squarely on his head. Looking back to his left, he thought he saw a figure move in the thick bush by the highway they had left. But he couldn't be sure. All he could be certain of was they had all been on the verge of total disaster.

Thank God for Ruge. He had been just like a pointing bird dog, only Rommel hadn't believed him. Sitting up now, Ruge pulled a handkerchief out and lifted off his cap to wipe his perspiring, dust-covered brow.

The feldmarschall gave the admiral's knee a manly pat. "Thank you, Friedrich. Daniel and I owe you our lives," he said.

"I'm afraid poor Kramer owes me nothing."

Daniel had pushed Kramer's body almost to the vertical position with his shoulder. Now he shoved it until it fell against the right door. The cap was still on Kramer's head. His jaw was slack, and his eyes were fixed, the bullet hole between them oozing a red and gray mix of blood and brain.

The feldmarschall and the admiral watched the macabre movements in the front seat like spectators at a grim puppet show.

Rommel shouted over the now-deafening noise of the engine and wind to Ruge. "Your point is taken. Never again a favorite route. Every day out a different way and every day back a different way."

For the first time that day there was something approaching a smile on Admiral Ruge's face.

17 July 1944: Rommel

SPEIDEL HAD been kept informed from Paris about Operation Valkyrie but had chosen not to pass the information on to his chief. All he had told Rommel was that the operation had been postponed and that the plan for delivery of the letter to Montgomery, the final draft of the document itself, and the selection of the team that would negotiate with the Americans and British—all should be in place not later than the 17th. Furthermore, he knew that by that date the feldmarschall should be satisfied that he had all his generals, including the SS generals, on side. Success or failure would hinge on the response of Hitler's own man, Sepp Dietrich.

As for the Bargatsky draft, Speidel had many questions and reservations about it. In the seven days since he had received the document, he had gone to Paris twice to confer with Bargatsky and Stülpnagel. In turn, Stülpnagel had had to discuss questions raised by Speidel with his colleagues in Berlin, General Beck and Colonel Stauffenberg. Notwithstanding these negotiations on the 11th and the 15th, the impatient Stauffenberg had been prepared to kill the ruling Nazi trio—Hitler, Himmler, and Goebbels—even though the crucial scheme for a concurrent approach by Rommel to Montgomery had not been finalized. To the meticulous, methodical Speidel, Stauffenberg's impatience was an indication that the man did not really understand the necessity of having his parachute on before he jumped out of the airplane.

At 9:00 on the morning of the 17th, Speidel met privately with the feldmarschall in his study.

"What about the letter? When will it be ready for me to see?" Rommel demanded as he looked at a promotion recommendation placed in front of him by Speidel for signature.

"I'll have it for you tonight by the time you return from the front. Stülpnagel and I are close to settling two outstanding points. We'll have that done by noon, I expect. Then I will have to write it out in longhand in German for your approval and then in English for Montgomery. Obviously it is not a document I can give to a clerk to copy or put in a typewriter.''

"Why don't you just give it to them in German?'' Rommel suggested. "I'm sure Montgomery has people on his staff who can interpret it immediately. Let them do the work.''

"Yes, Sir, I guess I could do it that way.''

"Do it.''

Rommel was finished with his signing chore. He looked up at his chief-of-staff as he put the pen back in its desk holder.

"It's all arranged with Lüttwitz,'' Speidel announced. "As you know, Sir, there have now been two truces on his front—which is ideal. The last one was on the 9th, the very day that Hofacker was here. This time we'll ask for a truce to hand back some injured American soldiers. It will be a large transfer, probably in the range of eighty to a hundred men, so we'll need a large number of ambulances . . .''

Rommel could see where he was going. " . . . and a large number of escorting personnel.''

"Correct, Sir. Among the escorting personnel will be General Stülpnagel, three of his trusted staff officers, Bargatsky, and myself. We will be in camouflage paratroop battle gear covering our uniforms, so no rank will be disclosed.''

"But you'll be dealing with Americans when you have to get to Montgomery.''

"I don't expect a problem there, Sir. Montgomery's headquarters is located just east of Bayeux. It's about twenty-seven kilometers from the proposed exchange point. Unless he is sick or absent, we expect he can be at the American divisional commander's headquarters in half an hour.''

Rommel stood up and walked to the opened French doors.

"And what about Montgomery's authority? Do you really think he can make an armistice without getting political approval?''

Speidel shrugged, "You know the answer to that question better than I do, Sir.''

Rommel reflected for a moment, then said, "Yes, I'm sure he could. Given that Hitler had been arrested and there was clear evidence that the German army had revolted. In any event, he could get instructions from Churchill by telephone. Yes, Montgomery would seize the opportunity, no question about it.''

"Even with the implications for the Soviets . . . the withdrawal of our forces to the east of the Siegfried Line fully armed and with the intent to use them against the Soviets?"

Again Rommel paused to think. "It may be wishful thinking, but I cannot believe that the British perception of the Soviet threat is different from ours. And if the terms of our withdrawal make no mention of the potential use of our forces against the Soviets . . ."

Speidel broke in, "The written word will not. I've been careful about that."

Rommel turned in the doorway to face Speidel. "So. Everything is arranged then, except for the letter, which will be ready for me when I get back this evening."

"Correct, Sir."

"Good. My plan today is to visit the 276th and 277th Infantry Divisions. I'll go via Falaise. They're complaining that they aren't being supported because the Panzers are too far back. I want to see the situation firsthand. Then I'll go east to St. Pierre-sur-Dives to visit Sepp Dietrich. If the enemy launches his big attack today, I'll come back here as soon as it begins."

"Dietrich is the final link in the chain," Speidel observed.

"Yes, the final link. The one thing I don't want to do is have German troops fighting German troops on Valkyrie Day. If Dietrich and what's left of his division don't go along with the armistice and everyone else does, then we will indeed have the SS fighting the Wermacht. And they'd still be fighting the Anglo-Americans at the same time—or would they? Dietrich's no fool, but as you say, he's the last link in the chain and a strong one."

"What about Feldmarschall Kluge?"

"Kluge? A strange man, Hans, a strange man. He knows about our plan, at least the basics of it. Hofacker went to see him in St. Germain-en-Laye after he left here on the 9th. So far he appears to be with us. If one can believe Hofacker—and I'm not sure about that—Kluge is convinced we must have an armistice in the West." Rommel paused. "If anything happens to me before we approach Montgomery, my legacy to my successor, whoever he is, will be my armistice scheme, the absolute and urgent need for an armistice. Remember that."

The owlish Speidel's head shook from side to side slowly, deliberately. "Nothing's going to happen to you, Sir. Nothing. You've been leading a charmed life from the day you joined the army.''

''True, but unlike the cat that has nine lives, I've already spent eighteen of them.'' Rommel sighed as he reflected momentarily on the myriad close calls he had had. Then he walked toward his desk. ''Tell Lang to have Daniel bring the car around now. I'm ready to leave.''

It was close to 4:00 in the afternoon. The sky was blue and cloudless, excellent weather for the Jabos, which were swarming over the area like hornets. On the way to visit the combat positions of the 276th and 277th Infantry Divisions and then on to St. Pierre-sur-Dives, Daniel had had to take evasive action at least half a dozen times. He had headed for shelter under trees or down sideroads at the call of Feldwebel Holke, Captain Lang, Major Neuhaus, one of Rommel's staff officers, or even the feldmarschall himself. On each occasion they had avoided an attack by a hair's breadth. But Rommel insisted on pressing on. The car churned its way down sideroads, past burnt-out vehicles, some still smoking or in flames, past horse-drawn wagons, artillery, and loaded ambulances. Virtually all the mobile vehicles were off to the side of the road under trees and in sheltered areas. Only the most reckless drivers were on the move.

They had arrived at Dietrich's headquarters at about 3:45. Rommel had hoped to spend some time with his SS Panzer commander, to have supper and a long talk before putting to him the question of support for an armistice. But the time for that was not available.

As soon as he arrived at Dietrich's headquarters, he was presented with a signal from Speidel requesting that he return to La Roche-Guyon as quickly as possible because the Americans were launching a major attack on Eberbach's troops at St. Lô.

Dietrich had already seen the signal. He told the feldmarschall that he had no problems other than the heavy casualties and lack of replacements he had been screaming about for days if not weeks.

With the few minutes now available, Rommel did with Dietrich as he had with Hausser. For privacy, he invited the weatherbeaten, round-faced general to walk with him in the field next to his headquarters, even though there would be no refuge from the hot, late-afternoon sun and the humidity that filled the air that day.

The question was—had Dietrich been sufficiently disillusioned by Hitler and the OKW that he would disavow the Führer? For Sepp Dietrich, the stocky, rough Nazi of lower-class origins who had been at Hitler's side as his chauffeur and one of his early assassins, owed everything to his Führer and until recently had been totally loyal to him. Hitler had raised him from the ranks of the non-commissioned to be a Panzer Oberstgruppenführer in the SS.

So with Dietrich, Rommel was far less open, much more circumspect, than he had been with Hausser. There was no discussion whatsoever of the Schwarze Kapelle group. The two men simply had a reasoned discussion concerning the faults and diminishing leadership of the OKW and, as well, the Führer.

Even though Dietrich acknowledged certain of Hitler's failings, a sixth sense kept cautioning Rommel that he should not disclose the plan for an attempted armistice with Montgomery.

He knew that Dietrich respected him enormously. He also knew from the look on the lined, weather-chiseled face, that the best he could do was to put a hypothetical question to him.

"You know how desperate the situation is, Sepp. We are right in the front line and have to make decisions, minute by minute, hour by hour, regardless of what OKW, Jodl, and even Hitler are thinking as they're looking at their maps, drawing lines, and arrows. My question to you is this—and I want you to think about it carefully because if you say yes and you have to live up to your promise to me sometime in the near future, I may have to remind you of the answer. The question is this: Even if I gave you an order that didn't follow the Führer's instructions, would you obey it?"

Out of the corner of his eye, Rommel could see that his man, Lang, was still within earshot, and like any good aide, was listening intently while not appearing to.

With barely any hesitation, Sepp Dietrich replied, "You are my commander, Sir. I will obey your order." And he offered his right hand in confirmation of his pledge.

The road to armistice negotiations was open.

At 4:00 the Horch left Dietrich's headquarters heading east toward the village of Livarot only fifteen kilometers away. The feldmarschall was in the front seat beside Daniel, maps on his lap. In the back seat were Lang, Holke, and Neuhaus.

Traveling at high speed it took them just a few minutes to reach the western outskirts of the village. Rommel could see some Jabos attacking targets to the north of Livarot and other fighters coming toward it from the north. There was no sense in driving east into the village and inviting attack. Rommel made the decision. Looking at his map he shouted to Daniel, "Let's get off this road. Turn right at the next road. It runs south parallel to the main highway from Livarot to Vimoutiers. About five kilometers south of here it swings east, and we'll pick up the main highway."

Eagerly Daniel swung the Horch south on the road Rommel had pointed out. As he began to accelerate after the turn, Holke screamed, "Four Jabos, at 4 o'clock, about nine hundred meters, about one kilometer."

All heads in the car, including Daniel's for a second, swiveled to the right as they looked behind. The four Jabos were there in absolutely perfect position to attack. But there was no place to hide except a clump of trees straddling the road about a kilometer ahead.

Rommel shouted instructions calmly. "Keep your speed where it is. You're only doing about fifty. Start slowing down. If they start to dive on us, stop the car, foot brake, hand brake, everything. Everybody out and head for the nearest ditch. All the windows down? Good. Then that's all we can do."

All eyes in the Horch, except Daniel's, who could only take furtive glances, were glued on the four Jabos. As the aircraft flew south, parallel to the road, and came abreast of the still-moving Horch, the leader could be seen to lower his left wing to take a better look. There was no doubt he had seen them. The only question was whether he would attack.

To the amazement and relief of the five men in the Horch, the four enemy aircraft that looked remarkably like their own ME109s but with British-style camouflage and Allied marks at the wingroots, began a slow turn to the west toward Caen.

"Let's get going," Rommel said urgently. "Those are bludhunds-Mustangs. The intelligence people say they've stopped attacking the last few days. What the leader will do is report by radio where we are. The message will be passed to other Jabos in the area who'll then come to find us." He spoke as loudly as he could so everyone could hear him over the roar of the accelerating Horch motor. "So all of you keep an extra sharp lookout!"

Because of the turns and twists in the backroad they were following, Daniel could do no better than keep the speed between eighty and one hundred kilometers an hour as they swung east to the main road between Livarot and Vimoutiers.

As ordered, Daniel turned the car right, onto the highway to Vimoutiers, the tall trees flanking the road on each side flashing by as the car thundered on at high speed. As the Horch hurtled south through the village of Ste. Foy-de-Montgommery, Rommel checked his watch and the map. It had taken them seven minutes to travel the five kilometers from the point where they had been sighted. Now that they were on the main road, they could get up to really high speeds.

In the back seat, Neuhaus, Lang, and Holke were doing as told, keeping an extra sharp lookout. In the center, Feldwebel Holke was on his knees facing the rear, ready to pick up any aircraft approaching from behind. On the left side of the car, peering through his spectacles, Lang swept the horizon and sky to the east, while the west was covered by Major Neuhaus. The Horch had just crossed the railway line about two kilometers south of Ste. Foy on a stretch of straight open highway that had no protecting trees when Holke screamed, "Two Jabos, coming straight at us from behind, low level, about nine hundred meters!"

Again all heads swiveled to look back. In the front seat, Rommel turned his head to the right, pulling his shoulders and body around so he could see.

There they were, coming straight at them, one following the other, heading for them like flying arrows. They still were not in range, but Rommel knew that the Horch was in their gunsights. It was only a matter of seconds before they would open fire.

"Faster, Daniel. Faster!" Rommel shouted. "There should be a little sideroad on the right with some trees just ahead. Try for it!" Rommel, still looking back, felt his mind and body gripped with fear as he saw the flashes from the cannons in the wings of the first oncoming fighter.

The car had just started down a slight incline leading toward a bridge when the cannon shells struck.

It all happened in a second. The lefthand side of the car was hit. A shell caught Daniel, taking off his left arm and shattering his shoulder. Not yet unconscious, he started furiously applying the brakes. The car was instantly out of control. The second aircraft was about to open fire. Rommel was still turned watching it as the car slowed down the hill, Daniel desperately braking. The Horch headed toward the left side of the road near the bridge at the bottom of the hill. Rommel, looking behind never saw the tree stump coming up.

When the Horch hit the stump, glancing off it, the impact drove Rommel's head against the right windshield post, and at the same time threw him out of the car, which then went off the road and turned over on its side in the ditch.

Miraculously, Hauptmann Lang and Feldwebel Holke were uninjured by the strafing and rode the Horch safely through its crash. As soon as the car came to rest on its side, they jumped out and took shelter as the second Jabo returned to drop two bombs. They exploded harmlessly well wide of the Horch. Neuhaus had been unable to follow Lang and Holke. A shell from one of the Jabos had hit the holster of his revolver and the force of the impact had broken his pelvis. All he could do was roll out of the tipped car and lie in the ditch, unable to move.

As soon as the second enemy fighter had left, Lang and Holke rushed to the unconscious feldmarschall, who was lying on the pavement about eighteen meters from where the Horch had come to rest. His face was cut by shards of windscreen glass. Blood flowed freely from the many wounds in his face, especially from his left eye and his mouth. The left temple was smashed in and facing upwards.

While Lang was tending to the feldmarschall, Holke dragged Daniel from the front seat of the car to the ditch and immediately pulled off the wounded driver's jacket. With his knife he sliced a long piece from Daniel's shirt, wrapping it around the stump at his left shoulder as a tourniquet in an attempt to stop the heavy flow of blood. Holke then turned to Major Neuhaus lying in the grass in the ditch, writhing in pain. He spoke to Neuhaus, comforting him. But there was nothing he could do about the injury to the hip area. Holke could hear Hauptmann Lang calling, so he left the two men in the dry ditch and went to help Lang, who was kneeling on the road beside Rommel.

Distraught, Lang was checking Rommel's pulse. It was weak but still there. "We have to get him to a hospital. But first we have to get him off the road in case those Jabos come back. There's a house just up there by the edge of the road. Help me carry him."

Lifting the feldmarschall as gently as they could, they

carried him to the steps of what appeared to·be a gatekeep-house and laid him on the ground at the foot of the steps. There was no one in the house, and there were no telephone connections to the place. Lang decided that all they could do was wait for the next passing vehicle and commandeer it.

A local worker bicycling by informed them that Vimou-tiers, only a little over a kilometer away, did not have a hospital. He suggested that they take the three injured men to Livarot where there was a pharmacy.

It was forty-five minutes before the first vehicle came up the road from Vimoutiers. A German soldier was at the wheel of a small, French-made car only big enough to take the feldmarschall, Daniel, and Lang.

With Holke's assistance, Lang laid the unconscious feld-marschall on the back seat. He cushioned Rommel's injured head with his own uniform jacket, which he had stripped off and rolled up for that purpose. The inert Daniel, not a tall man, was laid on the floor of the back seat on his right side.

"I'll send a vehicle for you and Major Neuhaus as soon as I can lay my hands on one," Lang told Holke. "When you get to Livarot, go to the pharmacist's—he can give Neu-haus a shot of morphine or whatever. The pharmacist will know where we've gone from there. It'll be the nearest hos-pital, wherever that is."

His final words as he got in the car, "But I don't really know whether either of them is going to live."

In Livarot, ten minutes later, Lang quickly found the pharmacist, who was in the café on the square, sipping on his evening Calvados. The local doctor was nowhere to be found, but the pharmacist knew that something had to be done for the very senior officer, perhaps even a general, who wore medals and gold braid. There was no way he could help the man lying on the floor.

The pharmacist examined the large open wound above the unconscious Rommel's left eye and noticed he was bleeding from the ears. There was only one thing he could do for him. It must be done quickly. He hurried into his shop, just a few steps away. Quickly he collected a needle and the medication he wanted. In a few seconds he was back at the car where he gave Rommel two injections of etherated cam-phor, a treatment the doctors later agreed saved the feld-marschall's life.

"That's all I can do," the chemist told Lang. "You should

take him to the Luftwaffe hospital at Bernay. It's only sixty-five kilometers from here. But I'm sorry, Sir, I don't think he has a ghost of a chance of surviving that head wound. As for the man on the floor . . .'' A Gallic shrug said the rest.

An hour later, close to 8:00, Lang telephoned General Speidel from the hospital at Bernay. The shocked chief-of-staff listened intently, asked a few questions, and hung up.

Should he report to Feldmarschall Kluge first or to Jodl? Earlier in the day Speidel, without having first received approval from OKW, had given the beleaguered Hausser permission to withdraw in the St. Lô area. There just hadn't been time to call. So he knew he might well be in trouble with Jodl again, even though Kluge himself had later confirmed Speidel's action.

Speidel decided to go directly to the top. Hitler had to have the news first. He immediately put through a Führungsblitz call to Jodl at the OKW location at Rastenburg in East Prussia.

He told Jodl about the strafing of Rommel's Horch and then the diagnosis. ''Three doctors have examined him. Their finding is that the feldmarschall has a fracture of the base of the skull, two fractures of the left temple, and his cheekbone has been broken in. The left eye is damaged, the scalp badly torn, and he is seriously concussed. If he survives, it will be several months before he is fit again.''

Jodl gave no hint of sympathy or concern. Rommel had been nothing but a thorn in his side for months now and really was a bothersome, overrated egotist. As he listened to Speidel, Jodl was realizing that the entire Anglo-American side would get a tremendous psychological lift, a taste of victory, if they knew that Rommel had been removed from the battle by their Jabos. They would know soon enough that he had been injured—or, for that matter, that he had died. But they and the German nation should be led to believe that his injuries were caused by an automobile accident, not a strafing by enemy fighters.

''A shame about poor Rommel. How unfortunate.'' Jodl's voice was dry and unemotional. ''I have just decided, and I'm sure Herr Goebbels will approve, that the feldmarschall was injured in an accident and not by enemy action. You understand, Herr General?''

''I understand perfectly, Sir. I'll pass the word at his headquarters.''

''I will report this to the Führer immediately. You'll be

wondering who will succeed the feldmarschall because that affects you very directly—but I can tell you who it won't be.''

''Who is that, Sir?''

Jodl's voice was cold and sarcastic. ''Since you gave permission to Hausser to withdraw from St. Lô today without approval from me, you can be sure that it will not be you, Speidel!''

When word of the tragic accident—as Speidel announced it—spread through the headquarters at La Roche-Guyon, a sense of disaster enveloped the officers and men in the chateau and was to spread throughout the German forces in France. Speidel was to write:

> *Rommel was in fact eliminated in the very hour that his Army and his people could spare him the least. All those who were groping with his help to find a way to a new and better world, felt themselves painfully deprived of their pillar of strength.*

About Rommel's removal from the scene, Ernst Jünger, the philosopher, historian, close friend of Rommel, and member of the Schwarze Kapelle, wrote:

> *The blow that felled Rommel on the Livarot road on 17 July 1944 deprived our plan of the only man strong enough to bear the terrible weight of war and civil war simultaneously, the only man who was straightforward enough to counter the frightful folly of the leaders of Germany. This was an omen which had only one interpretation.*

The omen was of disaster: disaster for the members of the Schwarze Kapelle, disaster for the assassination attempt on the Führer, and disaster for Rommel's successor in the battlefield, the inheritor of Rommel's armistice legacy.

PART TWO

Rommel's Legacy

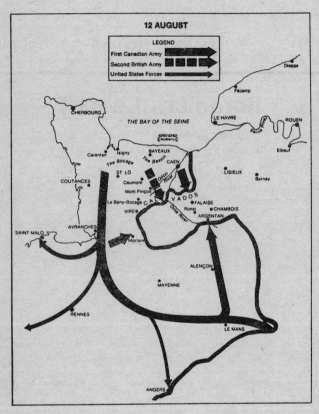

The Falaise Gap

17 July 1944: Kluge

THE COMMANDER-IN-CHIEF WEST, Feldmarschall Hans Günther von Kluge, was having a quiet dinner with his old friend, the military governor of France, General Karl-Heinrich von Stülpnagel, in the privacy of the cloistered small dining room in the Pavillon of Henri V. They were deep in discussion.

Halfway through the trout meunière, Kluge's aide tapped on the door, opened it just far enough to see his master, and announced in a quiet voice, "Sir, there is a telephone call from General Speidel. He says it's most urgent, Sir."

One thing Kluge did not like was to be disturbed in the middle of a good dinner, especially when he had an important guest with whom he could share confidences and ideas. However, Speidel would have been told that he was at dinner with Stülpnagel, and since Speidel still insisted on talking to him, the matter must be urgent.

He excused himself and went to his office to take the call. Speidel's report to him was the same he had given to Jodl, but Kluge's reaction was much more humane. In the short time he had known Rommel, his view of the man had changed completely. While he still did not particularly like the little feldmarschall, he had developed a high regard for his integrity, ability to lead, and dedication to the German nation. He also recognized that it was Rommel's leadership in the field that had kept the Seventh Army and the Panzer Army fighting so tenaciously against enormous odds. But now he was out of it. Kluge was disturbed as he assessed the ramifications. Who would succeed Rommel?

"You've confirmed all this with the doctors?"

"Yes, Sir. I've also talked to Generaloberst Jodl." Before Kluge could react, Speidel quickly added, "I tried to get through to you first, but your lines were tied up, so I decided to pass the word directly to him. And General Jodl has instructed that the incident be described as an accident, Sir. So if you're telling anyone about . . .''

The often petulant Kluge accepted the explanation without argument. He concluded the conversation by asking Speidel for the name and telephone number of the doctor at Bernay.

He pushed the call button for his aide and instructed him to give his apologies to General Stülpnagel but he would be perhaps another ten minutes.

The doctor at Bernay confirmed everything that Speidel had said. Rommel had not yet come out of the coma. "If he survives, it will be a long time before he's fit for action—if he ever is," was the doctor's summary.

It crossed Kluge's mind that he should telephone Frau Rommel in the morning to offer her words of sympathy and hope for recovery, or should the little man not make it through the night, words of condolence.

Kluge then put a Führungsblitz call through to Generaloberst Jodl at the Wolfsschanze in East Prussia where Hitler and the OKW staff were now directing the battles on all fronts.

He had no trouble reaching Jodl immediately. "You already heard about Rommel from Speidel, I understand," Kluge opened.

"Yes. A pity. It's a wonder it hadn't happened sooner, the way Rommel has been rushing around the front in broad daylight. What's the word on him now?"

"Still in a coma."

"Let me know if there is any change. I suppose you want to know about Rommel's replacement. I've been talking to the Führer about that, but I haven't any decision for you yet. I hope to have one by sometime tomorrow."

Kluge made his move. "I will take over Rommel's duties myself until the Führer decides what he wants to do. The great need is for strength in command."

He stopped short of recommending that he himself be put in Rommel's place. But the hint was there and Jodl did not miss it.

Jodl asked, "What would you think if the Führer appointed you commander of Armee Gruppe B, as well as Commander-in-Chief West? I really can't see the need for finding another feldmarschall when you could handle both jobs—what do you think?''

"I think your suggestion," Kluge was careful to credit Jodl, "would be most acceptable to me."

"Good. I'll make that recommendation to the Führer. Now tell me what's happening at the front."

"We are still holding at St. Lô against a strong American push. I've moved the Panzer Lehr Division there to bolster the situation. At Caen we've created seven distinct lines of defense using every available antitank 88 we can find, so we're ready for Montgomery's next attack."

"My people," Jodl observed, "tell me that attack is going to start tomorrow."

Kluge countered, "My people tell me Montgomery won't be ready for another three or four days."

"If you're wrong, I'll let you know. You'll hear from me on the other matter tomorrow."

Back in the dining room a tense, pacing Kluge recounted the Rommel accident to Stülpnagel, who appeared profoundly shocked.

"Rommel severely injured?" The consequences of Rommel's being out of Operation Valkyrie were racing through Stülpnagel's mind. The armistice attempt was essential to its success, and Rommel was surely the only man who could have brought it off. And time was running out. Stauffenberg was to go to Rastenburg with the bomb any time now, and there was no way to stop him.

What Kluge then said gave Stülpnagel a ray of hope. "I just talked to Jodl. It may well be that I will assume Rommel's duties as well as my own. What do you think of that, Herr General?"

Stülpnagel watched the tall aristocrat lower himself into his chair, lift off the warming cover that had been put on his unfinished trout, and begin to eat.

"It makes it all the more important, Herr Feldmarschall," Stülpnagel said cautiously, "all the more important for you to know, if you're taking on all Rommel's responsibilities, that he was to have played an important role in certain plans for a transition to a new government."

The burly Kluge knew exactly what Stülpnagel was talking about. Stülpnagel was not sure how much Kluge knew, but only twenty minutes ago Kluge had been talking about his changed view of the prospects in Normandy and the impossibility of Hitler's orders. Kluge clearly had been brooding on Rommel's report with its final paragraph about "the proper conclusion to be drawn." Furthermore, Hofacker had reported that Kluge was with him, although one could never quite be sure about the reliability of a Hofacker claim.

Kluge replied, his mouth full of trout, "You must remember, Karl, that I don't know about any plans for such a transition and right now I don't want to know. But I assume Rommel's part had to do with—at the right moment—an approach to Montgomery."

Stülpnagel nodded, hoping Kluge would say he would be prepared to make the approach. Instead, Kluge was noncommittal. "Interesting, my dear Karl, interesting. What more can I say?"

He continued eating.

Stülpnagel was satisfied. "Nothing. You should know that an armistice offer has been drafted."

"Did Rommel see it?"

"No. It was to be delivered to him this evening when he got back to the chateau."

Kluge lifted his eyebrows. "Poor bastard, now he'll never see it." The eyebrows came down and furrowed. "And I don't want to see it. Remember that, Karl!"

18-20 July 1944

"WHAT ABOUT IT, Freddie?" Montgomery wanted to be reassured. "Should we do a press conference? Goodwood's doing bloody well."

"Yes, it really is, Sir. The reports from Dempsey look good. You told him to 'step on the gas' and that's just what he's doing."

Montgomery's massive Operation Goodwood was designed, as he had told Dempsey, to "open up the southeastern exits from Caen and to mop up the enemy in that area." It had been thoroughly planned. At first light, between 5:45 and 7:50 hours on 18 July, some 1,100 Royal Air Force and Royal Canadian Air Force aircraft of Bomber Command and 1,000 bombers from the Eighth and Ninth U.S. Air Forces had unloaded more than 7,000 tons of bombs on Caen and its surroundings—the city that was mocking the British commander forty-two days after he had planned to take it. In Goodwood that morning, Montgomery had struck forward with 1,500 tanks and 250,000 men against the German defenses around Caen. Then three tank divisions and three armored brigades had moved out behind an advancing barrage laid down by all available artillery. Some 45,000 shells fell on the area of the Second SS Panzer Corps alone in the matter of a few hours. More than 800 fighter-bomber missions provided close support to the army while in excess of 1,800 missions were flown by RAF and RCAF Typhoon Squadrons against Eberbach's and Dietrich's tanks, vehicles, and gun emplacements. Montgomery had planned it to be—and it was—the most violent, intense, concentrated assault made in western Europe by the Allies during World War II.

Late that afternoon an exuberant Montgomery did two things that he would much regret. First, at his press conference he made a special announcement in which he in effect claimed to have broken out when in fact he had not. Second, he sent a message—dispatched at 4:30 p.m.—to Field Marshall Alan Brooke, chief of the British Imperial General Staff, saying, "Operations this morning complete success." That was not the case. The "southeastern exits from Caen" were not opened up. The breakout that the press had been led to believe in did not happen on the 18th of July. Nor on the 19th.

The signal from Jodl was cryptic. Kluge had read it late on the evening of 18 July when he returned from an intense day of working with Hausser and Eberbach at the Caen front. The message read: "You were wrong. Also your appointment as commander Armee Gruppe B confirmed by the Führer."

Acting swiftly on the confirmation, Kluge moved out of his headquarters at St. Germain-en-Laye on the 19th and took over Rommel's office and suite at La Roche-Guyon.

By the morning of the 20th, the enemy had breached six of the lines that Rommel with Hausser and Eberbach had set up south of Caen. What could be done to strengthen that seventh line—a deadly antitank barrier of 88s guarding the entrance to the plains? That morning Feldmarschall Kluge met with Eberbach, Hausser, and their corps commanders in the cool depths of the Forêt d'Ecouves, where Hausser had originally assembled the Panzer divisions he had brought from Poland. They were sixty-five kilometers away from the battlefield and totally concealed from the Jabos.

As they stood around the hood of his car, on which his chinagraph maps of the battle area were spread, Kluge could sense the feeling of pessimism and foreboding that everyone had about the apparently inevitable defeat. The meteorologists had told Kluge that a helpful weapon might just be coming in the form of rain, but there was no certainty.

His commanders had nothing but complaints.

Eberbach told him, "I have lost 40,000 men since the Battle of Normandy started, and I've received only 2,300 replacements. The Seventh Army is on its knees."

Dietrich pounded the hood and said, "My losses are just as bad, my tanks are almost finished. The orders I receive from OKW are mad, absolutely impossible. They order us to do things that are a mad waste of men. I tell you, Herr Feldmarschall, it's insane."

The Panzer general's fists were clenched, and his arms were raised in frustration.

"Here we are in Normandy, being ripped into pieces like a rotten cloth when the whole of the Fifteenth Army and all of their Panzer divisions could be down here and in the battle instead of sitting up there north of the Seine sucking their thumbs. Everyone knows that there isn't going to be a second assault in the Pas-de-Calais area. Everybody knows that Patton's right here in Normandy. He's up there somewhere." He pointed furiously to the northwest. "He's not going to lead any sixty divisions across the Channel. His successor isn't going to lead sixty divisions across the Channel because there aren't sixty divisions. It's all been a hoax, a ploy, a deception to keep Salmuth's army away from Normandy. For God's sake, when will those assholes in Rastenburg come to their senses and let us withdraw and get out of Normandy before we're completely overrun."

No one spoke against Dietrich. They knew he was right.

"I cannot argue with your line of reasoning, Sepp," Kluge admitted. "But we have our orders from the Führer himself. There can be no further retreat. He demands that we hold the line in the vicinity of Caen at all costs." He spoke emphatically. "The last line, the seventh, has been reinforced with every tank, every 88, every man we can find. We can do no more. We will hold and if nothing can be found to better our situation, then we will die like men on the battlefield. Gentlemen, this conference is at an end. Heil Hitler."

The feldmarschall went to Eberbach's operations tent and made telephone calls for half an hour. When he was preparing to leave for La Roche-Guyon shortly before 1:00, the first drops of rain splashed on the windscreen of the new Horch. By the time the driver got the canvas top up, the rain was falling, as Eberbach later put it, "as if the good Lord had turned his water bucket upside down." Even the foilage of the great forest was no protection from the outpouring from the heavens. As Kluge walked smiling from the tent to get into the car, the rain soaked his uniform and hat, and mud covered his boots. But he did not run or move quickly. Instead he walked slowly, and just as he went to get into the car, he stopped, lifted his head toward the clouds to feel the rain beating on his face, and spread his arms out wide, his baton in his hand, welcoming the mightiest defensive weapon he could have hoped for, the rain.

At the very moment Kluge was savoring the Normandy rain, Stauffenberg, the Schwarze Kappelle's assassin, was enter-

ing the map room in a large wooden hut at the Wolfsschanze, deep in the East Prussian woods at Rastenburg,
where a Führer Conference was under way.

Stauffenberg, a one-armed man with three fingers and a
black patch over an empty eye socket, carried a briefcase.
He moved through the score of officers surrounding the map
table and Hitler, who was following on the situation maps
a briefing by his deputy chief of the General Staff, General
Adolf Heusinger. Hitler, in his customary black trousers
and gray tunic, interrupted the briefing to receive Stauffenberg, telling him he would hear his report next, then continued with Heusinger.

Stauffenberg moved around to the far side of the table
from Hitler and placed his briefcase on the floor. He then
left the room, saying that he had to make a telephone call.

In the briefcase was a bomb, its fuse mechanism just seconds away from detonation.

One of Hitler's staff officers standing beside the briefcase
thought it was in the way and placed it against one of the
thick upright legs of the table. The leg stood between the
bomb and Hitler at the far side of the table.

Stauffenberg went outside, walked about one hundred
meters away from the conference hut, and lit a cigarette.
He waited. Suddenly the wooden building shuddered. Black
smoke and orange flames blew out of its windows. The roof
collapsed as the thunder of the explosion shook the ground
under Stauffenberg's feet.

Certain that Hitler had been killed, Stauffenberg moved
quickly to escape and pass the word of the Führer's death.

With the coming of rain on the 20th, the whole battle area,
which until then had been several millimeters deep in Normandy dust baked by the hot July sun, turned into a sea of
impassable mud, giving Montgomery no choice but to call
off Goodwood. In two days Montgomery's forces had penetrated six of the seven heavy lines of defense south of Caen,
but the seventh line had held. He had been denied the wide-
open plains that led to the Seine and Paris.

That same day, Tedder, the deputy supreme commander,
now deeply concerned about Montgomery's leadership,
wrote from his vantage point at SHAEF (Supreme Headquarters, Allied Expeditionary Force) in England that he
and the Marshal of the Royal Air Force Sir Charles Portal,

chief of the British Air Staff, "were agreed in regarding Montgomery as the cause." Montgomery could be replaced by Eisenhower as Land Commander if Eisenhower was prepared to go take over, and Tedder was taking the lead in having Montgomery removed.

On 18 July, over on the western flank of the battle area, Omar Bradley had taken St. Lô in the bloodiest fighting his army had experienced since D-Day on the Omaha Beach. West of the Vire River the American forces had also taken the ground necessary for mounting the major breakout operation southward. The Battle of the Hedgerows, which had started on 3 July, had brought the First U.S. Army into St. Lô at enormous cost. Bradley's twelve divisions had progressed only eleven kilometers in fifteen days, losing in the process some 40,000 men, dead or wounded, thereby seriously impairing the capability of his force.

Bradley called for reinforcements of 25,000 infantry as quickly as possible, but they were not in England and would have to be brought in from the United States. His ammunition supply was extremely short and his momentum temporarily spent in what General Dietrich von Choltitz, the German Corps commander at St. Lô, described as "the most monstrous bloodbath, the likes of which I have not seen in eleven years of war."

The news that Montgomery had shut down Goodwood reached Patton at his remote Néhou headquarters at the same time word arrived about the attempt on Hitler's life at Rastenburg. The general was sitting in his tent reading, the rain drumming on the canvas roof, when an orderly from the operations room brought the message about Hitler. He read it and shouted at the orderly, "Codman, find Captain Codman now, boy, now!"

Within five minutes the general was in his jeep, Codman at the wheel and Willie in the back seat, heading for Bradley's command post east of Isigny at Colombières. It was a seventy-two-kilometer ride in the driving rain to deliver a message that he could have given by telephone. But this was too important. He had to look Brad in the eye. When he reached the First Army's command post, he found his commander in the operations tent.

"Georgie, what are you doing here?" There had been no warning that Patton was going to descend like an excited demon.

Patton went straight to the point. "You've heard the news about Hitler? For God's sake, Brad," he pleaded, "you've got to get me into this fight before the war is over. I'm in the doghouse now, and I'm apt to die there unless I pull something spectacular."

"Georgie, I can't get you into this fight yet. The 1st of August is still set for you to bring the Third Army in, 12 noon on the 1st of August, Georgie, that's it. But I tell you what. I'm planning to start Operation Cobra in four days, on the 24th. My aim is to break through and take Coutances and be heading for Avranches. As soon as Cobra meets its objectives, even if it's before the 1st of August, I'll call you in and you can take command. How's that?"

Patton still was not satisfied. "You're sure it isn't Montgomery who's keeping me out of this thing and just telling you what to do?"

"Come on, Georgie." Bradley was exasperated. "I'm running my own show here. Monty gives me free rein. I tell him what I'm going to do, and he makes comment. But this is my army, and I'm giving the orders. As of the 1st of August I'll be an army group commander just as he is. No, he's got nothing to do with it."

Somewhat mollified, Patton saw there was nothing he could change. "Okay, Brad, okay. But remember, goddamn it, you've got to let me into this son-of-a-bitching war before it's over!"

On his return from the front on the 20th, Feldmarschall Kluge went directly to the chateau at La Roche-Guyon. On the desk in his study, as he now called the room that Rommel had used as an office, was an urgent message. He picked it up and read it with astonishment. The message, signed by General Erwin von Witzleben, a Schwarze Kappelle member, said that Hitler had been assassinated that day and that a new provisional government had been established under General Beck, who had been declared the acting Chancellor of Germany. The new Commander-in-Chief of the Wehrmacht was General Witzleben himself. In the order Witzleben instructed the Commander-in-Chief West to eliminate the SS leadership throughout France.

Kluge was still attempting to digest the incredible message when Speidel came into the room. The feldmarschall could see that Speidel was flushed and agitated.

"Have you seen this message, Hans?"

"Of course I have, Sir. The operation appears to have been successful. General Blumentritt called me about half-past three. He has some information, so I suggested that he come here and give it to you directly. He should be here any minute."

Kluge was still not satisfied. "Do you really think the Führer is dead?"

"That's the best information we have, Sir. If he isn't, surely that signal wouldn't have been sent by Witzleben."

Speidel left to go back to the war room as Kluge's telephone rang. It was old General Beck himself calling from Berlin. He gave Kluge a quick summary of what was going on in Berlin and throughout Germany and told him that all steps were being taken for the assumption of power by himself, Witzleben, and others.

Beck finally came to the point of his call. "I'm asking you to announce publicly that you are in support of us, and I want you to give the word to your generals for a military revolt under your leadership. I want you to ask the other generals of the German army staff to join you."

While Kluge was listening to Beck and rapidly calculating his response, Speidel brought in a slip of paper with the text of what Goebbels had just said on the radio at 6:30 p.m.: "An assassination attempt has been made on Hitler's life, but it has failed. The Führer lives and has been only slightly hurt."

Kluge had read this before Beck had finished putting the question. If the Führer really was still alive—if that was not just another Goebbels ploy—then he would have to consider very carefully which way he was going to jump.

"What is the actual state of affairs at the Führerhauptquartier?" He did not yet mention the radio report.

Beck replied, "In the long run does it make any difference, provided we're determined to go ahead?"

"No, but . . ."

"Kluge, I'm asking you for a straight answer: Do you approve of what we are doing here, and will you place yourself under my command?"

"Look, Herr General, I have in my hand a report that Goebbels has just announced Hitler is alive and only slightly injured. I have to know what the situation is. As Commander-in-Chief West, I must know the actual state of things before I can commit myself and my generals."

Beck would not be put off. "In order to avoid any misunderstanding, I must remind you of your conversation with Stülpnagel and your commitment to us. Whether or not Hitler is dead is beside the point. We have started the revolution and it will only succeed if you are with us and are prepared to move toward an armistice. We had that commitment from Rommel, and we thought we had it from you. Now I put it to you. Will you unreservedly accept my command?''

Kluge hedged. "I must tell you, General Beck, that if the assassination attempt has failed, that puts a new light on the situation. I must first consult my people here. I'll ring you back in half an hour.''

When he put the telephone down, Kluge reflected on what Beck had said. Whether or not Hitler was dead, the revolt was on. It would only succeed if Kluge was with them, which would put the head of "clever Hans" right on the block—and Hitler could swing a mighty ax.

On the other hand, surely Witzleben's proclamation would not have been sent unless the assassination attempt had been successful. At a time like this, no one could believe the master propagandist, Goebbels. Kluger was beginning to think that perhaps he should go with Beck after all.

Shortly after 7:00 p.m., his chief-of-staff was shown in. General Blumentritt, whom he trusted implicitly, had served with him for many years.

The two of them discussed the situation from all sides. Finally Kluge said, "I think I should side with Beck. I don't trust Goebbels' report. And the obvious thing now is to try to get an armistice as Rommel had planned. The second thing is to stop the V-1 fire against London. That will convince the enemy that we mean business. It will be an olive branch they will find very attractive. If we stop the V-1s, they will stop the bombing of Germany. An armistice would allow us to withdraw to the Siegfried Line and evacuate all the occupied areas in western Europe.''

Again the telephone rang. It was an officer from the headquarters at St. Germain-en-Laye. From OKW had come an announcement by Keitel that the Führer was alive and almost uninjured. All commanders were to ignore any orders received from anyone but himself and Himmler.

Thunderstruck, Kluge repeated the message to Blumentritt. Shaking his head, the feldmarschall said, "This is impossible. If Keitel's message is true, then I don't see how I can support Beck.''

Annoyed and frustrated, he turned to Blumentritt and to
Speidel, who had just entered the room, and shouted, "Find
out what is true and what is false. We must get the facts
first and until then let things stay as they are."

Kluge left the two of them while he went into his bed-
chamber for a much-needed bath and a change of clothes.
While he was gone, it was Blumentritt who made the telephone call to the Wolfsschanze in East Prussia in an unsuccessful attempt to reach Keitel, Jodl, or Jodl's deputy,
General Warlimont. Finally he made contact with General
Stieff at the army headquarters next to the Wolfsschanze.
Stieff, a one-time member of Kluge's staff, gave Blumentritt
the full and true story. Klaus von Stauffenberg's bomb had
gone off, but the Führer had been only slightly hurt. Others
were mortally wounded, including Rudolf Schmundt, Rommel's "Apostle John."

Kluge came back into the study while Blumentritt was
speaking to Stieff and took the telephone to hear for himself.

"A great deal depends on what you're telling me, Stieff.
Are you absolutely certain?"

The unfortunate Stieff, who had flown with Stauffenberg
to East Prussia that morning, was attempting to distance
himself, if he could, from the assassination attempt. Since
it had failed, he had decided he would have no part in the
rebellion.

"Yes, Herr Feldmarschall, there are officers here with me
listening to what I am saying. They were there when the
bomb went off. Hitler was injured but only slightly."

There was now no question in Kluge's mind.

Slamming the telephone down in its cradle, he muttered
to himself but loud enough that Blumentritt and Speidel
could hear. "My God, what a bungled business!"

He turned to Blumentritt, saying, "I suppose you know,
or you strongly suspect, that these people were in contact
with me once . . ."

He reached for the sherry decanter on the small table near
his desk. His hands were shaking as he poured a glass for
himself.

The sound of cars coming up the Rue d'Audience could
be heard. Speidel immediately got up and left to meet the
visitors, whoever they were, at the front door.

While he was gone, Kluge kept talking as if compelled.
"In the summer of '43, emissaries, I suppose you'd call
them, emissaries from Beck and Witzleben came to see me

twice. As you know, Günther, I was in command of Armee
Gruppe Center at Smolensk at the time. They tried to win
me over to a certain political plan. The first time I spoke to
them at length. The second time I began to have my doubts.
So I broke off the conversation and told them I wanted to
be left out of this highly dubious business. I really should
have reported it. I really should have.''

He lifted the sherry glass to his lips with both hands to
control the shaking.

Speidel appeared at the doorway from the corridor to announce, ''General Stülpnagel is here, Sir, with Oberst
Finckh and Oberstleutnant Hofacker.''

Kluge was alarmed. ''My God! What the hell are they
doing here? They'll implicate all of us.'' He shook his head
in disbelief. ''Take them to my study, I'll be there in a
minute. And, Hans, dinner. It's almost 8:00. Tell the kitchen
I will dine at 9:00 and that I will have guests.''

Speidel departed. Kluge put down his empty glass and
pulled himself stiffly erect in Prussian form, saying to Blumentritt, ''let us go hear what they want.''

''You know what they want.''

The feldmarschall smoothed down his jacket front, then
his straight silver hair. ''Of course I do. Come.''

When the formal greetings were over, Kluge settled into
his desk chair, waited until the others were seated, then
played his opener, his hooded eyes watching three faces for
their reactions.

''Gentlemen, you should know that I have it on confirmed
authority that the assassination attempt on the Führer was
unsuccessful. I assume you know that the Führer was only
slightly injured.''

There was no reaction. Obviously the news was old. Operation Valkyrie had failed. But then why were they there?
It was Hofacker who spoke.

''Herr Feldmarschall, what has happened in Berlin is not
decisive. Much more so are the decisions that will be taken
in Paris. I appeal to you, for the sake of the future of Germany, to do what Feldmarschall Rommel would have done,
what he said he would do in the secret conference I had
with him in this very room on July 9th. Cut free from Hitler
and take over the task of liberation in the West yourself. In
Berlin power is in the hands of Generaloberst Beck, the
future head of the state. Create the same *fait accompli* here
in the West. The army and the nation will thank you. Put

an end in the West to bloody murder. Prevent a still more
terrible end, and avert the most terrible catastrophe in German history.''

Kluge had heard what he thought he might hear. Even so,
the consequences appalled him. The Führer was still alive.
He had sworn allegiance to Adolf Hitler, renewed just a few
months before. It was Hitler who had promoted him to the
highest rank, general feldmarschall, after the fall of France,
and given him command of Armee Gruppe Center on the
Russian front in 1942. He was deeply beholden to the Führer—and for more than his military rank and position. On
Kluge's 60th birthday, 30 October 1942, the Führer had
written a letter of congratulations and sent him a substantial
sum of money, some 250,000 marks, half of which could
be used for the improvement of his estate. He had gladly
accepted the gift, whereas others of the general staff to
whom Hitler had made similar gestures had refused.

If Hitler had been killed today, Kluge's ties to the man
would have been severed. He would have been free to go
with Beck and the Schwartze Kapelle. Indeed the challenge
of liberation in the West was highly attractive to Kluge, as
was the prospect of putting an end to the war.

But Hitler was alive, very much alive. And so was Kluge's
sense of self-preservation. He stood up, clasping his hands
behind his back, his face flushed and taut with apparent
indignation. He looked down at Hofacker and Stülpnagel.
''This is the very first I've heard about any such assassination attempt.''

Stülpnagel's face blanched as the surprise and shock sank
in. ''Herr Feldmarschall, I thought you knew all about it,
about the plan.''

''Good heavens, man!'' Kluge shouted. ''I had not the
slightest inkling, otherwise I wouldn't have been out at the
front . . .''

Up to that moment, Stülpnagel had believed Hofacker's
assurance that Kluge was with them, certainly if Hitler was
dead and most likely even if he were not. But now Kluge,
his friend and his commander, had abandoned him and the
Schwarze Kapelle's cause.

Stülpnagel was on the verge of panic as his mind raced
with the consequences of the order he had given earlier,
which was at that moment being carried out: the arrest by
troops under his command in Paris of all the SS and the
Gestapo in that city.

Stülpnagel's stunned mind turned in on itself. He got to his feet, turned, and walked out through the French doors and down the steps to the courtyard. He was oblivious to everything—the blooming rose bushes climbing the ancient walls, the massive gates, the black staff car sitting in the dusk-shadows at the far end of the courtyard, the sound of his feet on the gravel.

What was done was done. Stülpnagel pulled himself together and returned to the study, there to be greeted by his ever hospitable friend, Kluge. Knowing that he had just devastated Stülpnagel and his companions and probably cost them their lives, Kluge gave Stülpnagel an invitation that protocol required him to accept, however distasteful it was. "Well, Stülpnagel, you'll stay and have a meal."

The taking of that meal was pure agony for Stülpnagel, Finckh, and Hofacker, but for Kluge it was as if all were normal. The host ate and drank heartily and talked incessantly about his experiences on the eastern front and his proposed tactics in Normandy. Blumentritt ate silently. Speidel was in and out of the dining room in response to telephone calls. Through it all, as the candles on the dining-room table slowly burned down, Kluge's guests picked at their food and barely touched the excellent wine. Their thoughts were on themselves and their hopeless futures. They heard the feldmarschall but they were not listening, except late in the ordeal when Kluge expressed relief that no action had been taken in his command that would indicate support for the treasonable action against the Führer.

Kluge was appalled when he heard Stülpnagel break his silence. "But I've already taken steps. I've given the order to arrest all the Gestapo in Paris."

More than that, his order had been to arrest the SS as well. The process of finding and arresting some 1,200 of the most vicious people in Paris was in full swing at that very moment. It was also Stülpnagel's order that the most powerful among them be immediately tried by drumhead court-martial and executed forthwith in the courtyard of the Ecole Militaire. Sandbagged execution structures were being hastily thrown together.

Kluge could not believe his ears. He dropped his cutlery on his dinner plate and jumped to his feet in extreme agitation. He looked down at the hapless Stülpnagel, shouting, "Heavens alive, man, you couldn't do that without my consent!" It was an unacceptable, insulting act of insubordination to issue such an order without the authority of the Commander-in-Chief. Red-faced and furious, Kluge deserted his friend completely. His loyalty, whatever its former strength, had totally evaporated. ''Well, my dear Stülpnagel, you'll have to save your own skin then!''

Kluge's words to Blumentritt were terse. ''Ring up and see whether action has already been taken.''

Within moments Blumentritt returned. The entire SS and Gestapo hierarchy, including Hitler's ambassador, Otto Abetz, and all SS and Gestapo leaders, had been arrested by army troops and were to be executed in the morning. Kluge now had no choice. He had to distance himself totally. He told Stülpnagel, ''I must ask you to give orders immediately that the Gestapo are to be released. As for you, the best thing would be to get into civilian clothes and disappear.''

Kluge wanted these men out of the chateau. It was nearly 11:00 p.m. Ever the aristocratic host, he led Stülpnagel out the dining-room door and down the hall toward the courtyard, with Blumentritt close behind and listening. The words to Stülpnagel were precise and for the record. ''You must get back as quickly as you can to Paris and release the arrested men. The responsibility is fully yours.''

The proud Stülpnagel, who had put his life on the line for the German people against the ruthless excesses of Adolf Hitler, replied, his voice calm, ''I accept the responsibility. But we cannot withdraw now, Herr Feldmarschall. Events have spoken for us.''

Hofacker was to have his last say to Kluge. ''It is your honor that is at stake, Sir, and the honor of the army. The fate of the nation is in your hands.''

Kluge brushed off this final plea, replying, ''It would be so if the Führer were dead. But, of course, he is not.''

There was a final word for Stülpnagel before he entered his waiting car when Kluge ordered, ''Regard yourself as suspended from duty.''

The next day Stülpnagel was summoned to Berchtesgaden by Keitel. Rather than face the Führer, he shot himself, but failed in the attempted suicide, succeeding only in blinding himself. However, in the delirium that followed, he implicated Rommel by murmuring his name. This inculpating evidence would soon be passed to Hitler.

Before Stülpnagel's staff car had left the dark courtyard that night of 20 July, Kluge had made up his mind to cover his tracks and do so quickly. He knew that the Führer would move heaven and earth to find out who the conspirators really were and how far their net had spread. The Gestapo would be given a free hand. Himmler would never rest until he discovered through torture, blackmail, or whatever means, the names of all those who had a hand in the assassination attempt and revolt.

And Hans von Kluge knew that, except for some magical stroke, he would be implicated. He could trust his chief-of-staff, General Blumentritt, but he wished he could turn the clock back and obliterate two events. The first was his meeting in Berlin in 1943 with Goerdeler and Truscow, leaders of the Schwarze Kapelle. Even though he had said nothing during that meeting that could implicate him, the fact was that he had met with them.

And then there was this meeting with Stülpnagel and the others. Even though he had put on a convincing performance, and for the record disassociated himself from their plot, the fact that he had received them at all and listened to their pleas without throwing them out, or for that matter, arresting them, would sooner or later be sufficient to involve him.

At that moment his sense of guilt and foreboding compelled him to sit down at his desk immediately to write a personal signal to the Führer.

What Kluge wrote that night as he sat at the historic desk in his study at La Roche-Guyon was this:

To the Führer and the Supreme Commander of the Armed Forces:

Thanks to a merciful act of Providence, the infamous and murderous attempt against your life, mein Führer, has miscarried. On behalf of the three branches of the Armed Forces entrusted to my command, I send you my congratulations and assure you, mein Führer, of our unalterable loyalty, no matter what may befall us.

Next came a brief order-of-the-day to his armies in the field:

The Führer lives! The war effort at home and the fighting at the front goes on. For us there will be no repetition of 1918, nor of the example of Italy! Long live the Führer!

Both the messages were given to a duty officer for immediate transmission. The last thing Kluge did for himself, his family honor, and his future before he retired to his bed shortly after 1:00 a.m. was to put in a blitz call to Jodl at Rastenburg. A full report on Stülpnagel's actions and words would be appropriate from a Commander-in-Chief who knew absolutely nothing about a plot against Hitler's life or a plan for revolt or a scheme for an unthinkable armistice.

21 July 1944

"IT WAS very unwise for you to have seen them—Stülpnagel and his people. Their keeping you informed was one thing. But for them to come here, for you to actually receive them and talk to them . . . Hitler will have the Gestapo out like a bunch of hornets. Stülpnagel, Beck, and all of them will be strung up like pieces of meat. And if any one of them talks, you and Rommel are bound to be implicated."

Kluge was listening carefully to his son-in-law's words. He could not argue against the logic of Dr. Udo Esch.

"Even if I had no part in the plot?"

"It's called guilt by association, Father." Esch shrugged. "All that Hitler needs is for Himmler or anyone to tell him they were here yesterday, the very day of the assassination attempt."

Kluge protested. "But I turned them away. I would have nothing to do with them. Even my staff can certify to that!"

Esch shook his head. "That may well be. I understand the point. But Hitler is going to be absolutely paranoid now. Everyone will be, I suspect. He'll blame all you generals for what happened to him and for the loss of the war. He'll hang every last one of you if he can. On the other hand . . ." Esch stood up, stuffed his hands in his pockets and walked to the French doors where Rommel had so often stood, " . . . the Führer may accept your version of being confronted by the others and the complete rebuff you gave them. Only time will tell. Certainly you've covered your tracks the best you could."

The near midday sun beating down on the chateau caused Dr. Udo Esch to squint as his eyes moved around the courtyard taking in the features of the ancient stone structure, its elaborate gates, the towering cliff, the reds and yellows of the cascading rose bushes in the perimeter gardens. "My God, this is a beautiful place. The building is magnificent. It takes you back hundreds of years."

Kluge, sitting at the desk, looked at the broad back of his son-in-law, whose huge figure seemed almost to fill the doorway. Apart from his own son, Oberstleutnant Günther von Kluge, whom he had brought with him to La Roche-Guyon as a member of his staff, there was no man in the world whom he trusted more than Udo. Kluge certainly didn't want to confide any further in Speidel or in Blumentritt at present concerning his views about the Führer, the assassination plot, or an armistice. No, for now there were just Günther and Udo. As soon as he had been appointed Commander-in-Chief West he had installed Esch as director of one of the German military hospitals in Paris. Esch had been an almost daily visitor at St. Germain-en-Laye, for lunch or dinner or drinks. Not only did Kluge respect the intelligence of this 40-year-old man, not only did he trust him completely, but there was also the bond of family.

Esch turned in the doorway, moving out of the sunlight, his broad, ruddy head with its gray eyes and heavy eyebrows under a full head of wavy brown hair. His brow was furrowed as he turned over the elements of the situation Kluge had presented.

"What's your assessment of the heavy fighting in the last three days?" Esch asked.

"The enemy came within a hair's-breadth of breaking through at Caen. They threw at us everything they could. They came at us like armored locusts. But we held, Udo, we held."

"Well, I know the enemy mounted a major attack because of the flow of casualties into my hospital. Our soldiers are taking a terrible beating."

"No reserves. No replacements." The feldmarschall went on: "The situation is appalling. But the rain stopped them. Montgomery may not know it yet, but he almost made it through. If they'd pierced the last one, Montgomery would have broken out into the plains. His tanks and men would have poured through the opening like water through a crack in a dam. Then they would have swung around to the west behind us. It would have been the end of the Battle of Normandy."

"The enemy also must have suffered heavy losses," Esch ventured.

"My intelligence people estimate between five and six hundred tanks, perhaps six thousand men. But then that's nothing, Udo. Kill one tank and they have five more to replace it. Kill one soldier and they have ten more to replace him. And we have nothing!'' His fists pounded the desk in frustration, his face flushed beet red. For a moment, Esch thought he was going to cry. ''I cannot bear to think of the hundreds of thousands of fine young German men—boys, many of them just boys—who are going to die just to satisfy Hitler's ego.''

Esch looked toward the document on the desk. ''When you telephoned you said you had something you wanted me to read?''

''Yes, it's this,'' Kluge replied. ''It's a status report to Hitler. An assessment of the battle situation.''

It was in Esch's mind to point out the obvious—that he was not a military person and would not understand the significance of the report—but he said nothing. He knew Kluge would not ask him to read it unless there was some part of it that he needed advice on.

''Let me give you some background. About ten days ago, no, I guess it was the 12th, I had just finished my tour of the front, the first time I'd been there. I can tell you, Udo, it is disaster. I came here to see Rommel to ask him to prepare a situation assessment. His report was delivered to me on the 15th, just two days before he was injured. That's almost a week ago. I just can't sit on it any longer.''

''You could tear it up.''

Kluge took his eyes from Esch's and looked down at the desk momentarily. ''Yes, I suppose I could do that, but what Rommel says is correct. As the Commander-in-Chief West I have an obligation to the Supreme Commander, to Hitler. I have a duty to him and a duty to Germany. I must tell the Führer what the true situation is. After all, he's off hundreds of kilometers away in Prussia. He's concentrating on the Russians, not on this front. But at the same time he and Jodl are trying to run the battle in Normandy, and they've never even been on the ground.''

Kluge looked up at Esch, waving his right hand as if to signal the termination of the argument in his own mind.

''Before I show what I've written, I'll read you part of Rommel's report. The part I think is the most important. Then you'll understand my approach.''

Kluge lifted the document that he had written, and under it was a second: Rommel's report. His eyes ran down the first page and then the second. Esch left the doorway to slump in the chair across from Kluge, four fingers to his nose, pensive, waiting.

"Ah, yes, here we are." Kluge read:

> *In these circumstances we must expect that in the fore-seeable future the enemy will succeed in breaking through our thin front, above all, Seventh Army's, and thrusting deep into France. Apart from the Panzer Group's sector reserves, which are at present on their own front and—owing to the enemy's command of the air—can only move at night, we dispose of no mobile reserve against such a breakthrough.*

Kluge hesitated, again looking at Esch. "He's absolutely right, you know. Montgomery will break through at any time. Whether it's in the Caen sector or over in the American area under Bradley, somewhere that thin line is going to give, and that's what I have to tell the Führer. He has to be made to understand."

"Maybe he doesn't want to understand."

"What do you mean?"

"Just that. As he watches the oncoming horde of Russians and his forces are being driven back farther and faster in the East, he probably wants to believe that everything is going well in this backwater where you're fighting the Americans and the British. And even if you're defeated by them, it's not nearly so bad as being defeated by those primitive, lesser beings, the Soviets. So perhaps he doesn't want to know of any bad news from you. Perhaps his staff may not even tell him about any message that says that things aren't going well. You know the man. You know his staff."

The feldmarschall nodded glumly.

Esch continued: "Why put your head on the chopping block? Why tell him?"

Kluge thought about the question for a moment, then said, "Let's leave that for now, because there's something more that Rommel said . . ."

"That you agree with?"

"That I agree with. He's urging that an armistice . . . that peace be worked out with the Allies. Since it's obvious we can't win, he says we should seek an armistice in Normandy—and in Italy—when we are still strong and can therefore negotiate terms, terms that would allow any of our forces on the western front to be moved to the East.''

He had Esch's full attention now. The doctor was sitting bolt upright in the chair, his eyes wide with incredulity. ''You don't really think that Churchill and Roosevelt would be prepared to abandon Stalin and the Russians?''

''More than abandon. It would be more like turning on them. Of course they would. Churchill and Roosevelt know full well that when they've defeated Germany, they're going to have to take on the Soviets. So why not take them on now? I think Rommel's right. Dead right. This is what he says in the last paragraph of his report. He's somewhat oblique but the meaning is perfectly clear:

> *''The troops are everywhere fighting heroically, but the unequal struggle is approaching its end. It is urgently necessary for the proper conclusion to be drawn from this situation.''*

It was the feldmarschall's turn to stand. He pushed the chair back, pulled himself up to his full height, and paced up and down the study.

''There is something else you should know, Udo. Speidel told me that when Rommel added the last paragraph, he used the word 'political' before the word 'conclusion.' And of course he was right. He means an armistice and peace authorized by the politicians—by Hitler and the Nazis.''

''Or by whoever is in political power at the time.''

Kluge grunted. ''If things had gone differently yesterday, it would be Beck and Goerdeler who would be making the political decisions.''

'And you, yourself, would be part of that decision-making process, Father. At this very moment, you would be planning the armistice approach to Montgomery and with full authority to do so.''

Kluge stopped pacing. His response caught Esch completely by surprise.

''I *am* planning that armistice approach, Udo. I know what I have to do and how I'm going to do it. It's simply a matter of when the time is right, when I know I have no choice.''

He returned to his chair. ''In the meantime, I must carry out the orders of the Führer . . .''

"Even if they don't make sense, if he doesn't understand the situation on the battlefield?"

"My dear Udo, he is still the Supreme Commander."

Esch knew what the response would be to the suggestion he was about to put to his father-in-law. "You don't have to go on with this. You could always retire. Ill health. I could certify to that."

"A coward's way out. Absolutely not. It would be a terrible disgrace for my family, including you, Udo. Impossible."

Esch pointed at the paper on the desk. "You wanted me to read your report to Hitler?"

Kluge shoved the documents across the table. "Tell me what you think his reaction will be."

"The real question is whether you should send it at all. His reaction? I don't know that I can tell you that. I've never met the man, but my guess is he's on the verge of insanity. That bomb will have destroyed his ability to trust anyone. How will he react to your report? God only knows."

Kluge managed a weak smile. "Well, he might know better after you read it. Take your time. I'm going to the toilet."

It did not take Esch long to read what his father-in-law had written in his meticulous hand. It was a devastating account of the battle situation: a confirmation, including new evidence from Caen, of Rommel's report and his conclusions. The memorandum ended by saying:

> *I can report that the front has held, despite almost daily losses of terrain, as a result of the magnificent valor of the troops and the resolution of the commanders, especially in the lower echelons.*
> *However, the moment is approaching when despite all efforts the hard-pressed front will break. And when the enemy has erupted into open terrain, considering the inadequate mobility of our forces, orderly and effective conduct of the battle will be hardly possible. As responsible commander on this front I feel responsible, mein Führer, to bring the consequences to your attention in time.*

Kluge came back into the study just as Esch was mulling over the impact of the last paragraph.

"Well, Udo?"

Esch shrugged. "I don't know, Father. You've told him in no uncertain terms that the Battle of Normandy has been lost, that there's no way it can be won. He won't like that news. In fact he might be mad enough to want to kill the messenger."

"And the author might be considered the messenger?"

Esch looked his father-in-law in the eye. "That's what I'm saying, and it's also why I'm saying you shouldn't send this report. It's like putting a loaded gun to your head and pulling the trigger."

Esch laid the document on the desk. "I notice you don't call for any reinforcements, more tanks, more troops. You simply say that the Anglo-Americans are going to break through and that he should understand the consequences— meaning he should get on with the business of making peace with them."

Kluge was slightly exasperated. "My dear Udo, there is no sense in calling for more tanks, more troops, more ammunition. Rommel has been screaming for them. His commanders have been screaming for them. In the very short time I've been here, I've been screaming for them as well. The fact is there isn't anything the Führer is prepared to give to us. He could authorize me to move infantry and Panzer divisions down from the Fifteenth Army still waiting in the Pas-de-Calais area for the attack across the Channel— an attack that will never come."

"Waiting for the Armee Gruppe Patton."

"Exactly. Supposedly a force of more than a million men. He could give me authority to transfer those divisions to Normandy, but he simply won't do it. *Perhaps*, if I send him this report, he'll let me have those divisions. And *perhaps* he'll order a retreat back across the Seine toward the threshold of Germany . . ."

"But what you're hoping is that this report will cause him to think seriously about the unthinkable: an armistice with the West?"

Once again Kluge's head shook. "In my heart of hearts I do not believe that the Führer, a megalomaniac who thrives on sending signals to fight to the last man, would consider for one second pleading for peace with Churchill and Roosevelt—or with anyone else for that matter."

"Don't be too sure, Father. Remember, he's a human being. When he realizes defeat is inevitable he might change his mind, particularly if he thought he could come out of it with a whole skin. The primitive wish to survive is undoubtedly alive in Hitler. But why would you send such a message if it isn't your objective to persuade him an armistice is needed?''

''So that if and when—sorry not if, but when—I personally open negotiations for armistice, with or without Hitler's approval, the record will show that I gave Hitler full and ample warning of the consequences and that he ignored my warning. I have to think of Germany and the lives of my troops. All that Hitler has to think about now is his own skin, his own reputation. And obviously he doesn't give a damn for the lives of German civilians or the cities of Germany—nothing but his own ego.''

''So,'' Esch summarized, ''you're going to send this report regardless of my advice.''

''Which is exactly what you expected, my dear Udo.''

The son-in-law smiled. ''True. I would expect nothing less of you, Father.''

Kluge nodded. ''Ours is a family of honor and respect for traditions, of dedication to the Fatherland—total dedication. And so, while I hear what you're saying, Udo, you know that I must send this report. On the other hand, I cannot tell you how much it means to me to be able to talk to you and get your counsel.''

Dr. Udo Esch was moved. He did something that was never done. He reached across the desk to touch the hand of his father-in-law, only momentarily, as he said, ''I understand what you're saying. I understand the Prussian principles of honor under which you have always lived. It's simply that I cannot bear the thought of losing you. God knows you've put yourself at prejudice by even talking to the assassination plotters. But this report by itself could cost you Hitler's confidence and therefore your life.''

Kluge had been leaning on the desk with his elbows. Now he sat up straight, pulled his shoulders back. ''You must understand one thing, Udo. Life is short. I am almost at the end of mine, whether by natural causes or by the act of the enemy or by the judgment of the Führer. I am not afraid of dying. But, above all, I must die with honor.''

''That is something Hitler might not permit you to do.'' Esch spoke softly. ''He might want you, along with countless of your colleagues, he might want you to die in disgrace. The better to be able to say that you and your colleagues of the General Staff were, as he has long claimed, totally incompetent, totally incapable of taking his infallible instructions, totally disloyal.''

Kluge was hurt by those words. He shut his eyes and bent his head down to touch his hands to his forehead. He was silent for a moment, then looked up at Esch. "Did you bring what I asked for?"

"Yes, I brought two." From his right suitcoat pocket Esch took out a small pill bottle, which he placed on the desk within Kluge's reach. "I made them myself this morning. There are two ampules of waterless acid cyanide in there."

"Why two? Only one is needed for eternity."

"But if you misplace one or you can't get at it when you need it—the second provides certainty. I only pray to God, dear Father, that it never comes to this, that we will share your love and affection until you are at least 90."

Kluge managed a wan smile. "At least 90? That, coincidentally, is the number of Hitler's generals who have taken their own lives since this madness began five years ago." This time the hand of the father-in-law reached across to rest affectionately on Esch's. Just a touch. "I thank you, my dear Udo, for everything you have done for me, for loving my daughter, for my grandchildren, and for being a son."

The hand moved away slowly. "You and Günther I trust above all men. You understand." It was a statement, not a question.

Esch nodded. There was nothing to be said.

Kluge looked at his watch. "It's quarter to twelve. I have invited General Speidel to have lunch with us."

"What does Speidel know about the assassination plot?"

"Everything. I suspect he was a major player in trying to get Rommel to be part of the group and to take over the military leadership once Hitler was out of the way. He's an extremely intelligent man, Udo, extremely. Speidel will have lunch with us but you must not raise anything that relates to the possibility of an armistice negotiation, even though Speidel may have worked out the mechanics of actually making contact. I'll talk to Speidel myself, but I want to choose my time."

Esch had to ask, "So how do you think you will get in touch with Montgomery?"

Kluge smiled broadly for the first time that morning. "This is what I am planning to do. My ability to commu-

nicate directly by radio with Montgomery's headquarters—
I'd have to be in the Caen sector with my wireless van to
do this—my radio contact is the key. Now here's what I
propose to do—at the right time . . .''

24 July 1944

CHURCHILL TAPPED the ash off his cigar. He knew that Montgomery didn't like anyone smoking in his precious van. But then he, Churchill, was the Prime Minister, the late-afternoon cigar was delicious, and he had flown to France especially to talk to his beleaguered general.

"How did you get on with Marshall this morning?" General George Marshall, the American chief-of-staff, alarmed by what he was hearing from Eisenhower about the progress of the battle in Normandy, had flown across from Washington to see for himself. His arrival had been a clear signal to Montgomery that he was in trouble, deep trouble, with the biggest military hawk of them all, Marshall, circling to see if it was time for the kill.

"I think you should ask General Marshall that question, Prime Minister, but I'll tell you one thing. When he got here this morning, he didn't have a bloody clue as to what my strategy was. I don't know what Eisenhower and Tedder and that lot have been telling him, but they have the whole thing botched. They don't understand what I'm doing and they're refusing to listen." Montgomery spun on his heel and strode over to the war map on the wall.

"I told them what you and my battlefield generals understand: that with my British and Canadian forces I'm attracting the German armor to Caen, that's my pivot point. With the German armor at Caen, that leaves the Americans open in the west to break out past St. Lô, down into Avranches, then they're away. Goodwood wasn't necessarily supposed to be a breakthrough. Certainly I hoped it would be, and at one point I thought it was. That was my mistake. Anyway, my overall strategy is working beautifully, Prime Minister.

"On the 15th of July, for example, opposite Bradley's army there were only two Panzer divisions with one hundred and ninety tanks. Just two Panzer divisions, Prime Minister, but opposite the Second British Army and the Canadians at Caen, there were six Panzer divisions with six hundred and thirty tanks.''

Churchill looked up sharply from his seat in Montgomery's upholstered chair. ''All right, Monty, it's apparent to me that the Supreme Commander and Tedder really don't have a grasp of what you're doing, though it's plain enough to me. I don't understand what they're trying to do. Tedder's after you, you know.''

Montgomery's mouth twisted in disgust. ''Bloody air force twit, sitting behind his desk, hundreds of miles away. Certainly I know he's after me, saying that I should have broken out on the eastern flank with Goodwood. I never had any intention of going for the Seine. If Tedder and his lot would refer to all the orders I have issued, they would see that. It's a false conception that exists only at Supreme Headquarters and among people there who, how shall I put it, Prime Minister, are not very fond of me—and I'll tell you why. The original plan made for D-Day by General Morgan was that we should break out from the Caen-Falaise area on our eastern flank. I refused to accept his plan and changed it myself. Now Morgan is deputy chief-of-staff at Supreme Headquarters. He considers Eisenhower as a god. And since I disregarded many of his plans, he now places me at the other end of the celestial ladder. So now Morgan and Tedder are trying to persuade Eisenhower that I am defensively minded and that we are unlikely to break out anywhere! Prime Minister, this cufuffle is nothing but the politics of jealousy combined with stupidity.''

Churchill accepted the views of the mighty little general who had saved the Prime Minister's political hide by gloriously defeating Rommel in the desert. He owed Montgomery much just as the general owed him.

Montgomery went on to describe the plans for his next attack, then added, ''Tomorrow is the start of Operation Cobra, Prime Minister. Bradley's forces will do exactly what I had planned: press forward from St. Lô after a massive bombing. Within two or three days they will break out of the bocage, rush down to Avranches, and out into the tank country. Then they'll swing west toward Le Mans and we'll have put paid to the Germans and their new commander.''

''Ah, yes, Ultra has told us about Kluge,'' Churchill recalled. ''We don't know yet what's happened to Rommel. Goebbels still hasn't made any announcement. Strange.''

''A pity if Rommel's gone: I would have loved to have

defeated him a second time. As for my planning and conduct of the battle, Prime Minister, if you can find anything wrong with it I would be obliged if you would tell me, Sir. And if it is your wish—not Eisenhower's or Tedder's or anyone else's—if it's your wish that I should stand down, you have only to say so.''

Churchill struggled to his feet. His cigar was almost done. ''Monty, I have the fullest confidence in you. You may count on me.''

25-28 July 1944

AFTER A false start on the 24th, Bradley's Operation Cobra got under way the next day. At 9:40 a.m., three hundred and fifty bombers of Major General Elwood Quesada's Ninth Tactical Air Command began a twenty-minute all-out attack against the enemy in a narrow path on each side of the Périers-St. Lô road to the west of St. Lô. Then followed the intense bombing of an area some 2,200 by 6,400 meters containing German concentrations in the Marigny-La Chapelle-La Mesnil area. More than 1,800 heavy and medium bombers and more than 500 fighter bombers returning for a second assault unleashed their lethal cargoes of bombs, this time augmented by napalm canisters. All told, more than 4,000 tons of explosives hammered the target area that morning. Concurrently, the big guns of the American artillery pumped in more than 140,000 shells.

The devastation was beyond belief. In the inferno thousands of German troops were killed, tanks obliterated, and command posts consumed. A parachute regiment went missing. The ground shuddered and shook incessantly as cascades of earth, explosives, and metal soared high in the air. The atmosphere was filled with dust.

At 11:00 in the morning, American armor and infantry of the Seventh Corps under Collins moved out against the smashed German sector to the west. Under and behind the heavy onslaught of artillery, his divisions engaged the enemy in a ferocious battle.

On 28 July the Germans began to fall back, retreating southward through the coastal towns including the key highway hub of Avranches. It was Kluge's intention to form a new line to the south of Avranches but that was not to happen. To Bradley all resistance seemed to have disappeared while the American army charged after the retreating Germans under an expanding arc of operations by the ever-present U.S. Tactical Air Force's fighter-bombers. That same day Coutances was taken, and with its fall the long, costly battle for the breakout was successful.

As soon as Bradley heard the news, he put a call in to Eisenhower in England.

"Ike, we've done it. We've got Coutances, and the Germans appear to be in full retreat. We're taking every calculated risk, and we believe we have the Germans out of the ditches and completely demoralized."

"Brad, that's fantastic. Congratulations. Now's the time you need Georgie."

"That's what I think. As you well know, Ike, he wasn't my choice to be the Third Army commander—he still doesn't know that, and I hope you'll never tell him. And I'm still a little wary of how he will accept our reversal in roles. I worry about how much of my time I'll have to spend curbing his impetuousness. But I also know that with Georgie in the field, there won't be any need for me to be out whipping the Third Army to keep it on the move. All I have to do is point him in the direction I want him to go."

"Look, Brad, on the battlefield, away from speechmaking and the press, the old boy has got to be the best damned field general you'll ever put your eyes on. And he's dying to do it. Go ahead. Call him up right now and tell him he's in charge. Give him Middleton's Corps to start with and then throw the rest in under him on the 1st of August. That's the switchover date. You'll have the First and Third Armies and you'll be the Twelfth U.S. Army Group commander, and as far as I'm concerned you'll be of equal status with Montgomery. However, until I can move my headquarters over there—probably by the 1st of September—Montgomery will have to stay as the Land Commander. What I'm saying is that Monty will act as my agent, exercising temporary operational control over your army group, his function limited primarily to coordination and the settlement of boundaries between your groups. What do you think of that?"

Bradley didn't hesitate, "That's okay with me. Look, Monty hasn't limited my authority or given me any directives that would make me angry. So I'm happy to remain under his command until the tactical situation dictates a change. What does Monty think about all this?"

There was a pause, then Eisenhower spoke ruefully. "I don't know. He's madder than billy-be-damned at me. He won't take any telephone calls, and he won't respond to any messages I send."

"My God, what's happened?"

"Well, Brad, it goes this way." Eisenhower sounded reluctant. "What with Monty's inability to move—he keeps on pivoting at Caen—I decided I just had to do something. So I had lunch with Churchill two days ago to tell him what was on my mind. Then there was dinner with Churchill, Brooke, and others last night. It's a real hornet's nest now."

A real hornet's nest indeed.

Eisenhower had taken lunch with Churchill at 10 Downing Street on the 26th, with just the two of them present. At the instigation of Tedder, Coningham, and Morgan, Eisenhower had said to Churchill, "Sir, I'm really worried about what the American and British press are saying about Montgomery and the British not taking their share of the fighting end of the casualties. As far as I can see, Monty's forces in the Caen area could and should be more offensive. They're not fighting as they should, and as far as I'm concerned, it's Montgomery's fault. He's not providing the leadership."

"Whatever makes you say that, Ike? He's drawing the German armor to Caen against the British and Canadians on almost a four-to-one basis compared with what they have against Bradley."

"Well if you look at the figures, you'll see that Bradley has suffered at least double the casualties. He's up over 40,000 now, way ahead of Monty and Dempsey. Prime Minister, Monty's simply not capable of moving. According to Tedder—here's the letter that he wrote to me when I was in Normandy just three days ago—he says, 'All the evidence available to me indicated a serious lack of fighting leadership in high direction of the British armies in Normandy.' That comes from the failure of Goodwood. Frankly, Tedder says Montgomery's had us for suckers at SHAEF. He doesn't believe Montgomery didn't intend to make a clean breakthrough at Caen."

"My dear Ike, these allegations are of the greatest seriousness. I hear them, but you should know that I am not in any way persuaded. If there's one thing that Monty knows and understands, it's the necessity of keeping the front aflame, of pushing on aggressively. I'm afraid that your staff are not communicating with him, nor he with you. It may well be that your people don't understand his strategy or don't want to."

Eisenhower appeared ready to object, but Churchill stopped him by holding up his hand. "It is not my custom to act precipitously. You know that very well, Ike. You also know that you're dealing with the reputation and future of Britain's greatest hero of this war, a man who has a track record that no other Allied general can match."

"And that includes me," Eisenhower acknowledged glumly.

"Be that as it may, give me time to think on this and to let the accused have his say. Have you told Montgomery your misgivings?"

Churchill's eyebrows went up when Eisenhower answered, "No."

"I need some time now, Ike, but I think we ought to come to a decision. I need others to hear what you have to say. So I would be obliged if you would come to dinner tomorrow night. I'll have Brooke there as well. After all he is the Chief of the Imperial General Staff, and Monty's responsible to him. I take it you can come. Seven-thirty for 8:00, if you please."

Churchill ruminated on Eisenhower's allegations for the rest of the day. His decision to be in touch with Montgomery was triggered by a SHAEF announcement that evening that the British forces at Normandy had sustained quite a serious setback.

Sitting up in his usual location, his ample bed, the next morning, Churchill dictated the following message to his male secretary, which was immediately dispatched:

Prime Minister to General Montgomery
27 July 1944

1) It was announced from SHAEF last night that the British had sustained "quite a serious setback." I am not aware of any facts that justify such a statement. It seems to be that only minor retirements of, say, a mile have taken place on the right wing of your recent attack, and that there is no justification for using such an expression. Naturally this has created a great deal of talk here. I should like to know exactly what the position is, in order to maintain confidence among wobblers or critics in high places.

2). For my own secret information, I should like to know whether the attacks you spoke of to me, or variants of them, are going to come off. It certainly seems very important for the British Army to strike hard and win through; otherwise there will grow comparisons between the two armies which all lead to dangerous recrimination and affect the fighting value of the Allied organization. As you know, I have the fullest confidence in you and you may count on me.

Churchill's message and a letter Eisenhower had written to Montgomery arrived at his headquarters almost simultaneously at noon on the 27th.

De Guingand brought the letter and the signal. By the time Montgomery had finished reading Churchill's message, he was furious. There had been no setbacks whatsoever. Obviously it was a SHAEF plot to do him in. Next came Eisenhower's letter. One sentence leaped out of the letter causing Montgomery grave misgivings. In dealing with what Churchill had said at the luncheon, Eisenhower wrote: "He repeated over and over again that he knew you understood the necessity for 'keeping the front aflame' while major attacks were in progress."

The little general's face was red with fury. "Look at this letter, Freddie. You already know what this signal says. Now lock the two things together."

When his chief-of-staff had finished reading, Montgomery said, "It seems to me, Freddie, that Eisenhower and his bloody lot at SHAEF have a plot on to get me removed. I'll wager my last quid on it."

"You're right, Sir. No question about it. I've just had a telephone call from my special source at 10 Downing Street. Winnie is all a'twiddly-bang about Eisenhower's allegations. Ike and Brooke have been summoned to dinner tonight to thrash the whole thing out."

Montgomery clenched his teeth. "Spineless bastards! I'll talk to Brooke now, tell him what's going on, and ask him to call me after this great dinner. Find him for me, Freddie. Probably in his London office."

After he talked to Brooke, Montgomery sat down and wrote a reply that Churchill would receive well in advance of the dinner.

General Montgomery to Prime Minister
27 July 1944

*I know of no "serious setback." Enemy has massed
great strength in area south of Caen to oppose our
advance in that quarter. Very heavy fighting took place
yesterday and the day before, and as a result the
troops of Canadian Corps were forced back 1,000
yards from the farthest positions they had reached.*

*My policy since the beginning has been to draw the
main enemy armoured strength on to my eastern flank
and to fight it there, so that our affairs on western
flank could proceed the easier. In this policy I have
succeeded; the main enemy armoured strength is now
deployed on my eastern flank, to east of the River
Odon, and my affairs in the west are proceeding the
easier the Americans are going great guns.*

*As regards my future plans. The enemy strength south of
Caen astride the Falaise road is now very great, and
greater than anywhere else on the whole Allied front. I
therefore do not intend to attack him there. Instead I am
planning to keep the enemy forces tied to that area and to
put in a very heavy blow with six divisions from Caumont
area, where the enemy is weaker. This blow will tend to
make the American progress quicker.*

As Brooke had promised, he put through an after-dinner
call to Monty, even though it was almost midnight.

"You were bang on, Monty. Eisenhower's SHAEF syco-
phants have convinced him that you're not doing the job. I
really don't think he understands what's going on in Normandy. In any event, Ike's main complaint is that Dempsey
is leaving all the fighting to the Americans on the right and
that you're not moving. He says your attacks have been failures. You haven't been able to break out at Caen. The Prime
Minister and I both drew his attention to your basic strategy: to fight hard on your left and draw Germans onto your
flank while you push with the Americans on your right. I
gave him the statistics again on the Panzer divisions facing
Dempsey—six of them."

Montgomery interrupted him, "It's five now, because an
SS Panzer division was shifted from the Odon sector against
Bradley three or four days ago."

"Well, either way, up until then there were six against

Dempsey and two against Bradley. I pointed out that Eisenhower had approved the strategy himself and that it's working: the bulk of the German armor has been kept continuously on the British front."

"And what did he say to that?"

"Monty, old boy," Brooke replied, "there was no way he could refute those arguments."

"The Prime Minister raised the allegation from SHAEF that the British had sustained, what were the words? Yes, 'quite a serious setback'."

"Yes. But Eisenhower brushed it off saying he didn't know where that had come from in his organization. He said he'd look into it."

"It's all part of the plot, Alan, the plot by Tedder, Morgan, and the rest to denigrate me and get me out of this job. They'd like nothing better than to see their boy Eisenhower take over as Land Commander while I grovel in the dirt."

"I told Eisenhower," Brooke said, "that as Supreme Commander if he had any feelings that you were not running the battle as he wished, he should tell you in no uncertain voice. I told him it was for him to order what he wanted and put all his cards on the table. The Prime Minister seconded that and also stated emphatically that he has the utmost faith in you."

A flood of bitterness and anger welled up in Montgomery. "Alan, can you believe Eisenhower's going to Churchill and complaining about me without having had enough guts to come here and look me in the eye, confront me directly. He's a coward, Alan, a devious, gutless coward."

Those were harsh words, too harsh for Brooke. "I'm not so sure Eisenhower deserves that description, Monty. It's probably that he's, as the Americans put it, too nice a guy. On top of that, he's probably afraid of you."

Alone in his darkened van in the heart of Normandy, Montgomery thought for a moment.

"Alan, my dear chap, you may well be right—and if he is afraid of me, he has bloody good reason to be."

With Eisenhower's words of encouragement fresh in mind, Bradley made the decision. The capture of Coutances meant that Cobra's objectives were met and so he would fulfill his promise to Patton. He picked up the telephone and put a call through to Third Army headquarters, Lucky Forward, at Néhou. Instead of Patton, he got his chief-of-staff, Major General Hugh Gaffey.

"Where is he, Hugh?"

"He's off inspecting the 101st Evacuation Hospital. He says you won't let him fight, so he's got to inspect the hell out of everything."

Bradley laughed. "Well, you can tell the old boy that as of now, he's got to give up his inspecting. We've taken Coutances, and Cobra is a complete success. It's time for General Patton to get in the saddle. Tell him I want him to take control of Middleton's Eighth Corps immediately. I'll tell General Middleton that General Patton will unofficially control him and his corps. Tell your general that his first objective is to take Avranches. The final thing is that General Eisenhower has approved the Third Army becoming operational at noon, 1 August."

Bradley laughed as he heard a loud whoop of joy from the usually sedate Gaffey, "Yahoo! Goddamn! Will the general ever be happy to hear this!"

Gaffey sent a young captain out to find his general. He located him at 3:30 p.m. at the headquarters gas dump and gave him the good news. The delighted Patton could scarcely believe his ears. He was finally back in the war. In the interests of the Fortitude deception, however, his presence at the head of the Third Army in France was still to be kept secret. Any war correspondent's story about Patton would still be censored. Now Lieutenant General George S. Patton Jr. was in the war in three capacities. He was the commanding general of the Third Army, but it was not yet operational; he was also the deputy commander of Bradley's Army, the First, but over it he had no control; and he had verbal control of Eighth Corps, but its actual commander was General Middleton.

But none of those constraints meant a damn thing to Patton. When the captain brought word to him at the gas dump, he had Codman drive him immediately to the operations tent. There he collected his officers.

"Gentlemen," he announced, with a smile from ear to ear, "I'm finally back in this goddamned war. We're going to get into our goddamned jeeps right now and go down to Middleton's headquarters and take charge. Before they know it, those goddamned German dogs are gonna raise on their hind legs and howl: 'Jesus Christ, it's that goddamned Third Army and that son-of-a-bitch, Patton.'

"Let's go!"

30 July 1944

KLUGE AND SPEIDEL had dined alone in the feldmarschall's suite. It was time, Kluge had decided, to talk frankly to Speidel. There was so much happening and no one other than Esch with whom to discuss the problems, let alone the solutions. Kluge had sensed that Speidel was on edge, more so with each passing day after the assassination attempt. Hofacker had just been arrested by the Gestapo. Would he be singing like a bird during interrogation? If he was, would he implicate Speidel? After all, it was perfectly clear to Kluge that his chief-of-staff had Schwarze Kapelle connections, although he had no way of knowing whether they were direct or indirect.

One thing Kluge believed was certain was that anyone who had been mentioned by Hofacker, let alone visited by him or Stülpnagel on the very day of the attempt, would be indicted by the Gestapo. Moreover Hofacker would want revenge—would feel that Kluge had abandoned both him and Stülpnagel. At the top of the list, then, would be Kluge himself.

So the feldmarschall's reality was that both he and Speidel were in the same kettle. Speidel knew that his chief was contemplating an armistice move. With Hofacker in the Gestapo cage, time was running out.

The cognac and coffee had been presented, and the steward had left.

"There is a matter of some delicacy I wish to . . . how shall I say? . . . open with you, Hans," Kluge ventured. "I must be assured of your complete confidence."

"You have that, Herr Feldmarschall."

"Yes. Well, it is the question of the contact plan you and Feldmarschall Rommel were working on."

"The armistice approach to Montgomery?"

"Exactly. It seems to me there is no choice now but to get on with it. The enemy is certain to overpower us, yet

Hitler refuses to recognize what's happening. Each day brings a new disaster not only here in Normandy but on the eastern front as well.''

Speidel observed, ''And you know that front better than anyone else.''

''Indeed. And I know all of the army commanders there. Each and every one of them served under me. I'm sure they're as concerned about Hitler's orders and his mental state as I am. Now, if we can get Montgomery to the bargaining table, what terms would you suggest we offer him?''

''Well first of all, you won't get Montgomery to the bargaining table. If you get anybody, it will be his chief-of-staff, General de Guingand. Intelligence tells us that Montgomery sends him to conferences on his behalf, even to meetings with Eisenhower, which just makes Eisenhower and his staff furious. When you do get them to the table, I don't know who will be sitting across from you, or for that matter, whether you'll even sit at a table. If this goes the way I think it will, and it will have to be done in total secrecy, you'll probably do it in a field somewhere.''

''And what about the terms, the offer?''

''I would stay with the Bargatsky letter.''

''The what?''

''The letter drafted by the lawyer, Bargatsky. He was a member of the Schwarze Kapelle. He put together the letter that Rommel was to use if Operation Valkyrie had been successful.''

''The Schwarze Kappelle. Is it finished?''

''Totally, Sir. Himmler has hunted down most of the members. Witzleben, Goerdeler, Roenne, Hofacker, Stülpnagel, and the rest. The movement is gone, destroyed.'' He shrugged, then went on: ''The Bargatsky letter covered all the details: discontinuation of the V-1s, the stopping of the bombing of German cities, the retreat of our forces intact behind the Siegfried Line—everything's in it. There will be changes necessary, but it's an excellent opening document.''

''You've seen it?'' Kluge asked.

''I have it, Herr Feldmarschall. I will bring it to you immediately.''

''No. There's no need to do that. You know what's in it. That's enough.''

''The key is to get our forces back to Germany without having to lay down their arms,'' Speidel said. ''If that can be achieved we can then reinforce our forces on the eastern front.''

''But what about Hitler? Surely the Rommel approach and the Bargatsky proposals were predicated on the success of the assassination attempt on Hitler. Would the same thing not apply now—the assassination or overthrow of Hitler would have to go hand in hand with an armistice package?''

''The only alternative would be if Hitler himself authorized the armistice negotiations''—Speidel shook his head—''and that would never happen.''

''Never say never,'' Kluge responded. ''But, you know, even as we talk, I can clearly see a precondition to the approach to Montgomery, and it involves the eastern front. Unfortunately, it will take some time to arrange. If you will help me, Hans—I cannot do this without you.''

Speidel smiled. ''We are doing this for the German people, Sir. Our duty is to the nation, above all. I will do whatever you require.''

1-4 August 1944

"IT'S FIVE minutes to 12:00, Paul. At noon my whole god-damned Third Army becomes operational. Imagine that!"

Patton's deputy chief-of-staff, Colonel Paul Harkins, said, "That calls for a little celebration, General. I have messages from all your commanders congratulating you, and I've also got a bottle of local stuff—it's supposed to be brandy. Maybe we could have a little drink to celebrate."

Patton was standing at the opening of his personal tent looking around his new command post north of the Granville-Saint Sever-Lendelin Road. "Why not, Paul? God-damn it, this is one of the best moments in my life. Sure, why not?"

Then he looked down at his dog, Willie, collapsed in a heap by the tent post, obviously exhausted. "As for you, Willie, you little bastard, you're all worn out from shacking up with that French lady dog, aren't you? And digging up that dead German this morning. Shame on you, Willie. You're a disgrace to the military service!" He laughed and reached down to give Willie a scratch behind the ear and a pat on the bum. Harkins opened the bottle of brandy and poured some into a metal canteen cup. Patton took it from him saying, "We'll have a loving cup. It's twelve noon, high noon, so here's a toast to the Third Army. We're going to pull those goddamned Germans by the nose and kick them in the ass!"

With that he took a first swig. His eyes popped and face went red as he coughed while the stream of French fire burned its way down his throat. When he was able to speak he gasped, "Jesus Christ, Paul, what the hell is that stuff?"

"The natives call it Calvados. It's apple brandy."

"The hell it is. It's goddamned rat poison. Here, it's your turn. Drink up, Paul. A toast to the Third Army." He shoved the cup at Harkins, who, grimacing and gagging, downed his portion.

"Now let's grab a bite to eat. We'll find Codman and get our asses out of here. I want to get to Avranches and see what's going on there."

Patton's tanks had entered Avranches on the 30th of July, and on the 31st the town had been secured with all its bridges intact. All roads lead to Avranches from the north and all spread out from it to the south, so Patton had ordered two army corps to pass through Avranches as quickly as possible. Unfortunately both corps, with their masses of men and tanks and vehicles, had to do it at the same time.

Two hours after drinking the toast of Calvados, Patton, Harkins, and Codman, who was driving the jeep, fought their way through massive lines of traffic into the center square of Avranches, which was jammed with a hopeless snarl of trucks.

"Jesus Christ, why doesn't somebody direct traffic!" Patton shouted as he leaped from the jeep and jumped into the abandoned umbrella-covered police box in the center of the square. The three stars at the front of his shining steel helmet blazing in the sun, arms waving, his voice shouting shrill orders, he directed traffic for at least an hour and a half until a military policeman appeared to relieve him.

When he walked back to the jeep, he was pleased with himself. "Did you see the way I got those bastards going? And did you see the expression on their faces when they saw it was Old Blood and Guts? Scared the shit out of them."

Patton's Eighth Corps went swinging west into Brittany and south toward Rennes, while his Fifteenth Corps under Haislip turned east as did Seventh Corps of the First Army, toward Mortain. The breakout, so massively orchestrated by Bradley, was becoming a breakthrough.

At Montgomery's headquarters far to the east, 1 August was not a day for celebration. Rather it was time to recognize an erosion of the general's power and authority. Bradley was now an equal as an army group commander, even though Montgomery remained, at least temporarily, as Land Commander with—as Montgomery, but not Bradley, saw it— operational control over Bradley. The American felt that Montgomery's authority would be limited primarily to the coordination and settlement of boundaries between the British and American army groups. Eisenhower was still not in the position to take over command because there was no city or town yet in Allied hands big enough to take his staff.

All along the British and Canadian fronts, fighting continued to be intense as armor and infantry clashed head-on in huge masses. Dempsey's army was striking hard against the enemy. To the west of Caen a new attack began at 6:00 a.m. on 30 July, but progress was slow owing to enemy counterattacks and the great difficulty of the country. On the Falaise road the last Canadian thrust had been halted on 25-26 July.

The British press repeatedly noted that Montgomery was still pivoting while the Americans were moving like greased lightning.

Monty's hands were shaking as he held a prestigious London newspaper printed that day, 1 August, and read the cruel editorial criticizing his inability to move his forces south against the Germans, commenting disparagingly on his leadership and calling for his early replacement.

"This is too much, Freddie, altogether too much. What they're saying is false and wrong-headed!" He rolled the newspaper up in a ball and threw it toward the door of his van.

"They say I've failed. Good God, it's *my* plan that's working, *my* plan that's turned the Americans loose to Avranches. And what are my troops to think? They're getting these bloody papers the same way I am, every day. What are they to think of their Commander-in-Chief when they read this kind of rubbish? And on top of that, there's Eisenhower and his little troop of knife-wielders and whisperers. When's he going to come here to tell me to pack it in? Well, he hasn't got the guts, Freddie. As the Americans say, he has no balls."

De Guingand stayed silent as his general raged on. "It's my plan and it's working brilliantly, but it makes me look cosmetically bad, while the people who are carrying it out, the people who want to get rid of me, are basking in the glory I've created for them."

"What would you do, Sir, if Eisenhower turned up and asked you to pack it in?" DeGuingand ventured.

Montgomery stood up, pulled on his beret, whipped off his spectacles, and stared at de Guingand. "I'd tell the incompetent, inexperienced, sniveling bastard to get stuffed!"

At his new headquarters location on the southeastern fringe of Forêt de Cerisy, Montgomery was pleased when he read the supportive letter from Churchill that Bill Williams had brought him.

"By Jove, at least the Prime Minister understands that it's *my* plan. Decent of him to send such a kind message. Yes, jolly decent."

"Do you want to send a reply now, Sir, or wait until morning?"

"No, I'll wait until morning, Bill. I'll write something for the record that will demonstrate conclusively that it's *my* plan and that *I'm* running the battle, that *I'm* telling Bradley where to send his armies and his corps. I have no choice now but to put on the record everything I can to substantiate that the credit for the plan and for the great victory that is coming is mine and not Bradley's or Patton's or that wobbler, Eisenhower."

General Sir Bernard Montgomery's message was dispatched the next morning.

General Montgomery to Prime Minister
4 August 1944

1. Thank you for your message.
2. I fancy we will now have some heavy fighting on eastern flank, and especially on that part from Villers-Bocage to Vire which faces due east. The enemy has moved considerable strength to that part from areas south and southeast of Caen.
3. I am therefore planning to launch a heavy attack with five divisions from Caen area directed toward Falaise. Am trying to get this attack launched on August 7.

The next paragraph would confirm that he was still in control over the Americans.

4. I have turned only one American corps westward into Brittany, as I feel that would be enough. The other corps of Third United States Army will be directed on Laval and Angers. The whole weight of First United States Army will be put into the swing around south flank of Second Army and directed against Domfront and Alençon.

5. *Delighted to welcome you here next week or at any time.*

Montgomery would indeed be delighted. He desperately needed the Prime Minister's face-to-face encouragement.

7 August 1944: Kluge

THE TELEPHONE call was ominous. It had been made from Berlin to Speidel from a ''friend.'' Hofacker had indeed been singing, telling the Gestapo at length about his visits at La Roche-Guyon with Rommel and then the significant one, the meeting with Kluge on the evening of the failed attempt, while at the same time protecting his friends and the real leaders of the Schwarze Kapelle. It would probably be a week before the report went to Hitler. After that it would merely be a matter of time before Hitler would demand his blood revenge.

Icy fear went to Kluge's gut when Speidel reported the call to him. He knew the Führer would be ruthless. There would be no opportunity to explain, no chance to tell him that he had repudiated Stülpnagel and the rest in the presence of Blumentritt who could verify his actions. Kluge was Hitler's man. The Führer had heaped accolades and money on him. Before the assassination attempt Hitler might have given him a hearing. But now Hitler was over the brink. No one was to be trusted. And those—even Rommel or Kluge—whose names emerged from the lips of the Schwarze Kapelle traitors would be purged regardless of guilt or innocence.

Kluge looked as though he was ready to panic. ''What am I to do? I am loyal to the Führer, Hans. You know that. I carry out all his orders, and I will continue to do so. I repudiated Stülpnagel. What more could I have done?'' Then he answered his own question. ''Yes. I could have refused to see them. I could have sent them packing. But I didn't. Now I will probably have to pay the penalty. Hitler has become a madman. Am I to follow a madman blindly, Hans? Am I? A madman who squanders the lives of German troops like a drunken loser in a gambling casino? No, this war has to be stopped.''

Speidel asked quietly, "The commanders on the eastern front, Sir?"

"Yes. I have hesitated. But now it is time to get on with it. Place the first call immediately. I am ready to talk to them. We must save Germany."

Kluge shook his head as he read the signal. It was as if the Führer had no concept whatsoever of the battle situation in Normandy notwithstanding the mountain of information that was being fed to him daily in Rastenburg. For the past ten days the litany of bad news being passed by Kluge to Jodl had been unrelenting. It had started with the massive American attack at St. Lô, which had led to the collapse of Hausser's Seventh Army on its western flank and the capture on 30 July of the highway-axis town of Avranches.

Kluge had reported to Jodl that American armored divisions were passing through Avranches. Some were heading west into the Brest Peninsula, but others were swinging east with great rapidity heading for Le Mans, thus creating a southern flank for Kluge. Their almost unimpeded movement to the east Kluge saw as the harbinger of total entrapment of his armies.

The breakthrough for the Americans in the west against Hausser's forces combined with Kluge's need to commit all his forces to the holding of the Canadians and the British in the Caen sector had put Kluge in the position of using every man and weapon he had. There were no reserves. His armies were being decimated. Only now was Hitler beginning to turn loose forces from the Fifteenth Army in the north, and from southern France, ordering them to the Normandy sector.

But with the air forces of the Anglo-Americans in total command of the skies, the question in Kluge's mind was whether those reinforcements would get there intact or get there at all. Then on 2 August, when he was pleading with Jodl for reinforcements before the whole front collapsed, Hitler had produced an order that in theory showed the light of brilliance but in reality demonstrated to the commander in the battlefield—whose tanks and vehicles and men could not move in daylight, except in bad weather that grounded the Jabos—that it was created in cuckoo land. Hitler's directive required Kluge to assemble five Panzer divisions to attack from the area of Mortain, some thirty-two kilometers to the east of Avranches, and drive straight through to

Avranches and the sea, thereby sealing off the American
divisions that had passed through that chokepoint and were
racing eastward. Hitler's plan, if successful, would see the
cutting off of their lines of supply, thereby leaving the
American forces that had been passed through Avranches
open to annihilation by Kluge's forces.

Blindly following the Führer directive, Kluge had done
his utmost to bring his Panzer forces together, assembling
them with great difficulty under the cover of darkness. Notwithstanding that his infantry and armor were not to the
strength he wanted and might have been if he had waited
three or four more days, and ever concerned about the threat
of the American armored divisions moving toward Le Mans
under his southern belly, he had decided to launch the Mortain attack—another Operation Lüttich, as Hitler called it—
at 12:01 a.m. on 7 August, without artillery support, in
order to take the enemy by surprise.

Reports on the Mortain attack had been coming in to Armee Gruppe B headquarters throughout the day, and it was
becoming clearer that all was not going well. The tanks had
not reached their initial objectives. One Panzer division under General Schwerin had not even appeared. Mortain had
been captured, but Kluge's powerful Tiger and Panther tanks
were impeded in the bocage, where they were being picked
off by the antitank weapons, artillery, and of course, the
Jabos.

Pounding the map in the war room that morning, Kluge
had said to Speidel, "Look at where those Americans are
right now! They're way over here to the east approaching
Le Mans, and here at Mortain I have all the armored forces
I have left trying to drive through to the sea to the west. I'm
in an absolute pocket, Hans, a pocket from which there is
no escape if we do not make it to Avranches and the sea."

It was in the middle of that afternoon when the second of
Hitler's directives arrived at La Roche-Guyon. As Kluge
read paragraph two it became very clear that Hitler himself
was taking charge of the battle. Obviously the Führer and
his planners at Rastenburg, totally remote from the situation, had decided that Kluge was incompetent and that *they*
were going to run the battle. It was a bitter pill to swallow,
but there would be worse to come.

The order was short in comparison with Hitler's usual
battle directives, Kluge thought:

The decision in the Battle of France depends on the success of the attack on the southern wing of Seventh Army. The unique opportunity which will never return has been proffered to the Commander-in-Chief West to drive into the extremely exposed enemy area and thereby to change the situation.
Therefore I command:

1) The attack will be prosecuted daringly and reck-lessly to the sea.

2) Regardless of the risk 11 SS Panzer Corps *with* 9th *and* 10th SS Panzer Divisions *and either* 12th SS Panzer Division *or* 21st Panzer Division *(attached) will follow the first (*116th *and* 2d Panzer, *and* 2d SS Pan-zer Divisions) and second (*1st SS Panzer Division*) waves as third wave.*

3) The rear echelons of the attack will veer north-ward in order to bring about the collapse of the Nor-mandy front by a thrust into the deep flank and rear of the enemy facing Seventh Army.

4) Incipient gains will be expanded and exploited by attacking with the adjacent infantry divisions.

5) Greatest daring, determination, and imagination must give wings to all echelons of command. Each and every man must believe in victory. Cleaning up in rear areas and in Brittany can wait until later.

Der Führer, Adolf Hitler

Kluge was incredulous.

"Jodl and his planners can't get it through their thick heads that the divisions they are ordering around aren't di-visions at all, they're bits and pieces of what's left of divi-sions. But on the planning table at Rastenburg they'll be telling Hitler that they're full strength, which is absolute nonsense."

"And 'Imagination must give wings,' " Speidel ob-served, "—the wings of the cuckoo bird. In addition to the Mortain battle there is another problem, Herr Feldmar-schall. Intelligence reports indicate that the enemy has greatly stepped up his radio traffic in the Caen area. Our front-line units can hear a great deal of tank movement."

"Another major attack, I suppose," said Kluge, disheart-ened.

"Yes, Sir. There's not much doubt about it."

"That's all I need is to have Montgomery put on a major assault at Caen. That would stop me from moving two Panzer divisions from Caen west into the Mortain attack force. My Mortain spearhead is virtually stopped, and I have the Americans—I don't know who's leading them, but he's certainly taking advantage of every tactical opportunity—pressing me at Le Mans. So I have to put some forces down there to head them off. God in heaven! And here is the Führer saying each and every man must believe in victory." He shook his head in despair.

Speidel looked around the war room to make sure no one was close enough to hear. Then he whispered, "Perhaps it's time for the armistice route, Sir. Every moment counts."

"No, Hans, I still need a few more days. I'm not sure you understand how complex this is. I have to work out every move of the chess game—through an armistice and well beyond. Whatever I do will affect the fate of Germany—and of Europe—for years to come. The future lies in my hands, so I have to have all the pieces in place."

Speidel knew he was right. But he also wondered—for a brief moment—whether some of Hitler's megalomania might have spread to Kluge.

7-8 August 1944: Montgomery

ONCE AGAIN Churchill was in Montgomery's van, now located with his entire headquarters at the southeast edge of the Forêt de Cerisy, closer to the battle action. The flight across from England had been relatively easy for the Prime Minister, the air smooth and the sky once again clear.

"Well, Monty, are things any better between you and Eisenhower? I understand he's setting up a small headquarters near Bayeux."

Monty shook his head. "I'm afraid not, Prime Minister. He avoids me like the plague. He spends a lot of time with Bradley. I get the odd signal from him. And odd is a good description. Always urging me to do this or suggesting that I move with greater speed. Impossible." He turned to the map and pointed toward Bayeux. "Yes, you're right. He's setting up a personal camp at an ideal spot near Tournières—sorry Prime Minister, I give the man too much credit. Choosing a location like that is probably beyond his capability. His staff would have to do it."

"Now, now, Monty," Churchill chided.

"Yes, yes, Prime Minister, I know. But I'm afraid that chap and what he's been trying to do to me behind my back have become a bit of an obsession."

"And you've been here in this bloody van in splendid isolation with virtually no one to talk to except Freddie for two months now."

Montgomery managed a wan smile. "Well, you come to see me once in a while, Prime Minister. Yes, a spot of leave would be a good thing. But not until this battle is finished, the Battle of Normandy—or unless Eisenhower succeeds in getting rid of me."

Churchill's jaw stuck out. "That won't happen so long as I'm Prime Minister. You can be sure of that. Now what are your plans that I should know about?"

Again the general related to the map. "It's Operation Totalize. The Canadian army, now under General Crerar, is going for Falaise again, starting tonight. Actually the attack is being led by Simonds, the man I regard as the top Canadian fighting general. Bright, innovative young man. Good leader. Jolly good leader.

"We've negotiated with Bomber Harris for a big attack of his chaps starting at 23:00 hours. Simonds wants to penetrate between the forward German strong points with columns of tanks accompanied by infantry riding in what he's calling defrocked Priests—self-propelled guns. He's had about seventy priests stripped and plating put around the sides, so that his troops can ride in them with a good measure of protection. The idea is, having penetrated some three miles, the infantry will de-bus, and attack the second belt of German defenses under cover of darkness. The bombers will saturate the defenses on either side of the corridor and seal off its flanks."

"How in heaven's name will they know where to bomb? We've had enough short bombings as it is."

"Simonds' people worked out a solution. His artillery will lay down green target-indicator shells on the targets as the bombers come in. They'll bomb on the green."

"And the tanks and the Priests? How will they keep in this column, go in the right direction in the dark?"

"The lead tanks will move on a radio directional beam. On the flanks, Bofors guns will fire bursts of tracers. And the moon should rise just before midnight. Its light will be supplemented by searchlights pointing in the right direction. Falaise is the objective and the Canadians will go straight down the road from Falaise to Argentan to meet the Yanks there.

"So that's what the Canadians are doing, Prime Minister. Now let's see what's happening over here with the Americans." He moved to the left of the map and pointed at Mortain. "Operation Lüttich that Ultra picked up in a Hitler signal to Kluge on the 2nd finally started last night. It's a Panzer operation designed to take Mortain, go on to the sea, and cut off the American forces—Georgie Patton's forces, which are now through and to the south of Avranches. I'm quite sure that Bradley can contain the Panzers. What will really do the Panzers in is this weather today. I had word just before you arrived that the recce pilots have found the first gaggle of tanks, about two hundred and fifty, out in the open near Mortain, and every Typhoon and fighter-bomber we can find is attacking them.

"And you can see, Prime Minister, what Hitler's doing is concentrating all his reserves, all his armor, over here in the west. He's actually taking some of his tanks away from the Falaise sector and putting them at Mortain, so with Georgie racing east underneath," his hand swept in an arc, "what you've got shaping up . . ."

Churchill smiled broadly, " . . . is a bloody great pocket. Put a cork in the end of it and you've got him."

"And"—Montgomery couldn't leave it alone—"who'll get credit for this? The bloody Americans!"

After the briefing and lunch with Montgomery, Churchill was driven west to Bradley's headquarters in a chateau at St. Sauveur-Lendelin. The cordial Bradley talked to the Prime Minister about the overall situation, but especially the battle at Mortain, where the fighter-bombers had been "cleaning the clocks" of the Panzers,

Churchill was uncomfortable at Bradley's command post. He could feel the great tension with the battle at its height and messages arriving for Bradley every few minutes. Sensing he was in the way, he cut his visit short to drive back to the Dakota aircraft waiting at a strip near Bayeux. He was about to get on board when, to his great surprise, Eisenhower appeared. He had just flown in from London to go to his newly organized advance headquarters.

"Being here will give me a better chance to keep an eye on things," Ike said.

"Jolly good idea, and you'll be fairly close to both headquarters," Churchill agreed. "Both Monty's and Brad's."

"That's right. About an hour's drive to either one."

"You might keep in mind, Ike, that Monty could do with a little chatting up from the Supreme Commander—at the right time, of course." His pouty lips curved into a knowing smile.

Eisenhower nodded, but he did not return the smile. If anything, his face had a hint of a grimace. "Message received and understood, Prime Minister." He intended to defer that painful meeting as long as he could.

Eisenhower saw Churchill off, then was driven to his new headquarters, left his gear there, and went straight on to Bradley's command post, where he was quickly briefed. It was shortly after 6:00, and the day's air destruction tally was coming in.

"We've got them stopped, Ike," Bradley reported, obviously pleased. "Typhoons and fighter-bombers are claiming more than 80 tanks destroyed, 56 damaged; and more than 100 trucks destroyed, and 120 damaged. The Germans have been stopped about six miles west of Mortain, and I think we're going to be able to hold them. Our artillery and antitank people have done a hell of a job and so has Leland Hobbs' Thirteenth Division." He was speaking of Major General Hobbs, whose infantry division stood between the Panzer spearhead and Avranches. By noon, Hobbs had been in difficulty and his corps commander, General Hodges, had rushed in reinforcements to stave off a cave-in. "And we're still holding Hill 317, right here. It's a thousand-foot peak that dominates the Mortain countryside, and my artillery spotters can pick off any Panzers coming in. It'll be tough to hold that hill, but right now we've still got it."

Technically Eisenhower was not the commander in the field, but he could certainly make suggestions. "Okay, Brad, what are you going to do? Put the reins on Patton and stop him where he is in case the Krauts break through to Avranches and cut it off? Or are you going to keep Georgie going? Let me tell you that the Air Transport Service has told me they can deliver up to 2,000 tons of supplies a day to Patton's troops. How many divisions have passed through Avranches now?"

"Twelve."

"Okay, ATS can keep those twelve going. So what do you think?"

Bradley replied cautiously, "It's too early, Ike. I'll have to see in the morning. I'll know by then how Hodges and Hobbs are doing and we'll take a look at the weather. If it's still good and it looks as if it will continue good, then we'll shoot the works and rush east with everything we've got."

By 9:00 the next morning, Bradley was satisfied that he could hold Mortain and let Patton go. Eisenhower was at Bradley's headquarters again.

"Okay, we'll shoot the works," Bradley told him. "I've already sent the order to Georgie. Now, Ike"—Bradley went over to the map—"I know your friend, Monty, wants to make a wide enveloping movement. He'd like to see Georgie go straight for the Seine at about Paris and at the same time drive the British and Canadian armies at Falaise and Caen straight east for the river. That's Monty's long-hook-to-the-Seine plan. But what's happening here is the opportunity for a short hook to Argentan. Patton can send Haislip up there with four divisions and cut those German bastards off from behind at Falaise. What do you think?''

''Sounds good to me. Why don't you call Monty and get his approval? After all, he's still the Land Commander. You talk to him. I'm sure as hell not going to.''

''Don't I know he's the Land Commander. He lets me know at every possible opportunity.''

In Eisenhower's presence Bradley put through the call to Montgomery, careful not to say that Ike was with him. He explained what he wanted to do. Montgomery expressed some concern about Mortain. ''But the prize is great, Brad. So I'll leave it entirely up to you. If that's what you want to do, I'll issue orders immediately requiring the whole force to conform to your plan. Then I'd like you and Dempsey to meet with me here to coordinate the plans, say, tomorrow morning at 9:00.''

''Yes, Sir.'' Bradley still insisted on calling the British general ''sir'' and of course received no objection at the other end. ''But what about Crerar, shouldn't he be in on this, too? After all, it's his army that's hammering away at Falaise, not Dempsey's.''

''Brad, my dear chap, Crerar and Simonds have just launched Totalize, the operation that's going to get them through Falaise and down to Argentan before your people get there. I can't take Crerar away from running that battle. On top of that''—Montgomery couldn't restrain himself from adding a barbed comment—''Crerar would have difficulty in understanding what was going on anyhow, if you know what I mean.''

Bradley concluded the conversation as quickly as he could, then dictated the order: ''Twelfth Army Group will attack with least practicable delay in the direction of Argentan to isolate and destroy the German forces on our front.'' Georgie Patton was ordered to ''advance on the axis Alençon-Sées to a line Sées—Carrouges prepared for further action against the enemy flank and rear in the direction of Argentan.''

Patton's Lucky Forward headquarters had just been established to the north of the newly captured Le Mans. He and a welcome visitor from Eisenhower's staff, Major General E.S. Hughes, had driven that morning to Dôle. ''It has the biggest goddamned phallic symbol in the world,'' Patton had declared as they had driven away from Lucky Forward, but Patton couldn't find the symbol at Dôle, much to his regret. They went on to see Middleton at Eighth Corps, then to Saint-Malo.

It was late in the afternoon when Patton and Hughes returned to Lucky Forward. Awaiting Patton was Bradley's signal and Bradley himself, with General Tooey Spaatz, the renowned United States Air Force general, and Air Chief Marshal Sir Arthur Tedder.

"I'll be goddamned," Patton exclaimed, delighted, when he saw his surprise visitors. He hadn't seen them since the North African campaign.

When the exchange of friendly greetings had subsided, Bradley asked, "Did you get my order to turn north?"

"Yes. It was handed to me as I got out of the jeep, but the bastard who gave it to me didn't tell me you three turkeys were here. I'd prefer to go on to the Seine and Paris, but if you want the short hook up to Argentan and Falaise, I'll be happy to oblige. I'd just love to whip the asses of every goddamned German I can find at Falaise!"

Two days later, on the 10th, Simonds' Operation Totalize came to an end with the failure to take Quesnay Wood. The Canadians had advanced fourteen kilometers in a stark straight line on 7 August, but the enemy, inferior though his forces were, had maximized the use of his high-ground positions, his 88s, and his Panzer units, and had successfully contained the Canadians. The Americans were rushing north for Argentan, but in order to take Falaise, Montgomery would have to mount yet another complex, large-scale, southward attack.

11 August 1944

KLUGE HAD many disturbing telephone calls during the afternoon of 11 August. One of them warned him that the Gestapo was almost ready to present the Führer with its comprehensive report on Hofacker's confession, Stülpnagel's murmurings, and other sources. Time was running out for the harassed feldmarschall, whose conversations with both eastern and western commanders in the field were well advanced. Now he had no alternative but to get on with his approach to Montgomery.

The feldmarschall had made a quick trip to St. Germain-en-Laye that morning. When he returned to La Roche-Guyon mid-afternoon, he ordered Speidel, "Have the communications people who are monitoring the British get me the frequency that Montgomery's staff are using for their transmissions in the clear—that is, from Montgomery's headquarters."

"I already have that, Sir."

"Where's his headquarters now?"

"He's at Le Bény-Bocage—here." Speidel went to the wall map, pointing. "We've been monitoring his radio traffic-broadcasts in the clear and the men that operate the direction finders tell us that's where he is, although we haven't been able to confirm it by aerial reconnaissance."

"I'll bet you haven't," Kluge snorted in derision. "The Luftwaffe wouldn't be able to get near that place in daylight. So if I want to make contact with him . . ."

"You should be all right in the area south of Falaise. The closer you are the better the chance of getting through."

"All right. So have you picked a good place near the front lines and Montgomery's headquarters, and a place where I can take a staff car and a radio truck and be hidden from the Jabos, and for that matter, from my own troops?"

"Yes, Sir. I have the spot. I've got it laid out on a map in my office."

In less than a minute Speidel was back in Kluge's office with a large envelope and a map, which he spread out on the ancient desk. He took a pencil from his tunic pocket to use as a pointer. The map was a large-scale one, showing in detail buildings and bridges as well as the contours of the land.

"This is the spot here, Sir, just to the west of the main Falaise–Argentan highway and slightly to the west of a village called Ronai, just here."

"Yes, I see it."

"Now just down this road that leads west out of Ronai, a dirt road, there is a large grain field—it's just been cropped and its in stubble—surrounded by trees that make it impossible to see the field from the road. In other words, when you get in there with your staff car and radio truck you won't be seen from the ground, and certainly not by the Jabos if you stay under the trees."

"You seem pretty sure about this place."

"I'm positive, Sir," Speidel smiled. "I can even tell you that the field is 1,219 meters long north and south and 305 meters east and west. The reason I know is that I sent one of my aides out yesterday—he'll never know why—to do a reconnaissance of this field and to take a good look at the surrounding area. You're approximately fifty kilometers from Montgomery's headquarters van."

"It's probably the same one he picked up from us in North Africa."

"The same one."

"So far what you've told me looks good—if I can get there without being shot up by Jabos. But assuming I get there and make contact with Montgomery or his staff, what do I propose about meeting?"

"Sir, as I see it, they're in the driver's seat. If they're prepared to meet, they'll be telling you where, how, and when. I don't see any truce being fabricated in order to exchange prisoners or anything of that kind. It's too late for that sort of thing. On the other hand, maybe that's what they'll want to do. They may propose some scheme of passing you and me through their lines . . ."

The feldmarschall shook his head. "Not you, Hans. Somebody has to run the shop and cover my tracks while I'm away from this headquarters, particularly if I'm secretly trying to negotiate an armistice. No. I would take Tangermann and perhaps Behr. Tangermann can handle the English language reasonably well, something I can't do. This stubble field and the woods, you say it's 1,219 meters long. Is the surface fairly flat and smooth?''

''It's flat but rises slightly toward the south end. It's smooth, no ditches. That's the reason I picked it, Herr Feldmarschall, it can handle any kind of machine.''

Kluge contemplated that response for a moment. ''I want to move on this immediately, Hans. Immediately. I've made all my changes to the Bargatsky letter, but I might not use it. Just the points in it. In any event, there's no time to waste.''

''In that case, Sir, you can leave immediately after an early dinner. You can be at Sepp Dietrich's headquarters at Fontaine-l'Abbé by 10:00 this evening. If you're up at 4:00 in the morning you can be in the special field by 6:00 at the latest—before the Jabos start flying in strength.''

''All right. I'll do it.''

''I have a special radio truck and crew on standby at Eberbach's headquarters waiting for my call. It will be in the field at the rendezvous point before you get there, probably by 5:00. The wireless truck will have a special radio operator and translator.''

''Who is he?''

''Hauptmann Peter Richter. Intelligence experience, studied at Oxford for three years before the war, languages. He's the officer in charge of Eberbach's headquarters communications. Very bright. Totally reliable. Eberbach rates him very highly.''

''Has he been briefed?''

''No. I'll brief him by telephone as soon as you give the order.''

''Good. I want this Hauptmann—what's his name?''

''Richter, Sir.''

''Yes, Richter. I want Richter's sworn declaration in the name of the Führer that he will not disclose any information to any person about this operation, what he sees or hears. And I want the same oath from Tangermann and my driver and any crew on the radio truck.''

Speidel ventured. ''What about me, Sir?''

''Not from you, Hans. It's not necessary. In any case, it's different. I've decided that Tangermann and the others must think I'm acting on the Führer's orders. And so, by the way, must Montgomery.''

Speidel's jaw dropped. This was a new twist. Just what was Kluge planning to do?

12 August 1944

THE DAWN mist had almost dissipated when Kluge's Horch, a virtual replica of Rommel's destroyed vehicle, drove through the woods of the designated rendezvous point to the west of Ronai and out into the smooth golden grain stubble of the field. To the east but hidden by the wall of trees, the sun was lifting above the horizon, a bright orange ball glowing through the thick dark haze of smoke and dust particles from the incessant firing of artillery and anti-aircraft guns and the bombs and rockets of the American, British, and Canadian fighter aircraft. By day they were decimating the German forces from Caen as far west as Mortain at the end of the pocket now clearly taking shape as American forces advanced northeast toward Argentan.

Kluge was concerned that they might thrust beyond Argentan to Falaise, where the encirclement of his armies would be complete. The feldmarschall had no information on who was leading the Americans in their charge to the east. But whoever he was, he was clearly a brilliant tactician.

"There they are," the feldmarschall exclaimed as he pointed south toward the woods at the far end of the field. Just inside the trees at the top of a slight rise stood a small car and a squat gray radio truck, with its canvas top down, its half-dozen aerials standing high and ready for action.

Kluge and his aide, Tangermann, were greeted by the crew: Hauptmann Richter and the driver, Schmidt, an unteroffizier and also an experienced radio operator. The crewmen then went to their stations on the deck of the open vehicle. The whirring sound indicated that the radio had already been in operation for some time.

Richter explained to Kluge, "I switched the radio on as soon as we arrived here, Sir, about a half an hour ago, and I've been listening on the main frequency Montgomery's headquarters uses, but I haven't heard anything yet. It's now

ten minutes to 6:00 our time—ten minutes to 7:00 theirs—
so we should be getting something very soon. Schmidt is
monitoring their standby frequency.'' He motioned toward
the unteroffizier, headset firmly clamped over his ears, listening intently. Richter went on: ''So if you'll pardon me,
Sir, I'll get my earphones on. Here's a set for you, I've
plugged them into my radio so that you can listen in case
we get some action, and I have a set plugged into Schmidt's
radio for Leutnant Tangermann. I've tested the microphones
and the equipment, and everything is in working order. All
we need now is for Montgomery to wake up.''

It was about ten minutes later that the first transmission
was heard. It came in clear and so loud that it startled all
four men clustered on the radio truck.

''Twenty-one Army Group to Eight Corps headquarters,
good morning, how do you read? Over.''

The reply, weaker in volume, probably because of the
greater distance, was immediate. ''Twenty-one Army
Group, this is Eight Corps, good morning, reading you five
and five, over.''

Richter translated for the feldmarschall. Tangermann and
Schmidt could handle the English themselves.

The message was a request for information. Had Brigadier Bill Williams yet departed Eight Corps headquarters to
return to Twenty-one Army Group? The answer was affirmative. Williams had departed at 06:30 hours.

Richter looked up at the feldmarschall.

''Everything's set, Sir. Shall I proceed?''

Kluge gave a curt nod. Richter spoke in English into the
microphone, his words measured and precise. ''Hello
Twenty-one Army Group, this is the mobile headquarters of
the commander of Armee Gruppe B of the German Armed
Forces. How do you read? Over.''

His Oxford accent deceived the operator at Montgomery's
headquarters, who responded, ''This is Twenty-one Army
Group. Come off it mate, whoever you are. You're putting
me on. It's probably you, Higgins, at Thirty-one Div!''

As Richter translated, Kluge smiled. Someone was in for
a shock at Twenty-one Army Group. Then Richter was
transmitting again.

''Twenty-one Army Group, this is not Higgins, and this
is not Thirty-one Div. This is the mobile headquarters of
Feldmarschall Kluge, the commander of the German forces
in Normandy. So that you will understand, I will repeat my

message in German, if you have someone there who can translate.''

From the sound of the British voice, it was clear that Richter was beginning to penetrate the disbelief. The man at the other end decided that he had to have confirmation. ''Stand by one.''

It was not one but five long minutes before the next transmission from Montgomery's headquarters. It was the voice of another man. To Richter's ear, he had a much different accent—probably Oxford or Cambridge—and was clearly an officer.

''Twenty-one Army Group to unit calling. Please repeat your message. Over.''

Richter did so with the offer to deliver it in German. He was pleased, but not surprised, when the response came in fluent German, the language in which the rest of the transmissions that morning took place.

''We need a call sign, please. Over.''

''The call sign is 'Kluge'. Feldmarschall Kluge, the Commander-in-Chief West, is standing by at his mobile headquarters and wishes to communicate with Feldmarschall Montgomery most urgently. Repeat, most urgently. I request you make arrangements forthwith. Can this be done?''

''Stand by, Kluge. I'll have to get instructions. What does your feldmarschall want to talk about?''

Kluge took the microphone from Richter. ''This is Feldmarschall Kluge speaking. Tell your commander that I wish to discuss a meeting and an armistice.''

In the compact communications van at Montgomery's headquarters, some fifty kilometers to the northwest, the officer concerned, the normally unflappable Major Peter Corby, shouted excitedly, ''Christ, he wants to talk about an armistice!'' Turning to the corporal who had received the first messages from Richter and had hurriedly found Corby, he said, ''Potts, go and find General de Guingand. He'll be in the commander's van. Chop, chop!''

Potts raced down the steps and sprinted the forty-five meters to Montgomery's van. Corby could see him knock on the door. It was immediately opened by de Guingand, who listened intently, a growing look of astonishment on his face. De Guingand then turned and disappeared from the doorway. In a few seconds Montgomery himself appeared and questioned Potts briefly. Then, with de Guingand, he strode across and up into the communications van to stand beside the seated Corby.

"What's going on, Peter?" Montgomery had to hear it directly.

Corby repeated the Kluge translation verbatim.

De Guingand asked, "Are you sure it's Kluge, or is somebody pulling your leg?"

"All I can tell you, Sir, is that the people out there are speaking to me in fluent German, and the voice that says it's Feldmarschall Kluge is the voice of an older man, I would say in the 60s range."

Montgomery turned to his chief-of-staff. "Freddie, I think we have to assume that this is Kluge. If he wants to talk about an armistice, I think we should be prepared to meet him somewhere."

"The problem, Sir," de Guingand responded, "is that you haven't any authority, you haven't any instructions from either Eisenhower or the Combined Chiefs-of-Staff. You have no authorization to conduct armistice negotiations. And Churchill, Roosevelt, and Stalin have agreed that there has to be an unconditional surrender."

Montgomery frowned. "True, Freddie, true. But I am the commander of all the land forces in Normandy, and from a military point of view I have a responsibility to respond to any legitimate overture for an armistice."

Corby sat listening intently, fascinated as always by Montgomery's high-pitched, nasally voice with its peculiar lisp. As he talked, the scrawny general with his famous two-badged beret squarely on his head looked up into de Guingand's mustached face. "There's every reason to hear what the man has to say. Corby will do the translating for us. He'll tell Kluge I'm not available, but say you're here with him. I don't want to deal directly with Kluge, certainly not at this stage." He turned to Corby. "All right, Peter, you know what to say. Let's get on with it."

Corby nodded, "Yes, Sir," and picked up the microphone.

"Hello, Kluge, this is Twenty-one Army Group, over."

Richter replied immediately. "Twenty-one Army Group, this is Kluge, go ahead."

"Kluge, the Commander-in-Chief is not available, but I have standing by his chief-of-staff, General de Guingand, who can assess the matter. I have already told him that your feld-marschall wants to talk about a meeting for an armistice.

General de Guingand is prepared to discuss the matter. He does not speak German so it will be necessary for me to translate your transmission. Please speak slowly and give me time to tell him what you've said. Understood? Over.''

It was the German commander himself who responded. ''This is Feldmarschall Kluge. I will go slowly as you suggest. Both sides must keep in mind these transmissions are not secure, and I want to be as brief as possible. On the instructions of the Führer, Adolf Hitler''—he managed to conceal the slight catch in his voice—''I wish to meet with General Montgomery as soon as possible to negotiate an armistice.'' Kluge paused to allow the translation to be made.

''Kluge. How do we know you have Hitler's authority or that he has approved of what you're going to propose? Over.''

''You must take my word.''

The reply came after a brief delay. ''Kluge, your statement is accepted. Please carry on with your proposal. Over.''

''The proposal is for an immediate cessation of hostilities here in Normandy and at the same time on the eastern front. The German forces in western Europe, all of western Europe and Scandinavia, would withdraw into Germany as quickly as possible. The same would happen on the eastern front. I have made the necessary arrangements with the generals there. As I have said, all hostilities would cease, including the bombing of German cities and the use of V-1 weapons.'' Another pause for translation.

Corby's voice again. ''Kluge. Do you mean that the German forces retreating into Germany would remain armed and take their equipment with them? Over.''

''That is correct.''

''How would a full-scale armistice be reached?''

''When the withdrawal into Germany is going on, the Führer and his staff could perhaps meet in Berne, or such other place in Switzerland that might be chosen—meet with Churchill, Roosevelt, and Stalin after his and their staffs had worked out an agreement.''

In the communications van at Twenty-first Army Group, Montgomery muttered, ''Bloody incredible. Ask him what Hitler's prepared to do personally. Is he prepared to hand over control of the government?''

Corby put the question.

''All I can say,'' Kluge came back, ''is that the Führer may be prepared to hand over the government provided that he and Eva Braun and certain members of his staff are given safe passage to a South American country of his choice.''

''Kluge. What does 'turn over the government' mean? Over.''

''It means abandon his authority to a German government that has Allied and Soviet approval. If these basic terms are acceptable, they can be put in written draft form by General Montgomery's legal staff. It would be an interim armistice document. This whole matter must be conducted in the utmost secrecy, and directly through me. If there is any breach of security both the Führer and I will deny any knowledge of the matter. Is that understood?''

Montgomery ordered, ''Tell him to stand by. I want to think about this for a minute. Well, Freddie, what do you think? Let's step outside a moment.'' He did not want Corby and Potts to overhear. Outside and out of earshot, de Guingand said, ''I think you have to take Kluge at face value, Sir. This is the first opening, the first chink in the armor. I think you have to take it seriously.''

Montgomery nodded. ''I agree, but, as you say, I don't have the authority to negotiate an armistice. No instructions whatsoever. In fact, I don't know whether the Combined Chiefs or that donkey, Eisenhower, have even thought about it.''

''Even if they had, Sir,'' de Guingand observed, ''this one is so complicated and . . .''

''And it involves the Soviets, and getting them on side will take time,'' Montgomery interrupted. ''It means that someone will have to get to Moscow and talk to Stalin. Even then the Russians are so damn slow about everything anyhow. I think it's going to take at least three days to get instructions.''

''That takes us to the 15th.''

''Yes, the 15th.'' Montgomery looked out across the fields to the east of the woods that enclosed his headquarters, saying, ''This may be the very break I've been hoping for, Freddie, for me personally, that is. All this criticism by the press and by Eisenhower and his staff. Eisenhower, that gutless bastard—every time I think of him going to lunch with Winston, trying to get me fired and not having even spoken to me about it first . . .''

His voice filled with bitterness. ''And who's getting all the kudos for my planning? Bradley and Eisenhower, and now Patton. The great and glorious Georgie, racing across

France but only because I made it possible. And what do I get? Nothing but criticism. So here is my chance, Freddie, my chance to demonstrate to the world that *I* brought this off, not the bloody Americans. They've been one-upping me left, right, and center, but if I can pull this off, it will be *my* armistice, negotiated by the Commander-in-Chief of all the land forces in Normandy. I've just got to bring this off, Freddie, not only for my own ego, but for my soldiers and England.'' The general turned to de Guingand. ''So tell Kluge that at this moment I have no authority to enter into armistice negotiations with him, but I will do my utmost to obtain that authority. My target is to be able to meet three days from now. Explain that we have to deal with Stalin. I'll meet with him on the 15th . . .''

De Guingand intervened. ''You personally, Sir?''

''If I can arrange it. Find out the exact location he's transmitting from. If he thinks it's an acceptable place for him on the 15th, then he should be there at twelve noon our time. We'll be in touch with him at that point as to how and when and where we will negotiate. When you've done that, Freddie, come to my van. As soon as you get there I'll report what's happened by telephone to the decision makers. If they get Stalin's approval and give me carte blanche, I could wrap this thing up pretty bloody quickly.''

As he turned to walk to his van, de Guingand said, ''I'll get a line cleared through to General Eisenhower.''

''Eisenhower? After what he's done to me? No bloody way. That call will go directly to the Prime Minister.''

As Feldmarschall Kluge waited for the response from Montgomery's headquarters, he said to Tangermann, ''Now you can understand why I had to have an oath of secrecy from all of you. What you have heard can never be repeated to anyone. Never.''

Like the others, Tangermann was astonished by what he had heard, particularly that Hitler had ordered the negotiations. He shook his head in disbelief. ''I really can't believe that the Führer's prepared to surrender, Sir.''

''Surrender. Never.'' Kluge was adamant. ''Negotiated peace and armistice for the sake of the German people, yes. But surrender, never. Remember also that if there's no agreement, the Führer will renounce me. He'll repudiate me, tell the world I'm a liar and a traitor. He will have my head—literally.''

Richter spoke up, alarmed at the implications for himself and Schmidt. "And what about us, Sir?"

The feldmarschall dismissed their concern with a wave of his hand. "Don't worry, Herr Hauptmann. You and Schmidt are innocents. So is Leutnant Tangermann. You are merely doing your duty. With me, the situation is quite different."

At that moment the voice from Twenty-first Army Group came through the earphones again. The response of General de Guingand was received and understood. Richter passed the coordinates of their exact location and gave a description of the woods and the field. On behalf of the feldmarschall, he acknowledged the need for time for Montgomery to get instructions. The feldmarschall would return at 11:00 hours German time, 12:00 hours Double British Summer Time, on the 15th to receive rendezvous instructions—if there was to be an armistice meeting.

Kluge had no choice but to accept the three-day delay. It was in his mind to ask if there could be a truce in that period. That would stop the Americans who were now moving east on his southern flank almost unimpeded. But he dismissed the thought. There was no chance whatsoever that Montgomery would consider stopping the battle that his land forces were so clearly winning.

When the final transmissions were over, Kluge looked up at the brightening blue sky and said to Tangermann, "Three days. My God, the speed with which the Americans are moving now—in three days, they could swing up and meet the Canadians at Falaise, come up from the south behind my forces there. What I have left of my Panzer Army and my Seventh Army would be trapped—finished. And so would any hope of an armistice. It would simply be a matter of surrender."

That morning the mobile headquarters of General de Panzertruppen Eberbach was some twenty kilometers to the west of Ronai. Hitler had placed Eberbach in command of the new attack to be mounted toward Avranches for the exact same purpose as Lüttich at Mortain: to drive through to the sea, thereby cutting off the supply lines of the American forces now moving rapidly eastward.

Hitler's order to attack had been delivered to Kluge on 9 August. Quite apart from the impossibility of carrying it out, the tone was highly critical of Kluge, accusing him of ordering the Mortain attack

too early, too weak, and in weather which was favor-
able for the enemy air force and therefore did not suc-
ceed. It must be resumed elsewhere with strong forces.
I command hereto:

> *under the command of General de Panzertruppen*
> *Eberbach, the new attack will be mounted sud-*
> *denly . . .*

It was obvious to the resentful Kluge that Hitler intended
Eberbach to be directly responsible to the Führer and not
to him. However, Kluge had no choice but to follow the
order, which went into great detail on the utilization of the
forces to be under Eberbach's command. As Kluge had seen
it, the attack could not succeed. Indeed it might never begin
because it contained instructions to wait for all the reserve
forces coming in from northern and southern France and for
weather "unfavorable for the enemy air force". Unfortunately on the 9th a massive high pressure area with cloudless, clear skies had begun to move into the Normandy area,
bringing with it perfect flying weather. According to the
meteorologists, the high-pressure area was moving slowly
eastward and might even become stationary for a few days.
Their best prediction was that there would be a change in
the weather about 20 August. The Eberbach attack would
have to wait until then. In the meantime, all available forces
would have to be directed against the thrust of the American
spearhead coming up from Le Mans toward Argentan.

Kluge had so informed the Führer early on the morning
of 10 August. Hitler was distraught about so late a date.
Who could attack the Americans at Le Mans? When? Yes,
Hitler recognized that if the Eberbach attack could not go
in before 20 August, Kluge must attack the American spearhead. Looking at his maps in Rastenburg, the Führer could
see that he was on the verge of losing his entire force in
Normandy unless some miracle occurred or unless he took
some dramatic action himself.

As Kluge's Horch began its dangerous, Jabo-interrupted trip
back to La Roche-Guyon, the Twenty-first Army Group
communications staff was patching Montgomery through by
telephone to 10 Downing Street. Churchill's principal secretary advised de Guingand that the Prime Minister was still

in bed although he was reading his mail and dictating. If de Guingand would put the general on the line, the secretary would ring through directly to the P.M.

"How are you getting on, Monty?" Churchill bellowed into the telephone. He sat in the bed propped up with the cushions behind his back, the bedcovers pulled up to his chest, his half-glasses perched on his nose, an after-breakfast cigar in his free hand, documents scattered within easy reach over the bed. "I hope you've got some good news for me for a change."

That remark nicked the sensitive general, but he had the best of all possible answers.

"I do have good news for you, Prime Minister. Hitler's made an armistice offer."

Churchill's round face showed his astonishment as he sat bolt upright in the bed. "He's what?"

"Offered an armistice, Sir, through Kluge. He contacted me by radio this morning to pass the armistice offer."

"Unconditional surrender?"

"No, Sir. An armistice with terms. Actually a preliminary armistice."

"Preliminary hell," Churchill grunted. "You know we've agreed on an unconditional surrender."

"I know that, Prime Minister. But it's my responsibility to report to you and get instructions, and there's no way I'm going to tell Kluge to bugger off when he approaches me with an offer from Hitler."

Churchill had to agree. "Quite so, Monty, quite so. So what's this offer?"

Montgomery gave him the whole proposition. Churchill listened in silence, puffing on his cigar. When Montgomery said, "That's it, Sir, that's the lot," Churchill's reaction was one of indignation. "Us, sit down with that swine, that consummate and most evil criminal, that murderer—never!"

"But Prime Minister, you won't have to sit down with him. You can tell him what *your* terms are. And one of them can be that he'll have to sit down with your representatives, not with you."

Churchill nodded into the telephone. "I understand that, my dear chap, I understand that." His mind was working over the proposal. "I suppose it's not up to me to make a decision. It's really up to the three of us to decide what to do. I'll talk to Roosevelt first, and we'll decide whether we'll even raise the matter with Stalin. I'll call the President at noon, catch him just as he's having breakfast. He's not well, you know. Not well at all. By the bye, Monty, I assume you've reported this to Ike?''

The general knew that Churchill knew that he hadn't. He just wanted to hear Monty say it.

"No bloody way, Sir. I'm the Land Commander. This is my victory, this is my armistice if it comes off, not Eisenhower's, not that strutting Georgie's. Mind you, I have nothing against Patton. He's the only good general the Americans have got. The way I see it, Prime Minister, is this: the Americans are represented in this theater by Eisenhower, the British by Montgomery. I am your appointment, and in a matter of this magnitude, I report to my political master, not to the military representative of the President.''

Churchill was amused by Montgomery's rationalization. He chuckled. "Yes, my dear Monty, I understand what you're saying. But you realize that if Roosevelt and I, quite apart from Stalin, decide that something should be done, any instructions will have to be given to you through Eisenhower, who will be most unhappy to find out that you have been dealing directly with me.''

In his captured van on the edge of the Forêt de Cerisy, with his faithful Freddie de Guingand at his right hand listening to every word, Montgomery responded, a smile on his face. "Pity, my dear Prime Minister. A pity. I hope that the great armchair general who has never fought a battle in the field but who has made judgment that I, Montgomery, am incompetent—I hope he has apoplexy when he finds out.''

Churchill chuckled again. "One final thing, Monty. In the event the decision is made to meet with Kluge in the field— and I assume there would be some considerable personal risk in this, physical risk—who would be your nominee?''

The answer was immediate. "Either myself or Freddie. Whoever it is, it must be a British general. But I would prefer to do it myself.''

Churchill was pleased. "Jolly good. As I say, I'm not sure we'll be prepared to negotiate. However, it could be said that we have an obligation to do everything in our power to bring this mindless mutual massacre of humanity to a stop, put the dogs of war back on their leashes, and be done with the carnage. Perhaps we should be prepared to put our massive egos into locked boxes and negotiate. But never would I sit down to negotiate with that Nazi swine, Hitler. Never. Eden would have to do it for me, and I don't know who would do it for Roosevelt." He took a puff of his cigar. "But we'll see, Monty, we'll see. What an interesting turn of events."

Montgomery cast a glance at de Guingand before saying, "One final word, Prime Minister. I strongly urge you to negotiate."

"As you well know, that's a political decision."

"Of course I do, Prime Minister. But you've asked for my opinion countless times before. This time I thought I'd offer it before you asked.

"You may not realize this, Prime Minister, but my great commander, Eisenhower, and his multitude of staff have never issued any orders giving me instructions as to how I and my field commanders are to cope with an offer of an armistice or of surrender. We need such an order very badly and quickly. I can put one together, but it's really their bag. The order must deal with how we handle large formations and small ones. Somebody's got to get them off their duffs, Prime Minister. It's urgent."

"That's dreadful," said Churchill. "It should have been done some time ago. I'll see to it immediately. But it's not Eisenhower's fault. It's something that should come from the Combined Chiefs-of-Staff because it involves the whole matter of unconditional surrender. But leave it with me."

In Normandy, Montgomery put down the telephone, saying to de Guingand. "My hunch is that the P.M. and Roosevelt will come up with a counterproposal and will be prepared to negotiate. I haven't any idea what Stalin will do."

De Guingand took off his flat hat, pulled out his handkerchief, and wiped the moisture off the front of its headband. "Frankly, Sir, I don't know how they can lose, how they can be prejudiced by negotiating. It will be totally secret and it will be indirect, that is, between you and Kluge. If it doesn't come off, the negotiations fail," he shrugged, "and only a handful of people will ever know that there were any negotiations."

"All right, Freddie, we should put our thinking caps on. If we get a negotiating go-ahead, how are we going to get Kluge here?"

"Here? You mean here in the van?"

"Yes, dear boy, right here. We can't afford to make a bollocks of this one, so get on with it, Freddie. You can talk to Bill Williams about this and no one else." Brigadier Edgar "Bill" Williams, an Oxford don, was Montgomery's intelligence officer. "I want a preliminary plan by tomorrow at noon."

There was a knock at the screened door of the van. "Speak of the devil," said Montgomery. "Bill. Come in."

Williams, a tall man, stooped as he entered, than stood erect to salute his chief. "Good morning, Sir."

Montgomery, now without his beret, nodded to acknowledge the salute as Williams went on: "I've just arrived back from Eighth Corps, Sir, and I have this message from General Bradley asking about the inter-army boundary line. It's set . . ."

Montgomery cut him off. "Yes, I know very well where it's set. I set it after all. It's east and west just south of Argentan at Sées."

The inter-army boundary line was set by Montgomery as commander of all the allied land forces. The area to the north of the line was allocated to the British and Canadian armies even though they had not reached that line in their drive southward. Similarly the allocation to the south was to the Americans, and in particular, Patton's Fifteenth Corps under General Haislip. The Americans had not reached Argentan, but their spearhead of two armored divisions, the second French Armored Division under General Leclerc and the American Fifth Armored Division under General Oliver, was about twenty-five kilometers to the south of Argentan and advancing steadily while encountering little resistance.

The Canadians, on the other hand, coming down from Caen toward Falaise, were meeting the usual stiff resistance. The Canadians and British "rush" was stalled, and again it would look to the British newspapers and the public that Montgomery was not able to move his forces, while Bradley and his American armies were doing it all. But if the Canadians could break through in the next few hours, they might still be able to meet the Americans at Argentan and complete the encirclement of the entire German force.

"So what does General Bradley want?" Montgomery asked.

Williams looked at the paper in his hand, then at his commander. "I don't think he wants anything except to know whether—because Patton's forces are moving north toward Argentan and are meeting little resistance—whether you're considering moving the inter-army boundary line to the north, closer to Falaise."

Montgomery got to his feet looking up at Williams. "No

bloody way. Tell him I'm not about to move that boundary line north. It's much too early. I'll move it when the tactical situation requires it."

"Yes, Sir. I'll call him and tell him."

As his intelligence staff officer was leaving the van, Montgomery turned to de Guingand. "If I change that boundary line now and the Americans come up north of Argentan and close the pocket, I'll look like a bloody laughingstock. The press will be saying there are the Americans doing it all again, while Monty's stuck at Falaise. The Americans won the war. No, that boundary line has to stay where it is for the moment. Do you agree?"

De Guingand had long since learned that when his chief had stated a conclusion, it was too late to argue the other side of the matter. De Guingand was in fact of the view that the boundary ought to have been moved north to a point immediately to the rear of the German forces holding the Canadians. But he did not say so. At that moment Montgomery wanted to hear only words that confirmed his decision, so that was what de Guingand gave him. "I think you're absolutely right, Sir."

Churchill could hear static on the transatlantic line as he held the telephone to his ear, waiting for his good friend, Franklin Delano Roosevelt, to be connected. "Hello, Winston?" Roosevelt's distinctive American voice was unmistakeable.

"Franklin, my dear fellow, good morning to you. How are you feeling?" Churchill growled, in his lisping English voice. Thus the two most famous voices in the world began a discussion that had the potential of bringing the war to a close in August 1944, with an incalculable saving in lives and weaponry and the saving of untold thousands from injury and suffering.

At the outset, the Prime Minister made it clear that Montgomery had gone directly to him rather than Eisenhower and explained why, using Montgomery's rationale in a way that Roosevelt did not find unpalatable. Furthermore, the President was aware of the "dust-up" that had occurred after the 26 July luncheon at 10 Downing Street. "Don't worry, Winston, if I was in Monty's shoes I'd probably have done the same thing. Mind you, Ike is going to be mad, goddamn mad, when he finds out. Maybe that'll even the score between them. Now, what's this armistice proposal? I'm all ears."

As Churchill recounted the offer as he understood it, Roosevelt broke in several times with comments or questions. Eventually Churchill said, "Well, that's it. Now what do you think? Are we to stick with unconditional surrender, or do you think we should negotiate?"

His question was met by another question. "Are you sure Kluge has been authorized by Hitler?"

"Who can be sure? He's probably put an intermediary between himself and Kluge so he can deny everything if it falls apart—that would be vintage Hitler. And even if it's *not* from Hitler, it's something we may still need to take very seriously."

"All right, let's assume the offer is valid. Frankly, I like the concept: stop the fighting, the German forces pull back inside the German border and we come up to it. Hitler abdicates—I guess that's a good word for it—abdicates and goes to, let's say, Argentina. As I see it, we may then have to have a joint occupation force with the Russians and a joint commission to administer the changeover to a democratic form of government."

"Democratic? Franklin, my dear fellow, you're dealing with Joseph Stalin, a Communist and a dictator. Democracy be damned, so far as he's concerned."

Roosevelt agreed. "Yes, I guess you're right, Winston. Perhaps I should've said a joint commission to supervise the eventual transition to a civilian-controlled government using the existing German constitution. Does that sound better?"

"Much better. Just so long as we don't use the word democracy. My own guess is that he'll want to partition the country so he can occupy the eastern half and we can occupy the western. He'll want a divided Germany that he can control physically—so there won't be any further phoenix."

"God knows what Stalin will want out of this deal," Roosevelt said. "I think we, the two of us, have to decide whether we think there should be negotiations. If we do, we should get our own act together, agree, and get an emissary to Stalin to ask him to join us on our terms. But the issue is, Winston, should we negotiate?" The President answered his own question. "In my opinion, I think we should. I think we've got something here. We owe it to our soldiers and our people to make an effort to stop the war."

"I share your opinion, Franklin. The unconditional surrender principle can never publicly be set aside. But privately, secretly, I think we should negotiate."

"Good. I suggest we deal with the proposal item by item and decide what we can agree on or what counterproposal we should put."

Twenty-five minutes later they had sorted out their counterproposal. Churchill, the scribe, had written down each point when they had agreed on it. Then, as a precautionary measure, he read the items back to Roosevelt.

"That's fine, Winston. Now what?"

"This matter must be dealt with in the utmost secrecy. The fewer people who know, the better. It would have a devastating effect on morale if we were to fail and word got out."

"I agree. I agree."

"Let me make this suggestion. I will write an order—and I'll do it in my own hand, Franklin, I won't give it to a secretary—I'll write an order that will by-pass the Combined Chiefs-of-Staff. There will be the original only, no copies whatsoever—except my own. I will hand the order to Ike myself. He will be instructed that there will be no copies made, with one exception. He will be given authority to make two copies in his own hand of our counteroffer, which is contained in the order. Those copies can be used as the signature documents. They could also be amended in the field on our instructions, but only on our instructions."

"Sounds good, Winston. I like it. I think the instruction to Ike is that the original order and the two handwritten copies should be destroyed—burned is the only way to do it—in the event the negotiations fail. And everyone involved should be sworn to secrecy for the usual thirty-year period."

Churchill observed, "We'll all be dead by then, anyway."

"Precisely, Winston, precisely. Now, who's going to meet Kluge face to face in the field, and how's it going to be done? The 15th you say, and this is the 12th."

"I think we have to leave it up to our military people to decide how and where they're going to meet. That should be arranged by the Land Commander," Churchill suggested.

"With the approval of the Supreme Commander, of course." Roosevelt had to protect American interests. "But who should do the negotiating for us?" An astute negotiator himself, he once again answered his own question. "I really think it should be one of my people, and I know you think it should be one of yours. But we have by far the biggest force on the beachhead. We supplied a lot of the equipment that you people are using. We're the ones who have broken out, and we're about to capture the whole goddamn German army in a bag. At least that's what it looks like now."

Churchill bit his tongue. It was not the time for a nationalistic argument. "Well, you know, Franklin, it's been Monty's plan that's been followed, and we've taken the brunt of the fighting at Caen and now Falaise, holding the German main forces there, so your people could break. Between us, Monty's been under such criticism, he needs something like this. If he could do the negotiating himself, it would polish up his reputation again and do wonders for his ego."

That brought a snort from Roosevelt. *"His* ego? Monty's? He's no different from any of my generals. They've got egos as big as all outdoors. I don't think it's a function of mine, Winston, to polish those egos when they get a little tarnished. I'm concerned about Monty, and I'm concerned about what would happen to him if he was conducting those negotiations and he failed. I'm thinking about how we would feel personally—that ego again. No, I don't think we can afford to let our Land Commander put himself at risk here. I think it should be us, as I've said, one of our people."

The Prime Minister knew he had lost the point. No sense in pushing it any further. Monty would be beside himself again. Pity.

"Pray, tell me, whom do you have in mind?" Would it be Eisenhower himself, or his chief-of-staff, Bedell Smith, or Bradley? That's who it would be, Bradley. Bradley, the soft-spoken former schoolteacher. Churchill waited. When the name came he could scarcely believe his ears.

"Georgie Patton. He's the most successful of all my generals. He's the one American general the Germans fear and respect, with good reason."

"But Franklin," Churchill protested, "he's caused trouble wherever he's been. Talks too much, hits soldiers in hospitals."

Roosevelt laughed. "Trouble? Georgie Patton? Off the battlefield, he's caused me more trouble than you can shake a stick at. But on the battlefield, there's no leader like him— in the American army," he added diplomatically. "Listen. Patton is one of the most intelligent, well-educated, articulate men in this country. He is absolutely brilliant. Sure he's got the cuss word vocabulary that would shock the hell out of a sergeant-major. But he's a man with great compassion. I bet he could negotiate Kluge's Iron Cross right off his neck. And I can tell you, Winston—when Patton presents himself in front of Kluge for the first time, that poor Prussian bastard will be overwhelmed by what he sees. Patton will have on his best shiny steel helmet, his battle-dress jacket will be flowing with ribbons, he'll have on his cavalry jodhpurs, riding boots and spurs, and his riding crop will be tucked under his arm. And on each hip will be a beautiful ivory-handled revolver.

"And Patton's tall, Winston, he's tall. Kluge won't be faced by some little sparrow general in a beret and sweater, no sir—no offense intended, Winston. It's just that when we're negotiating with those bastards, we've got to go in there tough. And I can't think of a tougher guy to send then Georgie Patton."

The voice of his friend, Winston Churchill, sounded downcast. "I hate to think of what Monty's going to say when he hears about this." In his 10 Downing Street office, the face of the Prime Minister reflected his unhappy tone.

In the White House in Washington, the President, sitting in his wheelchair, still at the breakfast table, was lighting up a cigarette in his cigarette holder. "So, Winston, if you will write the order?"

"Yes, yes, I'll do it straightaway and get back to you within the hour. One final thing, Franklin. When we've settled the matter between ourselves, what about Joe? How shall we handle him? We just can't do it by signal or message. I've been thinking we should send Eden. Stalin knows him well from the Teheran Conference. I can lay on a bomber that can fly him to Moscow. Probably get him out of here this evening. He could be at the Kremlin tomorrow."

"Good idea. Great choice." Churchill had been allowed a crumb in making his own selection. "But he won't take a copy of your order with him, will he?"

"Absolutely not. All he has to know is the proposal and our counterproposal. I'll brief him."

It took Churchill less than an hour to write the armistice instructions in his own unique prose. Roosevelt agreed to what he had written without change, admiring the concise and masterful English of the order.

Churchill's next step was to call for his foreign secretary, Anthony Eden, to come to 10 Downing Street on a most urgent basis. After a briefing by Churchill at 3:00 that afternoon, he would be flown in a Royal Canadian Air Force Lancaster bomber to Moscow. The crew had made the trip several times and were hand-picked: all were of Ukrainian descent and could speak Russian. The departure time was set for 9:00 that evening, which would give Eden sufficient time to pack and make the drive up to the Canadian air base near York.

Eden, slender and elegant, sat at Churchill's desk opposite the Prime Minister. "I've laid everything on with the Russians through their embassy here," Churchill said. "The ambassador's a bit of a clod but he's cooperative. He wanted to know the details of exactly why you're going, but I simply told him that you are taking a special confidential message from the President and myself to our good friend, Stalin, and that it was of the utmost urgency. I haven't heard back from him yet, but I assume that the head of the Russian Bear will be only too pleased to receive you."

"What are my instructions?" Eden asked. "What do I do if Stalin wants changes made, or if he won't agree at all—should I send a signal to you for instructions?"

Churchill's jowls shook as he moved his head. "No, no, Tony, there isn't time for that. Moreover, the Soviets would monitor anything that went on between us. No, you'll have to make your own decisions. Roosevelt has agreed with me on that. If you think we can live with the changes he wants, so be it."

"And if he won't agree, if he says no to an armistice, what then?"

Churchill smiled, gave Eden a knowing look, and took a puff on the omnipresent cigar.

"Persuade him, Tony, persuade him. He likes you. I could see that at the last conference. He pays attention to what you say. Wheedle, cajole, be patient. The Russian Bear likes to have its belly scratched. You won't have much time. You'll probably see Stalin for the first time tomorrow afternoon. When he's heard what you want, he'll probably have to collect the Politburo members. They'll probably take the whole of the 14th. Remember, Tony, the Russian Bear is not swift. You'll have to kick its large posterior, and very hard, very hard indeed, to get an answer out of it by noon on the 15th." Churchill smiled across the desk at him. "Now, dear boy, take this bloody masterpiece of a document into my study and memorize it. I've ordered up tea for you. Ike will be here at 4:00 for his marching orders, so I'll need the document back from you by that time."

"I'll be long gone by then," Eden promised and went into the adjoining study and shut the door. By ten minutes to four, the foreign secretary had returned the order to Churchill, said his goodbye, and gone.

At 4:00, General Eisenhower arrived. The two men greeted each other warmly. Notwithstanding their many differences—of political station as against military rank, of nationality, customs, accents—they had become good friends over the months since Eisenhower had been designated to fill the American-allocated post of Supreme Commander. Churchill had found the amiable Kansan to be "a most agreeable chap", while Ike, as Churchill called him, found the Prime Minister "a really great guy".

It was tea time, tea for Churchill and black coffee for Eisenhower, served in front of the unlit fireplace, where the two men sat in comfortable high-backed, stuffed chairs. When the pleasantries were out of the way, Churchill told Ike about the telephone call that morning from Montgomery. Ike bristled when he heard that Montgomery had bypassed him but accepted the Prime Minister's conciliatory explanation. "I guess that evens the score between Monty and me," Ike ventured hopefully.

"I wouldn't be too sure, Ike, I wouldn't be too sure. If the truth be known, I don't think Monty will ever forgive you for trying to get him sacked. He's simply not the forgive-and-forget type. If I may venture a word of caution, I think you'll have to keep that in mind in all your future dealings with him, especially when you have to take over from him as Land Commander."

Eisenhower nodded. "He reminds me of a cocky little bantam rooster, the kind we used to have out on the farm in Kansas. He acts like one and he looks like one. And if I'm going to enter his barnyard, I've already learned that I'm going to have to watch my ass."

Churchill's mouth twisted in a grin. "Both cheeks, dear boy, both cheeks."

He stood up, walked to his desk, picked up his handwritten armistice order, and brought it back to Eisenhower. "This is how the President and I have decided to handle the offer. Read it while I go to the toilet." As he headed for the door he was already pulling down the zipper on the front of his siren suit, the comfortable, one-piece jumper he had become fond of wearing. "Too much brandy last night," he muttered as he left the room.

Eisenhower had read the document by the time Churchill returned, but was busy reading the Churchill-Roosevelt counteroffer and the instructions for negotiations. He looked up at the Prime Minister, saying, "I think the counterproposal will work. I think Hitler will buy it. Really there are just three or four variations."

Churchill agreed. "Yes, although the one where we require Hitler to meet in Switzerland not with us but with my foreign secretary of state will disturb his ego."

Ike added, "And the one about laying down their arms in Normandy and on the eastern front rather than being able to take them back into Germany—he may balk at that. But designating Georgie Patton to do the negotiating with Kluge"—a broad grin crossed his face—"that's a stroke of genius. Kluge will be simply dazzled.''

"If not dumbfounded," the Prime Minister added. He went on to inform Eisenhower about Eden's mission. "What happens there will be crucial, because if Stalin won't go along with this, then we cannot consider a separate armistice in the West. And there's always the possibility that Hitler will change his mind—or that we're not dealing with Hitler at all."

"What authority will Georgie have to make amendments in the field?"

"Well, he can agree to things in principle, but he should then radio to you at Montgomery's headquarters."

"Yes, that's in the order."

"And you, in consultation with Montgomery and Bradley, can make a judgment as to whether or not the change is acceptable. If the three of you cannot agree unanimously, then you'll have to come to the President and me. We'll clear all the telephone lines."

Eisenhower nodded. "Sounds good to me, Sir."

Churchill threw himself back in the chair. "Oh for God's sake, Ike, please call me Winston or Winnie. This continuing formality when we're in private just isn't on."

The general was embarrassed. "I appreciate what you're saying, but I'm just not trained that way. Perhaps some day when the war is over, and I'm out of this uniform."

Churchill added mischievously, "And you're the President of the United States."

"Good grief. Me a politician? Not on your life. By the way, what about Monty, does he know about this order or about Patton's being involved?"

"No, he doesn't," the Prime Minister rolled his eyes upwards. "I wouldn't want to be in his presence when he finds out. I don't propose to talk to him, Ike. It's up to you to deal with him. You're his superior."

"Thanks a bunch, Prime Minister. Yeah, thanks a bunch. Okay, I'll take it to Monty myself. I'm going back over this evening. I guess we'll have to work out a plan for getting Patton and Kluge together."

Eisenhower's brow was furrowed. "I'll send Monty a signal to have Patton and Bradley join us on the evening of the 14th and be prepared to stay through the 15th. Through my own backchannel, I'll tell Patton to travel in his L5."

Churchill reached inside his siren suit for a new cigar.

"In God's name, what is an L5?"

"It's called a Bird Dog. It's a light aircraft made by Beech in the States, a two-seater tail-dragger used for artillery spotting, things of that kind. Georgie has two of them with his headquarters. He used the L5s to jump around to see his division commanders. A hell of an idea. When his generals are way out in front, miles from Lucky Forward, and they see this funny little airplane appear, they goddamn nearly die because they know the old man's going to get out of that airplane, all six-foot-two of him, all blood and guts, and give them what's for. I'll make sure he gets to Monty's headquarters in one of his little L5s. Otherwise he'd have to drive all the way from Le Mans back to Avranches and then around almost to Falaise—a hell of a long trip."

Churchill's highly inventive mind was at work. "And on top of that, you're thinking that the little airplane would be the way to get Patton across the lines to meet Kluge. Correct?"

Eisenhower was startled by Churchill's perspicacity. "Right, Sir."

"Good thinking. And I suppose you're going to tell me that Patton is also a pilot."

Ike laughed. "As a matter of fact that's exactly what I'm going to tell you. Georgie is a qualified light aircraft pilot. In fact, back in 1940 he owned his own airplane. I don't know what the damn thing was. But, as you know, he's a very wealthy man and can afford things like horses and airplanes. Anyway, he is a pilot. There are few people in the world who know that, but it's a fact."

"And I'll wager he flies that little Bird Dog every chance he gets."

Eisenhower admitted, "They tell me he never sits in the

front seat. That's where his pilot sits. But he's got a stick
in the back seat. The word is he can fly like a bird.''

"A turkey probably. Well now, my dear Ike, you seem to
have everything in hand. Pray let me know on the 15th if
there's any change of timing so that the President and I can
be standing by."

"I'll do that, Sir."

It was shortly after 8:00 on the evening of 12 August when
de Guingand handed to his chief, General Sir Bernard
Montgomery, the warning message from Eisenhower advising that the Supreme Commander would arrive at the headquarters of Twenty-first Army Group at 17:30 hours on 14
August, for a one-hour visit, with Bradley and Patton to
arrive not later than 18:00 hours.

Montgomery was upset because he had not heard back
from Churchill about the armistice proposal. Surely the
Prime Minister would have the graciousness and common
sense to call his senior commander to tell him what had
transpired and what the plan of action was going to be. The
general had been on tenterhooks as the day wore on. Once
again his pride was suffering.

For Montgomery, the SHAEF signal from Eisenhower
was evidence that he, Montgomery, and the British had been
sold out again. Eisenhower and Bradley were going to run
the whole show. He didn't need them. He could do this by
himself. And on top of that he was the Land Commander.
It was his responsibility, not Eisenhower's. And Patton—
what in hell was Patton going to be doing in this? Patton
was just an army commander. He could see Bradley's involvement, but if Patton, why not also Dempsey, his own
army commander? Something was fishy, very fishy. And
Montgomery was very angry.

When he read the Eisenhower signal, Montgomery
stormed up and down the confines of his van, his high,
lisping voice loud with fury. "Goddamn it, Freddie. Here
I give the Prime Minister a chance of a bloody lifetime to
make the British army look like heroes instead of lapdogs
to those glory-seeking Americans. And what does he do?
He just throws it away. Look at this! They're sending Eisenhower here—Eisenhower to conduct the armistice negotiations. I tell you, Freddie, I won't have it. I'm the one
who's going to run these armistice negotiations, not Eisen-

hower. I brought the Hun to his knees here. This is going to be my bloody show and not the Americans!''

In the middle of this tirade, Brigadier Bill Williams entered the general's van, another signal in his hand. When Montgomery saw him, he stopped, saying with sarcasm in his voice, ''Well, Bill, what other bloody awful news have you got for me?'' Without a word Williams handed him the signal. It was from Bradley's headquarters, informing him that Leclerc's Second French Armored Division, part of General Haislip's Second Fifteenth Corps under Patton, had crossed the east-west road at Argentan and had started up the highway toward Falaise.

The meaning was clear. Patton's forces had crossed his inter-army boundary line just south of Argentan without his, Montgomery's permission. If they were allowed to continue north toward Falaise, come up behind the Germans defending against the Canadians, Patton would effectively seal off and entrap Kluge's entire force. Patton and the Americans would, once again, claim all the credit while he, Montgomery, would be an ignominious spectator at the event he, himself, had created. And the golden opportunity to end the war on all fronts, the opportunity that he had engineered through his masterful conduct of the entire Normandy campaign—that too would be lost.

He would tolerate neither of these affronts. He handed the signal to de Guingand, saying through clenched teeth, ''Tell Bradley to get back.''

De Guingand began to protest. ''But, Sir, the signal says that Leclerc and Oliver have had little opposition. They've already been in touch with the Canadians . . .''

''I don't give a damn what the signal says, tell Bradley to tell Patton to get back to the inter-army boundary. Is that clear?''

''Yes, Sir.''

It was this order that created the Falaise Gap through which the bulk of the German army was to escape during the next seven days. It was not until the 16th that Montgomery would give the order to close it.

Patton was asleep in his tent at his Lucky Forward headquarters near Le Mans with his bulldog, Willie, curled up on the floor beside him when the ''get back'' order from Montgomery arrived through Bradley's headquarters. It was Codman who woke up his general—and Willie.

Patton was fully dressed except for his boots and his battle-dress jacket. He reached for his steel-rimmed glasses, and smoothing his short white hair, demanded, "Goddamn it, Charles, what the hell are you doing waking me up? It had better be important."

"It is, Sir. I have a signal from General Bradley."

"Well go on, read it to me."

Codman turned up the low-burning kerosene lamp, and holding the signal close to it for light, read:

French 2nd Armored division and 5th Armored Division are ordered back south of the inter-army boundary line at Sées-Argentan and are not authorized to cross it until further orders received.
SIGNED COMMANDER 12TH U.S. ARMY GROUP.

Patton jumped to his feet, shouting, "Jesus Christ! How stupid can those bastards be? We're well north of Argentan. Leclerc and Oliver are in radio contact with the Canadians. We're right behind the Germans defending Falaise. We've got the whole German army trapped and some stupid son-of-a-bitch is telling us to get back!"

"But, Sir," Codman protested, "it's General Bradley's order."

"If it was Bradley, he should have consulted me first. I don't give a shit who gave the order, it's the craziest thing I ever heard of. You know what this means, Codman? The Canadians aren't able to move south, the Germans have them stopped at Falaise. We're sitting at Argentan, so there's a fifteen-mile gap. Fifteen miles, Codman! Every German in that trap is going to be able to get out. He's going to get his tanks out, his trucks, his guns, everything. And we're just going to be sitting there watching them."

"The air force," Codman ventured, "the air force will take care of them."

Patton was putting on his boots. Willie was barking and wagging his tail in the middle of the shouting.

"Bullshit. Sure the air force will get some of them, some of the tanks, some of the men. But it's only the army, Codman, my tanks, the infantry, and the guns, who can destroy the German army. A fifteen-mile gap, Codman! Jesus Christ!" Captain Codman helped him into his battle-dress jacket. "You go on ahead to the operations tent. I'll be there in a minute. Patch me through to General Bradley. I don't care what the hell he's doing, I want him on the line.''

Five minutes later, with at least a dozen members of his staff within hearing distance, General Patton opened a fusillade at his commanding general.

"Omar, for Christ's sake, what's going on? What's this goddamn order telling me that Leclerc and Oliver have to get back to the inter-army boundary line? Christ, Omar, we have no resistance. The German force is still milling around in the Mortain area. We can go right up the assholes of the Germans defending Falaise. We can trap the whole German army. I mean, goddamn it, Omar, this is the stupidest order I've ever seen!''

Bradley's calm voice came back down the line. "Take it easy, Georgie. Take it easy. Sure, on the face of it my order looks stupid. When you assess the situation, it might not be so stupid, after all. I mean the possibility of Canadians shooting at Americans and that sort of thing. Best to keep the two sides well apart.'' Bradley was not about to attribute the order to Montgomery, knowing that Patton's reaction might be violent. He could envisage Patton arriving at Montgomery's headquarters in his airplane and punching Montgomery in the teeth. So far as Georgie was concerned, Bradley thought, best to lead him to believe that it was his order and that he and Montgomery had not consulted.

Patton was not to be deterred.

"Look Omar, there's no way my armor is going to get close enough to the Canadians to fire at them or vice versa. On top of that, we'll be talking to them. Your line of reasoning is, to say the least, specious. Got that, Omar, it's specious. Sure I know the inter-army boundary line is set by Montgomery, but that little twat can move it. All you have to do is ask him.''

"I asked him earlier in the day, and I got a negative. He expects the Canadians to break through in Falaise and at any moment to rush down the road to Argentan to meet us.''

"But, goddamn it, Omar, the situation's changed. We're already approaching Falaise.''

"I'm sorry, Georgie, that's the order, and I expect it to be followed.''

Despite the fact that Bradley was much junior to him in service, and, indeed, had been his junior in the Sicily campaign, Patton was a great disciplinarian, not only with his men but also with himself.

His response was a dejected, "Yes, Sir."

He put the phone down. The staff in the operations tent were all intent on their business, trying to avoid the old man's eyes. He looked at Codman. "Find Borders for me and tell him to get his ass over here right away!"

Five minutes later, the bleary-eyed Colonel Bill Borders, one of the general's operations officers, presented himself to Patton in full combat gear.

"Bill, boy, I want you to find General Haislip, and I don't give a damn where he is, you've gotta find him. You will give him my verbal order that he is to get back south of the inter-army boundary line, south of Argentan. That means Leclerc and Oliver both have to get their tanks and men back immediately. Tell him the order didn't come from me, it came from higher headquarters. You can also tell him that I'll bet my bottom dollar it wasn't Bradley who originated the order. It was that little prick, Montgomery. Tell him I'll confirm the order in writing in the morning, at dawn, with an airdrop from my L5."

When Borders found Haislip at his command post near Boucé at dawn, Haislip had his shirt off and was shaving, getting ready for breakfast and the day's assault on the Germans.

"What the hell are you doing here, Bill?"

"An order for you from General Patton. He knows damn well you won't like it. But I have to pass it on to you anyway. What I've got to tell you will be confirmed by airdrop as soon as a Bird Dog can get here."

"So what's the bad news?" Haislip asked as he toweled his face.

"The order is to stop any further movement north, withdraw Leclerc and Oliver's divisions south of the inter-army boundary line at Sées. That's it."

Haislip's face had a look of total disbelief. "What! You've gotta be kidding!" He had his shirt on only partway buttoned. It stayed that way. "Goddamn it, yesterday afternoon Patton ordered me to capture Argentan and push on slowly in the direction of Falaise until I contacted our Allies. Now he's reversed himself."

"Sorry, General, but that's the way it is. The order came from higher headquarters, so there's nothing General Patton can do about it except bitch."

General Haislip was almost shouting. "Look, I can consolidate my position by midafternoon. I can be right up against the Germans' asses at Falaise. They've got their guns dug in, everything they've got is dug in, and it's facing *north*. Do you understand that? North and we're attacking from the south, the south, goddamn it. We've already been in contact with the Canadians, and they're expecting us. We can turn this whole goddamn war around today, Bill, today and there's nothing to stop us.''

He undid his trousers, tucked the shirt in, and started to do up the buttons while he talked. ''No. I will not do it. I'll stand at court-martial and be vindicated. Stopping us now is a criminal act. The person who gave the order should be court-martialed. Jesus Christ!''

He put his steel helmet on and put his arm around Borders' shoulders. ''Bill, it isn't your fault. Come on. Let's get some breakfast.'' The food seemed to pacify him. By the time the meal was finished, he had calmed down and resigned himself to obeying orders.

As Borders stood up to leave, Patton's little Bird Dog aircraft flew overhead. He watched as a small canister trailing a long, red cloth tail like a kite fell from the plane hitting the ground just a meter away from the mess tent.

Borders turned and walked away as the general was opening the canister. Borders had decided that he just couldn't stand to see a grown man cry.

Patton was completely baffled by the rationale behind the order to halt and get back. Looking for excuses, he accepted information from an intelligence officer at Bradley's headquarters who had told him that the British had sowed the area between Argentan and Falaise with a large number of time bombs, which was not true. Totally frustrated and rightly suspicious of Montgomery, he wrote in his diary: ''I believe that the order . . . emanated from the 21st Army Group, and was either due to (British) jealousy of the Americans or to utter ignorance of the situation or to a combination of the two.''

On 13 August, the first trickle of German withdrawal began through the Falaise Gap. It was to turn into a flood.

14 August 1944

"I DON'T know whether I have the strength to go on. I really don't, Hans." Speidel thought the feldmarschall looked terrible. There were bags under his eyes. His skin was ashen, his hands shook. He was physically and mentally exhausted.

Kluge had just returned to La Roche-Guyon from a conference at his St. Germain-en-Laye headquarters to discuss the defense at Paris. He had met with the Commander-in-Chief of western naval forces, the officer commanding the Air Fleet 3, the new military governor in France, Air General Kitzinger, and the newly appointed commandant of greater Paris, General von Choltitz. After long wrangling and discussion, prompted by the distasteful order from Hitler that the sixty-eight bridges of the Seine were to be blown up, as well as any monuments or buildings that might have military importance to the enemy, the conference had finally agreed on the order of retreat for the armed forces and the method of handling the bridges.

While that meeting was going on, Kluge found his mind wandering away from the Parisian problems to the calamities that were going on in the battlefield. God in heaven, what was he doing in Paris when he should be at La Roche-Guyon, if not at the front? And then there was tomorrow. Would Montgomery be prepared to negotiate? What had Churchill and Roosevelt done with his offer?

Kluge was satisfied that at least he had all his ducks in a row. His myriad telephone discussions with the commanders both in the East and the West had brought them to his camp. All SS units expected to be loyal to the Führer had been ordered into full engagement on all front lines so they would be unable to turn their backs on the enemy in order to attack the Wehrmacht. The plans for the seizure of power inside Germany were complete. His mind went over and over the arrangements as the conference droned on.

The battle in Normandy had turned into an absolute

shambles with confusion everywhere. Still there was no order from Hitler that even hinted at withdrawal, even though the Americans were sitting at Argentan, and the Canadians were hammering to break through at Falaise.

Things were so bad that Dietrich had put into words what Kluge and Speidel and the generals in the field had been thinking. In a telephone conversation the day before he had told Speidel that it was high time to begin an escape while the resupply of fuel and ammunition was still possible and before Allied artillery converging its fire from all four winds began peppering every part of the closing trap. But without orders, and pending the completion of the armistice negotiations, Kluge had no choice but to instruct Dietrich, Eberbach, and Hausser—the Fifth Panzer Army and the Seventh Army—to stay and fight as Hitler required.

Kluge had reported starkly to Jodl the evening before on the state of the battle and the prospects. "The enemy seeks with all his power to encompass the encirclement of the bulk of the Fifth Panzer Army and Seventh Army. That encirclement is imminent." He had not asked for a general withdrawal through the gap, merely that the Seventh Army should pull back from the western end of the pocket to Flers, some forty kilometers west of the Falaise-Argentan gap line.

About 6:15 that morning, the 14th, Speidel had awakened his chief with a signal from the Führer himself. It authorized the move west to Flers, but the opening words of the signal were extremely disturbing to Kluge. As he read them his face showed no outward sign, but inwardly he was seething.

The present situation in the rear army group is the result of the ill-planned and miscarried first attack on Avranches. Now that the enemy has turned sharply west, there is danger that Panzer Gruppe Eberbach, *which was committed much too far north, will again be involved in an inconclusive frontal conflict.*

The blame for the failure of Lüttich at Mortain and Avranches was now being placed totally on Kluge's shoulders by the Führer—completely unjustified blame on a man who had served his Führer well. The order instructed him to attack the Americans in the Alençon area to the south of Argentan. He struggled to read on to the end:

Therefore the general mission for the next few days in
OB West *territory is:*

Destruction of the enemy near Alençon.
Defense of the coast in the sector of Nineteenth Army
against the coming landings.

Hitler anticipated the landings in southern France. Still
groggy with sleep, Kluge had told Speidel, "Impossible,
Hans, impossible. There is no way that we can cut off the
American spearhead by attacking at Alençon. We just
haven't got the strength. But this is a Führer Order. Advise
Eberbach and Hausser they are to meet me—I don't want
them to travel far—at Nécy, a little village just south of
Falaise that I drove through yesterday. It sits high on a hill.
The church there, at 10:00 tomorrow morning. After the
Paris conference today, I'll come back here, change, then
go on to Dietrich's headquarters at Fontaine-l'Abbé. Arrange for the radio truck and crew to accompany me. I can
have a good sleep there and get an early start in the morning."

"Yes, Herr Feldmarschall," Speidel had replied. "I assume Tangermann is to go with you, and I suggest you take
Major Behr as well. His English is excellent and you might
need a translating backup if something happens to Richter."
The suggestion was accepted.

During the Paris conference, Kluge's mind also kept going back to the Führer Order, working over the injustice and
inequity that Hitler was dumping on him, thinking about the
report that came at noon that the Canadians had just
launched a massive assault toward Falaise, led off by heavy
smoke screens and hundreds of tanks. It was apparent to
Kluge that if this time Montgomery and the Canadians were
successful and breached his lines of antitank 88s, they would
break out down the road to Argentan and, with the Americans, seal off his forces in Normandy. That would be the
end of the Battle of Normandy and the end of hope of any
armistice negotiations. God in heaven, would this conference never end?

Finally, in exasperation, Kluge declared when the meeting resumed at 1:30, "Gentlemen, I must leave this conference at 2:30 at the outside. The Canadians are attacking in
strength toward Falaise at this very moment and may well
break through. I must return to my headquarters to super-

vise the battle. Furthermore, I have explicit orders from the Führer that require me to be at the battlefront early in the morning, which means I must leave for Normandy this evening. Now can we get on with this, please?''

When the last item had been decided shortly before 2:30, Kluge departed for La Roche-Guyon. On his arrival, Speidel reported that all the arrangements had been made, only to hear Kluge admit that he was exhausted. For the first time, Speidel had a feeling of sympathy for the man. Kluge had kept him, and indeed the rest of the staff, at arm's length during his brief tenure as commander of Armee Gruppe B. He had been haughty and distant, sometimes almost impossible to communicate with. Speidel simply could not gain his trust as he had with Rommel. Kluge had even been close-mouthed about what had happened during the opening contact with Montgomery's headquarters on the 12th.

''Would it help, Sir,'' Speidel asked, ''if I came with you on this trip?''

He was surprised at Kluge's reaction. It was almost violent. ''No, no, for God's sake, Hans, it's much too dangerous, and on top of that you must be here to keep the headquarters running. No, I have to do this alone.''

Shortly after 7:00 p.m., Feldmarschall Kluge and his party left La Roche-Guyon in his Horch, preceded by two motorcycle outriders and followed by the radio truck manned by a crew of four. By 10:30 they were at Dietrich's headquarters at the castle of Fontaine-l'Abbé near Bernay where the worn-out feldmarschall went straight to bed, leaving instructions to be wakened at 5:45 a.m. for departure at 6:30.

As he lay in bed that night, Kluge turned over in his mind exactly what the Gestapo would have extracted from Hofacker, Goerdeler, and the rest.

What Kluge suspected had indeed taken place that very day, 14 August. The Gestapo report that Germany's top feldmarschalls had been involved in the 20th of July assassination plot had been given to Hitler by the SS chief, Heinrich Himmler, himself. The report was, ''West. Kluge-Rommel.''

The time remaining for Kluge to achieve his plan could now be numbered in hours.

''Well, Simonds,'' Montgomery asked, ''you're satisfied that Operation Tractable is ready to go?''

The tall, dark-haired Canadian lieutenant-general, his chiseled, handsome face freshly shaven except for his black mustache, was with Montgomery in the latter's van. Guy Simonds looked at his watch. It was 6:30 a.m. He had come over at Montgomery's instructions to brief the commander of Twenty-first Army Group on how the critically important attack would be conducted. It would be a Canadian show all the way. The one thing different about Tractable was that instead of going in at dawn or at dusk, or at night, for that matter, the attack would be launched at midday.

"Yes, Sir, we're ready and we're going to smash every German line until we break through. It's Falaise first, then down the road to Argentan."

Simonds outlined his plan, which was to Montgomery's satisfaction. After all, Montgomery regarded Simonds as being by far the most able of the Canadian generals. Battle-seasoned and clever, he was Monty's sort of chap.

"Good show," said Monty finally. "We simply have to do it this time. This is our chance to close the Falaise-Argentan gap and show the Americans how to fight a *real* battle. Guy, a very great deal depends upon your success today. The casualties will be high, but good luck and God bless."

The attack went in as planned, the artillery beginning to fire their marker shells at 11:37 hours and laying down a tremendous smoke screen at 11:55. By 11:40 medium bombers were bombing enemy positions. At 11:42 wireless silence was broken by the command, "Move now!", and the Canadian armored brigades began to roll toward the start line in solid phalanxes some seventy meters square. The smoke screens were now augmented by massive clouds of dust mixed in with the smoke. The tank commanders could not see ahead, but they were able to fix on the sun, which showed through the thick haze like a great red ball.

Driving blindly they penetrated farther and farther south, closely followed by the infantry. But even with the thick, dust-laden smoke, the Germans were still able to destroy scores of Canadian tanks. The German gunners knew which way they were coming and could hear them. They simply kept blasting away with their 88s in the direction of the clanking roar of the tanks.

At 14:00 hours heavy bombers arrived overhead. Some 870 of them unloaded their bombs on the assigned targets.

But unfortunately for the Canadians, a series of errors resulted in a short bombing in which 65 Canadian troops were killed and some 300 were wounded or went missing. By dusk the leading troops of the Canadian Third Division went barely four-and-a half kilometers from Falaise but were still meeting heavy antitank fire.

By nightfall, Operation Tractable, which came to be known as the "Mad Charge", was still being pressed by Simonds' forces, but the Canadians were short of Falaise and the vital high ground that dominated the Germans' escape gap. Once again, with tremendous losses on both sides, the German forces had held the Canadians from a breakthrough. There would be no "rushing down the road to Argentan". There would be no surrender or entrapment of Kluge's forces to the west of the gap.

And, once again, it had been the Canadians who had carried the brunt of the British fighting.

"Goddamn it, Codman, what's this all about, this signal from Montgomery that I'm to report to his headquarters not later than 18:00 hours?"

"I haven't any idea, Sir. All I have is a signal that says you're to be there for twenty-four hours—until 18:00 hours tomorrow."

Patton raised both arms, fists clenched, above his head. "Good God A'mighty, how can any sane human being spend twenty-four hours at Montgomery's headquarters?" He lowered his hands to rest them on the ivory-handled revolvers on his hips. "And you know what, Codman? It's that little British bastard who's keeping the secrecy lid on me, sure as I'm standing here. I've been leading the Third Army, beating the shit out of the Nazis since before August 1st, traveling farther and faster than any army in history. The American and British press are filled with the advances of the American army, but they don't know who the hell the commander is. And it's me, goddamn it, and it's about time the world knew about it. As I told Bea when I wrote to her yesterday, 'When I've actually emerged from obscurity, it will be quite an explosion. I've stolen the show so far, the press is very mad they can't write it.' "

Patton whacked his trouser leg with his riding crop. "Well, I'm not going to fight this whole war with no recognition—with the American people not even knowing I'm here!'' He shook his white-haired head in disgust. ''I was up in the middle of the night working on a plan.''

Codman commented, ''So what else is new, Sir?''

''I've decided that I can't just let Haislip and his people sit on their ass at Argentan, waiting for Montgomery to give us permission to close the gap. I'll never understand why that little bastard ordered me to get back.''

''We don't really know it was Montgomery who gave the order, Sir. General Bradley hasn't said that it was Montgomery.''

''Don't give me any of that bullshit, Charles. It was Montgomery! History will prove I'm right someday. Anyway, the first thing you and I are going to do this morning is to strap those two little Bird Dogs on our asses and fly up to see Haislip. I'm going to tell him he's got to hold the shoulder there at Argentan with two divisions and be prepared to drive north if the insufferable Montgomery finally allows him to drive north to Falaise. I'm going to tell Haislip he's doing a hell of a job. Then we'll go on to General Bradley's headquarters so I can sell him my new plan. So have Jones and Lipson get their toy airplanes ready right away.''

''Will do, Sir,'' Codman acknowledged. ''About going to Montgomery's headquarters, you should know that General Smith—''Eisenhower's chief-of-staff, General Walter Bedell Smith—''called this morning before you were out of the pit. He suggests that you fly to Monty's headquarters rather than drive, and that you take both the L5s. He said it's really General Eisenhower's suggestion.''

''Suggestion?'' Patton's eyebrows shot up. ''Suggestion be damned. When Beetle Smith calls, that's an order, boy, an order. Now why in hell are we going to be there for a full twenty-four hours?'' Patton was perplexed.

''I guess I'll find out soon enough.''

Patton's L5, followed by Codman's, jolted down onto the rough surface of the stubbled field at Bradley's headquarters shortly after 11:00 hours. The visit to Haislip had gone well. While the younger general had been frustrated beyond belief by the previous day's ''get back'' order, he'd worked it out of his system.

''Haislip's all hepped up. He's hot to trot,'' Patton was pleased to tell Bradley, as they sipped coffee in the latter's van.

"Good. Now Georgie, what's on your mind—I know you've got something you want to sell me."

"Sell you!" Patton put on an expression of mock astonishment. "You know I never try to *sell* anything."

They both laughed.

"Okay, Omar," Patton's high-pitched voice urged, "I've got to get my army moving. I just can't sit on my ass at Argentan and watch the Jerries move out. I want you to give me permission to take two of my four divisions under Haislip at Argentan and let them go east on Dreux. I'd like to point Twentieth Corps at Chartres and Twelfth Corps at Orleans." With his reading glasses on, Patton pointed at the map spread out on the table in the van as he talked.

Bradley nodded. "It sounds okay to me, Georgie. If Montgomery wants to help to close the gap he can ask for it. He hasn't yet, and I don't think he will. So sure, Georgie, go ahead."

Patton looked Bradley in the eye. "It was Montgomery who gave you the order to tell me to get back to Argentan, wasn't it?"

Bradley looked away and stood up to go to the coffee pot. "Look Georgie, we've got enough animosity between the two sides as it is. I gave you the order. For the record I'm going to tell you I didn't consult Montgomery before I did." Which so far as Bradley was concerned was a fact—it was Montgomery who had consulted *him* and given him the order. "So, that's it, Georgie, I really don't want to talk about it any more. We're going to be at Monty's headquarters tonight and all day tomorrow, and it's going to be difficult enough as it is."

He sipped on his coffee and walked back to the table to sit down.

"Okay, Omar. You're the boss. Now what about this business at Monty's headquarters? Do you know anything about it?"

"Not a thing. I do know that Ike's going to be there, so it must be pretty important."

"Anybody else?" Patton was curious.

"No, that's it. Ike, Monty, myself, and you."

Patton's brow furrowed. "What the hell am I supposed to be doing there with all you goddamned high-powered brass? It just doesn't fit."

Bradley smiled. "You'll find out soon enough." The smile disappeared. "It's going to be difficult meeting. This is the first time the two of them have been together since Ike tried to get Monty kicked out—the lunch with Churchill, you know.''

''Everybody knows.''

''Well, something's happened today that'll make matters even worse.''

''Which is?''

Bradley shifted uncomfortably. ''It's the agreement that my army group is to be on an equal footing with Monty's army group and that Monty's supposed to give up being Land Commander. Eisenhower is supposed to take over on August 31st, and I'm to be Monty's full equal. It was supposed to happen on August 1st but got delayed. This has all been arranged, even Montgomery's promotion to field marshal on that date. But it's all secret. The British are very concerned about face. They can't stand to lose face. They have this tremendous shortage in manpower in comparison with us, so their bid for face in this campaign depends largely on Montgomery's retention of his role as the Allied Land Commander. Giving up that post to Ike on August 31st will probably be the most difficult thing Montgomery's ever done. And having me as an equal will be tough enough on his ego.

''But what's happened today is that an Associated Press reporter has blown the story. While lots of people have known about it, it wasn't supposed to be reported yet. Well, the British press are screaming. They claim making me equal to Monty is a deliberate affront to him. They're claiming Montgomery has been slurred. Some editorial writers are even calling it a 'demotion' for Monty and a rebuke to the English people. And Monty gets the newspapers from London the same day they're printed. He'll be sitting there seething over this.''

Patton had no sympathy at all. ''We'll, isn't that too bad. The poor little thumb-sucker has had more recognition, adulation, and glory than Kelsey's got wheels, in spite of the fact he hasn't been able to get his armies going. Here I am leading an army across France, capturing everything in sight, moving faster than any other general in the history of war—under your guidance, of course, Omar—and the American people, the British people, the German people don't even know I'm here! All I can say is it's too goddamn bad about that strutting little rooster. Christ, he's always getting his feathers ruffled about something.''

* * *

Eisenhower was the first to arrive at Montgomery's headquarters. It was 5:25 p.m. when his unescorted jeep pulled up to the gate of the heavily guarded, barbed-wire-fenced Twenty-first Army Group compound. Major-General Freddie de Guingand, affable as ever, was there to meet the Supreme Commander and escort him to his chief's van. Monty was standing outside waiting, his double-badged beret squarely on his head, his beribboned khaki battle-dress uniform freshly pressed. He was actually wearing a shirt and tie. Montgomery saluted as Eisenhower, his superior, clambered out of the jeep, a broad, friendly smile on his face. After he returned the salute, he held out his hand, which Monty took rather limply, Ike thought.

"Good to see you, Monty."

His broad Kansas accent was immediately counterpointed by Montgomery's lisping, thoroughly English tones. "Welcome to Twenty-first Army Group headquarters, Sir."

The use of the word "sir" did not escape Eisenhower. He detected no sarcasm in it. It was simply part of the British general's courteous welcome of an officer senior to him. But it was the last time during Eisenhower's visit that Montgomery would use that word.

He showed Eisenhower into the van, saying, "I've ordered some tea. I thought we might have a little chat before the others got here."

When they were seated in the van, tea in hand, Montgomery opened, "I assume you're here because of the armistice offer."

"That's right, Monty, that's right."

"I also assume because you're here and Bradley and Patton are coming that negotiations with Kluge have been authorized."

Eisenhower nodded, "Right again. The President and the Prime Minister decided they'd put together a counteroffer."

Montgomery leaned forward. "Can you tell me about it?"

Eisenhower hesitated. He decided he would have to bite the bullet. "If you don't mind, Monty, I'd like to brief you and Bradley on this thing at the same time, so you'll both hear the same words."

"Well, I do mind. You're bloody right I mind," Montgomery bristled. "Kluge came to me with this offer, not to you or Bradley. And I'm still the Land Commander. You better than anyone else know that I'm the Land Commander—even though you tried to have me fired behind my back.'' Montgomery's high-pitched voice was steely.

"That's all behind us, Monty.'' Ike tried to be conciliatory. "It's gone, done, put to bed. My staff and I have the fullest confidence in you.''

The British general's mustache twitched as his mouth grimaced into a sneer. "There's a word you Americans—and Georgie in particular—a word you use with much frequency. It's 'bullshit'. According to the British press today, you've demoted me to coequal status with Bradley. I thought we'd agreed to the 31st of August. But no, you had to leak it to the press and they had to print it. So what you're telling me is that you haven't got enough confidence in me to tell me the instructions for dealing with Hitler and Kluge. Is that right?''

"I understand what you're saying, Monty,'' Eisenhower replied. "I know you're hurt and I know you've been under a tremendous amount of criticism which you feel is unjustified. But the fact is I'm the Supreme Commander, not you. You report to me, even though you took this armistice proposal directly to Churchill and went around me. And yes, Bradley is now your equal as commander of the American army group. Theoretically, he's supposed to consult you and take your supervision, and I'm sure he's doing exactly that. But as far as I'm concerned, right here and now I'm telling you that the two of you are equals. Surely it's not that hard to take? So I'm not going to tell you what the orders from Churchill and Roosevelt are until Bradley's here.''

Montgomery swept off his beret, threw it on the table, and leaned back in his chair, stuffing his hands in his trouser pockets. "Well, all right then, surely you can tell me about Patton. What the hell is George Patton doing here? He's no more than an army commander.''

"Patton's role will be explained in the briefing. All I can tell you right now is that I didn't invite him here. Roosevelt and Churchill gave that order.''

"Very well, when do you propose to do this briefing?''

"Immediately after dinner, supper, or whatever you Brits call it—assuming you're going to feed us.'' There was no levity in Eisenhower's voice.

"Ah, indeed, my dear Ike, I'm going to feed the lot of you. And you don't have to worry about tasting the food to see if it's poisoned. If nothing else I pride myself on being an officer and a gentleman. I have laid on dinner for 20:00

hours. Freddie's set up a special mess tent complete with white tablecloth and my best regimental silver candelabras, cutlery, wine goblets, the lot. And a bar for you hard-drinking Americans. Even after-dinner liqueurs.''

"My God, Monty, that sounds like quite a spread for Britain's most austere general.'' He managed a smile. "Suppose I do the briefing over coffee and liqueurs. How does that sound?''

"Fine. I assume that you would have no objection if Freddie sits in on the dinner and the briefing and my intelligence lad, Brigadier Bill Williams. After all, I can't take on the three of you all by myself.''

"Go on. You could take on a dozen of us. No, I don't have any objection. De Guingand and Williams will have to be in on what we're going to do, anyway. By the way, since we're going to be in a tent, I don't want anyone eavesdropping . . . cooks, or stewards, no one. The place must be secure.''

"Not to worry. I'll make sure no one's about to hear what we're saying—unless, of course, we get into a shouting match, which, I daresay, is a possibility.'' He managed his first smile. It was wan.

The mild-mannered Bradley arrived at the compound as Eisenhower and Montgomery were talking. He was met at the gate by de Guingand, who escorted him directly to his assigned tent.

"Any idea what this is all about, Freddie?''

The tall, very British officer smiled, ''I haven't a bloody clue, Sir.''

"Has General Patton arrived yet?''

De Guingand did not have to answer, for at that moment, two American L5s flew at treetop height right over the Twenty-first Army Group compound.

As he looked up through his ever-present spectacles, Bradley's kindly face broke into a grin. "That's Georgie, now. I'll bet he's flying one of the airplanes himself.''

"Now if I can show you to your tent, General,'' de Guingand said, ''I'll dash off to the airstrip to pick up General Patton.''

"Gentlemen, I wish to propose a toast,'' Montgomery declared, shoving back his folding wooden chair on the grass and standing, lifting his glass of after-dinner port. The others around the table did the same. As he stood up at the head of the table, Montgomery looked at the scene: Eisenhower in the place of honor at his right, Bradley to his left. To Eisenhower's right, de Guingand, then Patton. To Bradley's left, Bill Williams. On the table, the candles had burned down to less than half height in their silver candelabras, their light glinting off the cutlery and regimental silver pieces Montgomery had acquired during his long service career. His elegant china and silver were set off by the white linen tablecloth, now tainted with flecks of wax, crumbs from broken bread, and a crimson red wine stain where Patton had missed his glass when he began to pour the port from its traditional crystal decanter.

All were on their feet under the cathedral ceiling of the tent, port glasses in their right hands.

"Gentlemen. His Majesty the King—God bless him," Montgomery proposed.

The response from the British was the traditional "The King, God bless him." And from the Americans, "The King." Then glasses to lips. Montgomery continued: "Gentlemen. The President of the United States." The echo was, "The President of the United States." Again the port was sipped.

They all sat down, with the exception of de Guingand, who spoke to the chief steward, asking him and his men to leave, go to the cook's tent, and wait there until called back. The headquarters provost marshal, a major responsible for military police, was standing inside the tent entrance. At de Guingand's signal the major did a tour around the outside of the tent to ensure that in the darkness no personnel came within thirty meters of the tent.

At the dinner table, following the toast to the King, three people lit up: Eisenhower, de Guingand, and Williams. The coffee and the Calvados had already been poured by the stewards.

The time had come.

"Well, General," Montgomery looked at Eisenhower, "now you can tell us what this is all about. I've a bit of a clue, of course, so do Freddie and Bill."

Eisenhower seemed almost diffident. "Okay. As you said, Monty, the three of you have a clue. That's because you were on the receiving end of the armistice proposal."

"Armistice proposal?" Bradley asked in astonishment. At the same time, Patton was blurting out, "What armistice proposal? What're you talking about?"

Eisenhower related the entire story as he knew it, augmented by bits and pieces from Montgomery and his team. What he left to the end was Churchill and Roosevelt's order and Patton's part in the game plan.

"I told you that Churchill wrote out one original order. It's on two pages. There are no copies to be made. None whatsoever. But we'll make two copies of the armistice counteroffer it contains. And if this operation doesn't come off, both the order and the copies of the counteroffer will be burned. The attempted armistice will not be a matter of record. It will never be spoken about again by anyone in this room. That's from Churchill and Roosevelt directly."

He didn't wait for anyone in the room to agree. It was simply a straightforward order.

"Okay, this is the order," he said, reaching into his inside jacket pocket. He unfolded the order, then held it upright, turning it so each man could see the precise handwriting on the front page of the foolscap-sized paper. "In Churchill's own hand, approved by the President, as I've said."

He read it out slowly. After a short preamble at the beginning, in which Churchill recited the terms of the original proposal as received from Kluge, it continued:

The President and I, after due deliberation, have concluded that it is in the interests of the people of the United States, the United Kingdom and the Commonwealth, and their Allies, that notwithstanding our commitment to an unconditional surrender on the part of the Nazi hordes, and having regard to the source of the armistice proposal, that being Adolf Hitler . . .

Bradley interrupted, "Good God almighty, Ike, are you sure? Is Churchill sure? An offer from Kluge is tremendously important itself, but if this is Hitler's doing . . ."

It was Monty who answered, "No, we're not really sure, Brad. I'm fairly satisfied, however, and so is Bill, that Kluge is in fact acting on Hitler's instructions. We have to make that assumption."

Bradley's eyes were wide and blinking with astonishment.

Ike went on: "Now this is the Roosevelt-Churchill counterproposal." He read it, and when he was finished it was Patton who observed, "It isn't a hell of a lot different than

Kluge's. One or two major points but nothing serious as I see it. If this comes off, it'll be a real shocker.''

''It'll be a bloody miracle, that's what it'll be,'' de Guingand commented quietly.

Ike went on: ''So that's the deal, gentlemen. All we have to do is negotiate it.''

''It's not as simple as that, not by a long shot,'' Montgomery said. ''What about the Russians? Churchill and Roosevelt can't agree to this alone. They have to have the Russians with them, totally. First, there's the matter of unconditional surrender. Then if they're prepared to waive that, they have to agree to each and every term of this document. If they don't, it's not worth the paper it's written on.''

Slightly flustered, Eisenhower said, ''Yes, you're right, Monty.''

''So, what's being done about it?'' his host demanded. ''What's happening?''

''Eden's in Moscow—at the Kremlin. We're getting word through your embassy there. There's no answer yet. Stalin has pulled the full Politburo together. Evidently they're debating the matter. Eden's optimistic on all points except Hitler's safe conduct, but the good Lord only knows what will happen.''

''It will depend, Sir,'' Bill Williams said, ''at least the way I see it, it will depend on whether the Politburo thinks its army has enough strength to smash through right into Germany, so the Russians can overrun a good portion of it and divide and subjugate the country forever. If they don't think they'll be able to, or that the cost in men and equipment will be so great now that it's *their* lines of supply that are extended to the breaking point, then they might well go along with the proposition. Then again, there may be a fight in the Politburo.''

Patton asked, ''What's the deadline the Russians have been given?''

'Three p.m. our time, Double British Summer Time,'' Ike replied.

''Which is what, about 7:00 or 8:00 in the evening, their time?'' Montgomery asked.

''Yes. It's 8:00. Eden arrived in Moscow yesterday morning.''

Looking at his chief momentarily and then at Ike, de Guingand said, ''There isn't anybody better equipped, anywhere, to get the right answer out of Stalin then Tony Eden. Stalin knows him from Teheran last year, and likes him. So if Tony is optimistic, I think there's real hope he can bring it off.''

Eisenhower shifted uncomfortably. He was about to read the next part of the order, which dealt with who was going to do the negotiating. He knew it would get a reaction, probably a violent one, out of Montgomery. But it had to be done.

''Okay, let's move on to the next point of the order. It says this:

> *As to the crucially important matter of who shall be charged with responsibility of face-to-face negotiations with Kluge, the President and I have considered the attributes of all candidates on both the British and American sides. We recognize the inherent equity in favour of designating our most able Land Commander, General Sir Bernard Montgomery, being the field officer to whom the offer was made and in accordance with his consummate abilities as a leader . . .*

Here Eisenhower stopped, deciding to pause for a moment. Montgomery was smiling.

But like a judge delivering a written decision, the wily Churchill had stated the positive and would now go on to the alternative.

> *On the other hand we envisage consummate physical danger in all aspects of bringing together the negotiating partners whether by way of an arranged truce or otherwise. We therefore believe that it would be inappropriate to place our most valued Land Commander in an unnecessarily dangerous position, especially if it is necessary to cross the German lines in order to meet, a possibility which, under the given fluid circumstances, is a most real one. Regard must also be had to the fact that our Land Commander should not be directly associated with this enterprise should it meet with failure and the fact of these negotiations should later be made public even though every effort is to be made to keep the negotiations secret during the lifetime of all who are concerned.*

Having regard to these factors, in our judgment it is appropriate that the person designated to conduct the negotiations with Kluge shall be an army commander. For a host of reasons which need not be written here, it is our joint decision that the person to conduct these negotiations should be a fighting general who has the highest possible regard and respect of the enemy—Lieutenant General George Smith Patton, Jr., Commander of the American Third Army.

Eisenhower stopped reading to look up at Montgomery's face. What he saw was a mixture of hatred and anger. Eisenhower thought, If he could breathe fire he'd burn this whole tent down.

Fists pounding the table, Montgomery shouted at the Supreme Commander, "Damn it, Eisenhower, you can't do this to me! You can't do this to the British people, you can't do this to the British army! This is the last bloody straw, you understand me! I won't have it I tell you, I won't have it! I'm entitled to conduct these negotiations, not you bloody Americans. I set up the whole bloody thing, and you people walk in and take it over. I will conduct the negotiations, not George Patton. You can tell that to your political master. I'll tell it to mine!"

Eisenhower had had enough. He leaned forward, stuck his face into Montgomery's, and snarled, "You are not going to go around me again. If you go to Churchill, the man who wrote this document, if you go to him around me, this time I'll make sure that you're out as Land Commander and of the command of the Twenty-first Army Group in one hour. And furthermore, that promotion to the rank of field marshal on August 31st—forget it! Listen, it was your political boss, Churchill, who wrote this document. I had no input. I didn't even know it was being written because you went around me!" Bradley and Patton, who had known Eisenhower for years, had never seen him so angry.

Eisenhower's arm pointed to the tent exit. "If you want to go talk to your Prime Minister, you go ahead, do it right now. But I'm telling you if you do that, I'll have you, Montgomery. The whole goddamn world will know, when, where, and why."

Seething, Eisenhower sat back in his chair. As his anger began to subside, his eyes were locked onto Montgomery's. The other men around the table were scarcely breathing. It seemed an eternity until Montgomery averted his eyes, shifted in his seat, and said, in his high-pitched but subdued nasally voice, "Freddie had worked up a plan with Bill to get our negotiator—Georgie, that's you now—together with Kluge. Perhaps Freddie would like to brief us on it."

The tension in the room dissipated immediately. It was as if all the mannequins sitting stiff at the table had suddenly been brought to life. Coffee and liqueurs were reached for again. New cigarettes were lit by the smokers, although there was no chitchat.

"Monty, all this is sure news to me," Patton spoke up, "and I'm certain that you would have done a far better job than I in these negotiations. You'll understand, Sir, that I didn't know about this until you did, until Ike read the order, so I haven't given any thought to the business of meeting with Kluge. I wonder if, rather than having Freddie go through his plan here, he and I shouldn't get together after this excellent dinner with its superb wines. He and I can sort it out between us. I have one idea boiling around in my head at the moment . . ."

"That's a pretty big place to have an idea boiling around in." Bradley couldn't resist the opportunity. Everyone, including Montgomery, laughed. Old Georgie took it in good humor.

"So, if it's all right with you, Monty," Patton went on, "Freddie and I'll get together and we'll come back to you with a plan later tonight or first thing in the morning. Okay? I tell you gentlemen, I have no idea why Roosevelt and Churchill would choose an old fart like me to do this job, but I guess it's because they're a pair of old farts themselves!"

More laughter.

"One final thing," Eisenhower said. "The order requires two handwritten copies of the armistice counterproposal to be made, so if a deal is worked out it can be signed or amended and signed, or whatever. As a penance for my sins, which are many and of which, yes, there is much witness around this table tonight, I'll write those copies myself."

"With an American accent, I presume," Monty jested, with a hint of a conciliatory smile on his face.

Ike returned the smile. "By golly, it won't have an American accent or an English accent for that matter, but it sure as hell will have American spelling, Kansas style."

That evening, back at his own headquarters, the Supreme Commander of the Allied Forces, Dwight D. Eisenhower, finished his copying chore and climbed into his cot at just about the same time that the worried Feldmarschall Hans von Kluge was getting into bed at the headquarters of Panzer Gruppe West at Fontaine-l'Abbée.

15 August 1944

KLUGE SAID goodbye to Sepp Dietrich sharp at 6:30 on the morning of 15 August and stepped into the right-hand front seat of his Horch. His driver, Unteroffizier Kraus, was at the wheel, with Major Behr and Leutnant Tangermann in the back seat, both of whom would act as lookouts for the Jabos that would undoubtedly be swarming on a day that promised to be cloudless and hot. The radio truck's crew of four was ready to go. With a wave to Dietrich from Kluge, the little party was off, its destination the church at Nécy in the heart of the Falaise Gap.

The trip was only some eighty kilometers. If he was going to make his rendezvous with Eberbach and Hausser at Nécy by 10:00—though he had the second rendezvous at 11:00 uppermost in his mind—a 6:30 a.m. start seemed like a good idea. He would have to stay off the highways and take the backroads all the way across, a time-consuming process in itself.

After what seemed to Kluge countless Jabo stops, they had passed Trun and were heading west over the last thirteen kilometers to Nécy. On the approach to the tiny village of Brieux, the narrow road was completely blocked by a burned-out, still smoking Tiger tank.

Checking his map, Kluge could see that he had no choice but to turn around and double back, then head southwest through the Bois de Feuillet. The woods would give him good protection against the Jabos. Then he would turn north for the last three kilometers into Nécy on another backroad. But when they arrived at the road north, it, too, was blocked. There was no choice but to continue to head west, cross the Falaise-Argentan highway—to drive north on it would be suicide—continue west to Ronai, where he had to be at 11:00 anyway, then north five kilometers to Nécy, again crossing the highway.

They had just turned north at Ronai shortly after 9:30

when the attack occurred. The Horch, closely followed by the radio truck, had crested the hill and was running down the open untreed road toward the Falaise-Argentan highway. Kluge could see the tall spiral of the church at Nécy some three kilometers ahead. To the east, the glaring sun was piercing the haze in the cloudless sky. The lookouts, Behr and Tangermann, did not see the two low-flying Typhoons until the road and turf around them began erupting in pockets of flame, earth, and sparks from the cannon shells. Miraculously, the Horch was not hit. The driver slammed on the brakes as Kluge screamed, "Stop the car. Everybody into the ditch!"

The two aircraft thundered past, their propellers just a meter above the ground. Then they turned to come back for another run. The car was almost at a halt when Kluge looked back to the radio truck. It was in flames in the ditch about ninety meters behind the Horch. His car was still moving slightly when Kluge threw open the door and leaped out, falling and rolling toward the ditch. As the car stopped in the middle of the road his two aides and the driver also jumped just before the first Typhoon opened fire.

Huddled in the ditches on each side of the road—they gave little protection—Kluge and his men could only pray that the cannon shells would not hit them. The murderous staccato firing of the 20-millimeter cannons, and the impact of the shells on the Horch and the road surface around it, started and was over in a matter of seconds. The roar of the aircraft engines was deafening as they passed over the cowering men. Then the Jabos disappeared over the hill, streaking northward toward their own lines.

Kluge stood up cautiously, searching the horizon for more aircraft. He could see several in the distance but none close by. He shouted to his men, "It's all right. They've gone." As the others emerged from the ditch, Kluge, panting from the exertion and the close brush with death, said, "Driver, you go back to the radio truck and see if there are any survivors. See what you can do for them."

He turned to look down the road the other way toward the Horch. It was shell-pocked and burning.

From the direction of Ronai came the sound of an approaching motorcycle. When it appeared over the hill, Kluge could see that it was being driven by a Wermacht dispatch rider. The feldmarschall waved him down. The motorcycle came to halt, its engine popping. Kluge shouted at its astonished young rider, "I'm sorry, but I must commandeer your machine."

He turned to Behr, saying, "I know you can ride one of these things, I've seen you do it. You go on to Nécy. When Generals Hausser or Eberbach get there, tell them what's happened. I can't ask them to send transport for me. That would be suicide. So tell them to forget the conference. I'll be in touch with them as soon as I can get to a radio. Tangermann will stay with me. You can report back to me here later." To the dispatch rider the feldmarschall said, "I'm afraid that wherever you were going, you will have to go by foot." Without a word the soldier shrugged, saluted the feldmarschall, and started to trudge down the road, toward the main highway.

With a roar of the engine of his new-found vehicle, Behr tore off toward Nécy.

He arrived at the church rendezvous at 10:01 and parked the motorcycle at the entrance gate, looking around for the vehicles that might have brought the generals. There were none. Cautiously he went to the church door, found it open, and went in. The place was empty.

Behr knew that the rendezvous time that Kluge had set was from 10:00 to 11:00. So he waited, examining the stained-glass windows, marveling at the ancient stone architecture, and listening to the guns firing in the far distance and the frequent sound of the Jabos ranging at will over the Falaise Gap.

At 11:15 he decided he had waited long enough.

When Behr finally arrived back at the place where the Horch lay smoldering and the radio truck was now a gutted, blackened wreck, the feldmarschall and Tangermann were nowhere to be seen. Kluge's driver was still tending to the three badly injured crew members of the radio truck who had survived, but Behr could get no information out of him about the feldmarschall. All he knew was that the feldmarschall had walked that way. He pointed southwest down the road toward Ronai.

Behr rode into the village, his head swiveling as he watched for Jabos. But there was no sign of Feldmarschall Kluge or Tangermann. Speidel had briefed him on the armistice negotiations but had not told him the exact location. Behr didn't know what to do. Finally he decided to go to the headquarters of the Seventh Army, to General Hausser. He knew where that was. He would wait there until the feldmarschall reappeared. Behr gunned his motorcycle and headed down the narrow road running southwest out of Ronai, making for Hausser's headquarters some fifteen kilometers away.

Major Behr did not notice the long wall of trees on his left less than a kilometer down the road he had chosen out of Ronai. He was too busy steering the motorcycle and looking out for Jabos. He knew they would love to catch him on an open stretch and kill him like a cat kills a mouse. Had he stopped at that wooded section and turned onto a small dirt road, he would have found a long, open field guarded on all sides by a thick stand of trees. At the far end, almost two kilometers away, he would have seen his feldmarschall, followed by Tangermann, walking up the slight rise to the bordering trees and the radio truck and car they sheltered.

Hauptmann Richter and Feldwebel Schmidt saluted the feldmarschall and reported to him that the radio equipment and the coded wireless were all in good working order.

Kluge looked at his watch. 11:38. "I'm forty minutes late, gentlemen. If Montgomery's waiting for me and prepared to do business, he's probably ready to give up just about now."

Kluge, followed by his men, pulled himself up onto the deck of the radio truck. When his earphones were on and Richter announced that everything was set for transmission, Kluge himself picked up the microphone and spoke.

"Armee Gruppe Twenty-one, this is Kluge. Do you hear me?"

Patton and de Guingand had excused themselves from the dinner table early to work on the rendezvous plan the previous evening. Both had been relieved to see that the tension and animosity between Eisenhower and Montgomery appeared to have been alleviated. Whether the new mood of cordiality would last was another matter.

Patton accompanied de Guingand to the latter's van where the British general produced mile-to-the-inch detailed maps and "on-the-deck" low-level aerial photographs of the field from which Kluge had established contact.

It was close to midnight when they wrapped up the planning session, both completely in agreement.

The next morning at 8:00 a.m., the two men met in

Montgomery's van with Montgomery, Eisenhower, and Bradley, to brief them and get their approval.

When their presentation was finished and approved, Patton was astonished when Montgomery said, "I must say, Georgie old boy, that your plan is probably the only way we could bring this off. But I must also say I think it's a bloody hairy way to do it. The risks are enormous, and I'd hate to see our very best army commander, our very best, go for a burton. You're much too valuable, Georgie old boy, to be doing this sort of thing." Ike and Bradley were also surprised to hear such concern in Monty's voice.

"I'll be damned, Monty, I didn't know you cared," was Patton's light-hearted reply. But he was serious. "And thank you for the compliment. Goddamn it, it isn't every day that an old cavalry warhorse gets a compliment from his commander." By referring to Montgomery as his commander in Bradley's presence, Patton was returning the compliment. Montgomery smiled. Patton continued: "Now all we have to do is wait for Kluge to appear on the radio at noon. If I can believe the stuff that Freddie's given me to read, he's quite a guy."

De Guingand had given Patton a package of biographical material on Kluge, which Patton had read before breakfast. It was important for him to have as good a handle as possible on Kluge as negotiator. What was his background? How did he think? What was his original relationship with Hitler? What was it now? The more Patton knew about Kluge the better.

"I take it there's no word from Eden yet?" Patton asked.

It was de Guingand who responded. "Nothing yet. I talked to Eden's undersecretary this morning. The Politburo still hasn't made up its mind."

"Should we proceed if we haven't heard Moscow's response?" asked Eisenhower.

"No question about it, Ike, none at all," said Patton. "Even if we haven't heard by the time I'm ready to leave, I should still go, carry on with the negotiations, try to get the goddamned thing wrapped up, and hang in there until Uncle Joe decides whether to shit or get off the pot."

No one argued against Patton's pungent opinion.

"I've spoken to the air force," de Guingand said. "All air commanders will prohibit any air-to-ground attacks in the pocket from 12:00 noon until 17:00 hours or until the ban is lifted, whichever is the earlier. It would be just like our chaps to shoot up Kluge and Georgie in the middle of negotiations. So that point is covered.''

Montgomery asked, ''What about protection for Georgie during that period?''

De Guingand looked at Patton, then turned toward his chief. ''Good point, Sir. I'll ask for three or four squadrons over the rendezvous area. If Georgie needs them, the simplest way would be for him to call through to us on the frequency Kluge's been using, and we can relay instructions to them.''

Patton shook his head. ''I don't think that would be a good idea. Those fighter jockies will shoot up anything and they're just as liable to shoot up Kluge and me as not. I don't mind them in the air circling, showing the flag, but with specific orders that they're not to attack anything.''

''Unless otherwise ordered,'' Montgomery persisted.

''Okay, unless otherwise ordered,'' Patton agreed reluctantly. ''I've told my pilots to paint out the stars on the side of my aircraft and under the wings. The same with the black and white stripes at the wingroots.'' The black and white stripes were painted on all Allied fighter aircraft so that the ground troops could identify them easily. ''If the Krauts on the ground can't see any identification marks, they'll still be trying to figure out who we are long after we're gone. They'll be so busy thinking, they won't shoot. On top of the wing the stripes and the stars will be left on so that when the aircraft is on the ground the identification marks can be seen from the air.''

''Well, it sounds as though you've got it well organized, Georgie,'' Bradley observed.

Patton nodded. ''I think so, Brad. I have the armistice papers.'' He pointed to his thin briefcase on the table. ''The maps are all set. I've been over the low-level photographs of Kluge's field. So I'm all set. All I have to do is brief my young pilot.''

''What'll he think of this? Will he think it's too dangerous?'' Eisenhower asked.

''Too dangerous? Hell, no. Jones'll love it. And if he doesn't like it I'll kick him in the ass and tell him he has to do it anyhow.''

Patton's prediction about how Captain Glen Jones, his pilot, would react was right. After the briefing session with his fellow generals, Patton went to the airstrip where Jones and Patton's other personal pilot, Captain Barry Lipson, were putting the finishing touches to the painting-out of the identification marks on their L5. "We're painting out the stars and stripes—but not forever," Jones shouted as his general got out of his jeep and approached them. "What's this all about, Sir? Why in hell have you got us doing this?"

Patton looked at the aircraft and shook his head. "As painters, you two would sure make good pilots."

"The paint job's no hell, General, but at least we're getting everything covered."

Patton had seen enough. "Come on over to the jeep and I'll show you what we're doing."

Spreading the maps on the engine hood of the jeep, after asking the driver to make himself scarce, Patton proceeded to brief his two pilots on the details of the flight. Jones would fly him, while Lipson remained on the ground as backup or to fly in and bring them out if Jones' Bird Dog became unserviceable while on the ground in enemy territory.

The general then told his pilots the purpose of the mission. "All you boys have to know is that I'm meeting the German commander, Kluge, to talk about an armistice offer he's made. So that's what it's all about. Any questions?"

There was a big smile on Jones's face. "No, Sir! This is fantastic."

Patton looked at Lipson standing beside Jones with a glum look on his face. "What's the matter with you, Lipson?"

"Nothing, Sir, except that I'm going to have to sit on my butt and do nothing while you two are out there having a ball."

Patton laughed, "You're right, son, you're right." He reached into the back seat of the jeep and pulled out two objects that looked to the pilots like green pumpkins cut in half with flaps hanging down from each side. "I've always wanted to make tankers out of you two bastards, anyhow. I want you to wear these helmets. They'll protect your thick heads."

Jones protested. "Do we really have to wear them? They've got to be the ugliest looking things I've ever seen."

"Yes, you're going to wear them and so am I." He reached into the back seat again and pulled out what appeared to be vests. "*And* these flak jackets. We have absolutely no protection in these little goddamn airplanes, so I thought we should wear both the helmets and the flak jackets."

Again Lipson looked glum. "General, I hope that this isn't going to be standard practice."

"No, no—not unless we have to fly over enemy territory again."

"God forbid," said Lipson.

"Amen," said Jones.

There was a flurry of activity and excitement when Kluge's voice came through the speakers and earphones in the communications van at Twenty-first Army Group at 12:39 hours, Double British Summer Time. De Guingand sent a runner to advise his chief and the other generals. In a few moments they were all standing just outside the van listening to the conversation in German, with one of Brigadier Williams' interpreters doing his best to translate for them.

Major Corby acknowledged Kluge's opening transmission, then asked, "What is your location? Over."

"My location is the same as before. What are your instructions?"

"Kluge, Twenty-one Army Group. You are to remain at your location. The representative to negotiate with you will arrive at your location by air at 12:30 your time."

"The field is clear. Who is your negotiator, and does he have authority?"

"Twenty-one Army Group to Kluge. Our negotiator is a general who has full political authorization to negotiate. He will not be accompanied except by the pilot flying the aircraft. As expected, you will do everything in your power to ensure his safety during the time he is with you. Over."

"You have my assurance."

Eisenhower turned to Patton. "Okay, Georgie. It's up to you. Good luck." He shook Patton's hand, as did the others. Patton saluted Eisenhower and Montgomery, got into his jeep, and was gone in a cloud of hot, billowing dust.

Jones got into the front seat of his L5. The general was already in the rear seat, strapped in, his polished steel helmet on the tray behind the seat. He wore his flak jacket over his battle-dress jacket and its multi-colored ribbons and shining general's stars. Patton had on his best cavalry jodhpurs and high boots. He wanted to look his impressive best for Kluge, so his two ivory-handled revolvers were both securely in place. But that tank helmet . . . Jones had laughed when Patton put the hard plastic protective helmet with its hanging flaps on his white-haired head and tied the laces together under his chin.

"General," he said, "that's got to be the funniest god-damned thing I've ever seen you wear."

"Listen, son," Patton had wagged a finger at Jones, "it's a privilege, a goddamned privilege for anybody to wear a tanker helmet. So get yours on, boy, and get your ass into that airplane."

Jones checked his watch. It was coming up to 1:10. The time of flight over the thirty-eight kilometers to the rendez-vous point was seventeen minutes. Jones was strapped in, the doors closed and secure. He made a quick pre-start check, then shouted, "You ready, General?"

The high-pitched voice came back, "Let's get going. Boy, you look great in your tanker helmet."

Jones laughed as the engine, spewing smoke for a moment, roared into action.

At 1:04, the little L5, with no identification marks except on the upper side of its wings, rolled down the field and lifted smoothly into the air heading due south at treetop level. Jones had clipped the map to the top of the instrument panel. That way he would be able to fly the aircraft as low as he could get, below treetop level and under wires if necessary, but at the same time be able to flick his eyes down to the map to read it as he crossed roads, woods, and rivers along the track line he had drawn. Patton had clipped his copy of the map to the back of Jones' seat so that he could double-check his pilot's navigation and yet have his hands free should any emergency arise.

It was bumpy. The hot sun, hitting open grainfields and the surface of roads, was churning up a lot of fast-rising air.

They flew east at low level over friendly territory. Fourteen minutes after takeoff from Le Bény-Bocage, Jones turned the aircraft south, then down right to the ground, wheels almost touching the grain. The village of Leffard was coming up just to the right and with it they entered German territory. No way of telling—yet. Then by Martigny and along the road going south to the main east-west highway leading to Falaise. There was the intersection dead ahead, and there were German trucks under that bush over there and troops in field-gray uniforms in those distinctive German steel helmets, white faces turning to stare at the little airplane as it sped by at one hundred and forty-five kilometers an hour. At the road to Falaise there was the railway track and the river just ahead. Jones turned slightly to the left to a heading of 120 degrees. Still no sign of anyone firing at them, but lots of tanks, trucks, ambulances, hidden under trees and men moving around them. There was the highway south from Falaise to Putanges. They crossed it at Cordey.

"Five miles to go, Sir." Patton could hear Jones' calm voice on the intercom. "I'm just following this river. It'll take me straight to Kluge's field."

At that instant Patton heard a sharp crack. At the same time a hole appeared in the plexiglass window just to the left of the pilot's head and at the level of his jaw. Jones's head fell forward, his body held back by the safety harness. Patton realized instantly that Jones had been hit. The aircraft was heading for a clump of trees, its wheels about one meter off the ground. Patton's right hand grabbed the control column, his left seized the throttle. He pulled back on the stick just in time to get over the trees then pushed it forward to go back down to ground level. There was the river. His eyes checked the map. Dead ahead was the church steeple of Rouffigny. Patton flew his L5 by the church steeple, well below its peak. Then he was over open rolling fields again, covering the last three kilometers. Ahead were the woods and to the left the village of Ronai silhouetted against the sky slightly above the level of the aircraft.

Looking intently past Jones' head he saw a slight movement of the tank helmet. God, he hoped the boy would be all right. That slight movement was a sign that at least he wasn't dead. The road west out of Ronai was clear of vehicles and troops as the aircraft raced toward the target woods, just skimming the ground. Patton thought through the maneuver that Jones said he was going to use to get into the field.

He turned the aircraft slightly so that it was pointing toward the west edge of the woods. The throttle was still near the wide open position, as it had been from the time of departure, the engine delivering maximum running power.

Half a kilometer away from the woods, Patton pulled back on the throttle, cutting the power to half. At the same time he pulled back on the control column to rise above the looming trees. As the aircraft crossed the woods edging the road, Patton recognized the long wild field from the photographs the air force had taken earlier. He cut the throttle right back. The air speed dropped rapidly and he leveled off, ready to touch down about halfway down the field. With a slight bounce the L5 settled on the stubble, heading for a point on a slight rise about ninety meters west of Kluge's radio truck. As the aircraft slowed down, Patton put on power to taxi up the rise. When he was almost to the trees he put the left brake on hard and swung the aircraft around so that it was facing north. It had been Jones' plan to park it facing in that direction so that if a tank or vehicle came into the field through the woods to the north, its crew would be looking at the aircraft's nose and from below and not be able to see any of the identification markings on the top of the wings.

The general put on the parking brake, then shut the engine off.

As he turned to his right to open the door, Patton could see three men in gray-green uniforms walking quickly toward him from the radio van. He threw the door open and stepped out onto the yellow stubble without a glance at the men approaching. He ripped off his tank helmet and replaced it with his shiny steel helmet, its three stars of his rank emblazoned across its front. The ugly flak jacket came off next. He was ready to meet Kluge. But first there was Jones. He opened Jones' door quickly to find the pilot just coming out of unconsciousness. Strange, there's no blood, Patton thought. Then he could see why. As Jones turned to look at him, the general could see a large gash across the tanker helmet just above the left temple. The bullet had hit the plexiglass window and, since it was fired from below, had traveled upward into the helmet where it had been deflected by the metal rim. If Jones hadn't been wearing the helmet, the bullet would have gone through his skull. As it was, the impact had knocked him unconscious.

Patton could see that his pilot's eyes were focusing. Jones would be fine.

"It's okay, Glen," he said. "You just stay in the aircraft for a few minutes. Just take it easy."

Jones mumbled a weak "Yes, Sir" and reached to untie the helmet that had saved his life.

Patton, bent over as he had been to get at Jones, backed away from the door and when he was out from under the wing, stood up and turned to face the three Germans standing at the wingtip, Kluge, Richter, and Tangermann.

Patton and Kluge exchanged salutes, then the American stepped forward, his hand outstretched, and said, "I am Lieutenant General George Smith Patton Jr."

The German feldmarschall was astonished by the offering of the hand, but more so by the totally unexpected presence of the famed Patton. As Kluge took Patton's hand, the officer next to him said, "Herr General, I am Hauptmann

Richter. I am a communications officer, and I will translate for you."

Patton replied, "Yes, Hauptmann, I understood that you would be here to translate. I can handle French, but I certainly can't handle your language."

"And this is Feldmarschall Kluge's aide, Leutnant Tangermann."

Kluge looked anxiously toward Jones, still sitting in the front seat of the aircraft. "Your pilot, is he all right?"

"Oh, yes. He's just stunned. Knocked out by a sniper's bullet a few miles back."

Again Kluge was astonished. "So you flew the airplane yourself?"

"Absolutely. I've been flying for quite a while, and I've flown this particular airplane a lot."

"Amazing," Kluge declared. Then with a wave of his hand he said, "Come, let us go to the radio truck. We can talk there. As you can see it's out of the sun and we have some coffee, such as it is."

Patton commented, "And it's also out of sight of our fighters."

As they started to walk the thirty meters to the radio truck, Kluge went on: "In the daylight in Normandy, particularly on a hot day like this, when there isn't a cloud in the sky, every vehicle, tank, horse, and man is under a tree somewhere, hiding from your aircraft."

At the radio truck coffee was served as each general continued to size up the other.

"Have you been in Normandy long, Herr General?" Kluge ventured.

"Yes, I came on July 7th and I've been leading the American Third Army since the end of July."

"My God, that explains why your forces have been moving so quickly and with such great daring. And all this time the Führer and the rest of us were led to believe that you were in England waiting to cross the Channel and attack the Pas-de-Calais area. In fact, the Führer still thinks that might happen."

Patton laughed. "Well, you can tell the Führer that the deception is over, that the real General Patton is right here in Normandy. Hauptmann Richter, would you please ask your man," he pointed to Schmidt, "to tell General Montgomery's headquarters that I have arrived safely."

Richter spoke to Schmidt and came back to the generals.

"Also would you ask Leutnant Tangermann to go to the aircraft. I have a briefcase in the back seat. I'd like him to get it for me, please. And when he's there, have him help my pilot out of the front seat and bring him over here out of the hot sun. I think he should be okay by now."

Patton took the briefcase from Tangermann who had returned with Jones. The airman looked all right to Patton except for a bruise on his left temple.

"You okay, Glen?"

"Yes, Sir, I'm okay. I've got a bit of a headache, but thanks to your goddamned tank helmet, that's all I've got."

"Well, take it easy, have a cigarette and some coffee."

Patton turned back to Kluge. "Churchill has sent Eden, his foreign minister, to Moscow to deal with Stalin—to present the proposition to him. If you people come up with some more changes, where you don't like our counterproposal, then there will be a delay. We'll have to get a message to Eden, and he'll have to take it to Stalin."

"So what is the counterproposal, Herr General?"

Patton opened his briefcase and took out one of the two copies of the armistice document. He handed it to Richter, saying, "Please read this to the feldmarschall."

Kluge listened intently, and when Richter was finished, the feldmarschall observed, "There appear to me to be one or two areas of difference, but I think the points are negotiable. Is there anything else?"

"No," Patton acknowledged, "I think that's it. The rest is really the same as your original offer."

"And what about Stalin—has he approved of this document?"

Patton had to "fudge a bit", as he later described it. "At this point we haven't had final word from Moscow. But we've told them what the deadline is, 3:00 this afternoon, our time, 2:00 yours."

"That doesn't give us much time." The feldmarschall averted his eyes, a look of guilt on his face. "There is something I must tell you, Herr General. I must confess that I do not have the Führer's authority. He knows nothing about this."

"Then why on earth did you tell us he was involved?" Patton demanded, anger in his voice.

"So Montgomery would take me seriously. So I would get the attention of Churchill and Roosevelt. So I could negotiate an armistice not just for Normandy but for the eastern front as well, an armistice for the whole of Germany.''

Patton shook his head in disbelief. ''But how could you possibly do that if you don't have Hitler's authority? He's the Führer, not you.''

Kluge hesitated.

''I have a dream, Herr General. A dream for Germany and for the end of this slaughter of innocent men, women, and children. A dream of peace. I am in a position to make my dream happen now, at this very moment, and no one else in Germany is in a position to bring peace.''

''Except Hitler.''

Kluge nodded. ''Yes, except Hitler. But he is incapable of thinking about peace because it means defeat, and he cannot face that reality. The man is sick, Herr General, mentally sick. The attempt on his life has pulled him over the edge. His orders to me and to my fellow generals on the eastern front are the orders of a madman who cares nothing for the lives of his soldiers.

''The German general officers in the fields have lost confidence in their Führer. Every key general in the German army is ready to turn against him, to destroy him and his henchmen. I speak for them, all of them, Herr General, and I am telling you I can deliver a cease-fire on all fronts.''

Kluge then quickly outlined his plan for the overthrow of Hitler and an armistice.

Patton listened intently as he grappled with the consequences of what the feldmarschall was saying.

''What you're telling me is quite different from your original proposal. I don't know what Roosevelt and Churchill, let alone Stalin, will think about it. I'll have to radio to General Montgomery's headquarters and ask for instructions. But before I do, what about these other generals you've been dealing with? How do we know they're with you? After all, you told us you had Hitler's authority when you didn't.''

Kluge smiled.

''True. But then I had to get your serious attention. As you know, I have spent most of the war on the eastern front. All of our generals there have served under me at one time or another. They are desperate as I am desperate. The difference is that I am here on the western front where I can negotiate with civilized human beings while they're in a position where they would have to negotiate with animals—

the Soviets. Impossible! So we have come together by telephone in the past week and agreed on a course of action."

Kluge stopped and looked momentarily up into the clear blue sky, his eyes catching the squadrons of Allied fighter aircraft on station above their rendezvous point.

"One thing you can be certain of, General Patton. I have spoken to my western commanders. I can deliver my forces here in Normandy, and I am prepared to do so. But only if our entire proposal is accepted. And since we are talking about the overthrow of Hitler and the Nazi Party, you now understand why the German armies must be allowed to retain their arms as they withdraw to the Fatherland."

Patton nodded.

"I'll get on the radio right away."

Five minutes later, Patton put down the microphone. There was nothing he could do now except wait for word from Roosevelt, Churchill, and Stalin.

In Moscow, thirty minutes after General Patton passed the information to Montgomery's headquarters, Anthony Eden was in the Kremlin. Summoned by Stalin, he was being escorted to the Soviet leader's office, which was located in an ancient baroque-styled structure in a secluded corner of the Kremlin, near the Grand Kremlin Palace.

Following his escort, Eden entered the building through a narrow, carpeted corridor, then up a few steps to an antiquated bird-cage elevator that groaned and shook as it lifted him to the third floor and Stalin's cavernous office. Eden was amazed at its size, estimating that it was at least twenty-five meters long and square in shape. He was impressed by the long conference table that had enough seats for all the Politburo members and their alternates. Beyond the table and at right angles to it was Stalin's massive desk with its bank of telephones and behind it, his well-padded, high-backed swivel chair.

Stalin, wearing his usual simple, high-collared uniform, was sitting in his chair talking across the desk to the young diplomat whom Eden had met at the Teheran Conference. His name was Andrei Gromyko. As Eden was shown into the room and his eyes took in Stalin and Gromyko, he could smell the tobacco smoke and could see that the filled ashtrays had not been emptied. Evidently, the last Politburo meeting had only just concluded.

When Stalin saw Eden, he pushed the button on his desk

to summon the interpreter. He stood up and, followed by Gromyko, slowly walked across the room to greet the foreign secretary, one of the Britishers he had come to like at the Teheran Conference, as had Gromyko.

The Soviet leader, hair combed straight back, mustache needing a trim, had a smile on his face. He led Eden to the Politburo table. Stalin sat at the end and placed Eden at his right and Gromyko at his left. The interpreter was at the table by the time they sat down.

Stalin lit a cigarette and began. "Well, Minister Eden, you have brought us a question which has divided the Politburo right down the middle. It is typical of that evil monster, Hitler, that even with an offer of an armistice he has caused division and animosity in the houses of his enemies."

In his ponderous way, Stalin was preparing himself and Eden for the announcement of the decision—whatever it was going to be.

"My country has lost millions of people, slaughtered by the Nazis. Millions, Minister Eden. And also we have found that entering into a protocol or agreement with Hitler is like signing an agreement with a snake. He will just slither out of it. On the other hand, we must recognize that an early opportunity to end the war, even if it is not unconditional, can save the lives of thousands of our young soldiers. That is why we have been prepared to look at the proposal and the counterproposal of my colleagues, Churchill and Roosevelt. So, Minister Eden, there are some in the Politburo who wish to conquer Germany, overrun that nation, and bring as much of its territory as we can conquer ourselves under the Soviet heel forever. Then there's the other group. They are in favor of stopping at the border and, with you, taking up joint control of the government of Germany."

He took a long pull on his cigarette, his hooded eyes watching Eden's face. "So, Minister Eden, the matter has been resolved. The Politburo has made its decision and I am prepared to accept it, even though my own judgment tells me I should reject it. Please be good enough to communicate to your Prime Minister and to the President of the United States my concern for their good health, my gratitude for their *finally* opening the front in France, and for sending you here to discuss the Hitler armistice proposition with us."

The preamble was over. Eden listened impassively to the measured tones of Stalin and the monotones of the translator as the General Secretary of the Soviet Union began to give the verdict.

At that moment his secretary hurried into the office saying that there was an urgent call for Eden from the British embassy. Eden took the call at Stalin's desk, then put the telephone down but did not hang up. He went to the conference table.

"Mr. General Secretary, that is our ambassador. The Prime Minister is in signal contact with him on a most urgent basis and is standing by in his office.

"His signal is in the clear, no cypher, to save time, so he's in direct touch. He says the situation has changed. Kluge now says he does not have Hitler's authority. Even so, he is making a new proposal. Perhaps it will cause you to reconsider your position."

Stalin glowered. "What is this new proposition, and what good is it if Hitler is not involved?"

"First let me tell you what the Prime Minister's saying. Since Hitler's out of it, there's no need to worry now about the odious business of allowing him to escape. Kluge can deliver his own army and claims to speak for the commanders of the armies against you on the eastern front."

Stalin held up his hand to stop Eden. "Do you and Churchill really believe Kluge speaks for those generals?"

"I think it is worth assuming that he does. It is logical that, with disaster and defeat facing them on all fronts and Hitler behaving irrationally, the German general staff in the field might be prepared to settle for an armistice and move to overthrow Hitler."

Stalin said nothing but gave a noncommittal nod.

Eden went on. "Kluge proposes a cease-fire, an armistice on all fronts, and an immediate withdrawal of all German forces to Germany. At the same time the army will seize power, arrest Hitler and all his henchmen, take all Gestapo agents and Nazi officials, and hold the whole lot for trial by the government of occupation that our three nations would set up."

"This cease-fire," Stalin asked. "They would lay down their arms before they withdrew to Germany?"

"Kluge claims his troops must remain armed in order to cope with any SS units that wouldn't give up—or any units that remain loyal to Hitler."

"A civil war scenario," Stalin mused. "I do not find the

possibility of the Germans destroying each other in a civil way unattractive.''

"Our forces would stand at the German border. When Kluge and his cohorts have completed their takeover they would transfer power to our joint government of occupation, hand over Hitler and the rest. At that point they would lay down their arms. So that is the proposition, Sir. Churchill says he and Roosevelt are prepared to accept it in order to stop the carnage. He says if Kluge brings it off, it will be as close to an unconditional surrender as we can get.''

Stalin fondled his mustache for a moment, then said, "Frankly, Minister Eden, I do not trust Kluge nor do I trust your Prime Minister or Roosevelt. How do I know this isn't some kind of a trick—a plot your people have worked up with Kluge so the German armies, fully armed, I repeat, fully armed, are allowed to return to Germany—overthrow Hitler, yes, I can see that—then join forces with the Americans and British to attack us on the eastern front?''

Eden understood the basic paranoia of the Soviet leader whose lands, both under the Communist regime and earlier under the Czars, had been invaded countless times by would-be conquerors from the West. Nevertheless, Eden was appropriately indignant. "We are your allies, Sir. What you suggest is unthinkable.''

Stalin snorted. "Hitler was my ally. We signed a pact. The possibility of his attacking me was also 'unthinkable'.''

Eden turned and went back to the telephone. He spoke to the ambassador, then waited. Stalin lit yet another cigarette, tugged at his mustache, and brushed the ashes off his jacket.

Eden repeated Churchill's reply verbatim as the ambassador relayed it.

"Pray tell our trusted friend and ally, General Secretary Stalin, that he has our solemn undertaking and pledge that the Allied forces in Europe will never turn their weaponry against our gallant Soviet comrades-in-arms. Victory in our joint united nations enterprise in the struggle against the Nazi hordes is almost at hand. Please be assured that our objectives are limited to the overthrow of Hitler and the total defeat of his nation. We hope the General Secretary might now see fit to reciprocate our solemn undertaking and pledge so that we can march securely together down the final road to victory.''

Stalin gave a grunt of appreciation and smiled as he listened to Churchill's closing words. He looked at Eden and said, "Tell the Prime Minister that he has my solemn undertaking and pledge. Also tell him that I will consider the Kluge proposal with my Politburo colleagues. You will have our answer within the half hour, Minister Eden."

The wait for Stalin's decision had seemed unending. In the late-afternoon shade of the woods southwest of Ronai there was virtual silence, except for the rustling of the leaves moved by a gentle summer breeze flowing through the trees under a cloudless sun-filled sky. No one spoke. Some were reading, others were dozing. But the silence was not true because of the sounds of far-off gunfire and heavy fighting to the north beyond Falaise where the Canadians were pushing hard. The undulating pounding of the British and Canadian artillery rumbled like distant rolls of thunder. From two kilometers above the golden stubble field came the buzz of many fighter aircraft, Jabos that moved in squadron formations, circling, ready to swoop down on command to attack any target in that hostile area and around Ronai.

Suddenly the radio came alive. Richter, followed by Schmidt, leaped up onto the truck and pulled on the earphones. Patton, who had been off by himself reading and rereading the armistice agreement, hurried to join Kluge and stand beside the truck to listen in case the message brought news of the Soviet position. The now-familiar voice from Montgomery's headquarters sounded loud and clear through the loudspeaker.

"Twenty-one Army Group to Kluge, do you receive? Over."

After a response from Richter, the voice continued: "I have a message for General Patton. It will be in English. Is he there? Over."

Patton stepped up on the truck, put on the earphones handed to him by Richter, and picked up the microphone. "Twenty-one Army Group this is Patton, go ahead with your message. Over."

"We have the answer from the Soviets, Sir."

Patton pushed the transmitter button. "Go ahead with the message, we are ready to copy. Over." He nodded to Richter, who was poised with pencil in hand.

"The message is one word, Sir. It's negative—no."

Patton could hear Kluge gasp.

"Any explanation? Any instructions for a counteroffer?" The general sounded like a man pleading for a second chance.

"No, Sir. Nothing. That's all we got. It came from the Prime Minister himself."

Patton pressed. "Did he talk to Monty?"

"That's affirmative, Sir."

"Didn't he say anything about going ahead with an armistice on this front regardless of what those Russian pigs think?"

The voice that replied was Eisenhower's. Patton whispered his name to Kluge as soon as the Supreme Commander started to speak.

"Georgie, it's over. Churchill talked to the President and they decided the risks are too great. They don't want to offend Stalin—at least not right now. So that's it, Georgie. There won't be any armistice in Normandy."

"But, goddammit, Ike, the field marshal's ready to make a deal regardless, and to hell with the eastern front. Look at all the American lives you could save!"

Eisenhower quickly added, "And British, Georgie, and British. I hear you, but I'm telling you that the orders from Roosevelt and Churchill are no dice. And that's final."

As Patton shook his head in frustration and anger, Eisenhower added, "Generals Montgomery, Bradley, and I extend our compliments to Field Marshal Kluge. He is a brave man who has fought honorably and fearlessly for his country. We regret that his valiant effort for an armistice has not met with success."

Kluge listened to the translation, eyes downcast as he contemplated not only Eisenhower's felicitous words but also the certainty of his own fate at Hitler's murderous hands.

Kluge fingered the cyanide capsules in his tunic pocket as he said to Richter, "Please tell General Eisenhower how much I appreciate those words. They are of much comfort to one who must now face the full wrath of his unforgiving Führer, the Führer to whom he has given his total loyalty, notwithstanding the events of this unhappy day. Above all my duty is to the Fatherland, and I am content that I have discharged that duty to the best of my professional ability. You are most kind, General Eisenhower."

There was nothing more to be said. Kluge turned and walked a few steps away, shoulders slumped, a man defeated.

Patton was uncertain what to do. Then he motioned to Richter to follow him and went to Kluge. It was time to leave.

As Patton spoke, Kluge, his bulging eyes on the verge of

tears, pulled himself erect, shoulders back, the very model of the proud Prussian that he was.

"It is time, Field Marshal," said Patton. "I just want to tell you that I agree with what General Eisenhower said. You're a brave man who has fought honorably and well for your country. That's the highest duty of any soldier. I am privileged to have had this short time with you—professional soldier to professional soldier. That snake, Hitler, doesn't deserve men as good as you."

Kluge took Patton's offered hand. A wan smile crossed his face as he said, "The Führer believes his marshals and generals are his enemies. So perhaps he does deserve us." Still grasping Patton's hand, Kluge said, "General, you carry yourself like a Prussian. You fight like a Prussian. You should have been one of us."

"I am, Field Marshal. I am."

Twenty-eight minutes later, with Jones at the controls, Patton's L5, the fabric of its tail section punctured by thirteen bullet holes, touched down in the landing field at Montgomery's headquarters. De Guingand was waiting by Patton's jeep to congratulate as well as console the disconsolate American general on his failed mission and tell him that Eisenhower, Montgomery, and Bradley were waiting for him in Monty's van.

By the time he arrived there, Patton had worked himself into a fit of anger pushed by an overpowering sense of frustration.

He brushed off the trio's attempts to praise him, saying, "What the hell are you congratulating me for? We've just crapped out on the biggest coup of this entire goddamn war! We had it right in the palm of our hands and we blew it."

He tore off his steel helmet and threw it into Monty's chair.

Eisenhower tried to calm him down. "It wasn't your fault, Georgie. You did everything you could."

Monty added, "And you did it right, old chap. Bang on. You really shouldn't take it personally. After all, the decisions were made by our political masters. If anyone's to blame, they'll have to carry the can."

"What can?" Patton blurted. "They've made sure no one will ever know about this. It's all super-secret, so their butts would be protected if it didn't come off. Right?"

"That's part of the game, Georgie," Eisenhower said. "And I think we all understand their reasoning. Now tell us what happened. We want a full debriefing.'' As his audience settled into chairs, Patton went to the wall map to tell the story from start to finish, his language punctuated by the cultured profanity that added color to the story and the man. His listeners were jolted by his account of taking over the controls of the aircraft and—except for Eisenhower—surprised to find out that he was a pilot.

When Patton finished, it was Ike's turn to do the talking. "Okay, Georgie. A great story. But one that will be recorded absolutely nowhere. We've all heard it here, but none of us will repeat it or any part of it again. Have you got your copies of the armistice agreement?''

Patton picked up his briefcase. From it he took the two handwritten copies and handed them to Eisenhower, who pulled from his inside jacket pocket the order that Churchill had written. He rolled all three documents together in the shape of a tube. That done, he said, "Gentlemen, please come outside with me.''

They all stood up to follow him out into the bright afternoon sunlight. A few paces from the van he stopped and they clustered around. He looked at the little group. "As you know, gentlemen, we have strict orders from the President and the Prime Minister that in the event of failure—and Uncle Joe has screwed us by saying no at the last minute—we are under the strictest orders to say nothing about this at any time in the future. So far as all of us are concerned, or anyone who knows about it, this armistice attempt never happened. It is not to be spoken about. It is not to be written about. It is not to be hinted at.''

He took his cigarette lighter from his trousers pocket, saying, "And, as you also know, my instructions are to destroy these documents.''

In his right hand the flame leaped from the lighter. Carefully he ignited the roll of paper in his other hand. In less than a minute the few handwritten pages that could have changed the history of the world were devoured in flame to become no more than ashes and smoke, wafting across an unremembered field in Normandy.